PRAISE FOR PAUL E HARDISTY

'*The Descent* is the best kind of thriller: one that makes you gasp, makes you cry, and makes you ask some very big questions. The writing is exquisite, and it unfolds at a breathless pace. Utterly compelling.' Eve Smith

'Concerning and completely engrossing, with characters you will naturally root for and those you will despise, *The Descent* demands your attention and your action. It is a must-read' Jen Med's Book Reviews

'The dystopian future landscape of *The Forcing* comes with a heightened realism that grips and shakes you ... provocative and insightful, visceral and terrifying' *SciFi Now* Book of the Month

'A superbly handled tale of struggle and survival in a maimed world' *The Times*

'Smart, gripping, and all too plausible ... announces Paul E. Hardisty as the true heir to John Christopher' Tim Glister

'A compelling, moving story of survival in a dying world ... a novel that might have actually predicted our future' Ewan Morrison

'A bold, beautifully written and imagined novel about an all-too plausible future – Paul Hardisty is a visionary' Luke McCallin

'Hardisty is a fine writer' Lee Child

'An excellent blend of deep suspense, thriller and – to be honest – horror. The message within it is all-too plausible, the solution to the problem distinctly chilling' James Oswald

'Fierce, thoughtful, deeply humane and always compelling ... the tension builds from page one and never relents' David Whish-Wilson

'Outstanding! Thrilling and thought-provoking. If there's any justice, this book will be HUGE!' Michael J. Malone

'A clear-eyed reckoning with social and political currents we don't like to examine ... tough, suspenseful and action-packed' Jock Serong

'The book I've been waiting and hoping for' Paul Waters

'With the biting intensity of a thriller and the majestic world-building of a classic dystopian tale ... This is a cataclysmic call-to-arms – a powerful warning about a world that could be' B.S. Casey

'This is a remarkably well-written, sophisticated novel in which the people and places ... all come alive on the page' *Literary Review*

'Laces the thrills and spills with enough moral indignation to give the book heft ... excellent' *Telegraph*

'The quality of Hardisty's writing and the underlying truth of his plots sets this above many other thrillers' *West Australian*

'Searing ... at times achieves the level of genuine poetry' *Publishers Weekly*

'A trenchant and engaging thriller that unravels this mysterious land in cool, precise sentences' *Catholic Herald*

'I'm a sucker for genuine thrillers with powerful redemptive themes, but what spoke to me more strongly than anything was the courage, integrity and passion with which this novel is written' *Cheltenham Standard*

'A gripping, page-turning thriller that is overflowing with substance to go along with Hardisty's atmospheric prose and strong narrative style' *Mystery Magazine*

'It's a measure of the wonderfully descriptive style of writing that *The Abrupt Physics of Dying* works as well as it does. The sense of place, and the way that the climate, the landscape and the people all combine ... is evocative' *Australian Crime*

'A page-turning adventure that grabs you from the first page and won't let go' Edward Wilson

'This is an exceptional and innovative novel. And an important one. Hardisty appears to know his territory intimately and describes in mind-grabbing detail its culture, its beliefs and its hopes. I can't praise it highly enough' Susan Moody

'Beautifully written' Tim Marshall

'Vividly written, utterly tropical, totally gripping' Peter James

'Beautifully written, blisteringly authentic, heart-stoppingly tense and unusually moving' Paul Johnston

'A smart, gripping, superbly crafted oil-industry thriller' Crime Review

'I read *Turbulent Wake* in a couple of days. Written with great poise and elegance, it's a big, bold, character-driven story so emotionally literate that it doesn't ring with authenticity, it clamours. Superb and highly recommended' Eve Seymour

The Descent

ABOUT THE AUTHOR

Canadian Paul Hardisty has spent twenty-five years working all over the world as an environmental scientist and freelance journalist. He has roughnecked on oil rigs in Texas, explored for gold in the Arctic, mapped geology in Eastern Turkey (where he was befriended by PKK rebels), and rehabilitated water wells in the wilds of Africa. He was in Ethiopia in 1991 as the Mengistu regime fell, survived a bomb blast in a café in Sana'a in 1993, and was one of the last Westerners out of Yemen at the outbreak of the 1994 civil war. In 2022 he criss-crossed Ukraine writing about the Russian invasion. He ran Australia's climate adaptation science programme from 2013 to 2016, and was CEO of Australia's national marine science agency from 2016 to 2023. The four novels in his Claymore Straker series, *The Abrupt Physics of Dying, The Evolution of Fear, Reconciliation for the Dead* and *Absolution*, all received great critical acclaim, *The Abrupt Physics of Dying* was shortlisted for the CWA John Creasey (New Blood) Dagger and was a *Telegraph* Thriller of the Year, and *The Forcing* (2023) was a *SciFi Now* Book of the Month and was shortlisted for the Crime Fiction Lover Awards. Paul is a keen outdoorsman, a conservation volunteer, and lives in Western Australia. Follow him on Twitter @Hardisty_Paul.

Also by Paul E. Hardisty and available from Orenda Books

The Abrupt Physics of Dying
The Evolution of Fear
Reconciliation for the Dead
Absolution
Turbulent Wake
The Forcing

The Descent

PAUL E HARDISTY

**ORENDA
BOOKS**

Orenda Books
16 Carson Road
West Dulwich
London SE21 8HU
www.orendabooks.co.uk

First published in the United Kingdom by Orenda Books 2024
Copyright © Paul E. Hardisty 2024

A catalogue record for this book is available from the British Library.

ISBN 978-1-916788-03-9
eISBN 978-1-916788-04-6

Typeset in Garamond by typesetter.org.uk

Printed and bound by CPI Group (UK) Ltd, Croydon CR0 4YY

For sales and distribution, please contact *info@orendabooks.co.uk* or visit
www.orendabooks.co.uk.

For Heidi

'How dare you.'
— Greta Thunberg, speech to the United Nations, 2019

It is always the same. She lifts me up and spins me around, a whirling explosion of colour. The blue of the sky, her hair a wind-blown cloud of sunlight, the water of the lagoon that exquisite aquamarine of my dreams. Palm fronds sway in the ocean breeze and the sound they make is like breathing. There is someone else there with us, just out of reach, someone I should know, and there is a threshold there, right there, but each time I get close and try to cross, it moves away, beckoning me deeper. She glances sidelong, something hiding behind her smile, and then she faces me and her eyes have gone cold and black, and then there is nothing there at all, just two fathomless sockets in a screaming skull and I am sinking deeper and deeper and the urge to breathe comes and then the spasms as the consumed oxygen bonds and builds and I can see that bright-blue surface falling away above me, and I know that I am drowning.

Ghosts

February 2024

The scientist squared the edges of his notes, adjusted his glasses and stared out at them with a nervous smile. It looked like he'd slept in his clothes, and he probably had. Though the room was AC cold, perspiration sheened his forehead and rolled like tears down his neck. He ran a finger under his too-tight collar and loosened his ill-matched tie. His name was James Trig, Professor James Trig, and he had a PhD in advanced computational simulation from MIT and several postdocs in atmospheric science and Earth-system dynamics. He looked fit, not the big, muscled gym type but the slender cyclist or runner's build that I've always been partial to. At the time of the meeting, he was forty-two years old, married with two children ages twelve and ten. He'd been on the payroll now for over a year, but this was the first time they'd asked him for a briefing.

Yu Wan leaned back in his chair at the head of the table and lifted his index finger towards the ceiling, held it there until the only thing you could hear was the dull hum of the gardener's leaf blower coming through the bulletproof picture windows from somewhere down by the lake. Then he turned his finger in an arc until its tip met the old-growth hardwood mahogany on the vertical.

'Begin, Professor,' he said. Wan's voice was thin and he spoke very quietly so you had to listen hard to hear everything he said. And it was worth your while, because he hated repeating himself.

Trig cleared his throat and put up his first slide. It was a graph of global average surface temperature differences from the 1901 to 2000 average, going back to 1890. Before 1940, all the bars were blue, meaning negative, below the average. Between 1940 and 1975 some were blue, but lots were red – above the average. After 1975 they were all red, growing left to right like the skyline of a booming city, Dubai, say, or Shanghai.

Trig began. 'This, gentlemen' – for they were all men there, the ones who mattered – 'is the very best data we have, collected and verified from the world's leading science institutions. As you can see, global surface temperatures have been climbing inexorably for the past six decades and have accelerated markedly since 1981. The ten warmest years on record have been since 2010. And 2023, the year just gone, has now been officially declared the warmest year on record, beating last year, which beat the year before that.'

My boss coughed and pushed back his chair. 'Yeah right,' he said under his breath.

Trig glanced at my boss, moved to his next slide, a Mercator projection of the world coloured different shades of red and orange and yellow. It looked like one of my dad's old lava lamps. The title was 'Temperature Trends Since 1990'.

My boss coughed again, that thing he does when he's not happy. I could see Trig's Adam's apple moving under the badly shaved skin of his neck as he swallowed once, then twice, then reached for a glass of water and drank.

We'd lured him away from a senior science position with the National Oceanographic and Atmospheric Administration, enticed him with ten times his normal salary – which wasn't that much, actually, I was surprised. He also got a nice new car, a house and unlimited first-class travel. He was, apparently, one of the world's best at what he did. By then we had a lot of scientists on the payroll, but this guy was different, he knew his stuff, and unlike the others, he was not allowed to speak publicly about his work, or publish. That was the deal. We set him up in his own laboratory on a remote property on the West Coast, and gave him a budget so big that when we showed him the number I thought he was going to pass out. He'd come across enthusiastically.

'This, ah…' Trig stumbled, continued. 'This shows the increase in temperatures up to 2023. The thing here is that warming is not the same everywhere on the planet. You can see that the Arctic is all red, and that the Northern Hemisphere, where most of the land is, has warmed much faster than the rest of the world.'

He fumbled with his laser pointer, and the red dot quivered on the ceiling then flashed across the wall before coming to rest on an area of white down at the southern part of Africa. The dot jumped with his pulse. His heart was racing.

'Areas like the southern cone of Africa, the southern tip of

Madagascar, the south-west coast of Australia, New Zealand, and parts of the Pacific have all warmed much less than the average and some not at all.'

By then I could tell from the veins in my boss's neck that he'd had enough. He stood, put both his fists on the table and sent his gaze around the room. 'Same old shit we've been hearing for forty years,' he flexed.

'Sit down, Derek,' said Wan. You could barely hear him.

My boss stood there a moment, appealing to his colleagues with those glacier-blue eyes, finally fixing on Yu Wan.

Wan stared back hard, and for a moment neither moved and all we could hear was the hum of the projector and the leaf blower still at it somewhere further away now.

Then my boss smiled, that big, amazing smile that he has, that he seemed to be able to switch on whenever he needed it, that he could direct in a way that made you think it was only for you. I swear, people would literally fall in love with him after having that smile directed at them, even when he was trying to throw shade. Then he looked over at me. 'Do I have anything better to do right now?'

'No, sir,' I said. 'Nothing until this afternoon.'

He winked at me, just a flash of ice, that way he did.

I smiled, could feel the heat rising in my cheeks, such a girl thing to do.

My boss said: 'Well, I guess I can stay then.' He sat back in his chair. 'But get to the punchline, would ya, Professor?'

Yu Wan shook his head and sighed like an annoyed and slightly embarrassed parent. After that Trig spoke quickly, skipping some slides altogether. And then he came to the punchline. Despite all the rhetoric and the efforts of the United Nations and the pledges of governments around the world – that got a laugh from the whole room – there was now little hope that the planet's temperature could be kept within acceptable, safe limits.

'And what does that mean for us?' said Pierre Valliant in that strong French accent of his.

'Well,' said Trig, 'in terms of the release of heat stored in the oceans—'

'No,' said my boss, an expert in the art of interrupting. 'Not the mumbo-science-jumbo. What does it mean for *us*?'

Trig glanced around the room, the laser-pointer-clicker hanging limp in his hand. 'Well, I … if you're asking about the economic consequences, it's not really my area of expertise.'

'Translate the physical,' said Valliant. 'Guess.'

'Guess?' stammered Trig.

Yu Wan nodded.

Trig took a deep breath. I could see his lungs rising and falling under his unironed and by now sweat-stained shirt. 'Well, if things don't change and emissions continue to track on their current course, widespread drought, fire, flood, significant changing of ecosystems, poleward shift of species that are able to move, extreme weather of all kinds, basically a lot more of what we've seen in the last few years.'

'Seriously,' said my boss. 'How many degrees does this guy have? Can't even understand a simple fucking question. Can someone please tell this egghead to get to the point?'

By now Trig was melting down. I'd seen my boss do that to people before, turn them into quivering masses of pure fear, and I was pretty sure that he enjoyed it. Power is such a turn-on for some people, I know.

Yu Wan raised his hand, shot my boss a warning look. 'Please, Professor, continue.'

I could see Trig making a supreme effort to compose himself. Even then, his voice came out sounding as if someone was choking him with both hands. 'Worst case,' he rasped, 'biological, social and economic collapse.'

He stopped there and everyone sat listening to the rattle of the AC and the interminable drone of that leaf blower.

Short-Wave

Two years to the day after Papa died, I read his manuscript over again from start to finish. It takes me the whole day and all of that night. I read until my eyes are burning and my heart is breaking.

The next morning, I walk up the hill to the little stone building that Lewis and I built the year Papa died. It was Lewis's idea, doing this. He'd made successive trips to Albany, worked with a friend of his and brought back all the necessary components, including the five-metre antenna. Shortly after, we started the weekly readings. We'd both read Papa's story about him and the others who were blamed for killing the old world that everyone seemed to love so much but not quite enough to save. And we decided that we needed to do whatever we could to tell whoever might be left out there about what he'd seen. Mum, too. It was her story as much as his.

From the top of the ridge, I can see all the way back down to Mum's place and the cove where *Providence* rests head to wind on her mooring, the one Papa put in all those years ago when I was still just a little boy and we'd arrived here and decided to stay. Further out, the headland we call The Hope glows for a moment in the sun and then vanishes behind a veil of rain. I glance up at the antenna, open the door and then open the shutters.

I sit in front of the set, place Papa's manuscript on the table in front of me, the one he called *The Forcing*. I open it at chapter nineteen, the part where Samantha Argent is executed. I turn on the transmitter, watch the dials come to life, position the microphone. We are broadcasting on 4.75 megahertz, bouncing our signal off the ionosphere and out to the world. A chapter a week is what we agreed on – pick a frequency and keep it there. And so far, we have heard absolutely nothing back.

I read the chapter, slowly and clearly. The short waves can travel thousands of miles. It is only a matter of someone out there somewhere being able to pick them up. When I'm done, I sit a moment staring at the glowing dials, these vestiges of another world, another time, the sigh of the empty carrier wave coming to me over the headphones.

The electricity flowing through the transmitter is provided by a solar array Lewis set up nearby, another salvaged echo. I always marvel at my younger brother's aptitude for anything mechanical. He's a genius, I reckon, or near enough.

I am about to shut down when the frequency crackles. There is a moment of silence and then a heavily distorted voice is there in my head. I can't make out what the voice is saying, but a moment later the signal clears up.

'To the boys telling us the story of *The Forcing*. Keep going. People need to know … Here is my part.'

I see Lewis standing outside and I wave to him through the window, signal for him to come inside. He runs in. I take off the headphones and unplug the jack so we can both hear.

We sit enraptured as she speaks, her voice warbling across the reflected miles. She recounts events of almost half a century ago, the time of my parents. It is as if we are living it with her, and as we listen, we can hear the years in her voice, and in her words we can glimpse the young woman she once was.

After she is finished there is a pause, and then she says: 'To whoever is broadcasting on this frequency. Please respond.'

'We receive you,' I blurt out. 'This is Australia.'

The frequency wavers, clears. 'Received, Australia. Thanks for your broadcasts. I thought I was alone.'

I key the microphone. 'So did we. Who is this, please?'

Lewis is standing beside me, a big smile on his face, his hand on my shoulder.

'That's not important,' comes the voice in reply. 'Just know that what you are doing is very important … And very dangerous.'

'Dangerous?' I key back. 'Dangerous how?'

'They are listening.'

'Who? Who is listening?'

We wait, the wave hissing over the speaker, but nothing comes back. The transmission is over.

March 2024

Three weeks before the Boss's big flight, we took the Gulfstream G800 to Paris for the weekend. The trip was part business and part pleasure, although I was never sure if business was the pleasure for the Boss, and the stuff he did with his wife was the chore. It was that way with him, with all of those guys, just go wherever they wanted at a moment's notice, the jet always waiting, ready to go, the rest of us lackeys left scrambling to organise accommodation and events and the whole business.

The Boss's wife arrived at the airstrip in her own limo. He pulled up a while later in his new whip, a black Ferrari. It was a beautiful car. He'd even taken me for a ride in it a few times, those leather seats so soft on my bare legs and ass. That's how he liked me, short skirts and pumps.

Before I am judged, in my defence I was very young, just out of college, armed with my shiny BA in psychology, working as a waitress in a swank restaurant in New York when we first met. He'd bought up the whole place for a big do, had flown in a bunch of politicians from Malaysia, all the dirty old men travelling without their wives, and he offered me ten thousand dollars just to be nice to these guys. You know, smile, wiggle my ass a bit when I walked, sit on their laps and put food in their mouths, that kind of thing. I had to slap one of them when he tried to grope me, but the Boss made it clear that I was off limits that way, and I could see they were all scared shitless of him, so there was no repeat. At the end of the night, he left me a card and told me to call him. There was a full-time job if I wanted it. A quarter of a mil a year. I told him to go fuck himself, not very smart but I was thinking no f'n way was this real. He just laughed that way he did, like there was nothing in the world that he couldn't do, and well, there I was, flying to Paris in a private jet. That's the way he was. He got what he wanted.

The flight was long, even with the flat bed. Somewhere over the Atlantic the pilot – Bryce Stephenson was him name – came back and we started chatting, the Boss and his wife asleep in their private room. He had a strong face and sandy hair with a cowlick in the front, and chestnut-coloured eyes. He looked quite young, maybe only a few years older than me. After a while he asked me if I wanted to sit up front a while, and I said yes. It was nice up there talking to him, watching him at the controls, his hands moving sure and deliberate across the panels, tweaking and pushing. I liked the way he spoke, very deliberate and confident, something gentle in the way he pronounced his vowels. I'd never really noticed him that way before. Strange how just one moment is sometimes all it takes.

When we landed in Paris the wife and her maid and bodyguard went to the hotel and the Boss and I and Paulo, his CFO, went straight to the meeting. We arrived in the armoured Merc and were led up to a plush conference room overlooking La Defense. I spent a lot of time in board rooms, back then.

There was a whole rank of them waiting for us, all suited up, short French guys mostly with greying hair and aquiline noses. They sat, ten of them, along one side of the board table, just the Boss and Paolo and me on the other. One of the guys smiled at me that way older guys do, and I looked away.

'Gentlemen,' the Boss began in English. He actually spoke perfect French, but as he'd told me on the way in, fuck 'em. 'It is deeply disappointing to me that I have had to come all this way to look at your hangdog ugly fucking stupid faces.'

That got their attention. They squirmed in their seats and glanced at each other as if to deflect blame.

'Can someone please explain why we are delayed? I need not remind you how much this is costing us.' He cracked his knuckles. 'Costing *me*.'

'Five point three million US a day,' said Paolo in his strangely inflectionless voice.

'There you go,' said the Boss. 'One of you sorry fuckers' annual salary, every goddam day.'

The man at the centre of the group, Breillard, the CEO, clasped his hands, bowed his head a moment and then looked up at us. 'I take full responsibility,' he said. 'The approvals we thought we had secured have been withdrawn at the last minute.'

I could see the veins in the Boss's neck starting to do their thing. 'What kind of approvals?'

'Development approvals from the government of Niger.'

The Boss threw his head back and laughed. 'Niger government? What the hell is that? We own those cunts.'

'There is a new director there,' said Breillard, visibly panicking. 'He is not acquiescing. We've tried all the usual means. He says our project will contaminate the aquifer and the rivers. Thousands of people depend on that water.'

'And will it?'

Breillard looked down the table and one of the younger guys nodded. 'Yes.'

'How much will it cost to fix?' said Paolo.

'According to our engineers, a new treatment plant and extra containment for the tailings ponds will cost about fifty million to build and another ten million or so a year to operate, low estimate,' said the younger guy. Actually, he was about the same age as the Boss. 'And it will take two years to put in place.'

Paolo pulled out his phone and tapped away for a couple of seconds. 'Too much,' he said. 'NPV is only thirty million a quarter.'

The Boss sat very quiet, like he sometimes did, thinking things through. Then he leaned forward in his chair. 'Tell me about this principled peckerhead standing in our way.'

Breillard looked to the younger guy again.

'His name is Rudolphe Asisi, a local. Mid-thirties, married to a local woman, three kids under the age of ten. He's smart – did a master's degree in hydrology at Imperial College in London – and knows what he is talking about. Highly respected in the community. The locals trust him.'

'Beautiful,' said the Boss, running his hand through his thick, sandy-blond hair. 'So goddamned frustrating. You offer people something that will transform their lives, and all they care about is some fucking river or some endangered useless tree frog. This project will bring jobs and prosperity to that blighted good-for-nothing hellhole. People, frankly, are idiots.'

The Boss paused a moment, turned his gaze on each of them in turn. He did it very deliberately, one after the other. 'All you people,' he said in a measured tone that surprised me, 'you have one job. One. Get this over the line.'

Breillard sat resigned, defeated.

The Boss stood up. Paolo and I did the same.

'Get rid of him,' said the Boss. 'Make it an accident.'

We walked back to the limo, and that night the Boss took us all out to the Guy Savoy for a thirteen-course dinner and bottomless five-thousand-dollar-a-bottle champagne. During dinner he fingered me under the table with his wife right there across from us.

Mother

Maybe it's because of the message on the short-wave. Or maybe it's the anniversary of Papa's death that has dredged this all up again, this feeling, these half-formed memories. Whatever it is, I wake in the morning from the dream, the one I have been having for years now. It's hard to explain, but it's more than some random feeling, or a vague sense of displacement. There are big holes in my life. I know that now. I can feel them, as real as the heart beating inside me.

I swim out to *Providence*, tied up on her mooring in our cove, and look through her log books, ranks of blue-bound hardcover volumes, the spines faded by decades of sun, the oldest frayed and worn, the ones yet to be used hard and crisp still, despite the years.

They go all the way back to her original owner, Daniel Menzels – to before the Repudiation, to before Papa stole her, or whatever he called what he did. But that's another story. Papa's entries begin in July 2039, the day he and Mum and Derek Argent escaped from a religious cult leader and his followers on the Gulf Coast of the United States. The days from then are numbered sequentially from one until day 124, when the log book is full, the entries detailed and precise in Papa's neat, legible hand. And then nothing again until a new log book starts six years later, as if nothing has changed. Papa's chronology is missing exactly 2,190 days. Everything from the moment they left Belize until they arrived here. Our whole transit across the Pacific, along the south coast of Australia. And then the log restarts: our trips as a family along this coast, those Lewis and I took alone, the solo trips I did as Papa got older, all recorded in book after book. But all of that time – those first five years aboard *Providence*, my birth, Lewis's – all of it gone.

Later that afternoon, after a full day's work with Lewis, cutting and hauling windfall from the forest behind the ridge, I walk down the hill and find Mum in her garden. I've been thinking about it all day, and I don't even greet her. I just walk up to her and ask her. 'What happened after you and Papa left Belize, Mum?'

She narrows her eyes, sets aside her hoe.

'I know you were pregnant with me and that I was born on the boat. But other than that, you've told us almost nothing.'

I can still remember some of it, vague childhood memories of sitting at the bow, watching the dolphins ride the wave, the silver darts of flying fish springing from the water, the way the silver droplets dripped from their translucent wings. And then there are the dreams. And the nightmares.

She looks surprised, stands brushing dirt from her hands.

'What happened, Mum? Something is missing. Something's always been missing. I've felt it for a long time.'

But she just frowns and waves this away. 'Nothing to tell,' she says, closing up the way she does more and more now.

'What happened to the *Providence* log books, Mum?'

She looks at me quizzically. 'They're not there?'

'Yes, they are. But some are missing.'

'Are you sure?'

'I'm sure, Mum, I've just gone through them. Those first five years of my life, gone.'

She looks out towards *Providence* swinging on her mooring. 'Maybe they're somewhere else,' she says. 'Maybe Papa was using them to write his book and forgot to put them back.'

'Have you seen them?'

'No. No, I haven't. Not for a long time.'

And that's it. She doesn't know. I scour her house, the bookshelves, ask Lewis, swim back out to *Providence* and check again, look through all of the other shelves and the chart table, everywhere I can think of. Nothing.

The next morning, I walk to the place where Uncle Liberty's mob camps in the season they call Makuru, when the first heavy rains start to fall. The trail is less well worn than it once was, but still clear enough, winding along the coast through shell hakea and catspaw heathland, across the six creek fords to Kwesi Point, then following our rough stone cairns up over the rounded granite headland and back down through the big valley trees to the camp.

The first time I did the trip I was seven years old. Uncle Liberty had arrived with news that his wife Jenny was going into labour. My mum had delivered Jennifer's first baby, and she'd asked Mum to help her through it again. I had insisted on going with her. It was the height of summer, and hot. The dark sand of the path burned the soles of my feet, and the sun seemed determined to crush me into insignificance. Mum kept asking me if I wanted to go back, but I just told her no and kept trudging along on my stumpy little legs. In her telling of it, I was stoically resolute. In reality I was afraid of walking back alone. I can still remember the urgency in Mum's voice as she urged me along, the impatience in her eyes as she glanced over her shoulder at me before surging ahead again on her long, powerful legs.

This time, eighteen years on, there is no one watching over me, no one pulling me along in her protective slipstream. I am alone. Squalls shake the wind-shaped peppermint and acacia, ruffle across the hills. Rain comes in angled sheets, passing over and then gone. I don't rush, not like back then with Mum. I am thinking, taking my time, turning it all over in my head.

By the time I reach Kwesi Point, a rocky promontory about halfway from our bay to Uncle Liberty's camp, the sun has passed its zenith and glows diffuse behind the clouds. Mum named this place after Aunty Jenny's first baby, on the day he was born. But she also named it after my father. He came from a place called Ghana, in Africa, and died in a place called Brownwood, in Texas, six months before I was born. Kwesi was his name – 'Born on Sunday' in Ashanti, the language of his people. I am Kweku, which means 'Born on Wednesday'.

And it's there, staring out across the bay, that I decide to write this history. This is for him, for both of them, the father I never knew and the one who raised me. And this is the first step.

By the time I reach the camp's outer picket it is dark. The rain has stopped and stars shine down through the bands of slow-moving cloud. I can see the lights of the camp through the trees, smell woodsmoke and meat cooking.

'Hey there, young fella.'

I look in the direction of the voice. A man is standing in the star shadow of a huge jarrah. I step closer, peer into the darkness.

It is Uncle Liberty, twirling the base of his spear in the root soil.

'Uncle. Hello.' I'd learned never to be surprised by Uncle Liberty's appearances and equally sudden departures.

He leans forward slightly so that one side of his face catches the faint firelight from the camp. His beard is longer than when I saw him last, the hollows under his cheekbones deeper. 'Been expectin' ya.'

'Anniversary of Papa's death.'

'Yes, I know. We don't talk about such.'

'I know, Uncle. But we do.'

'His time. We all got one. Mine coming soon.'

'If you want to live...'

'...You gotta die.'

One of Uncle Liberty's favourite sayings. I'd heard it since I was young, he and Papa reciting it like that, as a couplet.

'He was a good man, your papa. Too few of them nowadays.'

'He always said the same about you.'

Uncle Liberty straightens. It is a careful, deliberate motion, as with everything he does. His face recedes into darkness. Insects thrum and tick. A boobook owl calls, somewhere close. For a moment I think Uncle Liberty is gone, heard the news he needed, nothing more required, on his way.

'I know why you're here, young fella. Know you got questions. Your papa told me about you. Gonna write the next history of the world, a young Herodotus for our times.'

I smile, embarrassed as only parents can make you. 'It may take a while.'

'Well, I got as much time as I got.'

We walk into camp. A few old steel shipping containers converted into dwellings, grafted with plankboard and tin-roofed porches. The large stone house Liberty and Papa built together one year. Solar panels about, a few electric lights showing through the cut windows, all of it shaded by big, old trees, set in a henge of granite boulders.

Uncle Liberty motions me to sit by the fire. 'Eat first,' he says. 'Then we'll talk.'

A young boy brings me a cup of water and a plate of grilled roo, some fresh greens. Some of the elders come and sit with us, watch me eat.

'Teacher and the doctor's boy,' says Uncle Liberty. The elders nod. 'So, questions, young fella.'

'Yes, Uncle. About my mother.'

Liberty stares into the fire a long while, nods. 'A good woman. Strong. Smart.'

'Yes.'

'Stubborn.'

'Yes.'

More so over the last year, worse once Papa started going downhill. Lately we'd started to notice her memory failing, something that had never happened before.

'So.'

Walking here, through the forests and along the rocky coast, I considered this *so*. This question. So, young fella, what do you want to know? And now that I am here, I'm not sure anymore. Is there even a question, or is it all just something my imagination has dredged up?

Uncle Liberty listens as I tell the story of the log books, stroking his silvery beard, turning the base of his spear in little half-twists in the dirt between his bare feet, leaning in occasionally to add another piece of wood to the fire.

'What's she hiding, Uncle? Her and Papa.'

Liberty considers this until the last log burns down to a glowing coal. 'Stay the night, young fella. Tomorrow there is something I need to show you.'

April 2024

Three days before the launch, Bryce flew the wife and a few of us support staff down to the Boss's spaceport complex in Arizona. The Boss and the other crew had been in isolation there for two weeks already, getting ready. I was in the cockpit when Bryce did a low turn around the launch site, the rocket there on its pad ready to go. It was so close I could see the technicians on the upper platform working on the crew capsule. For a moment I thought our wingtip would clip the tower and I gasped, but Bryce just smiled, took his hand off the throttle and reached back to where I was in the jumpseat. He laced his fingers in mine. Those few moments, my God, I never wanted them to end.

When I came back into the main cabin the wife was staring at me.

'Don't you have work to do?' she said. I could tell by the way she narrowed her eyes under those fake eyelashes and by the tone of her voice that she didn't like me. She'd never liked me.

'Yes, ma'am,' I mumbled, demure, eyes to the ground. 'Sorry, ma'am.' That's my job. I do what I'm told. Like everyone else here. Whatever it is, just shut up and do it. No excuses.

With Bryce's sexy voice over the intercom telling us to prepare for landing, I went to my seat, strapped in. From the window I could see the desert big and brown and super flat for as far as there was, and the white buildings of the spaceport complex coming into view, the airstrip running alongside, and the big blue rocket aimed at the sky, ready to go. To be honest it looked more like a huge boner than anything else.

I handled all of the correspondence for this project. Paolo never liked it, said there was no way we would ever make a profit from it, competing against the government space organisations, NASA and ESA and the like. The Russians and the Chinese, too, were putting up satellites for cheap money, all subsidised by taxpayers, of course. But the Boss was adamant. He wanted his own space programme, kept talking about going to Mars, maybe putting a base on the moon. Anyone else, you'd call them downright crazy. But not him. It cost him plenty, but he didn't care. It was the one project that was given a blank cheque. Until the alpha project, of course, but that came later.

Bryce put the Gulfstream down so you didn't even know you were rolling on the ground until you heard the thrust-reversers going and the dust billowing back around us. Up in the cockpit he'd told me that he used to land planes on carriers for the navy. I stepped off the jet into desert air so hot and dry I could feel it pulling the moisture from my skin.

The Boss's chief of staff was there at the base of the stairs with a file in his hand. 'Boss wants to talk to you right away,' he said. 'Wants a briefing on Niger.'

I stepped into the limo, did a rush over with moisturiser and foundation using the mirror in the rear console, and ten minutes later I was waiting in the secure interview room, staring at a pane of sealed, bulletproof glass, beyond which was a room with a few armchairs upholstered in hideous orange and a full-length mirror set in one wall.

Five minutes passed, then ten. After half an hour I was getting a little pissed off, but I wasn't worried. The Boss liked to keep people waiting. In this case, even himself. I got out my phone, scrolled TikTok awhile. There was this one video of a super-cute puppy that could surf. No kidding. It just stood there balancing on the board, its little legs adjusting as the wave surged and carried him/her along.

Finally, the Boss came in. He was wearing a blue jumpsuit like you see astronauts wear on TV, with mission patches on the shoulders and his name on his breast in big white letters, so the cameras would have no doubt who was under the helmet.

He sat down, made a point of checking out my legs, smiled at me. 'So, tell me.'

'It's done,' I said, marvelling at the power surrounding me. 'It was pretty routine. Breillard reports that permits have been expedited and construction has started.'

The Boss nodded. 'And the river? The aquifer?'

'All dealt with. The official reports now show acceptable levels of heavy metals, neutral pH. No health risk.'

'Paolo happy?' But before he'd even finished asking the question, I could see he'd already moved on, dismissed the entire conversation from his mind. It was a thing he did, and it drove people crazy, and he knew it.

'Very,' I said, but he wasn't listening.

He turned side on to me, stood tall, or as tall as he could – he wasn't much taller than me – and said: 'What do you think?'

'The suit?' I asked.

'Yes, the suit. Nice, eh? Designed the mission patch myself.'

I pretended to look at it. 'Yeah, super nice, Boss. Awesome.'

'You looking forward to the launch?' he said, checking himself out in the mirror.

'Sure am,' I replied, injecting excitement into my voice even though he was no longer listening. I turned to leave.

'How did he die?'

I stopped, faced back up to the glass, the Boss still there admiring himself in his jumpsuit. 'Sorry, Boss?'

'I said, how did he die?'

'Who?'

'Asisi. Rudolphe Asisi, RIP.'

'Oh,' I said. 'His car drove off the road into a deep gorge near the mine site. The impact crushed his sternum and broke his neck.'

The Boss nodded and turned away, walked out of the interview room and I went outside and put on my hat against the sun while I waited for the limo.

Sister

I sleep badly, harried by dreams of loss, of things absent but indeterminate. Like an echo bounced from too many surfaces. Running through the darkness, hushed, strained, frightened voices whispering indecipherable words, a gate opening and then closing quickly behind me.

Under an overcast pre-dawn sky, I find Uncle Liberty's son Kwesi standing near the fire with a cup of tea. He offers me one and stands looking at the rekindled morning flames.

'How's Lewis?' he says.

'He's good. Mandy's pregnant again.'

'I heard. Don't see much of him these days.'

'Busy with the family, running the farm. I'll tell him you asked.'

'Thanks.'

'How are you travelling?'

'Okay. Dad's slowing down. I have to help him a lot now. Still won't wear clothes. Just them Eagles shorts. And they ain't played a game since long before I was born.'

I smile. Uncle Liberty's tolerance of the cold is legend hereabouts. His love for this thing he calls footy, too. He was a good player back then, some say. Back when things like that mattered.

'Any news on your other brother, the one Dad says is some big president up north?' Kwesi asks.

The name we saw in that Albany newspaper two years ago was Armstrong. Lachie Armstrong. Papa's son was Lachie Ashworth. Close but not that close.

'We've heard his name on the radio a few times since. Ashworth. Yeah, it's him.'

Kwesi whistles. 'Big stuff, for sure. Not my thing, mind you, politics. For me, here is enough.'

'Lewis says the same. Enough to worry about here.' I put my hand on Kwesi's shoulder, sip my tea.

Uncle Liberty joins us. 'Get the skiff ready, son,' he says. 'Fish ain't gonna catch themselves.'

Kwesi smiles at me in happy tolerance, one young man to another, flicks the dregs of his tea into the fire and starts towards the water.

'Good boy, that boy,' I say.

Liberty smiles. His teeth are still strong, a full set, dull oyster-shell white. 'Sure is. Lookin' after me now. Way it is. Everyone takes his turn.'

I nod, thinking about my own parents, alive and dead.

'Got somethin' to show ya, young feller.' Liberty turns and starts towards the trees.

He is old, but he is still quick, padding barefoot across the sand and through the scrub sheoak, gripping his way up the rounded granite headlands, slipping through the thick valley stands of marri and jarrah, fording the creeks back towards our cove. I have to work hard to keep up.

And then just past Kwesi Point he turns inland. I follow as we climb to the top of the ridge that runs along the coast, curving back towards our cove, the distant point of The Hope visible now across the sound. We follow the rock-strewn razor edge north until we come to a small, grassy clearing surrounded on three sides by granite pillars.

Uncle Liberty stands in the clearing with the pillars to his back and looks out across the bay. A few clouds scuttle across the horizon, but the rain of the last few days has passed and the sea breeze comes cool up the wildflower hillfront to meet us. I stand next to him and scan the horizon.

'So.'

'Was this what you wanted to show me, Uncle?'

'Yep.'

'I don't understand.'

Liberty taps the base of his spear on a small, flat rock at his feet. The rock is about the size of one of *Providence's* log books, maybe a bit bigger. 'This,' he says.

'A rock.'

'What's under it.'

I look at him, back down at the rock. 'What *is* under it?'

'A little fella.'

I swallow: 'Yours?'

'Not mine.'

I say nothing, try to compute.

'When you arrived here, all them years ago. There was five of you.'

'Five? No, Uncle. Four.'

'You, Lewis just a little capper, your mum, Teacher. And one more.'

'No, Uncle. You're wrong. I would remember.'

'Your mum. She was pregnant.'

I think about this for a while, looking out across the water.

'You had a baby sister. Healthy. Strong.'

I wait for him to continue, spinning unsteady.

'And then one day, she was gone. Your mum, Teacher, they said she died. Told me not to tell no one.'

Another silence, longer this time. Just the ruffle of the breeze blowing through the trees.

'Don't know they ever gave her a name.'

'Jesus,' I say. Hardly sufficient.

'It was a long time ago.'

I am still trying to process all of this, still trying to understand.

'Found her one day walking up here with the baby. Middle of a storm. Just the two of 'em. Cold it was. The baby crying. She wailing at the sky like a crazy woman, pulling her hair, near naked, soaked.'

Liberty goes quiet, just stands there tapping the base of his spear on the little slab.

'Uncle Liberty.'

He points to the thick clutch of acacia just beyond the pillars. 'I was there, watching her. Not sure what to do, women's business. You all so new here. Her carryin' on like that. Then she starts down towards the creek, the both of them still crying and wailing to raise the spirits. Last thing I see she has the baby at her breast. And then it all goes quiet.'

'The baby must have been crook, feverish.'

'Maybe.'

Uncle Liberty taps away on the stone, hardwood on Cambrian granite, resonant and hollow. 'When she came back, the baby was limp in her arms,' says Liberty. 'I watched her dig out a hole, right here. Used a stick. The baby set in the grass next to her, on its back as if it was looking up into the rain. No sound but her scraping and the rain in the trees. Me standing there watching this.'

I am hearing the words, but not understanding.

'Then she put the little tacker in the hole, pushed the dirt back in with her hands, and put this here stone on her. Like I said. Long time ago. Can still see it clear. So I've told you.'

May 2024

In the end, he had to settle for the flight being livestreamed on Maddisson's network. Yu Wan wouldn't broadcast it on his, was against the whole thing from the beginning. He didn't like the way the Boss flaunted it. Still, a hundred million people watched, all over the world. But the Boss was furious. He'd hoped for ten times that.

And Yu Wan was right. While the Boss was up there, a huge hurricane developed in the Atlantic, way earlier and faster than anyone had ever seen before, and within days it was bearing down on the East Coast. Bermuda was destroyed. I saw pictures of it on TV. It was as if the whole place had been bulldozed into the sea. Lots of people died, they still don't know how many. We all watched horrified as it gained strength and came straight for New York. Everyone called it unprecedented. You heard that word a lot those days. I remember sitting up in the Boss's Manhattan penthouse looking out over the city, all those huge buildings, and thinking there is no way this thing could ever hurt this city. The storm was so big the Boss had to stay up there in orbit looking down at it for an extra four days. The hurricane grabbed all the headlines and he barely got a mention in any of the mainstream press until after he got back.

I'd never seen anything like it, and hope I never have to again. I sat up there on the fifty-second floor and watched the wind rip up trees and tear roofs off buildings and send street signs flying like giant deformed frisbees down Park Avenue. And then the rain came and the streets flooded and the power went out. At first it was kinda fun, up there with the maids and the butler and the chef, all of us staff with the run of the place. We lit candles and drank champagne and the chef made us fabulous meals, and after the fresh food ran out, we ate oysters and pâté from tins.

But then, after the third day, we knew it was bad. I mean really bad. There was not a street or road we could see that wasn't underwater, and at night the city was so black, just a few lights like stars scattered around. We used our phones to follow what was going on, people posting like crazy, videos and more and more calls for help. We knew people were dying. Thank God the Boss had installed a separate battery system, so we had power for essentials like phones and the office communications and keeping the champagne cold.

On the fourth day, I got a call from the Boss.

'How's my penthouse?'

'Moving,' I said.

'Don't play smart. It doesn't suit you.'

'I'm not, Boss. The wind is so strong the building is literally swaying. I'm getting seasick.'

'I'm looking down at it right now. But the desert is clear. We're landing tomorrow. Get down there to meet me.'

I checked myself, didn't say what I was thinking. That time in the restaurant under the table was the first time he'd touched me, and by now I knew he really had the hots for me. 'I don't think that is going to be possible, Boss,' I said. 'The whole city is underwater. The airport, too.'

'I've been up here a week now,' he said. I could hear him cursing under his breath.

I said nothing, just let the line hang. What was I supposed to say? He was a man of large appetites.

'Fuck it,' he said. 'Call Asteroid and tell her to get her big ass to the spaceport. Tell her to wear that red dress I got her in Paris.'

Asteroid was his nickname for Astrid, a blonde he'd met on a business trip in Sweden a couple of years ago. He paid her three hundred thousand a year and set her up in a fancy apartment in Miami Beach, and all she had to do was fuck. Okay, she was beautiful, curvy everywhere and with skin any girl would die for. I mean this girl was thicc. Sometimes life just isn't fair.

'Will do, Boss.'

'And make sure you reschedule my meeting with that moron Bragg. The campaign is heating up, and I want him to know whose side he's on.'

'He's here in New York, too, Boss. So he's not going anywhere. I'll set up something for Wyoming, at the ranch, for the week after next.'

'Good. You can use the chopper to get him to an airstrip that's working. Have Stephenson meet you there.'

'Will do, Boss.'

'And tell Samantha to prepare the paperwork for Pharma.'

We were launching his next new venture in August, a huge investment into pharmaceuticals. He'd already raided the largest and most successful competitors, hired away their top guys, and bought up several up-and-coming smaller firms. He was waiting for the publicity from the space flight to consolidate before he announced this major new effort to improve people's lives.

There was a moment of silence, always a sign that he was changing gears.

'And you might want to review your terms of employment,' he said, 'before you get on that plane.'

I sat a moment, completely nonplussed. 'Sorry, Boss?'

'Have a look at clause sixteen.'

Before I could answer or ask what he meant, he terminated the transmission. I went back to the living room and sat with the others and watched the city flood.

Juliette

The next day I walk home from Liberty's camp. Rain pelts the hills, washing across the sound in wind-driven sheets. I detour up the ridge to the little grave and stand there a while thinking about everything, then I cut across the valley to the place where we buried Papa.

Everything I know is here, these rocky hills, the fishing grounds in the lee of The Hope, this lonely stretch of coastline much changed, all that accumulated inertia playing out still. But there was a world out there once, the world my mother and father lived in, Uncle Liberty too, in a time before the descent, when all of our possible futures lay spread before us like an ocean.

By the time I get home I am soaked. Darkness has come, and for a while the rain relents and stars pulse cold and distant between the clouds. I walk the pathway from our cove up past our vegetable plots towards the little stone house Papa and I built for Juliette and me after we married.

It's almost six years now since I first saw her on that street in Albany, outside the orphanage. She was seventeen, standing there with her friend Mandy, both of them in long dresses, shoulders bare, carrying baskets under their arms, looking as if they were off to a picnic or something. It was summer, hot, and the sea breeze blew in across the sound, whipping the skirts of their dresses around their ankles. And then she laughed, open-mouthed, and the sound of it carried on the wind and it was like a scattering of light, a melody of photons flung across the universe. Strange how one moment can change your life.

Warm yellow light glows in the windows. Smoke drifts from the chimney, that sharp home pang of burning jarrah and hot food. She greets me at the door, that same liquid embrace that always fills my senses. She takes my coat and shakes it out, hangs it on the peg in the wet room. I can see Leo sitting at the table by the fire, eating his supper. Julie puts her arms around my neck and kisses me and I kiss her back. I put my arms around her waist and pull her close, hold her like that for a long time.

Later, lying in the darkness beside her, I tell her what I learned from Liberty – all of it. She listens quietly, as she does, taking it in.

'Have you asked your mum about it?' she whispers.

'Not yet. I came straight home.'

'You need to, before you reach any conclusions.'

'I do. But I'm afraid. She's so fragile now. She might not even remember.'

'Something like that she'll remember, Kwe, believe me. It's only a matter of how much she wants to tell you. If it's true, then she's kept it a secret all these years. Maybe it's better that way, to let the past be. Maybe it needs to stay a secret.'

I think about this a while. 'Maybe. But it's all we have, the past. It's who we are.'

Julie takes my hand, squeezes it. 'This is your mother's past, Kwe. Hers. Not Liberty's. Not yours. Maybe you just need to respect that. If she wants to tell you one day, she will.'

'You're right, I know. But I can't help feeling there's more to this. Something important. This and the missing logs. She's hiding something from me and Lewis, from all of us, and I need to know why.'

The next day there is work to do, and for days after, and I am happy for it, losing myself in the familiar tasks that have helped keep us alive here on this remote and largely abandoned coast on an emptied continent. Lewis and I in our saw shed, the two of us working the big cross-cut saw for hours until our shoulders and backs ache. We talk about short-wave woman's warning.

'All the way down here, in the middle of nowhere,' says Lewis. 'I think we're okay.'

'Let's keep Papa's gun handy,' I say, 'just in case.'

We keep sawing, and later I split some of our stored logs and stack them for the fires. But I don't tell Lewis about the grave, or about what Liberty said. That evening we do our regular transmission of *The Forcing*, the next couple of short chapters, and listen to the woman's next instalment. After, we hang on for a while, thinking she might resume contact, but there is only the hiss of that empty band, all those photons ionising the atmosphere.

And then on the Saturday we all go to Mum's for lunch, as we always do. Me and Juliette and Leo, Lewis and Mandy and their little Becky. Mum has cooked up a feast, as usual, a nice emperor that Lewis caught, grilled up with onions and wild garlic and potatoes. The rain stops and the sun comes out, and after the meal we all go for a walk up to Chicken-Head Rock so we can look out over the sound and watch the whales playing in the deeper water beyond our cove. The kids take turns with the binoculars.

And then everyone starts heading back down. I ask Juliette to go on ahead with Leo, and then Mandy and Lewis with Becky, and soon it is just Mum and me up there. She takes my arm, leans in against me. She is older now, but still strong and fit. I stand beside her, tracing the ridgeline I walked a few days ago with Uncle Liberty, finding the three pillars, the rocky creek gully visible just beyond.

'What happened up there, Mum?'

She looks up at me. 'What happened where?'

I point. 'Up there, Mum. On the ridge. When we first arrived.'

She is quiet a long time, holding my arm. And then she sighs. 'Oh Lewis, what do you mean?'

'Not Lewis, Mum. Kweku.'

'Yes, of course. *Pardon, mon chou.*'

Mum spoke French, her mother tongue, to us when we were growing up, and even now reverts to it when we are alone.

'I mean the baby you had after we arrived here. The one that's buried up there.'

She lets go of my arm and takes a step back. 'I don't know what you mean, Lewis.'

'Kweku, Mum. Are you telling me it didn't happen?'

'Where did you get this idea? There's nothing up there. Nothing.'

'Uncle Liberty told me.'

'Uncle Liberty. You spoke to him?'

'Yes, Mum. I did. That's what he said.'

'Uncle Liberty. How is he?'

'Why would he tell me that, Mum?'

'Tell you what, dear?' Her eyes are clear, that same autumn gold, but clouded with confusion.

'Nothing, Mum. Nothing.'

She takes my arm again, smiles as if nothing was said. 'Let's go back now, Lewis. I'm cold.'

We start back down the hill.

June 2024

In the end, nothing about that space flight turned out the way the Boss wanted. The helicopter came to the roof the day after the Boss got back to Earth, and we flew to a small airstrip near Allentown. I had the full PR briefing report ready to go, just needed a couple of hours to polish my presentation. I'd arranged the meeting with Bragg's people, and the pharma deal was ready to sign – I had the papers with me.

By the time the helicopter landed Bryce was waiting for us with the Gulfstream. I could see him standing there beside the open stairway in his pilot's uniform, his arms bare, looking across the wet tarmac towards us as the turbine spun down and the rotors slowed. The door opened and I stepped onto the concrete with my bags. The wind swirled over my bare legs and flipped up my skirt before I could smooth it down, and he smiled and I knew that the smile was for me, and despite myself I couldn't help but smile back as he started walking towards us. He took my bags from me and as he did his fingers brushed my bare wrist and I could smell him and my pulse rate went crazy and I could feel my heart fluttering inside me like some big fat hummingbird, and it was as if her wings were wired directly to all the places I wanted him to touch.

The flight down to the desert was pure hell. Bryce came back to talk to me after we'd levelled out, but I had to work on my presentation so I brushed him off. All I could think about was clause sixteen of my personal employment contract. Basically, no romances or sexual relationships with other members of the organisation, or with clients or contractors of the organisation, unless okayed or directed by the Boss specifically. So far, I'd not been directed. That party with the Malaysians back when I'd first met him had been as close as it had come, but I knew some of the other girls had been told to do things. When I'd asked them if they had, they'd all said the same thing, more of less: of course. But still, it was clearly a warning. Somehow, he knew that I had the hots for his chief pilot, and I was pretty sure the feeling was reciprocated. It was probably the wife who'd brought it to his attention – it was definitely not something he would notice. She was such a bitch. I didn't know why she stayed with him. She knew about Astrid and the other women he had parked all over the world, about the parties he and the colleagues threw. And she had her own money. But then again, we were all in the same trap. Money and power are a gravity you can't escape, unless you own your own rocket, I guess.

So, after we landed and Bryce held me back for a second in the cabin after everyone had deplaned, and he tried to kiss me, one hand on the bulkhead, leaning over me, I pushed him away. He was a gentleman about it, straightened, smiled, said something like: 'Had to try, sorry.' I mumbled something stupid and entirely unconvincing like 'it's okay,' but every part of me was dying.

The Boss was sullen and withdrawn in a way I'd never seen him before, like a kid who'd been grounded or had device privileges taken away. Even Astrid's libidinous presence did nothing to buoy his mood. He sat in the meeting room at the head of the table, twitching and distracted as Paolo briefed him on the pharma deal and I laid out the documents for him to sign. And then I went through my presentation with him. I knew he wasn't going to be pleased, and I'd done my best to be positive, but there was no other way to say it: the space flight had been a PR disaster.

He sat a while, very still all of a sudden, looking out the picture window at the desert. Then he stood and walked to the sideboard, where the staff had laid out a working lunch: shrimp, lobster, and a selection of salads, cut fruit, Dom on ice. He picked up a shrimp and eyed it for a moment and then put it carefully back in the bowl. And then his body coiled and in one motion he swept the whole banquet to the floor in a crash of serving plates and smashing glass, then he stood looking down at all that beautiful food spread across the floor.

He looked at me then, with those eyes that destabilised you with their brute intensity. 'What about overseas, our target markets for pharma?'

'Same thing,' I said, my voice wavering. I gulped some air. 'While we were having that hurricane, Europe was being blasted by a record heatwave, and fires were burning out of control in Spain and Greece.' It sounded like what Trig had told us would be happening on a routine basis now. 'The press, social media, it was all the same. Billionaire goes galivanting to space at a cost of untold billions while normal people suffer through yet another disaster.'

'Fuck.'

'But very good for business,' said Paolo. 'Demand for electricity for cooling is through the roof, no pun intended. Our power stations all across Europe and the Middle East are going full bore. Spot prices are double what they were last year. We're making a fortune, Boss.'

This didn't seem to help. He stood there blazing at us. 'And what about that Swedish slut?'

'Astrid?' I said. 'What about her?'

'No, not Asteroid.' He rolled his eyes, but didn't call me an idiot, which I was. 'Dahlberg.'

'It's what you'd expect, Boss.' I didn't want to antagonise him further by going into detail.

'Tell me, for Christ's sake.'

I could see Paolo brace himself before he said: 'The events of the last few weeks are unequivocal expressions of a rapidly changing climate driven by our society's absolute addiction to fossil fuels, and are going to get a lot worse unless massive changes are made, now. She called you irresponsible, selfish, and a symbol of everything that's wrong with the world.'

The Boss stepped over the food and stood looking out of the window, his back to us. 'Get someone to clean that up,' he said.

I made a call.

'So, nothing new,' he said. 'Same old bullshit.'

Paolo started to speak again: 'Trig said—' But he didn't get any further.

'Fuck that egghead. Whatever he's spouting we have to kill it, once and for all.'

'We've been trying for years, Boss. They just keep coming back.'

'Maybe, but we've kept them at bay. It's worked. Our balance sheet proves that. But now we need to take it one step further. We need to end it.' He turned and faced me. 'Tell me about Dahlberg.'

I braced myself. 'In the wake of your trip, she's calling for a global tax on the super-wealthy to pay for massive emission-reduction programmes and climate-adaptation efforts.'

The Boss ran his hand through his hair. 'Go on.'

'She wants to tax all income over fifty million a year at ninety percent.'

The Boss laughed, genuine mirth. 'Right. Who the hell is going to take that seriously?'

'Apparently a lot of people,' said Paolo. 'Sweden is going to bring a motion to the UN.'

'I bet Bragg is incandescent. It will never fly.'

'Of course he is, and of course it won't,' said Paolo. 'But there are a lot of people here lining up behind the idea. In other countries, too.'

'Fucking liberals.'

'Not just them.'

The Boss directed his gaze at me. 'How is Bragg doing in the primaries?'

'He will get the nomination, according to our experts.'

'Good. Send him an extra twenty million.'

Paolo nodded, scribbled something in his journal.

The Boss walked back to the head of the table, sat down in his chair and leaned back. Just then a couple of maids came in and whisked up the spilled food and replaced the banquet as it had been before. He watched them leave then nodded to me, and I made up a plate for him the way he liked it, with the shrimp and the lobster tail set out just so. I put the plate in front of him and poured him a flute of champagne. Paolo and I made up plates for ourselves and we all sat and ate in silence.

When he was finished, the Boss dabbed his lips with a napkin. 'Sell it,' he said.

Paolo set his flute on the table. 'Sell what, Boss?'

The Boss swept his hand left to right in a broad arc. 'This,' he said. 'All of it.'

'Will do, Boss,' said Paolo. 'Good move.'

'And put half of what we get for it into charity.'

Paolo coughed, shook his head. 'Into what?'

'You heard me. I don't care what. Make me look good.'

And that was the start of it, a whole new play. I went home and violated clause four of my employment contract by writing it all down longhand in my diary.

Jennifer

That afternoon I walk to the transmitter cabin and send the next chapter of *The Forcing*, the part where Mum disappears and my dad and Papa are trying to find her. I finish the transmission, sit back in the chair, lace my hands behind my head and flex my arms. The band crackles and hisses. A voice emerges from the static.

'To the boys in Australia, come in please.'

I key back. 'We're here.'

'I am going to time my transmissions with yours. Please keep to this schedule. And keep going.'

'We will. What shall we call you?'

The line is quiet, warbling across the miles. And then: 'Just call me Sparkplug.'

'Understood, Sparkplug.'

She begins her transmission. I listen through as she describes her boss's space flight and its aftermath. And when it's over, I sit in the cabin, remembering how Mum and Papa used to talk about that world, before the Repudiation and everything that came after, running the transmission over again in my mind. I can't help but shake my head. So much of everything – a world of surplus for many, crushing deficit for others, but still, everything. What would I have done in such a world, if I had had the chance? What would I have called myself? Historian perhaps? Papa taught me and Lewis science and mathematics, about how the universe works, but I always loved history. I don't think about that stuff so much now, gravity and light and time, the forces that govern our world. But re-reading Papa's manuscript, and now hearing Sparkplug telling her story of that time, I find myself wondering about this recent history of the world. What actually happened? How could we have got it so wrong?

If there is one person who can tell me what my mother is unwilling or unable to, it is Aunty Jennifer. When you saw them together you could see they shared a special bond, two women cast away from all they'd known, raising small children together in a time of turmoil and isolation.

I set out a couple of days later, the weather still coming across the sound in ocean-blown ranks, the rain slanting down from dark, fast-moving clouds. When I arrive, Uncle Liberty and Aunty Jenny coax up the fire and put on tea.

Jenny hands me a mug, kisses my cheek. 'Kwe.'

'Suppose you've talked to your mum,' says Liberty.

I nod.

'And.'

'She said nothing's up there. I thought maybe she said something to you, Aunty.'

Jenny sips her tea, glances over at her husband. 'Uncle told me he took you up there, told you what he saw that day.'

'Yes.'

'When Uncle told me, all those years ago, I didn't believe it. Not her. A doctor, a mother. I know your mum, Kwe. We've been through a lot together.'

'That's why I wanted to talk to you.'

Jenny glanced at her husband a moment. 'Understand, Kwe, I didn't see it myself, what my husband thinks he saw. He shouldn't have told you.'

Liberty sips his tea. 'Feller deserves to know.'

'No, husband. Not everything. Did you tell him what you were doing up there that night?'

'Makes no difference what I was doin'.'

'It makes all the difference. Poor boy. Tell him, husband. Please.'

Liberty says nothing, stares into the fire.

'He was on walkabout, Kwe,' says Jenny. 'Fasting, speaking to the ancestors. Six days wandering without food. You saw all manner of things out there, husband. Real and spirit.'

Liberty grunts, tips the rest of his tea into the fire. 'Saw what I saw. There's reason for it.'

'*I* know, my love. But the boy deserves to as well.'

Next morning, I thank them both and start back. Aunty Jenny hugs me, kisses my cheek. Liberty tells me to walk well. A few hours later I am back at the stone Liberty showed me, looking out across twenty years of water. How am I to make sense of what happened to the entire world if my own family's story is beyond me? And suddenly it doesn't seem so unfathomable that we destroyed ourselves. Each of us an impossible complexity of fear and desire and sheer, burning will, half governed, animals still, and yet so much more. Divine. Psychotic. Atomic.

When I get back, I go straight to see Mum. It's evening, and she has a lamp burning. She is sitting at the table with a cup of tea and a book.

'Hello, Kweku.'

I kiss her and sit, place a small canvas bag on the table between us.

'What's this?'

'Open it, Mum.'

She looks up at me and smiles. That smile I've known all my life. She reaches for the bag, unties the drawstring. Her hands are strong still, sun-patched, the knuckles and fingerbones ridged in parchment.

She looks inside, and then back up at me. 'I don't understand, Kwe. What is it?'

'Take it out, Mum.'

She reaches inside, withdraws her hand. I watch as her mouth falls open and her eyes widen. She sits in silence, staring at the tiny skull cupped in her palm.

July 2024

It was about then, just after the Boss decided to sell the space programme and launch his new career as a celebrated philanthropist, that everything changed for me.

By then I knew that he liked me a lot. I'd caught him looking at me several times. Not just the leching stares he gave any pretty woman, but something else, some kind of longing there in his eyes. But each time I caught him, he just looked away and disappeared again behind those cold, clear blues. I knew I wasn't the prettiest of girls, not like Astrid and the other regulars, but I knew guys found me attractive. I still thought about Bryce now and then, but since I'd rebuffed him on the Gulfstream, he'd cooled right off, and now if we spoke it was all business and space.

And so that day when the Boss called me into his office, I was totally unprepared for what happened, not only there at his desk, but, more importantly, later on at the penthouse.

He was sitting at his desk when I entered, and I could feel him looking me over, lingering on my legs and my boobs. He told me to sit at the coding station, the one that he used for end-to-end encrypted high-level communication off-web. One of the military contractors had set it up for him a few years before. It kept his business dealings well away from anyone he didn't like and who didn't like him. And there were a lot of them, believe me.

I sat at the console and entered the password string. I'm good with numbers and letters, that sort of thing. We changed the password every week, and the Boss had a separate authentication. I waited while he authenticated on his phone, counted four blinks of the cursor. 'Ready, Boss.'

'Stockholm,' he said. I typed.

The cursor flashed and the response came up. 'Ready.'

'Order follows.'

'Ready.'

'Destruction order: Frederik Hedberg.' He spelled the name out for me. 'Senior partner, Lansing, Hedberg and Nylander, attorneys, Stockholm.'

'Confirmation.'

'Standard rate.'

'Acknowledged.'

'Confirm Completion.'

'Conclude.'

'Conclude.'

I shut down the console, sat staring at the blank screen. He stood behind me and put a hand on my bare shoulder, ran a finger up the back of my neck. Even now, looking back, I'm not sure what I felt. That fat hummingbird was there, her wingtips touching just about everything inside me. But there was something else too, something darker, and I knew then that I was being pulled into a place that I would never be able to leave.

'Hedberg?' I managed.

'That Swedish bitch's key adviser. I'm sending her a little warning.'

He stood back and told me to go and lock the door. I did it and he told me to come back. By now he was sitting behind his desk. He told me to stand before him and undress, as if I was being interviewed for a porno role or something. There was calmness in his voice. I guess I'd known this time would come, the way he was, but even so I was surprised at myself as I unzipped my dress and let it fall to the floor. I was wearing a G-string and a lacy half-cup bra underneath, and I could see his eyes glimmer a moment and a smile creep across his face. I found myself wondering if I'd picked this outfit to prompt just this, but pushed it from my mind. Some things are too dirty.

He left me standing there as he looked me over. Then he told me to step out of my underpants, keeping my shoes on.

'Good girl,' he said, making me wait. 'Now, play with yourself.'

I did.

He nodded, watched my hand moving. 'Most people, the vast majority, just want to be told what do. You know that, don't you?'

I said nothing, the afternoon sun warming my face and my body.

'Answer me.'

I moaned something.

'That's right. People are ruled by fear. I am not. That has always been one of my strengths. I don't feel fear. But I knows its effects. When others hesitate, freeze, panic, misjudge because of it, I am able to act.' He paused. 'Keep going.'

By now I was beyond it, barely listening to what he was saying.

'It's one of the biggest single reasons for my success. I started with nothing. Built all of this up myself. Not like that moron Bragg, inheriting it all from Mommy and going around making out like he's some kind of successful businessman. By the way, is that meeting set up?'

I nodded, breathing hard.

'I want you to know that I've always done what was required, without compunction. When it became necessary to put a bullet into my benefactor's skull, I did it without hesitation. Just stood behind him, one hand on his shoulder, this unsuspecting boss who had shown me so much kindness, had put me in charge of his empire. It was so easy. And after, when I pulled back his head, his silver hair slick with gore, and stared into the deep well where the face had been, I didn't feel fear, or revulsion, or even pride, just deep satisfaction. Because I knew at that moment that the rest of the organisation would now follow me, as blindly and stupidly as they had followed the lump of cooling flesh sprawled across the floor.'

By then my legs were quivering even as something inside me was dying.

'Come here,' he said, before I could finish.

I walked to the other side of the desk on wobbly stiletto legs and he pushed back his chair and signalled me to get on my knees. They don't call it a job for nothing.

Francoise

Mum turns the skull over in her hand, inspecting the open fontanelle, the little, toothless jaw, the partially knitted plates. Then she kisses the top of the head and places it back into the bag and ties the drawstring.

'Let me tell you about some of what was lost.'

She gazes straight into my eyes, completely lucid, my mother as I had known her all my life, all traces of her befuddlement gone.

'Ever since I was a little girl, I wanted to be a doctor. I worked hard, did well at school, got into the most prestigious medical university in the country. That was how it was, Kweku, back then. Women were respected, could do any work they chose. We could make our own decisions. We had control over our own bodies. After thousands of years as chattel, doomed to a restricted set of choices by biology, by our necessary role as mothers, finally we could be more. Leaders of countries, writers, scientists, lawyers and judges and policewomen. Even astronauts. Many helped make this change possible, women and men, and my generation was the beneficiary, for a time.'

She pushes the bag gently back across the table towards me.

'And then the Repudiation came, and war. And eventually, all that progress, all those possibilities, were extinguished as if they had never existed. And at the end, even with all my training and skill, I was treated as a menial slave and an object of lust to be controlled and used.'

She forces out the last hard consonant of that last word, and fixes me with her gaze. 'Do you understand, Kweku?'

'Yes, Mum. I understand.'

'It is why I raised you and your brother the way I did. There is a natural symbiosis between men and women, and when it works it is a beautiful thing. But if raw, unharnessed power defines our existence, the weak must submit. And without laws or mores, if civilisation collapses, it is worse. The strong take what they want, when they want it. Women become a resource to be managed and controlled.'

I can see the tears shining in the deep wells of her eyes.

'I feel so sorry for all of you. All of those choices gone. Look at Julie and Mandy. Your two lovely wives. The mothers of my beautiful grand-children.' She is crying now, silent tears slipping across her cheeks. 'When they first came here, they had never even heard of the contra-ceptive pill.'

'Mum.'

'It's true. I know both of those girls as if they were my own daughters. I taught them about their own bodies. When they arrived here that day with you and Lewis and announced to us that you were married, both of them so young, they knew nothing.'

I reach for her hand, take it in mine. I am trying to understand but I know that I cannot. I simply do not have the reference points. My life here has been full of love and learning. I've seen glimpses of that other world, relics like our radio, echoes of it in Albany, all the disused junk of that other time. But other than that, I've seen nothing of the plunge into darkness the two of them spoke about as we were growing up.

She squeezes my hand, knuckles away her tears with her other hand, sniffs. 'Your papa and I have devoted our lives to keeping the light burning. The light of hope and peace and truth. But Papa is gone now. And your father a long time ago. And I am an old woman now. It's your turn, Kweku. You have a responsibility.'

And then she tells me about my father, looking out at me through those old woman's eyes, still clear and green like the shallow water of our cove on a cloudy day. She tells me about what kind of man he was, about their great love and his gentleness and great physical strength and his respect for her, and them marrying against her family's wishes, and in the wake of the destruction of her hometown of Marseilles in a nuclear like-for-like exchange, their escape to North America. The rest, including her great sacrifice for love, I know from Papa's book.

'You are your father's son,' she says. 'I see so much of him in you.'

I run the palp of my thumb across the back of her hand, that thin rake of bones.

'There is something you must do, Kweku. For me, and for your father.'

'Of course, Mum.'

Suddenly she is very focused and all trace of emotion is gone. 'Something terrible happened in Africa, in your father's country.' She swallows, squeezes my hand. Her grip is strong.

Finally, I think. Some answers.

'The man who saved my life, who saved your life, Kweku, was called Derek Argent. He died in my arms.'

That is all in Papa's book, but I let her continue.

'His company won huge government contracts supporting the war effort in Africa. He made a fortune from it. But everywhere we went, your father and I heard terrible things. Rumours mostly. I was working in a hospital not far from Takoradi, where you father's family are from. Your father was my patient at the time, recovering from his wounds. Then one day I heard from a friend that there was an Argent camp nearby, built for refugees, people displaced by the fighting. I decided to see for myself.'

She takes a deep breath, as if to gather courage.

'I borrowed one of the hospital's cars and drove out through the town. There had been a battle there a few months earlier and I remember passing burnt-out vehicles, tanks and trucks, twisted rusted metal everywhere, such waste. And I'd seen what all of that had done, all those beautiful young boys ripped to pieces. It broke my heart, Kweku. I was never the same again.'

She pauses as if unsure how to continue, looks at me close.

'Sorry, dear, where was I?'

'The Argent camp, Mum.'

'Yes,' she says, smoothing her hair, composing herself. 'They'd built it in a clearing in the remnant forest, near a place called Kejabil. I smelled it before I saw it.'

She covers her face in her hands, chokes back a sob.

'Oh, Kweku, it was horrible. I can't even begin to describe it. Not a camp really, just rows of flimsy tents in the mud. The gate was locked. There was no one about, no guards, no minders, no doctors. I remember standing there watching a cruel mist reaching its fingers through the chain-link fence, a few smoking oil drums scattered about. And everywhere, as far as I could see, covered over in red dust, hundreds of bodies. The ground was paved with them. I can still see it now. It has never left me.'

I swallow, my mouth suddenly desert dry. 'What happened, Mum?'

She slumps in her chair. 'I don't know, Kweku. I reported it to the military governor's office but never heard back. If anyone did know, no one would talk about it. Everyone was so frightened. I met a nurse who told me it was an accident, but that the military was keeping it quiet. A few days later she disappeared. I never mentioned what I'd seen, and as soon as your father could travel, we left Africa to go to America, to start a new life, we thought.'

We sit in silence.

'You need to find out what happened there, Kweku. For me, for your father, for your family. I've met Papa's son. If he is still in government, he will know. And then you have to write it.'

I could feel a great weight descending on me, deep fathoms of it. 'I'll try, Mum. But please, what about you, about my sister?'

Her mouth straightens and there is a hardness in her voice. 'My story doesn't matter, Kweku. I am one of the lucky few. Millions of others, including your father, were not. Tell the world what they did.'

She slumps in her chair, exhausted, and closes her eyes. I sit there, her pulse even in my hand, considering everything that this means.

After a while she opens her eyes again and she says: 'Look after Juliette.' Her voice is barely a whisper now and it is as if with each word she is falling away from me into some great distance. 'She is strong, Kweku, and she loves you. I have taught her everything I know about medicine. She is a doctor now in all but name and diploma. She will look after you, keep you and Leo safe.'

And then, suddenly, she stops. It is like a switch being flipped. She looks into my eyes, as if searching for proof of my understanding, then pushes the bag towards me until it is touching my hand.

'Now go and put it back.'

Whatever she can't tell me will never be told. I will never see her again.

August 2024

All of that summer of '24 the fires raged. Most of Ontario and Quebec and big parts of Vermont were ablaze. Some days in New York the smoke was so thick you couldn't see across the block. My little place in Greenwich Village was hot even with the AC going full blast, and even in the penthouse, where I was spending more and more time with the Boss, the heat and smoke were almost unbearable. I couldn't help thinking about Trig and what he'd told us that day.

Then one day the Boss woke up early, like he did, and went and stood out on the balcony. I threw on the silk robe he'd bought me the week before and joined him. Normally from there you could see clear across Central Park to the Met, but today the smoke had settled in like a winter graveyard fog.

'Call Stephenson,' he said, putting his arm around my waist and pulling me close. It had all happened quickly after that day in his office, and now he wanted me around pretty much all the time. 'Tell him to have the jet ready to go in two hours.'

'Where should I say we're going?'

'I'll tell him when we get there. Tell him full fuel. And get the chopper ready – tell them on the roof in an hour.' He pulled out his phone and tapped a number, put the phone to his ear, always a cue for everyone else to leave.

I went to make the call, left him there on the balcony.

'And doll,' he called after me, his hand over the pickup. 'Pack light.'

Ten hours later we touched down on the island of Mustique in the Caribbean. It was just me and the Boss, Bryce and his co-pilot Smith up front, and Melody serving us in the cabin. Bryce hadn't said a word to me the whole way down, came back just the once to check on us, and when he did the two of us were drinking champagne and the Boss had his hand on my bare thigh and didn't move it as he spoke to him: yeah, all good, on time, yeah good, okay – zero eye contact between me and Bryce. I was pretty sure by now that he'd had the same clause sixteen warning as I'd had, and besides, the staff whisper moved at three times the speed of sound so I was sure he knew I'd been staying nights with the Boss over the last couple of weeks. He probably thought I was such a slut.

An hour and a half later we were sitting on the terrace of the Boss's place out on the point, drinking champagne, looking out at the dark sea, a gentle trade wind caressing the palm trees above us. He bought this place about five years ago. It used to belong to Mick Jagger.

Dinner came, amazing as always, with wines that he told me were fantastic and expensive but tasted just like normal wine to me. After dinner we went out onto the terrace again and I sat in one of the lounge chairs and closed my eyes and breathed the clean sea air. I must have drifted off because suddenly he was standing behind me, his hand caressing my throat.

'You thought I didn't notice,' he said.

My heart jumped. 'Notice what?'

I hear a faint creak, like a screw being turned in wood, and then felt his hands tighten around my neck, a new weight there.

I reached for my neck, moved my fingertips over the unfamiliar roughness of the thing. I turned to face him, breathing hard. 'What is it?'

He handed me a small hand mirror. Always prepared.

In the flickering torchlight I could see the stone glittering dark blue at my throat, the gold choker close to my skin.

'Sapphire,' he said. 'Fifty carats. Happy birthday.'

My speech centre had temporarily fled from my body. It was my twenty-first birthday and here I was sitting there with one of the richest men in the word with a gem on my neck that was worth more than my apartment. He kissed me, and that night I made love to him for the first time. Throughout he insisted I wear the choker.

The next morning, he got up early and went for a run around the island. I got the daily briefing together so it would be ready for him when he got back. I got all the secure communications, spoke to Paolo, who gave me the financial highlights – profits steady and solid; to the lawyers on the progress in Niger – on schedule; and to the PR people about the day's media – continued backlash from the spaceflight, more on Bragg's recent coronation at the Republican convention in Wisconsin and his latest rally in Pittsburgh.

I showered and changed into a bikini and a sundress, ate on the terrace, leafed through a day-old copy of the *Wall Street Journal*, waited for him to come back. None of it seemed real. A big part of me fully expected that I would wake up at any moment and be back in that crappy apartment with my three flatmates, holding down two waitressing jobs, wondering if I would ever be able to use my degree, trying not to think about whether I would get married or have kids someday. It was almost as if I was a different person now, divorced from that past. And despite the amazement, I could feel that dark fluttering inside me, and I knew then that all of this wouldn't last, couldn't last, and suddenly I could hear Trig talking in that boring monotone of his about how bad things were going to get if we didn't change. And then my twenty-one-year-old self clutched the paper and read again the page-three article.

Frederik Hedberg, forty-three, attorney and chief adviser to climate activist Ellie Dahlberg, had been accused by several underage girls of abusing them sexually over a period of ten months. The girls, aged between twelve and sixteen years, had come forward independently after seeing a video on social media that showed Hedberg seducing a teenage girl in the front seat of his Mercedes. Apparently, Ellie herself was aware of his penchant, but had done nothing about it. The fallout was rocking the liberal climate-action world. This was what the Boss meant by destruction.

Persephone

The day after that talk with Mum the rain clears and morning comes bright and cool. I ask Julie to walk with me up to the grave. She decides to bring a picnic – after we will go to our favourite beach and have a swim. I carry Leo on my shoulders. As we climb the ridge, I tell Julie about everything Mum said, about what she asked me to do, about what she didn't say.

'She's right,' Julie says, breathing hard as we move through the trees and the path steepens. 'We have a responsibility.'

'We?' I still haven't come to grips with any of it, what it means for us, for our future.

She reaches out and grabs my arm and turns into me so we are face to face, touching. 'Of course, we.'

By the time we reach the three pillars the sun is out and the hillside steams as if in grateful exhalation. The sandy soil is easier to dig the second time.

The rest of the skeleton is very frail-looking, there in its shallow grave. Bones nibbled clean, white as bleached coral. The flattened ossature of tiny fingers and toes splayed like the fossil wings of some small Devonian bird or reptile. Femur and rib and clavicle in perfectly formed compression. Little Persephone, I name her, goddess of the underworld.

Leo and Julie stand next to me. I place the skull as I found it, on one side, the empty little eye sockets directed towards Liberty's camp. We don't speak as I cover her back up. Like so many, she never had a chance.

After, we stand there together, looking out across the sound, the three of us holding hands. After the rain it is very clear and we can see all the way across to The Hope and the waves crashing white on the far rocks and the dark, almost black water of the Southern Ocean beyond and the sunlight flashing like stars on the rippled surface of the sound, and then the two little shapes moving very fast across the water as if suspended above the surface, and they are coming towards us now so quickly that our eyes have trouble registering the speed of them. And then the noise comes on the sea breeze, a grinding chop, and we stand there watching as they reach the cove and flare up to the ridge and I can see that they are helicopters, just as Papa had described them to me, and suddenly they stop and they are hovering there above our little radio building.

Julie moves close and grabs my arm, and before either of us can formulate words, two lines fall to the ground from each of the helicopters and we watch in horror as men slide down the ropes and move away and disappear into the building and down the slope towards our house and the house where Lewis and Mandy and Becky live.

At a full run I can be there in thirty minutes, maybe less. I pull Leo from my shoulders and put him on the ground. 'Stay here and stay out of sight,' I tell Julie and set off.

I formulate a plan as I run. Papa's handgun is at my house. There are two AK47 rifles on *Providence*, but it will take me too long to swim out there and get them. I have to go straight back. I am halfway down the ridge when I hear the first gunshots. The sound rips through my chest, the pain real and physical. I push myself on, flying across the rocks, running as fast as I can. My foot catches a root and I fall hard. I manage to roll out but not before ripping the palm of my left hand on some brush. By now I am not thinking. I am only reacting, running, trying to close the gap. A loud detonation echoes across the sound, and soon I can see a dark pillar of smoke rising above the trees. The two helicopters are circling now, and I stop and hug a tree as one of the machines flashes over me, the blades of its rotors strobing black against the blue sky, and I think of Julie alone up there with Leo and all I can do is hope that she has stayed hidden.

I keep going, dread welling up inside me dark and cold, and I feel as if I am going to vomit, and then I hear the distinct sound of Papa's handgun firing once, twice, three times, and then an eruption of automatic gunfire in reply and then just the hammering of my heart in my ears and the rasp of my lungs heaving as I sprint along the shore.

I duck into the bush as one of the helicopters approaches and stand frozen as it hovers a moment above me before it raises its tail like a scorpion and then turns back towards the smoke. As I near our cove I can see the evil machines hovering low and stationary, and then suddenly they raise up and drop towards the water, speeding away across the sound the way they came. And then they are gone.

When I reach my brother's house, I can see what's left of our short-wave building up the hill, the antennae toppled and twisted, the solar panels shattered, the stone walls blown apart, the twisted remains of our carefully assembled transmitter smoking in the ruins. Lewis's house is intact. I push the door open and double over. Mandy lies in a pool of blood, her belly torn open, eyes staring at the ceiling. On the floor nearby is a playing card, a queen of diamonds. I pick it up, stunned, and turn it over. Two symbols, Greek letters, are printed on the back, alpha and omega. I drop the card, call out for Becky and Lewis, but all that comes is an anguished rasp. I move through the house, but it is empty. I run up the hill to our place and find the door flung open and the windows smashed, everything turned over.

I re-emerge into the glare of day, and shout again for Lewis and Becky, but get no reply. I race down the hill to Mum's house and it's there that I find them. Mum is lying on the kitchen floor, shot through the chest and head. Lewis is nearby, my gun beside him in a pool of blood. I stand a moment staring at him and then my legs give way and I crumple sobbing to the floor.

It's there that Julie finds me an hour later.

Scavengers

Niece

I wander around our settlement in a daze. It is as if a clawed hand has reached into my chest and ripped out my nervous system, and I am left unable to process or feel or in any way comprehend what has happened. Sparkplug's warning comes to me over and over again, static-laden and discounted until I put my hands over my ears and try to scream it away.

Kwesi and Liberty arrive not long after. They've run the whole way. Each is armed with a rifle. They've seen the helicopters and the smoke, heard the gunfire, came as soon as they could.

'No words,' says Kwesi, looking at the bodies laid out on the floor. 'Who did this?'

I hand him one of the playing cards, Mum's, the queen of hearts. 'There were three of them, one for each body.' I show them. The queen of diamonds for Mandy. The jack of spades for Lewis.

Kwesi turns the card over, looks at the symbol. 'What is this?'

I shake my head. 'No idea. But whoever it is, I'm going to find them.'

'Where's little Becky?' says Liberty, respect in his voice, pragmatism.

'We've looked everywhere,' I say.

'Maybe she hid,' says Kwesi. 'Plenty of places to hide for a little tacker. We need to keep looking.'

'Poor thing,' says Julie. 'She must be terrified.'

'Unless they took her.' Liberty.

We all turn to face him.

'Heard about that kind of thing going on. Girl children especially.'

Julie shudders. I can see the tremors run through her whole body. 'It was in Papa's book.'

Liberty taps the base of his spear on the jarrah plank floor, nods. 'Better keep looking.'

We scour the whole area again, the four of us, up the hill, all around the houses, the places we know she likes, shouting out her name, telling her it's okay. We keep at it until nightfall. I run up to Chicken-Head Rock, but there is no trace of her. And then, just as the sky is darkening, I hear a shout. I'm up on the ridge, with the burnt-out hulk of the radio cabin there below me and Lewis's house beyond. Kwesi is standing near the trees Papa planted to screen the house from the winter storms. He is waving his arms over his head. I sprint back down, hurdling rocks and fallen trees.

When I reach the screen of trees, Kwesi is standing there with Liberty and Julie. He holds up a playing card. The same symbol as before. $\alpha\Omega$. Alpha and omega. Then he flips the card over. It's the three of hearts.

'It was pinned to this tree,' says Kwesi.

I know immediately and so does Julie. She wails to the heavens and collapses into me, and I hold her for a long time as the grief works through her, grim and uncompromising.

Liberty and Kwesi stay overnight, something they've only done a few times before, sleeping outside under a peppermint tree, a few sheets of paperbark each for a blanket. The next morning, we gather in Mum's house and we watch Julie clean Mum and Lewis and Mandy, washing away the blood, gentle as if they could still feel. Then we wrap them each in a blanket and Liberty puts a hand on my shoulder and I go to harness up one of Lewis's horses. We take Mum up first. Liberty and Julie keep vigil up on the ridge while Kwesi and I go back down for Mandy and then for Lewis.

It takes us most of the rest of the day to dig three deep graves next to Papa. The sun is out and a few clouds float unaware and dispassionate in a deep-blue sky. There is moisture in the sand so we cut the walls straight and square down through the layered Holocene sediment, use the pick to dig out the occasional limestone boulder. We lower them as gently as we can into the ground and cover them over. Julie weeps quietly by the graveside as we shovel.

And then we stand back and look down on the graves, and the immensity of what has occurred begins to crush me, fathoms of cold, heavy Southern Ocean water above me, deeper and deeper until my lungs start to compress and spasm and everything is pressing in on me. I stagger back from the graves, and suddenly it is as if I am at the bottom of some deep chasm looking back up at the surface and I can see the trees all liquid and dissolving and Julie's face a floating blur and I realise I am sobbing uncontrollably.

After a while I realise that Liberty is standing there next to me with his hand on my shoulder and has been the whole time. Slowly I swim back to the surface and when I emerge and breathe, he looks at me, and I look at him, and I am gazing deep into his old man's eyes, and I know what I have to do.

October 2024

With the election only a few weeks away, the whole team went into full campaign mode. The consortium – that's what we called it back then – met at the Boss's place in Mauritius. A couple of the guys flew in on their own jets, but most arrived on their yachts. The harbour was crammed with them. The guys who came by yacht helicoptered to the Boss's place, and as usual it was a competition to see who had the newest, fastest, most chop chopper. I watched them walking around the helipad talking about their machines like normal guys might do in a parking lot with their muscle cars. At least it made it easy for me to organise. And there was plenty of room at the place for support staff, as well as wives and girlfriends, and sometimes both.

Actually, these meetings could be a lot of fun, in short bursts anyway, all of us support people getting together in the evening after the work was done and the bigshots were all looked after. That first night we went to the back firepit. I'd arranged a roast pig on a spit and all the booze we could drink, and everyone had a good time. Even Bryce came, and I watched him across the fire sitting next to Melody, the Gulfstream's stewardess, and I could see her laughing at his jokes and frankly, it hurt.

But during the day it was all work. Again, I was assigned to minute the meetings. I was good at it, knew when to leave stuff out, how to focus on agreed actions and not clutter them up with a bunch of back and forth. The first day was all about the upcoming election. Yu Wan chaired the session, as usual. Everyone was there, twenty-four of them all up. Together, they figured they directly controlled almost forty percent of the world's wealth. And indirectly, through people who worked for them or they just plain out owned, it was more like half. Fifty-fifty they called it, with a grin. Win-win.

'Gentlemen, good to see you all here.' Yu Wan stroked his beard, the elder statesman of the group. 'Let's get started.'

I looked around the room. Frankly, it was scary. Most of these guys were older, fifties and sixties. Maddisson, the media tycoon, was way older, seventies at least. Some of those faces you'd see on the news pretty regularly, the ones who were heads of state in countries like Russia and Saudi Arabia. Those guys, you knew some of what they were up to, wars and assassinations and so on. But some kept so low key you'd never know they even existed if you didn't come to these meetings. They were the ones who really scared me. Guys like Li Sang and Valliant, and another guy called Auguste Leopold who almost never spoke, just sat quietly watching and listening carefully to everything everyone said, as if he was evaluating it all, locking it all away.

First up was a presentation from Pierre Valliant's chief of strategy, a preposterously huge Frenchman who I'd met briefly in Paris on an earlier trip. He heaved himself up, blotted his cheeks and forehead with a handkerchief and put up his first slide.

'The global strategic context is sitting on a knife-edge,' he began. 'On one side we have a possible future of untold expansion and wealth accumulation, and on the other ... well, severe contraction of our interests.'

He paused, put up his next slide, a collage of images from the news: activists gluing themselves to roads, Dahlberg addressing the UN, the big march for climate action in Paris the week before.

'The movement for serious climate action is gathering steam,' he said. 'Businesses around the world are promoting their green credentials, and citizens who can vote are increasingly choosing candidates who call themselves "progressive".' He raised two chubby fingers on each hand to put the last word in quotes. 'We've done our best to discredit this idea of a global wealth tax, but deliberations in the United Nations are well advanced. I would say that the vote is now down to a coin-toss. Fifty-fifty.'

'We know what a coin toss is,' said the Boss, shaking his head, frowning.

The president of the Russian Federation whispered something to his translator, who nodded and cleared his throat. 'The United Nations is meaningless.'

A general rumbling of agreement went around the table. He'd been waging his war in Ukraine for more than two years, and despite UN sanction and early setbacks, was making steady progress as the western democracies tired of pouring in money and weapons. I had a

Ukrainian-Canadian girlfriend whose twenty-year-old brother had gone over to fight. He'd been killed in a place called Bakhmut in 2023.

'Frankly, the key is the United States,' said the Frenchman. 'It is still by far the dominant nation on the planet, economically and militarily. It is imperative that Bragg wins the presidency. And this time, we need to ensure that he stays in.'

Everyone looked at each other across the table, right and left. He'd said it. You could hear people breathing.

Yu Wan looked at Maddisson. 'Well,' he said. 'Can we do it?'

A smile dawned on the media mogul's face. It came on slowly, as if he was deliberately stretching it out. 'Are you bloody kidding me? Of course we can do it. People are already scared shitless. This new tax will kill economic growth, kill jobs. I can see it now. People on the streets, millions unemployed and destitute, mortgage foreclosures. A few shocks here and there, another pandemic, say, a couple more wars, a bank run. That would be all we needed. Blame it all on the weak-ass liberal progressives. Flood social media with it. Fear. That's the ticket. Immobilise them with fear. Works every time. All they have to do is nothing.'

He leaned back in his chair, folded his hands across his overstretched belly. I wrote it all down, word for word. That last sentence I underlined.

Port Louis

Really, we have no choice. Julie and I talk about it for three days straight, going through all the options, the risks, and what we both know are the clear imperatives. Whoever killed Mum and Lewis and Mandy, and took Becky – and by now we are convinced she has been taken – they know where we live and they could return at any time. It isn't safe to stay. And then there is Becky. Sweet little Becky, not much younger than our Leo. Whatever it takes, we have to find her. On top of that, I have the promise I made to Mum, my own questions that need answering. The bastards came to stop us telling Papa's story, that much is clear, and I am going to find a way to keep telling it.

So we pack up everything that matters to us, everything we might need: guns and ammo and fishing gear and our little short-wave receiver, notebooks and pencils. We stock *Providence* with food, fill her water tanks and leave. Sail out of that sound for maybe the last time.

I have no plan for finding Becky. She could be anywhere. All I know is that it must have something to do with Papa's book, Sparkplug's tale and the gaps in Mum's story. It might take us the rest of our lives, but the one thing we have is time. Africa is as good a place as any to start. And along the way, I am going to write the story. Our story. Mum's, Mandy's, Lewis's, and Becky's.

❂

On August 17th of 2066 we arrive in Port Louis, Mauritius, after forty-two days at sea. Juliette and Leo are delighted to see land, but unsettled. They've done well, and I tell them so.

We anchor in Port Louis harbour in the late afternoon. The city is eerily quiet. No vessels we can see, no cars or people. The big warehouses and cranes of the port front appear intact, all bounded by newish-looking sea walls, but further along we can make out ranks of submerged jetties and the protruding tops of what were once waterfront properties, now slowly disintegrating in the Indian Ocean swell. Taller office buildings hulk beyond, terracing away inland, everything grey and powdered over in the sunlight, the country all around ravaged by fire, the trees burned to blackened trunks. A grey island, dead in the sun.

Leo's previous excitement has evaporated now, and he sits at the railing gazing out over the seemingly abandoned city in mute wonder. I don't want to stay, but we need supplies. Water is short, and with no rain for more than three weeks we are now relying almost completely on the desal unit. Food is running low, and we haven't had fresh vegetables or fruit for weeks. The next possible landfall is Reunion, a hundred nautical miles west, then Madagascar five hundred miles further again.

I leave Juliette with the gun, give her clear instructions about what to do if anyone tries to approach or come aboard. If I'm not back by nightfall, she should weigh anchor and stand offshore. Come back in the morning, if it's safe to do so, and if I haven't made contact within forty-eight hours, leave. Go home. Then I catch myself, realise that we don't have a home anymore. Go to Liberty's, I say.

I throw my big backpack into the dinghy and row in, looking down through the acid-clear water at that inundated shore. I tie up the dinghy and walk into the city. Buildings rise up canyonlike around me, their walls dripping with blistered, peeling paint. A thick layer of ash covers the street and powders up in little puffs of grey around my feet. Twisted signs hang forlorn and purposeless. Heat pours in waves from every scorched surface, sucking the air from my lungs so that I have to stop and force myself to breathe before I can go on.

Further down the street I find what looks like a store of some kind, and push open the door. Inside, the air is dank and humid. The stench of burnt rubber and plastic is overwhelming. My flashlight beam reveals aisles strewn with junk, banks of empty freezers and bare shelving, all filmed over in the same grey ash.

I keep going, past more empty stores, deserted buildings, the hulks of burnt-out cars, neat and orderly in their parking places. If there are still people around, they are staying hidden. Whatever happened here, it was relatively orderly. Not chaos, more like a hasty but well-organised departure. That explains the absence of any vessel in the harbour.

I come to the edge of the city, the base of a craggy, burnt-up spire of rock too steep to build on. A trail climbs up through the charcoal scrub – in places there are stone steps and steel railings. I start up, skin filmed in the fine grey powder that covers everything. From the look and smell, the fire had burnt not for hours or days, but for some altogether more protracted hell. Hard to believe that this is the same place Sparkplug described in her transmission. Hard to believe it's the same world.

From the top I can see the rest of the island curving away, all the hills, everything to the furthest reaches, burnt like here, ash grey and black against the blue sky and the deeper blue of the sea and the pale blue of the fringing reefs, nothing green that I can see. The city opens out beneath me, a shimmering mirage in the heat, the streets, the empty harbour, the big concrete silos, and there, so small, *Providence* swinging quietly at anchor.

Through the binoculars I can see Juliette sitting in the cockpit. She is facing the city, watching. I call out to her, wave. It isn't that far, and there is no wind. I call again, then see her look my way, stand, then disappear into the cabin, re-emerging a moment later with the other set of glasses. We stand looking at each other magnified, smiling and waving.

I start back down the hill to the city, heat still rising in corrugated waves, liquid and strangely buoyant so it is as if I am swimming in it. Most of the buildings are locked up, as if people left intending to return. But some are open, doors unlocked or ajar or blown in, bolts ruptured. I search a few, find nothing but ash and charred furniture.

By now, it's getting late. Maybe an hour and a half until sunset, when Juliette should be leaving to stand off. I come to a block of flats in an older-looking building, the inner courtyard spindled with the stubs of charred trees. I try a ground-floor apartment door but it's locked, then try another. After a few more I find one unlocked.

Inside it is dark, five degrees cooler out of the sun. As my eyes adjust, I can make out an ash-powdered living room, a dead television, and beyond, a kitchen with dishes and cutlery scattered across a table. A last meal rushed and then cut short? The sink taps yield no water and the fridge is empty but for a carton of mould. All the cupboards are bare. I keep going, a luckless intruder set on salvage, creep into the bedroom.

The closet is open, a few clothes still hanging there, a woman's dress, a man's shirt, two dozen empty wire hangers. Off the bedroom is a small office with a window that looks out over the street, a computer screen on the desk, my blank, grey face staring out at me, all of it filmed over in the same grey ash.

Suddenly there is a noise, something crashing to the floor. I spin to face it, my heart trying to punch through my ribs. A rat scurries away across the bedroom floor. I take a breath, steady myself.

Inside the desk drawers I find a few personal papers, bills more than a year old, and a small, black-bound journal. Inside are pages of hand-written scrawl, in French. The first entry is dated March 2063, three years ago, and the last is January 2066. I put it in my bag and retrace my steps. Back in the living room I scan the bookshelf and grab a copy of Homer's *The Odyssey,* blow the ash from the end band and the fore edge, and stuff it in my bag.

But you can't eat literature. I keep going, trying door after door, a lone scavenger loping through an abandoned world. By now, a blood-orange stain is wicking off the horizon. I check the other ground-floor flats, but they are all locked.

I come to the next door and stand back, staring at it, suddenly disdainful of these pointless barriers. I stand a moment, and then I kick it in. Blow the hinges right out of the tinder-dry doorframe. In the kitchen I find a locked pantry. This is good, I am thinking. I pull the hatchet from my pack, smash off the lock, that strange thrill, and open the door.

I stand there a moment taking it in, all that space, the fine powdered ash filming the bare shelves.

By the time I get back outside, the sky is erupting. I run back to the harbour, all those empty buildings glowing like embers in a dying sun, through this abandoned city on a burnt-up island in the middle of an empty ocean. And all I can think about is little Becky, a captive somewhere, alone and frightened.

November 2024

The Boss' charity PR campaign had been a big success, and although Yu Wan hated his flamboyance, he was more popular than ever. The combination of millions in giving and a steady message of economic security and jobs and the value of the products all his industries created was playing well on social media. Our private polling showed the Boss tracking pretty much with Bragg. And both were going north, fast. Social media was particularly valuable. We zeroed in on those already predisposed to our message, those who were basically scared shitless about losing what they had, no matter how little it was, and were well disposed to voting for things that were not actually in their best interest. That's how the Boss described it anyway. It was amazing to me how many of them there were, statically alike, all braying about how independent and individual they were. Sheep he called them.

Just before polling day, we met with Bragg's team in a Washington hotel meeting room. Like I said, a lot of meeting rooms.

I'd never met him before, only seen him on TV. The meeting was set for two pm, and the Boss had insisted on a big lunch and an extra bottle of champagne beforehand, so we were pretty much half in the bag by the time we arrived, fifteen minutes late. The lines in the back of the limo on the way to the hotel didn't help.

But when we got to the room, Paolo, the Boss and I, it was empty. The Boss was fuming. I ran to the front desk to make sure we had the right one – yes ma'am the Lincoln Suite – and raced back and told the Boss.

'Did he confirm?' the Boss said, barely keeping it together.

I checked my phone. 'Yes. His office confirmed yesterday.'

'Well, he's fucking late. Let's go.' The Boss turned and started back down the corridor and out the front doors and we got into the limo. 'Drive,' he said.

'Where?' replied Max, the driver.

'I don't give a shit, just fucking drive.'

'Yes, Boss.'

He glared at me. 'Find out where the hell that moron is.'

I made the call, talked to Bragg's chief of staff, listened to his apologies and excuses, ended the call. 'They'll be there in ten,' I said. 'They had a press conference that went over.'

But the Boss wasn't listening, just sat there staring at something on his phone. Max drove around for another half an hour, and then the Boss told him to go back to the hotel. When we arrived back at the meeting room, we'd kept Bragg and his team waiting for a satisfactory twenty minutes. Our dick was bigger than his.

Despite this, he was a big man, with a strangely overpigmented complexion that was more striking in person than on camera, and a mullet hairdo right out of the nineteen seventies. All up, the effect was part circus clown, part long-past-it surfer dude. They say some people's best friend is the camera. For this guy it was definitely the mirror. I'd never seen anyone preen and primp so much during an actual meeting.

We all shook hands and then sat, our people on one side of the table, his on the other. Bragg sat there staring at us, blinking. He looked confused. One of his aides whispered into his ear and he jerked upright.

'We're definitely gonna win,' he said. 'Clear-cut victory on the way.'

'I hope so,' said the Boss.

'We've fixed it so it's gonna be great,' said Bragg. He sounded like he was at the podium at one of his rallies. 'The best in the world.'

The Boss glanced at Paolo. It was one of his half-second 'this-guy-is-an idiot' glances that were common between them. They had a rapport that way.

'Damn right,' said the Boss.

'My opponent's an old man,' Bragg blustered. 'Falls down all the time. He's weak. I'm strong. That's what this country needs now, a strong man.' He strung the last two words together as one.

The boss and Paolo shared another glance. Bragg was only three years younger than the Democratic nominee.

'I'm here not only to help you win, Mister President,' said the Boss, 'but to make sure that once you do, you stay there.'

Bragg clasped his hands together and leaned forward on the table. His navy-blue suit was perfectly pressed, his orange tie hung long and loose across his puffed-up chest. All that were missing were the dangling balls. 'I'm listening.'

'We repeal the twenty-second amendment,' said the Boss. 'You can be the next FDR. How does four terms sound? Five. Your Russian buddy has set the standard.'

Bragg smiled big, displaying tens of thousands of dollars of dental work, and then put on that 'I am a serious businessman and I do deals' face. 'How?'

'Leave that to us. All you have to do is keep doing what you're doing. We'll feed you the script. There's going to be a big global crisis, another pandemic, for instance, worse than 2020, but this time you're going to be the hero.'

Bragg smiled again. He looked like a little kid who's just been told he's going to get a new bike for Christmas.

The Boss stood and walked to the door, Paolo and I behind him.

Then he turned back and faced Bragg. 'You'll be hearing from us,' he said. 'And try not to fuck it up.' He never could resist the opportunity to put a flex on.

And then we were out and back into the limo and on the way to the airport, and just like that we'd changed the world forever.

Indian Ocean

An ocean makes you think. Tracing that horizon across every blue meridian and ending up back where you started, there at the centre of your own little skull cap of water, it gets you to pondering. Maybe it's the scale, measuring one's own insignificance against such immensity. Perhaps the terrifying contrast between our own febrile passions and the ocean's implacable indifference drives some kind of current inside our brains. Whatever it is, out here at the far peripheries, most of the questions seem too big for answers.

Last night Leo asked me what happened on the grey islands. I told him I didn't know. Maybe there are some answers in that journal, the one I took from Port Louis, but I haven't had time to read it yet. But whatever I learn, whatever I tell my son, he's not going to understand. I still can't. Any of it. Part of me wants to turn back now. Two months and we'd be home. Home.

Hard to believe out here that half the world is gone – more, probably. Doubt plagues me. I am still not sure we're doing the right thing, launching ourselves out into the unknown like this. But then I talk to Julie and she reassures me, the way she does.

I was born on this boat, right there on the saloon table. We'd heard the story growing up, one of the few from that lost time, as if in the retelling Mum and Papa were cementing something in place. They would always hold hands as they told it, that sense of something shared between them, like witnesses trying to keep their stories aligned.

A copy of Papa's manuscript is here with me now. Mum copied it in her own hand after he died, like a monk working by candlelight in another dark age a thousand years ago. She gave me this pile of papers, but she wouldn't fill in the gaps. Her gaps. *My* gaps. As if some part of it was just too painful to tell.

I never knew my real father. He was killed in a riot in a concentration camp for old people before I was born. It's in Papa's book. He and Papa met in the camp, became close friends. A camp dreamed up by the youth government that took control in North America twenty years ago; a place to send the older generation – those the youth government deemed responsible for the cataclysm consuming the world, those who could have voted for change back when they should have known better, but didn't. Some kind of deep revenge. Mum was young enough to stay, but decided to go with my dad, who was well above the cutoff age. Papa's son, Lachie, was part of that youth government, high up enough that he knew everything that was going on. Must have.

I never went to school. Mum and Papa taught me and Lewis everything they could. They wanted us to know how far humans had come, before the descent. How much we'd discovered about ourselves, our world, about the universe and how it works. And they were careful to teach us about all the things we didn't know. 'Feet on the ground', as Uncle Liberty calls it.

And so, here we are, in the middle of the Indian Ocean, and all that remains are ghosts.

We are about four hundred nautical miles east of Madagascar when Leo spots the ship. It is the first one we've seen afloat and in open water since leaving home. It's on the port bow, a long way off. No wake is showing and there is no smoke from the stack. As we close, we can see she is listing, low in the water, in trouble. The superstructure is streaked black above gaping windows, and the masthead antennae lie toppled and twisted across the aft deck. Lifeboat davits hang empty, their lines dangling in the ocean. Some kind of aftermath.

'I don't like it,' says Julie. 'It looks recent. Let's leave it. Go past.'

I stand at the rail, scanning the ship through the binoculars. There is no sign of the crew. 'Could be supplies aboard,' I say.

'We're fine, Kwe. Really. Stretching things out, we can go another month easy.'

'There could be news,' I say. 'Information. Who knows.'

'It doesn't feel right, Kwe. Something bad happened over there.'

'Tell you what, we'll come alongside, check her out. See how you feel then. We'll take it from there.'

By now I know she's thinking the same thing I am. She takes my hand that way she does. 'Okay, let's see how it goes.'

It takes us another two hours to reach her. By then, Leo has been fed and we are squared away for quick running if needed. As we close, we can see that she is sinking. How fast, we can't tell, but definitely on her way down. Rope ladders drape the hull fore and aft, trail in the water. How long she's been like this is hard to tell. We circle her, bow to stern. Her rudder appears to be damaged, but she is sitting so low in the water it's difficult to be sure. The words *Ocean Transporter* are just visible across her stern, the port of registry submerged so just the tops of the letters are visible. Liberia, maybe. She is a Panamax freighter, designed specifically for the canal. I saw one in Albany, years ago, a refugee from Africa.

We manoeuvre within hailing distance and lower the sails, sit bobbing in the swell next to the stricken ship, peering up at its massive steel hull. I yell out at the top of my voice, wait, listen. And again. But there is nothing, just the sound of the swell surging under the great curved hull.

'I'm going aboard,' I say to Julie. 'There may be something we can salvage.'

'Take the gun,' she says.

I launch the dinghy and row towards one of the ladders that is draped over the side. I tie the dinghy to it, hail the ship one more time, and hearing no reply, start up. Rust blisters the hull, boiling up around the rivets. Every time the rope scrapes across one of the pustules it bursts, sending flakes of oxidised steel fluttering down to the water. Above me the sky is very blue and the ship's superstructure shines white in the sun, and now I can see that several of the upper windows have been blown open and it is smoke and the scorching of flames that have stained the paint black.

When I reach the main deck, I turn and look back down at *Providence*, so small beside this freighter, Juliette and Leo there in the cockpit waving up at me. I wave back, fish the gun from the bag, palm in a magazine and start towards the bridge.

The vessel groans as it heaves in the swell, a deep metallic rumble that I can feel through the soles of my feet as it echoes across bulkheads and through empty compartments. I climb to the bridge, an overpowering odour of rot and decay gassing from the ship's orifices. Halfway up I stop, stick my head inside one of the doorways and call out, my voice echoing through the bowels of the stricken ship, but no reply comes.

Eight storeys above the main deck, the ship's list cants the starboard bridge wing out over the water. *Providence* is there below, standing off. I call to Julie, and she waves from the cockpit. I can see the ship's three pairs of forward cargo holds gaping like dark pits dug into the steel plating. The big hatches have been thrown open and some have been forced and lie strewn at drunken angles across the main deck.

The bridge is empty. In the navigation table, I find charts for Madagascar, the Mozambique Coast and the Cape. I fold them up and put them in my pack. It's then that I notice the two symbols hurriedly spraypainted on the main window: α and Ω. I freeze, stand there not quite believing what I am seeing. And then it all comes back to me, that day of the attack and the unthinkable aftermath now as real as the graves on the ridge in that faraway place. The gun is shaking in my hand. I take a couple of steps back, bump into the chart table, lean against it. And then the fear comes, racing across the water towards me.

December 2024

Bragg won the election. It was a lot closer than he or we would've liked, though, and there was a moment there when we thought it would be a replay of last time with all of that coercion and trying to find the extra votes and the whole fiasco leading up to the storming of the Capitol. It has always amazed me that something like that could happen here in America. Not so amazed anymore, though.

The victory party was amazing. The Boss flew us all to Mustique for the weekend and brought in Rum Stacey and his band from New Orleans to play just for us and some Michelin chef from France. I'd done all of the organising, of course, and it was a lot of work. I had to fly down there three days before to make sure everything was set. It was only me and a couple of the IT guys in the back, Bryce up front with Smith, and Melody looking after us. I worked the whole way. Once we landed, the car came and we started to disembark. The guys were already in the car, Melody and Smith too, and I was halfway down the stairs when Bryce stuck his head out of the doorway.

'Boss wants to talk to you on the radio,' he said.

I waved to the car and they went off without me. I climbed back into the plane.

Bryce was waiting for me in the cockpit. 'Take a seat,' he said, jutting his chin towards the co-pilot's seat.

He handed me a headset and flipped a switch. His voice came to me over the headphones.

'What does he want?' I said.

'Nothing.'

'What do you mean?'

He turned in his seat to face me, his beautiful green eyes glowing in the afternoon Caribbean light. 'I lied.' Then he smiled.

And I smiled right back and that big, fat hummingbird started up inside me and she would not be quelled.

'I wanted to talk to you,' he said. 'I guess you must know how I feel about you.'

'Clause sixteen out the window.'

'Something like that.'

I reached my hand over and took his. I'd dreamed so many times of doing it, and now I'd done it and it felt good. Really good. 'We could get into a lot of trouble.'

'Fuck that,' said Bryce. 'We can just quit.'

'We can.'

'Or we can stay. Keep doing what we're doing.'

I sat up in the chair. 'What do you mean, what we're doing?'

'You know,' he said. 'Collecting.'

I shook my head. I didn't like the way this conversation was going.

'Smith and Melody are doing it,' he said over the intercom.

'Collecting?'

He smiled. 'Well, yeah. And fucking.'

'I'm not surprised. They're not hiding it too well.' Those wingtip feathers fluttering away again, having quite an effect.

'We need a plan.'

'A plan for what, Bryce? Collecting or fucking?'

'Both,' he said. Then he leaned over and kissed me. I thought I would pass out.

Just then the car reappeared and pulled up next to the plane.

He sat back in his seat. 'You need to get going,' he said, squeezing my hand as he pulled off the headset. 'See you at the party?'

I nodded, went out to the car.

The party started out with champagne cocktails on the terrace. Patio lights swayed in the breeze. A crescent moon rose over the sea. It was beautiful. Dinner was amazing, big tables set out under the stars, the best of everything. After the main course the Boss got up, took the microphone from the stand and stood on the stage in his navy suit and open-necked white collared shirt, looking exactly like what he was. It was a celebration, but I could tell right away that he was pissed off. That look on his face, the way he hunched forward, almost as if he was coiled up, like a cobra ready to strike.

He said a few things about Bragg's great victory and how we were going to change the world, together, teamwork, blah, blah, blah – the usual stuff I'd heard so many times before. And then he frowned and stopped mid-sentence, and I could see that he had jettisoned whatever it was he had planned to say. He stared out at us all, his hair moving in the breeze, and it was very quiet and no one said a word, and you could feel it growing there in the silence – the fear. He did that, threw shadow. It was spooky to see it.

And then he planted his feet and fixed his gaze on one spot and held it. You couldn't help but follow his gaze, it was that powerful. Soon we were all staring at that one table, at one couple sitting side by side, now visibly terrified. Smith and Melody.

'Everyone here, staff and guests, know how I run my organisation,' he said into the microphone. 'I am an honourable man. I do what I say I am going to do. I deliver. I keep my word, and I expect everyone around me to keep theirs.'

By then I was sweating fear, and the glow I had been carrying from the plane had gone as cold as an industrial freezer.

'You two come on up here,' he said.

Smith and Melody looked right and left, trying to escape the stare of four hundred pairs of eyes.

'Yes, you two. You know who you are.'

They stood, blinking in the lights, and walked unsteadily towards the stage, as if to the gallows. They climbed the stairs and stood next to the Boss, facing the silent crowd.

The Boss stood between them and put an arm around each and spoke into the microphone. 'Melody here has been with me three years now; Smith, just over four. They crew for me on the Gulfstream, and I just wanted to let everyone know that they do a great job. There'll be a little something extra for you both waiting for you when you get home.'

It was as if he'd announced a stay of execution. Everyone started clapping and cheering. Melody looked like she was going to burst into tears. Smith just stood there beaming, shaking the Boss's hand.

I looked over at Bryce and he was looking at me, very serious. I made a question mark with my eyes. He shook his head once. No.

It was then that I knew. Somehow, Bryce knew about my diary. This diary.

Ocean Transporter

I stand there a long time staring at the symbols, listening for any signs of movement on the ship. Once I have composed myself, I move carefully.

Inside the cramped corridors the air is close, heavy with that stench I first noticed when I came aboard. The heat is crushing, kilos rather than degrees, the way barely lit by the dim flickering of still-operating emergency power cells. Barefoot, I make almost no sound. I come to the officers' quarters, ransacked, drawers open, clothes and papers scattered. Deeper inside the ship, I find the mess strewn with broken glass and crockery and overturned chairs, what looks like a library with books accordioned in piles on the floor, crew quarters with beds unmade, doors and walls adorned with faded photographs and children's drawings, each cabin an interrupted life. This is now a ship of artefacts. Of bones and tools, coverings and implements dropped mid-use, flung aside in panic. It's hard to tell when it happened. Not history, this, more like archaeology. An archaeology of fear.

Back out on the main deck I gulp in a lungful of clean air, then another, trying to purge the stench from my nostrils. I call out to Julie that there are no signs of the crew and I am going forward to check the cargo holds. The ship has four pairs of holds, one aft and three forward of the tower and stack, port and starboard. I stay to starboard, keeping *Providence* in view. As I approach the number three holds, closest to the main superstructure, I can see that they are awash. The water level is now no more than about ten metres below the deck line. There is still some displacement keeping the ship afloat, but not much. It's then that the smell hits me again, stronger this time. I approach the edge of the hold and peer inside, looking straight down. And there, sloshing peacefully on the oily surface below, a raft of at least two dozen bodies. The corpses are bloated and stretched tight and black under stained and torn blue crewmen's coveralls, or the split, once-white epauletted shirts of officers. Some stare open-mouthed at an unseen sky, others, thankfully, float face down, arms and legs woven in gentle embrace.

I stagger back from the edge, double over, retch up whatever is in my stomach.

The other holds are also awash, empty of whatever cargo they contained. But there are no more bodies. One thing is clear, *Ocean Transporter* won't remain afloat much longer. And when she goes down, all evidence of what occurred here will disappear for ever, and it will be as if it never happened.

I start back to the stern. I am halfway to the tower, just abeam hold two, when I see a flash of movement up on the bridge. I stop, stare at the starboard wing, the one I signalled Julie from. There, looking down at *Providence*, is a person, a woman.

Just then she spins towards me, hair flying in the breeze. We stand there staring at each other. She is small, barely tall enough to see over the rail, dressed in black. Even from there I can see her eyes, big and wide, staring at me, at the gun in my hand. And then she ducks below the railing and disappears.

I stuff the pistol in my pocket and run back to the tower, sprint up the stairs. 'Please,' I shout. 'The ship is sinking. I won't hurt you. Please.'

But when I get to the bridge, she is gone. I stay up there for a while, calling out to her every few minutes, but she doesn't reappear. I go through the superstructure again, level by level, down to the engine room, awash too, but don't see her again. Whatever happened here, she managed to escape the fate of those I saw in the hold, and to survive here alone for who knew how long.

Eventually, I give up. There is no way that I am going to find her if she doesn't want to be found. She's lived in the guts of this ship for days, maybe weeks, and must know every vein and tract. I clamber down to the dinghy and row to *Providence*.

'I saw her too,' Julie says when I get back. 'Leo and I waved to her, but she just stood there staring at us. And then something spooked her and she vanished.'

'She saw my gun.' I tell Julie about the symbols.

Julie thinks about this a while. 'She's terrified. Who wouldn't be.'

'We can't stay here, Julie. It's too dangerous. They could be anywhere.'

'We can't just leave her. The ship is sinking, you said so yourself. She saw me and she didn't run. I need to go over there and try to bring her back.'

I run this over in my mind. She's right, I know, but I don't want her to go.

She smiles at me, takes my hand. 'I'll be fine, Kwe.'

I nod. 'Only an hour or so until nightfall. Make it quick.'

So she goes. I offer her the gun but she pushes it away. Feeling proud and terrified, I watch her row over, tie up, climb the ladder. At the rail, she turns and waves, smiles that beautiful smile of hers, and then she's gone. I sit with Leo in the cockpit, trying to answer his questions. Who was that lady? I don't know. Did she drive the ship all by herself? No, there was a crew, but they are gone. What happened to them? I have no idea, sweetie. Is the ship really sinking? Yes. When it sinks will it hurt the fish and crabs? No. It will happen slowly and they will have time to get out of the way. What about clams and oysters, Daddy? They can't move. It's very deep here, Leo, probably there is nothing on the bottom but mud, so you don't need to worry.

I fix him some warm weak tea with a bit of sugar. We play I-spy. After half an hour Julie still hasn't checked in, and I am starting to worry. What if the woman is armed? I should have made Julie take the gun. Stupid. I should never have let her go over there in the first place. After what happened to Mum and Lewis and Mandy, I should have known what we would find.

I can't swim out there and climb up and bring her back, leave Leo on his own. If Julie meets trouble, I won't be able to help her. It was a stupid idea, badly planned. I am an idiot. Suddenly everything we are trying to do out here seems very far away.

After an hour I still haven't heard from her, and the sky is taking on that high darkness of impending dusk, that paling on the horizon. I stand on the bow and yell up at the ship, calling her name. But there is nothing, just the surge and suck of the swell against the sinking hull. And then I realise how to do it.

Leo is in his life jacket. I tie him into the cockpit with a short line, sit him down. Then I break out a fifty-metre line from the aft cockpit locker, make one end fast to *Providence's* bow cleat, strip down to my shorts, tie the other end of the line around my waist.

'Daddy will be right back,' I say to him. 'I'm going to get Mum. Stay right here, in the cockpit. Understand?'

He nods, very serious. I explain what I am going to do, that *Providence* will be tied to the ship, so we are together. There is nothing to worry about as long as he stays in the cockpit where I can see him.

He nods, understands. Good boy, this boy, I can hear Uncle Liberty say.

I put the gun and a windup torch in a dry bag and slip into the water from the back step. The water is hot, like blood. It doesn't take long to swim over to the ship, the line spooling out behind me. When I reach the hull, I tie the line around two rungs and both ropes of the ladder above the waterline, where the rope is strong and unfouled. When it's done, I look back and wave, showing Leo the line securely fastened. He smiles, waves back.

By the time I've climbed to the deck, it is getting dark. I call out for Juliette, and a moment later she appears up on the bridge wing where we first saw the woman. She looks over at *Providence*, at Leo in the cockpit, and back at me.

'We're coming down,' she says. 'Wait there.'

A few minutes later Julie appears at the gangway carrying two big canvas bags. A small Asian woman follows a few steps behind her, furtive, glancing left and right, clearly terrified.

'Her name is Fema. She's from the Philippines. That's all I can get out of her. Except this.' She drops the bags on the deck.

'What's that?'

'Food. She showed me where they kept their supplies. Tinned fruit and vegetables. Meat. Flour and sugar. Far more than we can carry.'

'Will she come with us? We can drop her in Madagascar.'

'I've explained it to her. I think she'll come.'

'We need to get going, Julie. If she stays here, she'll die.'

Juliette turns to the woman. 'This is my husband, Kweku. He won't hurt you. Please, come with us. The ship is sinking.'

The woman nods, takes a step towards us. Then suddenly she turns and runs back into the tower.

Julie makes to follow but I grab her by the arm. 'Let her go, Julie. I don't want to leave Leo out there any longer than we have to. Every minute we're here makes us more of a target. We need to get going, now.'

'We can't just leave her,' says Julie.

'She doesn't want to come. You can't force her.'

We start for the rail. Just then the woman reappears, clutching two small bags. She stands looking at us with those big, wide eyes.

'Come,' says Julie to the woman, offering her hand. 'We'll go now.'

I let the women take the dinghy, load the bags in with them. When they are safely aboard, I untie the line and swim back to *Providence*.

For now at least, we are five.

That night we listen to Sparkplug's latest transmission.

January 2025

Bragg wasn't in power long before we started planning what everyone would end up calling the Repudiation. Maddisson came up with the name one day when the whole group was meeting at his chateau in Switzerland. Now that was a meeting room.

They were all sitting around after, having lunch in the dining room, everyone there except the president of the Russian Federation, who'd sent his lackey Piotrvich instead, when Maddisson clinked his flute with a cheese knife and said: 'Gentlemen, a toast. To all we've set in motion. To the complete repudiation of the left, and all they stand for.'

They all toasted and said, 'to the Repudiation,' and well, after that, it stuck. Not long after, Maddisson started getting all his editors to use it in opinion pieces and editorials all over the world and within days it was trending all over social media, and he got singers and sports personalities and movie stars to start using it, and it went ballistic.

The first step was simple, really. Li came up with it, and the Boss and Valliant executed it. I wasn't allowed to take minutes that day, but the conversation went something like this:

Li: 'Last time, the virus jumped from wild animals to humans, and millions of people were convinced that it was something cooked up in a lab. So, we flip it around. We cook it up and convince people it's one hundred percent the result of a jump, and we blame the greenies for allowing these unhealthy populations to be conserved. But this time we're ready beforehand with the vaccine.'

Valliant: 'We make it highly virulent and deadly. Let it run for just long enough to cause a major crash. Then Bragg puts American ingenuity and the private sector to work to find a vaccine and a cure. The government labs all fumble about in the dark. We wait just long enough, then release the vaccine, which we have developed beforehand.'

The Boss: 'We short everything that is going to tank over the next few months – airlines, cruise companies, you name it – build up our positions. We go long on everything that will do well – masks, hospital equipment, firms that specialise in medical construction and supply. And we make a killing on the vaccine.'

Everyone laughed at that one.

Li: 'Bragg ends up being the saviour, and along with our other, well let's just call them what they are, shall we? – puppets – they ride the wave of popularity and adulation. Bragg wins a second term and gets Congress and the Supreme Court to repeal the twenty-second.'

Valliant: 'And we all vaccinate ourselves before release, of course.'

Li: 'And then we change direction, take control.'

The Boss: 'And we all make a fucking fortune.'

It was all very matter of fact, almost jocular, as if they were talking about how to win the Super Bowl or something, who to draft, what trades to make. I swear, these guys actually talked like this. There was a lot of smiling.

Of course, to pull off something like that they needed a few key people to play ball. People like Dr Amie Zaruthstra, the CEO of the Boss's new eponymous pharmaceuticals business. By now, the business was growing so fast we couldn't keep up, and the amount of money we were making had even Paolo giggling.

Amie briefed us a week later back in the States. She was dark-skinned and very pretty for an older woman, and super smart. I guess for the amount the Boss was paying her she had better be. She made more in a week than I did in a year. Still, I wasn't complaining. I'd managed to pay off my apartment, had an awesome wardrobe, and had even started saving a bit of money.

'Cholesterol meds are one of the big money-makers,' she said, putting up some numbing numbers. Seriously, though, so much money. And these drugs were a perfect foil for the Boss's other-brand fast-food business, famous for deep-fried donuts and oversized burgers and fries. Fuck them up and then get them to pay you to fix them, he'd say. The heart of the playbook. Another winner was a new type of super-potent hard-on pill, balancing out the Boss's other-brand line of high-strength craft beers. When she showed us the earnings chart I though Paolo was going to have an orgasm.

And then she came to Operation Red. The Boss glanced at me and I closed my laptop.

'Go on,' said the Boss.

'We've done our evaluation,' she said, so cool, the archetype of the empowered twenty-first-century business superwoman: thin, confident, perfectly dressed, glowed up, childless, kick-ass, croaky-voiced. No one liked her.

'We will be ready to test the vaccine in July, and then, if that goes well, we will be able to release it in December. That's the best time, anyway, cold and flu season. Hospitals already under stress. Our models suggest that we will achieve global coverage within six months.'

That night I went back to my room and sat there on my bed for a long time thinking that I should cry but no tears would come. I went to go for a walk but when I got to the front door of the chateau one of the bodyguards told me I had to stay inside, so I went back up to my room and sat there basically catatonic until finally, sometime in the early morning, I fell asleep.

Fema

A few days after we've left the tanker to her fate, Fema tells us her story. We sit very still while she speaks.

Born at the start of the Repudiation, she left the Philippines with her mother when she was still small. They ended up in Mozambique, where her mother worked in a food-canning factory. When her mother died in one of the pandemics, she went to work for a shipping company. She was only thirteen years old. By this time, the African war was raging, and the continent's staples were keeping North America and much of the rest of the world alive. She'd made the journey around the Cape more times than she could remember, across to the East Coast of America loaded with Zimbabwean wheat and sorghum, returning with ammunition and weapons.

Ocean Transporter left Mozambique with a cargo of grain, bound for southern India, in early August of 2066. The crew, all volunteers, knew the perils of the journey but were enticed by the promise of triple their normal wages, paid in gold. A few were even motivated by the thought of helping alleviate the crushing, biblical famine unfolding on the sub-continent. The seventy-five thousand tonnes of grain would keep a few lucky thousand people alive for a month, or a dozen or so for several years. Given the scale of the calamity, of course, it was nothing. Worse than nothing, one might argue.

That night when the alarm went on *Ocean Transporter*, Fema was with the junior engineer in his cabin. She'd met him on a previous trip and they had become friends. He dressed and ran to the engine room while she assembled with the other non-essential personnel in the main mess. The first mate was there. He was young and looked scared. She noticed that he'd misbuttoned the shirt of his uniform and his breast pockets were misaligned. He told them all to remain there until given the all-clear, and then he left for the bridge. As he did there was a loud detonation and the ship lurched wildly, knocking everyone off their feet. People screamed. Crockery fell to the floor and smashed into shards. From outside they could hear the sound of gunfire and then, moments later, another explosion shuddered through the ship. There were four of them in the mess: her, the cook, the cook's helper, and a scared-looking young man who'd booked a passage back home to India. They did as they were told and waited there in the mess, terrified, as the sounds of the battle raged outside.

And then the door burst open. One of the mercenaries assigned to protect the ship, a young South African she knew only as Raven, stared in at them. His black uniform was smeared with a dark liquid.

'Hide,' was all he said before disappearing down the corridor.

Fema ran immediately to the laundry. She knew a place, deep in the ship, behind the washing machines, an access area she used to hide her valuables, just big enough to crawl into. As she fled, she heard the gunfire reach a crescendo and then quickly die away. She flew down the stairs to her hide-out.

By the time she'd pulled the access panel back in place behind her, the shooting had died down to a few sporadic pops that echoed through the ship's dark interstices. And then the engines shut down and quiet descended. A kind of peace. She waited in the darkness, shivering with fear.

And then voices, angry, gruff, getting closer. Shouted commands. The door of the laundry being thrown open. Footsteps on the decking, heavy, booted. A crash as one of the machines was pushed over. An endless, breathless moment as whoever was there just a few arm spans away searched the laundry. And then the footsteps receding again, and for a moment, silence.

It wasn't long until the unloading operation began. She knew the sound of it from previous trips, the capstans turning as the other ship was secured alongside, the clank and grind of the bucket elevators as the grain was removed from the holds.

The unloading went on for what seemed like a long time. She dared not leave her hiding place. She wondered what had happened to her friend. He was so nice, so gentle. This was the third trip they'd done together. They'd even talked of the future, maybe living together in Maputo. And then the noise stopped. They had finished unloading. It was quiet for a long time, and she began to think that maybe they'd left, whoever they were, had taken what they wanted and gone. And then that fearful, horrible crash of gunfire, many weapons being fired simultaneously for a brief, everlasting moment.

She stayed in her hiding place for a long time and then fell asleep. When she woke, several hours later, her throat ached from crying and her mouth was dry from thirst. In the end it was the thirst that drove her out. She worked up her courage and tiptoed to the galley, drank. She found Raven at the bottom of the level B stairway, his legs twisted beneath him, his pale eyes staring at the ceiling. She wept when she found the rest of the crew in the hold, her new love crushed before it had a chance to bloom.

The only thing the attackers left behind were the symbols we saw graffitied on the bridge, and a playing card with the same $\alpha\Omega$ crudely printed in black script, which she found tucked into Raven's blood-stained webbing. She still has it.

I still have my four.

July 2025

The Boss tasked me with keeping close track of Operation Red. Every couple of weeks Bryce would fly me down to Boss Pharma HQ in Charlotte, North Carolina, and I'd meet with Dr Zaruthstra. We'd go to the secure room and she'd brief me on progress. I was getting pretty good with the financial stuff by then. Paolo had helped me a lot, showing me how to read a P&L, what to look for in a balance sheet, and how to scan accounts receivable and payable, looking for anomalies and trends. He also showed me, bless him, a little trick he used to calculate internal rate of return and net present value quickly and accurately with only a pencil and a piece of paper. I thought he might have a bit of a soft spot for me. Too bad he was definitely not my type. My mum, God bless her soul, always told me the most important thing was to be honest with myself. And honestly, even though I did what I did with the Boss because, well, basically, I had to, or had convinced myself at that point that I had to, it was Bryce that really got my hummingbird girl fluttering.

Since that day in the cockpit in Mustique it had been a standoff with Bryce. I was still trying to figure him out, what he meant by 'collecting', and how he could have known about this diary. He was a bit older than me, eight and a half years, and so much more experienced. I looked at his personnel file. But with all of this work for the Boss, I was gaining ground. I wondered what Mum would have thought if she could have checked in on me.

The briefing that day was routine. Dr Z didn't like having to report to someone she considered so junior, but she put on her warpaint and came into the room and tried to be as imperious as she could, and she got on with it. She didn't have much of a choice. We both knew who called the game, and who had what on whom. So, good progress overall. The vaccine was coming along well. Initial trials showed it counteracted the pathogen perfectly, providing almost complete immunity. They were working with a new mRNA spike protein configuration and a modified coronavirus. She went on for a while about the technicalities of virus propagation, but I did a Boss on her and tuned out, already on the matter the Boss had asked me specifically to interrogate.

'So, Amie,' I said. 'Tell me about security arrangements.' We'd put a triple separation protocol in place at the start of the project, but the Boss wanted me to ask her straight how it was going.

'Doctor Zaruthstra.'

'Pardon?'

'Please refer to me by my title and family name.' There was real venom in her voice.

I wasn't trying to piss her off, but I couldn't help smiling, and she saw it, and it made her even angrier. Her cheeks blushed a deep ochre, the colour of a ripe eggplant, and I could see her heart beating in the veins in her neck, little pulses under the skin.

'Sorry,' I said. 'Doctor Z.' I couldn't help myself. I can be such a pain in the derriere, I know. 'Now please can you tell me about security.'

Basically, no one in Boss Pharma except the CEO had access to information on more than a single component of the operation. Alone, each of the projects looked exactly like what an aggressive and disruptive pharmaceuticals company should be doing, especially one that had just landed big new military contracts. They were researching new vaccines, working on prospective cures for various diseases, carrying out fundamental research on immunology and virology. So far, there had been no issues, and no unwanted prying.

I thanked her and the limo took me back to the airport. On the way I scrolled my phone. My feed told me that 2025 was already on track to be the hottest year on record, beating the record set in 2024, and that the world had now definitively breached the threshold of two degrees Celsius of warming since pre-industrial times. According to what Trig had told us, this was not good news, and hadn't been expected until at least 2030. I guess you could have said that we were ahead of schedule. Pretty soon, no one was going to give a shit anyway.

On the way back to New York that evening, it was just me, with a new girl in the back. Bryce came back after we'd levelled off and sat across from me. I ordered a gin and tonic and he had a water.

When the girl went to the back to fix my drink he leaned in and whispered: 'Smith didn't show up for work yesterday. I had to get Green to come up from Miami to right-hand for me.'

'Is Smith okay?'

'Don't know. No one has seen him since Tuesday.'

'Maybe he just decided to take some time off.'

'Like that? No way, he's gung ho. Wants every hour he can get.' He leaned back in his chair as the girl approached with our drinks.

'The Boss is freaking out about security right now,' I said. 'Across the board. Everything.'

'Well, here's the thing,' Bryce said, his voice barely a whisper above the hum of the turbofans. 'Melody disappeared yesterday too. No word to anyone. Just gone. Her mum's going crazy.'

We sat looking at each other, thinking the same thing. Clause sixteen. No, it couldn't be. There had to be something else, some other explanation.

Bryce went back to the cockpit and we landed a couple of hours later. I took an Uber home from the airport – Max was busy – and Bryce called me just after we got on the highway. Melody and Smith had died that afternoon in a sailing accident, he told me. Drowned. There were no further details.

Goddesses

Peace

Early that morning, the coast of Madagascar off to starboard, we spot a small freighter at anchor in a bay protected by rocky headlands. As we approach, we can see thick forest covering the mountains, deep green against a cloudless blue sky. Shearwaters slice across the waves, wingtip close. Terns and frigatebirds squall and dip around us. A warm land breeze carries the smells of earth and woodsmoke and blossoming trees.

The hills make a wide arc around the bay, leaning close over a gridwork of strangely protruding rocks set in regular geometric patterns. By the charts I took from *Ocean Transporter*, this should be the location of a small town. Through the binoculars I can see what looks like a submerged jetty running along the protected side of the northern headland, but no sign of the town. We need food, water and rest. We decide to take a look.

We navigate the passage through the outer reef with Julie at the bow calling directions, anchor in two fathoms of clear water. Within moments a pair of locals are paddling out towards us in a plastic canoe. We wave to them, but they keep their distance, watching us intently. Leo and I dive over the side and swim down to check the anchor. The bottom is white sand and the water is very clear and we can see the flukes well dug in, Leo looking at me with a big, tight-lipped smile. He pops up next to me, exhales and reports to his mother – anchor well set. The women in the canoe laugh, wave to Leo, and he waves back.

It is then that I notice a stone structure notched into the hillside atop a steep cliff of pale rock that rises above the new coastline. Faces line a balcony of some sort, a dozen or more of them peering down at us.

We secure *Providence*, lock her up and go ashore in the dinghy, all of us. My handgun, magazine in but no round in the breach, is tucked into the waistband of my shorts at the small of my back, covered by my shirttail. I have a bag of food from *Transporter* on my back and a few gold sovereigns in my belt. We paddle down the streets of what used to be a large town, the tops of the buildings crumbling into the sea. Below us in the clear water, a Pompei of rusted cars and market stalls, an abandoned bus, the building fronts still draped with ragged awnings that sway like anemones in the current. By the time we reach a little log-built jetty below the village, a group of people is there waiting for us, talking excitedly. Two dozen or more I count, but I can see no obvious way up to the settlement.

I tie up the dinghy, hold her steady as Juliette climbs onto the jetty, help up Leo and Fema. A tall, dark-haired woman steps to the front of the group. Like the others, she is swathed elaborately in brightly coloured cloth. They are all women.

'*Bienvenu a notre village de la paix,*' she says in heavily accented French. Welcome to our village of peace.

Leo, who was taught French by his grandmother since earliest childhood, giggles at the woman's pronunciation.

'Tell her, Leo,' I say.

Leo steps forward, very serious, and offers his hand to the woman. '*Je m'appelle Leo Abachwa,*' he says.

The woman takes his hand, a big smile creasing her handsome, weather-worn face. She introduces herself as First Governess of the village. We all shake hands, and she leads us up a steep, well-trodden pathway through thick forest. I keep the family together, Julie leading, me bringing up the rear, all of us glad to be back on land after so long, our sea legs rolling beneath us. It is the first time Julie and Leo have been on land in two months. As we climb, we come to a choke point in the rock. As we thread through single file I glimpse someone ducking away into the forest above us. We are being watched.

The village is made up of tightly packed stone and brick structures built into the mountainside. Narrow cobbled streets lead past slate-roofed dwellings, workshops, and what looks like a big communal kitchen. There are at least a hundred buildings of various sizes that I can see, everything tidy and well laid out. Water murmurs clear along stone canals the width of a man's hand, gardens burst with fruit trees. And everywhere we look are flowers, cascading over walls and overflowing from planters in every colour of the spectrum, as if all sunlight here is being refracted through a giant prism. A village of flowers.

We are led to a covered meeting place set with rows of plankwood

benches facing a stone platform on which is set a single chair hewn from
rock. The women who accompanied us up the hill usher us to our
places, Julie and Fema in front, Leo and I behind, and then crowd in
around us. I have yet to see any men, except maybe the shadowy figure
back by the trail.

The woman who introduced herself as First Governess sits in the
stone chair and faces us. She asks for news of the world. They've had
no visitors in more than a year. As she speaks, it's clear she is addressing
Julie, whose French is improving, but not yet fluent.

'S'il vous plaît,' says Julie. 'Mon mari. He speaks better French than I
do.'

The woman smiles. 'Parlez, monsieur.'

I tell her that we have come from Australia, found Mauritius in ashes,
and are bound for the Cape of Good Hope and then West Africa. We
hope to find my father's family there, and we are looking for the lost
daughter of my dead brother. We have food to trade and will gladly
accept any fresh vegetables or fruit they might have. We need to fill our
water tanks and rest for a few days before continuing our journey.

First Governess nods. 'Yes, there has been much loss,' she says in
French. 'The world is very dangerous now. But you are welcome here.
It is safe. We can offer you a place to stay for as long as you need. This
evening a meal will be sent to you, and afterwards, the women are
invited to join me at my home. And then tomorrow we can begin pro-
visioning you for your journey.'

'Thank you,' I say. 'On behalf of all of us.'

The woman smiles, and I notice that her teeth are strong and pale,
and that despite her age she is strikingly good-looking.

'All we ask is that you please respect our rules while you are here. Stay
within the village. Do not wander into the forest. It is very dangerous,
especially for children. Do you understand?' She sets her gaze on each
of us in turn.

I translate. We all nod.

Then she fixes her gaze on me. 'And no weapons of any kind are
allowed within the village walls.'

'I understand,' I say.

The woman narrows her eyes, still looking straight at me. 'Monsieur.'

'*Oui, Madame?*'

'There is another rule you in particular must observe.'

I nod. 'Of course.'

She straightens in her chair, begins. 'We decided many years ago, when we first came here, that we must change. It was men who caused all the fighting and the death that has destroyed our country. Pirates and armies and criminal gangs, always with their guns, as you have now, *monsieur*. So, we have decided that here, women will hold power. Our men work in the fields and the forest, fish the sea and defend the city, but within the village walls, they remain at home under the direction of women. It was difficult at first, for some, but they have come to see it as a better way to live, and have accepted it. They remain men, and are respected as such, and do men's work, but at home they must obey.'

'What did she say, Kwe?' Julie asks me.

'I'll tell you later.' I am not sure what to make of it.

'Your gun, please, *monsieur*.'

'Tell me what's going on,' Julie says.

'They want my gun.'

'Well give it to them,' she says.

I pull the handgun from my waistband and lay it on the bench beside me. 'I will take it back to our boat and keep it there,' I say.

'That is acceptable, *monsieur*. Thank you.'

November 2025

I got my first vaccine in November, along with the rest of the support staff. My shoulder was sore for a few days after, but other than that I felt fine. We were forbidden from mentioning anything about it to anyone, and were told that the consequences of violating confidentiality, as always, would be *severe*. I couldn't help thinking of poor Melody, drowned in that sailboat that Smith had bought with his little something extra from the Boss.

I had continued with my regular meetings with Dr Z, reporting back to the Boss on progress each time. I knew what was coming. But a part of me, a big part of me, still didn't want to believe that it was either real, true, or remotely possible. Surely, they would call it off, threaten to do it, extort whatever concessions they wanted from governments, like in the evil-genius comedy movies, but then back away at the last moment. It was all too, well, fucked up. And I was part of it.

By then I knew that the Boss was becoming obsessed with me. I'd pretty much moved into the penthouse, and his wife was living in her own house down in East Hampton. He'd helicopter down there to see her once in a while, but mostly now he just stayed in the city. Clothes would arrive for me, brand-new dresses from Paris and expensive lingerie, stuff he wanted me to wear for him. He was especially partial to shoes, the higher the better. I was spending more and more time under his desk at work, and accompanying him in the evenings to all his favourite restaurants, decked out in my new outfits, tottering like a ballerina *en pointe* in six-inch stilettos. Whatever turns your turbine, I guess.

Up until then, everything had seemed so, well, *normal*. The restaurants were full, traffic downtown was its usual snarl, even the crazy weather we'd been having for the last few years seemed now to be just how it should be. It all came down to that meeting.

We flew on the Gulfstream to Auguste Leopold's place in the Seychelles. This time, the wife came along. It was a long trip and she and the Boss spent a lot of it arguing. I could hear them over the roar of the engines screaming at each other in the aft suite, and every once in a while, the sound of things crashing against the walls. The rest of us just sat there in silence. We knew from experience that when they were fighting like this, things were going to be rough for everyone.

Over those last couple of years with the Boss, I'd seen some pretty amazing properties, but nothing like this. To say Leopold's place was a palace was like calling the Koh-i-Noor just a diamond. Each of the consortium guys was basically provided with his own chateau, with its own grounds, pool, everything. I had my own suite in the Boss's place, with a huge high-ceilinged bedroom, a balcony overlooking the sea, a walk-in bathroom the size of my whole apartment back in New York, and my own dedicated servants, a maid for my clothes, another to keep the place spotless, a masseur on call. It was ridiculous. These guys had so much, but it still wasn't enough.

The meeting was the next day. It will stay with me for the rest of my life. We assembled at Leopold's palace, which was set out on a point surrounded by lush tropical forest. The guys sat in big armchairs laid out in a circle on a shaded open-air patio overlooking the sea. The rest of us, we witnesses, accomplices, sat in a second larger circle behind them.

As host, Leopold chaired the meeting. He was a big man, powerfully built, late-forties by my guess, with a full head of silver hair.

'Gentlemen, welcome,' he said. 'I trust you are spending a pleasant time here.' He raised one hand and swept it palm up in a slow arc from left to right. 'What you see here is part of what I believe should be our vision for the future.'

He clapped his hands and two female servants made their way into the centre of the meeting area and kneeled at Leopold's feet, facing him, heads bowed, slaves before Pharaoh in some other time. I had to hold back a gasp. The women were both stunningly beautiful, very pale and fair with long slender limbs and perfect breasts.

'We are here to determine the fate of the world,' he continued. 'Never in human history has power and wealth been so concentrated in so few hands. The only questions that remain now are do we have the courage to seize this opportunity? And what are we going to do with this power? The future is ours to shape. Today, we are here to discuss one step towards shaping that future.'

Then the Boss turned in his chair and nodded to Dr Z and she got up and stood next to Leopold. She glanced down at the two women for a moment, and then addressed the circle.

'Operation Red is ready to commence as soon as you give the command,' she said, her frog croak more accentuated than usual. 'The virus will target the weak and the elderly. We have modelled ideal release locations for maximum spread, with peak mortality approximately twelve to fourteen weeks later. Inoculations for all key personnel are now complete as per your instructions. We have already manufactured enough vaccine to inoculate a billion people, and will be able to produce a billion doses every two weeks once given the word. Anytime in the next three months, during the Northern Hemisphere winter, is optimal for virus release.'

'Questions?'

'How many dead in that optimal period?' said Li.

'We estimate between five and ten million.'

'And how many hospitalised?' Li again.

'Hundreds of millions.'

Leopold nodded, and Dr Z made her way back to the outer ring and sat next to me.

Next was Paolo. He, too, glanced down at the two women as he stood at Leopold's side, but for longer. Once on a long flight after we'd had too many drinks, he'd told me what he liked, and while he liked money, he liked this more. Over the next few minutes, he described how the world's financial markets would react. The modelling was detailed and accurate, he said. If the decision was made today, they would need two months to position themselves optimally. That meant a February 2026 release.

'Like bringing out a new fragrance,' I whispered to Dr Z.

She scowled at me, and inside I felt sick.

'The information campaign is ready to go,' said Maddisson. 'We have some highly credentialled biologists and geneticists lined up to point the finger at conservationists in Southeast Asia who have been resisting the cull of infected animals. Unless someone inside one of our organisations talks – and quite frankly even if they do – we can absolutely control the narrative if we all work together and stick to the script.' Maddisson laughed, his belly fat rippling under his shirt. 'Quite frankly, we can give each of them exactly what they want. It doesn't matter if it makes up a coherent whole. People will digest and internalise the parts of the story that suit their worldview, as limited as that might be. Between me, Wu Yan and Leopold, we control over half of all media, more than two-thirds if you count social media, so we'll have good saturation.'

I would never look at an internet conspiracy theory the same way again.

They picked February 14th, 2026 for the release, Valentine's Day. Nice touch. That night, they threw a party to celebrate. But it wasn't like any party I'd ever been to before. There was food and dancing by the pool and booze and every kind of drug. At first, I was with Paolo and Dr Z, but after a while Paolo went off with two of Leopold's long, pale things and it was just Dr Z and I sitting there watching everyone, not talking. And then she went off with some extremely well-equipped male servant and I was all alone. Someone offered me pills and I didn't even ask what they were. I woke up two days later in my suite with a raging headache and no idea how I'd got there. The party went on for another day.

Women

By the time Julie arrives back from the First Governess's house that night, Leo and I are fast asleep.

The house they gave us is spacious and cool, with big, open windows that look out across the bay, and separate rooms for Leo and Fema. There are carpets and paintings, a table and chairs set in the main room overlooking the sea, wood-frame beds with comfortable mattresses in each bedroom.

I wake early and slip out of bed, careful not to wake Julie, the luxury of a full night's uninterrupted sleep something to be savoured. I dress, drink from a stone pitcher, the water cool and delicious. Below, I can see *Providence* on her anchor just beyond the submerged town. The morning sun bathes the headland, the rocks glowing helium yellow. The water of the bay shows pale blue over the sandy bottom, the outer reef dark teak, the colour of *Providence's* deck. Morning birdsong fills the air, calls I've never heard before, chimes and warbles and forlorn whoops that echo through the forest. It is one of the most beautiful places I have ever seen.

I tear a corner from one of the back pages of my journal and scribble a note for Julie: *Down at Providence. Checking all.* I leave the note on the table where she'll see it, weighted by a white ceramic mug with *I♥NY* painted on its side in black and red. By now I am confident that we are safe. The meal the women brought for us was delicious – vegetables and fruit, just what we needed most. Whoever these people are, whatever their story and customs, they seem as peaceful as the name of their community suggests.

I am halfway down the narrow lane that leads back to the main square when I hear a loud hiss. A woman dressed in swirling robes of ochre and sapling green is staring at me. She squares her lips and lets out another piercing hiss, her eyes set in deep disapproval. I keep going. Soon another woman has joined her, and another, following me, hissing. Soon I am being followed by half a dozen angry women. I raise my hands, show my palms, explain that I only want to go to my boat to check on it. One of the women points at my groin, shaking her head. After further admonishment, they let me leave.

I make my way down to the shore, wondering what law I have transgressed. The dinghy is where I left it, hauled up onto a small sandy beach not far from the log jetty. Aboard *Providence*, all is secure, lock in place, no sign of tampering, all deck gear in order. And in the cockpit, bunches of bananas, a ropework bag of coconuts, another of oranges. Carrots and potatoes and big ugly yams.

As I'm looking through it all, I see a group of men rowing out to *Providence* in what looks like a large wooden lifeboat, perhaps from the freighter, six of them. I watch them come, naked backs bent to the oars, the boat low in the water. The man at the tiller hails me. He looks young, but unlike the others has pale skin and pale eyes, long, blond, carefully braided hair, and a beard tinged with red. He is lean and tall, his arms and torso veined like twisted rope.

'Thanks for the food,' I call to them.

He nods. 'Brought you water, too.'

'Thanks. Come alongside.'

They manoeuvre the rowboat close, and I throw the helmsman a line. Once they are secure, I go below, grab the funnel and the key for the tank caps, and make ready. The men hand me up the jerry cans one by one, ten in total.

'That's two hundred litres,' says the blond helmsman. 'Need more?'

'One hundred more should do it.'

'Back soon,' he says, untying the line and moving off.

'We are very grateful.'

The helmsman nods once and turns away.

By the time they return, I've decanted the first ten jerrycans and dosed the tanks with chlorine. We swap empty for full.

'You live here, in the village?' I ask as I pour.

'Yes. All of us.'

'How long have you been here?'

The helmsman glances at the freighter. 'Me, five years. Came in that.'

'Does she run?'

'No oil.'

'Where are you from?'

'Amsterdam, originally. You?'

'Australia.'

'Where are you headed?' he asks.

'West Africa, and then, who knows. Maybe America.'

He whistles. 'Long way. Dangerous.'

I nod, hand him the empty can.

'Saw your family yesterday,' he says, 'when you arrived. Nice.'

'They're all up in the village.'

'What do you think of our little society?'

'Peaceful. Unusual.'

The helmsman smiles. 'No such thing as usual anymore,' he says.

'It's okay for you?'

He runs his hand through his beard. 'Took a while to get used to. But yes. It's good. We came here for this.'

This surprises me and I say so.

'Her grand experiment. You'll have heard the pitch. First Governess organised and paid for everything. She has a network. Like-minded people and all that. Me, I came with the boat.'

'You'll stay?'

'It works. Better than the shithole I was in before.'

After the water is loaded, I watch the men row back to shore, pull the boat up from the water and carry it into the trees. I strip off and am about to dive overboard to inspect *Providence's* hull and rudder, when a voice skips out at me across the water. I look up towards the village. There is Julie, her hair flying like a starburst, unmistakable in the breeze. She waves, and I can see she is smiling, and I wave back before diving in.

That afternoon I work on *Providence,* and then when it's time, I tune into Sparkplug's regular transmission. I sit in stunned silence as she recounts the meeting in the Seychelles all those years ago, her words echoing down to me through the decades although I know she is somewhere right now, in front of a microphone, reading to me, and it kills me that I cannot respond. And though I've read Papa's book, her story seems impossible.

Later that evening I climb the narrow, winding path up the cliff and pad barefoot through the village to our quarters. It is almost dark by the time I knock on the door. Julie answers, looks me up and down with a smile, puts her palm on my bare chest. She is dressed as the other women, wound into a bolt of blue-and-gold patterned cloth.

'Well, hello husband. What do you think?'

'You look beautiful.' I make to kiss her, but she raises her finger to my lips and gently pushes me back.

'Later, husband.' That smile again, the one that comes out when she wants to play.

I step inside and she closes the door.

'Leo is sound asleep,' she says. 'It's been a big day. For the first time in his life, he went to school. He was so happy, Kwe. So excited. Fema's asleep, too. She's been helping me. We cooked and preserved as much fruit and vegetables as we could. Tomorrow you can go to *Providence* and bring back all of the empty jars.'

'I'm ravenous,' I say, looking past her to the food set out on the table. A couple of candles glow in hooded clay pots. Through the big, open window that lets out to the sea, the first stars are shining. I tell her about my encounter with the women in the street that morning.

She kisses me and reaches for my waistband, undoes my shorts and lets them fall to the floor. I reach for her but again she pushes my hands away. Then she leans in and whispers close so I can feel her breath warm on my cheek. 'Come, husband. I will explain everything' She leads me to the table. I don't complain. We sit and eat.

Sitting at the other end of the table she tells me that she spent most of the day with the First Governess. Between them they know enough of each other's languages to communicate. They share similar views on many things. First Governess was a university professor before, taught political science and economics. She'd managed to escape the terrible fires that struck the north of Madagascar after more than a decade of drought. Under the strain, the country's economy collapsed. Money was worthless. And as the rest of the world fell apart, they became even more isolated. Gangs led by self-styled warlords roamed the country, looting and raping and killing.

'Pure anarchy, she described it as,' says Julie. 'All of her family were killed. Her parents and her sister. It's so sad, Kwe.'

I listen to Julie tell the story, think of all we have seen in the short time we've been away.

'She estimates that over ninety percent of the island's population perished. Ninety percent, Kwe. Maybe more.'

I say nothing, listen as Julie continues.

'She began developing this idea of a radically different way of living. A combination of neo-Marxism and radical eco-feminism, she calls it. She explained it to me. She collected followers, women and men, survivors searching for a better way to live. They started moving south into the more remote parts of the island to escape the turmoil. She's a leader, Kwe. Strong-willed, stubborn, but highly intelligent. It's been hard for her, I can tell. As they moved south, they heard that a civil war had erupted in the north, five gangs fighting for whatever was left. She says that they largely wiped each other out, and people who have come from there in the last few years say there is nothing left. And here we are.'

'I met some of the men today,' I say. 'Down at the boat.'

'I met some of them also, last night.' She smiles at me again, that same smile, narrowing her eyes.

Something hollows out inside me, and I am suddenly reminded of my own turgid nakedness. 'Tell me.'

'She explained more about her philosophy,' Julie says. 'Men are stronger, faster and more aggressive than women, and in that sense superior. They are builders and risk-takers and natural, instinctive warriors. But they need to be governed, regulated. Without the civilising force of women and left to their own impulses, violence rules. We have all seen how that has worked out. Here, men are provided the direction that is required for a healthy, happy society. Here, women govern, decide and manage. They raise and teach the children. Men work to provide for us, and when necessary, fight to protect us.'

'Us.'

Julie nods. 'Well, yes. Us women. You know, in many ways she sounded like your mum.'

'She's nothing like my mum.'

'If that's what you think, you weren't listening.'

We finish eating. The meal is delicious. A vegetable stew in a rich broth and fresh fruit for dessert.

After, Julie comes and sits on my lap and kisses me. 'It's so nice not to have to worry, just to relax,' she says, nuzzling my ear. 'Let me tell you the rest.'

I kiss her neck, the skin hot on my lips.

'They have very strict practices here, husband. Most of the women insist that their men remain naked while within the village. That is why you were hissed at today.'

I shake my head. 'What's the point of that?'

'To remind them of their station and to prevent them concealing weapons. And so they don't forget the vulnerability that others feel.'

'Well, my gun is on the boat. And I certainly feel vulnerable.'

Julie smiles. 'Economist that she is, First Governess says that the population must be carefully managed. It was one of the things that destroyed us, according to her. Too many people.'

'Now that sounds like Mum.'

'So they carefully regulate reproduction based on available resources, and what Patricia – that's her name – calls a sustainable optimum. You should put that in your book.'

That's Julie, why I love her. 'I will.'

'When it's time for a woman to have a baby, she chooses a man and they have sex until conception is achieved. After that, they go back to the system.'

'The system?'

'That's what she calls it.'

'And what is the system, wife?'

'Well,' she says, eyes sparkling in the candlelight, 'I was invited to witness it.' She can see the surprise on my face. 'With her husbands.'

'Plural?'

Julie blushes visibly. 'Three. I met them. Two were older, forties, maybe. The other was quite young, our age I would say. He had nicely braided long blond hair and a thick red beard, tall and very handsome.'

'The helmsman.'

'Pardon?'

'I met him today.'

'Oh.' Julie pauses, seems unsure of how to continue.

'The system?' I ask.

She gathers herself, continues. 'I didn't judge, of course. I listened and observed. First, she asked me if I wanted to be pleasured. That's what she called it. Pleasured. In any way I might like.'

Julie moves her face away from mine, still very close so I can feel her breath on my cheeks, and looks into my eyes. Lets me wait.

'She's crazy.'

'Not at all.'

'And did you?'

'No. But she did.'

'What, there in front of you?'

Julie closes her eyes a moment. 'And after, she showed me how they do it for the men – once every four days, to prevent unwanted pregnancy. There is no such restriction for women, by the way.'

Julie's voice catches on the words, and her pupils flash dark against the hot-flushed skin of her cheeks and neck. 'I watched her do it, one after the other. She was very experienced, and prolonged their pleasure expertly. She asked me if I wanted to try.' Julie raises her hands and examines them in the candlelight. 'After they were done, it was time for bed and I wanted you, but when I came home you were sound asleep.'

We sit there looking at each other in the flickering light, both painfully aware of the effect she is having on me.

'Time for bed,' I say. 'This time I'm awake.'

'I can see that,' she says through her grin. 'But tonight, husband, we're following the system.'

December 2025

That Christmas, I finally got some time off. Bryce had to fly the Boss and the wife down to Mustique. The day before Christmas Eve, I was walking around Central Park, without a coat or hat, just in my running outfit and my new Asics. It was that warm. A few big fires were still burning up in the Catskills, and the late-afternoon haze hung between the buildings and among the bare trees like some kind of lazy pestilence. Everything smelled of smoke. I'd reached the Tennis Centre near the reservoir and had started back – I didn't want to be in the park after nightfall – when my phone rang.

I looked at the number. It was Bryce.

I let it ring a few more times, did some breathing, and picked up. 'Hi.'

'Where are you?'

'Walking back to my apartment.'

'What are you doing for Christmas?'

'Oh, big plans. A few of us single girls are getting together and we'll talk about how great it is being single, especially on Christmas.' My parents both died, about a month apart, back in 2020. Mom of covid, my dad of cancer.

'You're not single.'

I chose to let that one go. 'What do you want, Bryce?' It came out more abrupt than I wanted it to.

'Come over and spend it with me and my mum.'

'I thought you were on call in Mustique, in case the Boss wanted to fly to Monaco for New Year's or something.'

'He's given me the week off.'

'Holy shit. Me too. What the f is going on?'

'Maybe he's grown a heart.'

'What about Emily, or whatever her name is?' Bryce's girlfriend.

'She moved out in April.'

'I'm sorry,' I said, lying though my pursed lips, my heart doing cartwheels.

'I'm not. Anyway, I don't want to talk about her, or him. Do you want to come over, or not?'

I had been picking my outfit from the moment he asked me, but I let the line hang a moment as I pretended to think it over. 'Well, sure, Bryce. Since you put it so nicely. Yes, I accept. What do you want me to bring?'

'Great.' I could hear the warmth in his voice, very unusual for him, normally all you got was his pilot voice, businesslike and efficient and clear. 'I'll text you the address and time. Just bring you.'

'What about clause sixteen?'

'Fuck clause sixteen. Just co-workers spending a day together with a lonely old woman.'

And suddenly, it was like being a kid again, counting down the days and hours until Christmas Day. On the way home I stopped and bought gifts, a model airplane kit for Bryce and an old 1950s hardback copy of *The Body in the Library* for his mum. Who doesn't like Agatha Christie, right? And as I walked around the shops, watching all those people searching for things that might make someone else happy, realising that this might be the last time many of them would do this, all I could see was Leopold's smug grin as he and Li walked around the party with their naked concubines that night in the Seychelles after making the big decision. And as hard as I tried to banish that image from my mind, it somehow pushed its way onto my retinae, and soon all the people in the store had his face and his grin, and it got so bad I had to rush outside onto the street, but even then the sidewalks were crowded with people and each of them was Leopold.

I leaned up against one of the big display windows and closed my eyes tight and tried to breathe, let the people flow past me like a river. It wasn't real, I knew that. I see things sometimes when I get anxious. After taking a Valium I felt much better, and after a while the faces of the people I passed in the street were again that comforting mix of dark and pale and handsome and stressed and not-so-pretty and absolutely stunning even without makeup and hairy and sly and sexy and downright dog ugly.

Christmas morning, I took the train up to New Jersey and then a taxi to Bryce's condo. In all the time we'd worked together I'd never asked about his family or where he lived. He greeted me at the door of his second-floor unit in a clean white collared shirt and navy slacks, almost exactly what he wore on duty except without the epaulettes. I could hear the football on in the background. He'd shaved and put on some aftershave that smelled like whisky and camp-fire smoke. I liked it. I had on my blue V-neck dress that showed off my boobs, not too much though, and accentuated my waistline, which my girlfriends always said they were jealous of. I could eat like a horse without getting fat, and they hated it. 'Wait till you have kids,' one of my girlfriends always said.

I gave Bryce the wrapped presents and he put them under the tree and introduced me to his mom. She was sitting in an armchair with a hand-woven blue blanket over her knees. I wished her a Merry Christmas and she smiled up at me as one might when being told your monthly electricity bill has been paid. The skin of her face was the colour of a sheet of copy paper and had that lack of elasticity that reminded me of dried-out apples. She smelled of an old folks' home – specifically, the one that my dad spent the last three years of his life in, God bless him – that strange medley of cheap face powder, institutional disinfectant and pork chops.

'Mom, this is…' And he said my name.

The old woman smiled at me again, another bill paid, and went back to staring at the TV.

'Do you want a drink?' said Bryce. 'Come into the kitchen and I'll show you what we have.'

I followed him. As soon as we reached the kitchen he spun around and took me in his arms and pulled me close and kissed me on the mouth. I couldn't say that I was expecting it, but I had sure thought about it a lot. I melted into him. He was quite a good kisser.

We necked for a while, leaning up against the counter, and though I would have let him, his hands didn't wander, just stayed there around my waist, strong and firm.

When we broke, he looked deep into my eyes. 'Thanks for coming,' he breathed.

'Fuck clause sixteen,' I said, out of breath and tingling.

He smiled at me. 'Funny girl. That's what I call you.' Then he narrowed his eyes and his forehead tightened up into parallel ridges. 'What do you know about Operation Red?' he said.

I took a step back. 'We can't talk about that, Bryce. You know the rules.'

He grabbed each of my forearms in his big hands, held me like that, at arm's length. 'I've only heard rumours. No one seems to know much, except that it's big, and it's going to start soon.'

'Have you had your vaccinations?' I asked.

'What does that have to do with it?'

'Just answer me, Bryce.'

He nodded. 'We all have. Company requirement. Just another covid booster.'

'Not another booster, Bryce.' There, I'd said it.

'What are you talking about?'

The whole thing had been burning a hole in me ever since the Seychelles meeting, that mixture of disbelief and horror and misplaced hope. 'I can't say any more, Bryce. Just please make sure you get your second shot in January.'

He thought about this a while. 'What about my mom?'

'Keep her at home.'

He looked at me as if I was an idiot, which of course I was. 'I fly for a living, in case you haven't noticed.'

'Find someone who can take her, then. Keep her away from people.'

'Jesus, what are you telling me?'

'Not more than that. I'm sorry.' I think that was the point when I really started hating myself.

Insects

We decide, after several long conversations, to stay in the village a while longer. It is Julie who pushes that we stay. According to *Ocean Passages of the World*, one of the original books that was onboard *Providence* when Papa and Mum found her all those years ago, the winds for the Cape won't be right for at least another couple of months. Leo is enjoying school, learning French, mathematics, science, ecology, and the village's peculiar mixture of history and philosophy. Julie has started working with the community's doctor, a middle-aged woman who is one of the governesses of this place, one of the original founders. Yesterday Julie helped to deliver a baby, and the day before she set a broken leg one of the men suffered while working in the forest. She says she is learning a lot, and I can tell that she is enjoying the feeling of peace and safety this place gives her. I also think she likes being the boss.

Fema is doing better, too. She works in the communal kitchen and helps look after Leo. Me, I work outside with the other men. Today I helped till a small plot about a kilometre from the village. It is hard work, all done by hand. Tomorrow, we are going to cut wood.

Still, I can feel the impatience simmering away inside me, all of these questions shoaling up like rivermouth sand, the promises I made carrying me out to sea on a cold current from that same river. I keep thinking of Becky, out there somewhere, alone and frightened, and it makes me want to run down to the boat and set sail and go find her. But where – where? It makes me shiver. And that little bone-white skull, and the image of Mum and Mandy and Lewis lying dead on the floor haunting me like stars, always there even when you can't see them.

I have started reading the copy of *The Odyssey* that I rescued from the flat in Port Louis, and last night I read the diary.

The diarist's name was Charles Antoine. By the time his entries begin, in 2063, the coral reefs that once surrounded the island have been dead a long time. Once the coral were gone, the fish, too, disappeared, until all that was left was a lifeless pile of rubble. Antoine likens what was left to the smashed concrete wilderness of a bombed-out city, collapsed and empty. From there, the entries are sparse and rushed.

March 12, 2065. Fires are now burning out of control on the far side of the island. I went to help. We fight hard, but are losing control. After months without rain, everything is a bomb waiting to go off. Three men died today that I know of, overtaken by the fires. The heat is unimaginable. The very air ignites. We need machines, waterbombers, but all we have is hand tools. Smoke covers the city.

Over three weeks, the fire raged. Every day the front moved closer to the city, driven by the wind, torching everything in its path. Every day they would pray for rain. People filled the churches, called to God for succour, for mercy. The fire was only a few kilometres from the city. Everyone knew it was the end. An evacuation was planned. The last supplies of emergency fuel were issued to the remaining ships in the harbour. His last entry, as best as I can make out, reads:

Leaving tomorrow for God knows where. When I was young, we had everything. We thought we would be happy and safe. You never believe it will happen to you.

The days string into weeks, and slowly we adjust to the rhythms of this principled, some might say idyllic, place. Julie reads Antoine's diary, appears shaken afterwards, says we are lucky to have found this place. I wonder how many other refuges like this remain in lonely outposts all over the world, people trying their best to survive, to rebuild. We must hope there are many.

Every day our work outside is assigned by a man they call Sabre, one of the originals. A hard man, scarred and tattooed, he watches over us in the manner of a hawk or a remote-surveillance camera – so you're never sure if he is actually seeing you, or if he's just focusing on something else.

One morning Sabre saunters up to me and informs me that I will be taking part in my first long-range patrol.

I'd done a couple of days of training the week before, and then a couple of short patrols – day-long affairs up in the hills beyond the village, always with the same team of four. Zana is our leader, one of the originals, a tough Malgache with tree-trunk arms, skin like polished teak and a big L-shaped scar on his left shoulder. Then there's the helmsman from Amsterdam, a teenage boy they all call Bird, and me. We carry food and water, AK47 rifles like I have on *Providence*, lots of ammunition, grenades, and mines that can be remotely detonated. Zana says there are more weapons on the island now than people. People die, weapons don't.

That day we set out east from the village, paralleling the coast single file through dense regrowth, Zana leading. After three hours of walking, we emerge onto a rocky outcrop, the blue of the Indian Ocean spread before us and the surf crashing in white fronts against rocks newly exposed to this power. Zana scans the coast with binoculars, and, satisfied, we turn inland.

We sweat through terrain razored with deep gullies and twisting ridges along overgrown tracks, the air close and hot. Zana leads, hacking with a machete as he goes, then Bird, me, and Amsterdam in the rear. Mid-afternoon we rest out of the sun, drink, eat something. I look down at my arms and legs. Blood oozes from dozens of grass cuts. Zana frowns, opens the medical kit and hands me a small jar and some clean cloths.

'Disinfectant,' he says. 'Put it on, and cover those over.'

We keep going. Towards evening we come to an old road, the surface frayed and crumbling at the edges, trees already pushing through in places, shouldering aside big chunks of tar. Zana says that no one comes here anymore because all the bridges on the main north-south road were destroyed, and most of the others too.

'One was standing when we first came here with First Governess.' Zana points along the road. 'Up there,' he says. 'It was many years ago. We blew it up.'

Zana leads us along the road as it twists through the ridged and serried jungle. In places the tar is almost gone and for long stretches has been completely reclaimed by the trees. After what I estimate to be four or five kilometres, Zana calls a halt. Just ahead, the outskirts of a small town, a few ruined buildings lining the road, roofs sagged and caved, vegetation growing green and vigorous between fallen beams and shattered brick.

'Careful from here on,' says Zana. 'Last year we ran into a pair of scouts here. Very bad people. From the north. We killed them, me and Amsterdam.' He slaps the receiver of the rifle slung across his bare chest. 'Got this. Nice, made in Russia. Only good thing they ever made.'

I take a breath.

'Let's get this over with,' says Amsterdam.

We walk into the ruined village, strung out ten metres apart, Zana in the lead. Many of the smaller structures are already gone, melted back into the earth, roots cracking concrete and pulling apart masonry, rain winnowing through mortar. Huge anthills burst up, twitching through patios and bedroom floors, insects everywhere boring through wood and turning over soil. As we penetrate further into the town, we pass wrecked storefronts and abandoned cars, side streets choked with vines and saplings, the charred ribs of burnt-out homes hulking in eerie silence. A bullet-punctured water tank lists on broken stilts next to a cemetery swollen with graves, the headstones tilted to every angle by the thrust of trees grown strong with the nutrients beneath.

We camp that night further up the road, in a small clearing just back of a ridge overlooking a deep ravine. Bird lights a fire and sets to preparing a meal, while Zana and Amsterdam and I hike to the top of the ridge. Zana works his way through a tangle of flaking boulders. Below us, what remains of a concrete bridge, the abutments and central pillars spouting tangled rebar, the intermediate spans gone.

'I did that.' Zana points to the far side of the ravine. 'Two charges. First Governess's orders. Tomorrow, we cross the river and keep going. Rest now. We start early.'

We eat and then smother the fire. As night falls, Bird takes first watch up in the boulders overlooking the bridge. I sit in the gathering darkness rebandaging my arms and legs, listening to the rising chorus of insects. Papa told us stories growing up about travelling through the famine lands and how the thing you noticed most was the total silence. It was good, hearing them singing.

'Better wear long trousers next time.' Amsterdam's voice in the dark.

'Now you tell me.'

'How long you been married?'

'Six years.'

A half-whistle. 'She must have been very young.'

'We both were.'

'Albany, right?'

'Pardon?'

'Albany, Western Australia. You were married in Albany. I was there once, a long time ago. Loaded a cargo.'

'How did you—'

I cut myself short, but it's too late. I already know the answer.

'We've talked, your wife and me. A few times. She's a beautiful woman.'

If Amsterdam thinks I am going to pursue this any further, he is wrong. I take a deep breath, glad of the darkness. 'What did Zana do before the war?' I ask.

'He's ex-military,' says Amsterdam, no change in tone. 'Fought against the insurgents for a long time, when they still had a government here. That's what some of the other originals say, anyway.'

'How long have you been doing this? These patrols.'

'Like you. Here for a few weeks and then it's part of what you do.'

'Why did you kill those scouts?'

'Orders. They were from one of the gangs. First Governess says we should kill any gang member we find.'

I catch a breath. 'I've never killed anyone.' Papa taught me to shoot when I was small, and I am good with a pistol. But I've never had to fire a weapon in anger. Mum and Papa always described themselves as pacifists. I've never had to fight physically, even in Albany during those trips for supplies with Lewis, and then alone. Strange, when you think of the world the way it is.

'Me neither. Before that day.'

I don't reply.

'But if you stay,' he continues, 'the way things are going, you may have to. Activity is increasing. More sightings. No shooting since that time with Zana and me last year. But close. It's only a matter of time. They're coming. And when they do, we won't be able to stop them. I've told First Governess, but she doesn't want to believe it. Thinks we can scare them off. If I were you, I'd take that pretty young wife of yours and leave.'

I don't like the way he says it, but stay quiet.

'What are you doing here, really?' he says in the darkness.

I tell him about what happened to Mum and Lewis and Mandy, about Becky being taken. 'All they left were playing cards with Greek letters on the back – alpha and omega.'

I wait for a response, but none comes. We string up our hammocks and lay down to sleep. The insects pitch higher and louder, a wild burst that ripples through the forest, and I can feel the jealousy rise up hot inside me, that hollowness in my chest. Anger, too, as my imagination boils up unwanted images. Why didn't Julie tell me?

I realise that I miss her. Over the last few weeks, she's been increasingly busy working with the doctor, and was recently invited to attend the daily meetings of the village council. Most nights after we've finished dinner and put Leo to bed, she goes to First Governess's house and stays there until late, leaving me alone with my books and my journal. I haven't asked her what they do there and after that first time she hasn't told me. The night before I left, after she got back, we made love. She knew I was leaving early for this patrol, knew I'd been training for it.

It has always been good between us, but that night she was different. I'd never seen her so aroused, with so much abandon. When she shuddered above me, I thought she would wake the neighbours. But before I could finish, she slid off and lay there beside me, warm and glowing, very quiet. I asked if she was okay, and she kissed me.

'Just wait, husband,' she said, stroking my hair. After a while, she got back on me and did it again, the same way. By then I was shaking for her.

'How long is your patrol?' she said, lying there beside me, wet and becalmed.

'Four days,' I answered.

'Perfect,' she said. 'Go to sleep now.'

I wake to Zana's hand on my shoulder.

'Your watch,' he says. 'If you see anything – and I mean anything – you come down here and wake me. Understand?'

I nod, grab my rifle and pack, and start up the ridge, a few clouds drifting silver against a hemisphere of stars, the din of insects sawing the night in two. As I reach the top of the ridge, I can see the amputated skeleton of the bridge shining pale against the dark of the ravine. I settle between two boulders, my rifle across my knees, the ravine below, the palimpsest of road disappearing into the forest. Somehow, I have become a soldier. For what, exactly, I am not sure.

That day we left The Hope, we rowed out to *Providence* and climbed aboard and made ready to weigh anchor. It was then that I noticed Liberty out on Kwesi Point, standing with his spear raised. I waved to him, and he swung the spear in reply. As we rounded the point, he was still there, a speck on the shore, a grain of sand. It felt like that now, sitting there overlooking that smashed bridge, as if the world were made only of questions to which there were no answers.

I check my watch. Half an hour until I need to wake Amsterdam. By now the moon is high, and the bridge shines white and clean. The shadows are very dark, and once I think I see movement on the road, a flash of black against the dark grey of the remnant tar, but it is gone before it comes and though I stare at the spot and the area around it for a long time I don't see it again and after a while I convince myself I haven't seen anything at all.

January 2026

It was now more than a year since Bragg's inauguration on that cold and windy January day. According to the president's press secretary, more than a million people had turned up, stood stamping their feet and breathing into their hands as the snow fell and Bragg rambled through a strange mash-up of attacks against the left, outrageous claims about the previous election, and more than a little bombastic gloating. I started watching it on TV, and then finally gave up about forty minutes in.

I hadn't been able to speak with Bryce since Christmas Day. After that kiss in the kitchen, I was ready and willing for a lot more, but then he was flying again a couple of days later – the Boss did want to go somewhere for New Year's after all, but it was Rio, not Monaco.

After the Boss got back, he was different. His ardour for me had cooled right off. He didn't want me in his office or in the penthouse, and to be honest I was glad. Astrid moved in and I moved out. I should have asked for a raise.

I came into work every morning, followed him around on his trips – all that was unchanged – but the sex part of it had disappeared. Talking to some of the other girls, that was his way. He'd go intense on someone for a few weeks or months, and then just lose interest.

So when the wife walked into my office that morning and closed the door behind her and stood there in her black leather pants and jacket and gold stilettos with one hip thrust out like she was some kind of aging model or something, I didn't know what to think.

'We need to talk, you and I,' she said, a cigarette burning between two manicured, red-nailed fingers.

I looked up from my laptop. 'Yes, ma'am.'

'Cut the ma'am crap,' she said, took a long drag on her cigarette and let the smoke pour back out through her nostrils. 'I know about you and my husband.'

I lowered my eyes. What I wanted to say was something to the effect that it didn't take any kind of genius to figure out what he was doing and that I had certainly not been the first or the last, and that it really hadn't been much fun at all – the sex part anyway – but I just kept quiet.

'I want you to know not because I blame you, which I don't, and certainly not because it is a surprise to me, but so you understand that you are not special. Girls like you come and go. This is the way we live, he and I. We have our own rules. He has his fun, and I have mine. But make no mistake, we are a team.'

'I understand,' I said. And I did. After all, she was one of the most ac-complished lawyers in the country and I was nothing but a glorified secretary. I knew my place. It was part of my job.

'And the one thing my husband and I do not tolerate is disloyalty. I suggest you and Bryce Stephenson think hard before you take your relationship any further.'

And with that she turned on her heels and strode out of my office, leaving me sitting there staring out of the window at the Manhattan skyline.

Bones

Zana has us back on the move before dawn. I don't mention what by now I am very sure I didn't see.

Last night's conversation with Amsterdam plays over in my head. I am now convinced that it was no casual mention – he wanted me to know about him and Julie. And though it's killing me, I am determined not to bite.

We thread our way down to the river in the dark. As we descend, the air cools and the sound of the river flowing through the rocks grows until we have to shout to hear each other. We cross over where the bridge spans have fallen, jumping from one chunk of smashed concrete to the next, then climb up the other side of the ravine. Back on the road, we keep going north, the sun rising in a clear sky, strung out as before, single file with Zana in the lead. Every kilometre or so he signals us to stop and runs ahead in a crouch, disappearing into the bush, reappearing a few minutes later and leading us forward again. The sun is high when we reach a place where the road turns sharply west. By now we are dripping from the heat. Zana calls a halt and tells us to drink and rest and check our weapons. Then he disappears again.

After half an hour he still isn't back, and Amsterdam is pacing. 'Should have been back by now,' he says. 'I don't like it.'

Bird sits with his back against a tree, fingering his rifle nervously. 'Never been gone this long,' he says.

'The next village is just up ahead,' says Amsterdam. 'Another bridge just beyond that. It's what he always does. Leaves us here, checks it out himself.'

I say nothing, wait like the others.

Another half-hour creeps by, then another. Zana still isn't back. We've heard nothing, no gunfire, no voices.

'Something's wrong. We should go,' says Amsterdam.

Bird sits back down. 'Zana said to stay.'

'He could be in trouble.'

'Zana said to stay.'

'I'm going. You two stay here.'

'We should stay together,' I say.

Amsterdam nods, looks at Bird. 'Coming?'

Bird gets to his feet again, picks up his rifle. 'Bad place,' he mutters.

We start towards the village, Amsterdam in the lead. It takes over an hour to work our way through the new-growth forest east of the village and approach from downriver. From the ridgeline we can see the wrecked bridge, similar in construction and destruction to the one we passed under that morning, and a ruined village clustered in the narrow tributary valley around its southern end. We hide in the rocks where the ridge falls away and there is a good view up along the valley.

'Bad place,' says Bird.

Amsterdam raises a pair of binoculars to his eyes, turns the focus wheel. 'They're all bad places, Bird.'

'See anything?'

'Nothing.'

Amsterdam scans the village and the bridge and the road both sides of the river.

'What do we do?' says Bird, fidgeting.

'Nothing,' Amsterdam says as he continues to scan the valley. 'We never go past here. If he's anywhere he's here. Maybe he hurt himself and can't walk. He'll signal us.'

We stand looking down at what is left of the village, a strip of disintegrating buildings set each side of a single road, all of it being swallowed up by the forest.

And then Bird stiffens. 'What's that?'

'Where?'

Bird points to the far end of the village. 'There. Is that smoke?'

Amsterdam swings the glasses. 'Where?'

'At the far end, where the road turns.'

The road verges shine white in the sun like twin tracks of freshly bleached coral threading through the smashed concrete. I can't see smoke.

'Wait,' says Amsterdam, focusing.

'There.' Bird's voice breaks. 'It could be him.'

'I see it. Fuck, your eyes are good. Can't see him though.'

'What do we do?'

'We've got to go down there.'

We pick our way down the ridge and into the village, moving quietly, hunched low, moving from building to building. We stop, huddle behind a crumbling brick wall. The road through town is just ahead, its verges piled both sides with the white coral.

Amsterdam draws back the bolt of his rifle and lets the action snap forward. Bird and I do the same.

'Let's go,' Amsterdam says. 'One at a time. I'll go first. Wait for my signal. You next, Kwek. Then Bird.'

Bird shakes his head. 'Bad place.'

Amsterdam shoots me a grin and sets off at a jog, slowing when he reaches the edge of the road. He stumbles for a moment on the white coral verge, picking his way through it as if the ground beneath him was somehow unreliable, then regains the tar and sprints across, clearing the white verge on the far side in one leap. We watch him reach a wrecked house, crouch down and look back at us. He waits a moment, then gives the thumbs-up.

I swallow hard, start towards the road, come to the coral. It is piled knee high, brilliant white in the sun. I slow as Amsterdam did, step up onto the pile, but my foot gives way, the coral stone brittle beneath me. I look down and my stomach lurches. This isn't coral, or stones. They're bones. Thousands of them, ranked and piled in gruesome order.

I shake off a shudder, keep going, leap the pile on the far side as Amsterdam did, join him beside the house. 'Jesus Christ,' I say.

Amsterdam signals and Bird makes his way across the road. 'Should have warned you, I guess.'

We move up a back street towards the far end of the village, going slowly from ruined building to ruined building. As we approach, we catch a whiff of woodsmoke.

'Fire alright.' Amsterdam points. 'There. Stay low. Keep quiet.'

We follow him through a graveyard of rusting vehicles, the bodies piled three and four high, to a mud brick wall. The smell of smoke is strong now, and there is something else with it, charring meat. Voices now, from the other side of the wall, several, speaking Malagasy.

My heart is running a sprint. We make our way to the far end of the wall. Amsterdam peers slowly around it, just for a moment, and then turns back to us. His eyes are wide, shining somehow. There is no trace of fear in them. He is enjoying this.

'It's him,' he says. 'Tied up. Looks bad.'

'I knew it,' whispers Bird.

'Three scouts. Rifles leaning up against the wall. We walk out, like this: me, Kwek, then Bird. Each takes the man in order, left to right. So Kwek, you take the middle one. Bird, on the left. Shoot when I say. Aim for the body. Keep shooting until they're dead. Understand?'

We nod. Blood thunders in my ears. My hands are shaking. Amsterdam glances at them.

'Breathe,' he says. 'You too, Bird.'

He lets us breathe.

'Ready?' Amsterdam steps out from the wall.

I follow, and it's as if some other mind is controlling me, an ancient reptile brain that does not understand fear and suffers no higher reasoning. It all happens so fast and slow that even though I have thought about it at length many times since, I am unsure of the sequence, if there was one. The three men turn to face us. They are dark-skinned, dressed in combat fatigues. The one in the middle is wearing a pair of sunglasses with gold frames and the bridge piece is held together with grey tape. I aim my rifle at him. I can see the expression on his face change. The corners of his mouth drop and his eyes widen. Amsterdam says, 'Now.' We all fire. As we do, the man on the right raises a handgun. At that range, the bullets tear through their bodies, shattering bone and shearing out cartilage in a bursting pink haze. When the smoke clears the three scouts lie dead, blood weeping from holes in their torsos. Amsterdam kneels in the dust, holding his arm just below the elbow. Blood seeps between his fingers and drips to the ground. Zana gazes out at us through the slits of his swollen eyes, stammers something in Malagasy through broken teeth.

March 2026

That month they held an unscheduled meeting, back in the Seychelles at Leopold's place – he was starting to emerge as one of the leaders of the group. We all flew in at short notice.

This time, Leopold and others had dispensed with all the displays of power and we met in a normal boardroom. Okay, not normal – huge, with cherry-panelled walls and a single picture window that looked out over the sea, but still, for them, restrained. No naked concubines. No 'entertainment' during breaks. This was business.

First on the agenda was the growing alarm about the weather, and how people and governments were reacting to it. Okay, most of us called it weather, but Trig was first up and he made it very clear that these events signalled long-term changes, so, climate.

He seemed a lot more confident than the last time he'd briefed us back in 2024 – had it really been that long ago, more than two years? 'Gentlemen, the climate signal is now unequivocal. The last two years have been by far the warmest on record. And there is no sign whatsoever of that trend changing.' He put up a slide showing a graph climbing away to the right like one of the Boss's now disposed-of rockets. 'In fact, our modelling, which is very robust, and that of every major academy of science in the world, shows that we are now locked into at least a century of runaway warming. The only thing that can change that is immediate, across-the-board, massive reductions in emissions.'

He stopped, blinked through his glasses. No one spoke for a long time.

After a while, Yu Wan said: 'How much of a reduction?'

Trig didn't hesitate. 'Ninety percent. At least. Ideally, near zero.'

The Boss guffawed. I really think that he still didn't believe it was real, was one of those who bought Bragg's line that it was all just a big leftie greenie hoax. 'Not going to happen.'

Yu Wan frowned. 'The reductions or the warming? Please, try to be precise.'

'Both,' the Boss said, triumphant.

'You are right,' said Trig, that newfound confidence coming through strong now. 'We estimate that there is now less than a one percent probability that we are going to be able to keep warming to less than four degrees by the end of the century.'

'So we are going to have to live with it,' said Leopold.

Everyone looked his way. He met their gazes, but didn't continue.

Yu Wan, who was chairing, thanked Trig. Then Maddisson lumbered to the head of the table. He looked heavier than the last time I'd seen him. His skin had a sickly pallor that made him look more like a corpse than a living, breathing mogul, and he was sweating profusely. It made me think that he was doing some bad drugs, or maybe trying to get off them. He took a gulp of water and began.

'Gentlemen, we have been hitting the climate issue hard for the last year. We have run several parallel narratives, basically one for every possible view. For those who still don't believe or don't want to believe that the science Dr Trig here tells us is true, we have a range of experts spreading doubt.' He threw up a short video showing clips of grey-haired scientists debunking the science. There was no proof that atmospheric CO_2 drove warming, in fact, it was the other way around. They had graphs that proved it. The loss of coral reefs worldwide to bleaching was not caused by elevated ocean temperatures. One talking head with a neatly trimmed grey beard claimed that the science agencies were deliberately falsifying the coral health data to make things look worse than they really were. He smiled as he said the reef was fantastic, as good as it ever had been, and anyway it had been around for a long time and seen much worse. It was an impressive barrage.

Maddisson was wheezing now – you could hear it over the hum of the AC – but he was on a roll. 'For those who understand that the climate is changing, we have the "it's not our fault" narrative.' He did that thing with his fingers to put the words into relief. 'Basically, the climate is changing because of natural phenomena, sunspots, volcanoes, natural variations in Earth's orbit, that kind of thing.'

I could see the Boss nodding. He liked this one.

'And then there's the "okay it's us but someone else is to blame and there's nothing we can do anyway" line' – that same thing with his fingers – 'and my favourite, the narrative that simply attacks any alternative to the current system as impractical, fearfully expensive and economy-and-job-destroying. So basically, fear. Solar is too expensive, wind turbines kill birds, and you are all going to lose your miserable little jobs if we try to change our economy.' He took another gulp of water, spilled some of it down his chin, wiped unsuccessfully with a flabby hand. 'So basically, something for everyone. Our monitoring shows that a majority of people and commentators in the media are very happy to mash up versions of each of these four together, even when they are contradictory.' He laughed, and the flesh wobbled with him and kept wobbling after he'd finished. 'Logic, gentlemen, is irrelevant.'

'So why isn't it working?' said Li.

Maddisson wiped his forehead and fumbled with the slide clicker. 'Well, it is working. We still have a solid fifty percent in America, maybe forty percent in places like Australia and Canada where they – we – have big energy and mining industries. And we are solid in the autocracies.' He nodded towards the state leaders in the room.

'But we are losing ground. Your graph shows it.'

'Well, yes. The counter-narrative is relentless. And basically, people can now see it for themselves.'

'What about Dahlberg and her constellation of idiots?' said the Boss. He didn't watch or read anything he considered left of centre or any shade of the colour of living plants.

'They've gotten louder, if anything,' said Maddisson.

'Good thing it's too late,' said Leopold.

Murmurs of agreement all round.

And then Yu Wan moved us to the final item, and the vote was one hundred percent in favour. Everything was ready. The virus would 'make the jump' – my fingers, my inverted commas – in a week's time, in three isolated locations in Southeast Asia.

To anyone who may be listening, please forgive me.

Calypso

A nightmare on a lost island in the time of goddesses and gods. An immortal nymph of temptation, beautiful beyond imagining, urging him to stay with her for eternity and forget the wife he loves. Daughter of the god who holds the world on his shoulders, prevents it from escaping the sun's orbit and spinning off into space. Goddess of the silent sea floor where *Ocean Transporter* and her unlucky crew now lie, she whispers to him in atomic hexameter, a new verse for a deadly time.

Seven years shackled, immortality beckoning. A golden weave of lies in a gilded prison as she comes and goes, her siren songs filling his days. And she is beautiful, her body full and soft, the work of the divine, made for pleasure. His for the taking, for all time. That silken promise. Who could resist, and why would they?

Her gentle power breaks him. He lies with her. The betrayal kills something inside him. To be mortal is to be imperfect, hopelessly flawed. She bears him two sons before Athena, goddess of warfare, takes pity on him and asks that he be freed. Calypso, temptress, outranked, must obey. In an infinite universe, even gods have limits. She provides him with tools, shows him where to find wood from which he may build a boat. The boat that will take him on the next part of a fantastic and perilous journey, back to the woman he loves.

Architect of and accomplice to her own demise, despondent and broken-hearted, Calypso ends her own life. As with matter, love cannot be created. Men and gods, women and goddesses, all subject to the same laws of physics and nature.

🌍

It takes us three days to get home. Zana and Amsterdam able to walk, but slowly. Both in bad shape. I apply one of Mum's leather and hardwood tourniquets to Amsterdam's arm, stop the bleeding. Later I pack the wound with a coagulating compound and release the tourniquet, and it seems to work. It's temporary but it gets him home.

Zana was pretty badly beaten, broken nose, concussion almost certainly, broken trigger finger among others. I splint his fingers, bandage what I can.

The scouts wanted to know where Zana was from, what was beyond the river, and if the disease was still there. He didn't tell them anything. Not that it would have made any difference. We took their weapons and ammunition, buried them in the forest, left no trace.

On the way home Zana tells me about the bones. It was at the start of the Repudiation. The government declared the whole region a quarantine zone, told people a terrible disease was running rampant through the population there. The army was called out, and the area was cordoned off. No one allowed in or out.

'There never was any disease,' says Zana. 'It was a ruse, designed to scare people off. But I don't know why or who for. I only know that they wanted the area depopulated. Completely. They sent in special troops in bio-med suits. Then they rounded up everyone, telling them the same story – disease, we are going to make sure you are okay. Brought them to the village by the river, and shot them all. Laid them out along the road, both sides, for miles, as far as you could see, three and four deep. A warning. Then they left, blew up the bridge. Whoever wanted it done never came. Probably died like everyone else.'

When I get home I tell Julie what happened at the bridge. All of it. She listens in silence. We are lying in bed together and I look to see if she is asleep, but her eyes are wide open.

'That's why they came here, Julie. Zana and First Governess decided it was the perfect place to hide. *La region de la peste*, people call it. The plague lands. But then you probably already know that.'

'How did Zana know what happened?'

'He told me he was there.'

'Patricia didn't tell me about that,' Julie said, her voice half an octave lower than normal. 'Her and Zana, they've been married a long time. They developed this philosophy together, slowly over the years as they watched society go wrong. They wanted to build a better world, learn from the mistakes of the past.' She takes my hand in hers. 'And they have. You can see it, can't you? They have. And it works. People are happy here, safe.'

'I killed a man,' I say.

Julie caresses my wrist with her thumb. 'You did what you had to do to keep us safe.'

'Maybe. But it doesn't change anything. How long does First Governess think they can stay hidden away down here?'

'People will think that the disease got them.'

'We can't kill them all. Someone is sending them, more and more. It's only a matter of time.'

Julie sits up and takes my face in her hands and kisses me on the mouth. As she does the sheet falls away and her breasts push into me, warm and soft. There are tears in her eyes and on her lips. 'Oh, Kwe, I was so worried.'

'I know about you and Amsterdam.'

Julie freezes, still holding my face between her hands, her eyes searching mine, saying nothing, her chest rising and falling. Then she moves slowly back and lies there in the dark, her hip touching mine, breathing hard so I can hear the air moving in and out of her in the dark.

I wait, the two of us like that, side by side, saying nothing.

After a condensed eternity she whispers: 'I'm sorry.'

'How many times?'

'Three, no four.'

'Tell me.'

'Oh, Kwe, no. Please. I'm so sorry. It won't happen again. It's this … this place.'

'Tell me.'

'First Governess insisted.'

'She wants us to stay. All of us. Amsterdam told me.'

'Yes, she does. We fit here, Kwe. Leo is blossoming.'

'She's manipulating you, Julie. Drawing you in. All of us, me too. I killed a man because of it.'

'No, Kwe. It makes sense. It works.'

'Are you saying we didn't work before?'

'No, Kwe. Of course not. But we can't live apart from the world. We need a society.'

'What's left of the world you mean.'

'That's the point, Kwe. We need to build a new kind of society, one based on respect, that nourishes rather than exploits. After all the death, love is the only thing that can save us.'

'You sound more like her every day.'

'Maybe I do. I respect her, Kwe. She is a remarkable woman.'

'What did you do, Julie, with this remarkable woman's husband, the guy from Amsterdam?'

She reddens, looks down at her hands. 'We didn't ... if that's what you're asking.'

I close my eyes, a rescue, open them again. 'What did you do?' I can smell the brine of tears on her skin.

'He pleasured me, with his mouth.'

I wince, glad of the darkness, fury boiling away inside me, barely under control. 'And then?'

'It was his fourth day. Each time. I followed the system.'

You don't think something you already know can hurt you so badly. It takes me a while to recover. I lie there trying to push oxygen to my brain, trying to settle myself.

'He loves you, Julie. He told me so, on the way back. Said he couldn't live without you, that he would die for you. Apologised to me about a hundred times, all the way back. Wanted me to know the truth. Said he owed me that, after everything that had happened, saving his life. He wants to take you away from here, Julie. Do you know that? Has he told you?'

Julie shakes her head. Tears stream from her eyes, run rivulets down her cheeks. 'No, Kwe. No. He hasn't. And it doesn't matter. I love you. And our children. Nothing is going to change that.'

I kiss her, hold her close. Forgive, mortal. Hold back the evil.

July 2026

Three and a half months into what was now being called the second pandemic, things were not unfolding the way Dr Z had said they would. The spread had been slower than expected, and while the Maddisson press and Yu Wan's media empire were doing a good job on the jump narrative, and blaming the lefties and greenies in general, the number of deaths was lower than expected, and the effect on the global economy was less severe than anticipated. It seemed the world had learned from the first time, and people and countries had reacted more swiftly and effectively than predicted. Turns out people weren't as stupid or incompetent as they'd assumed, at least where short-term self-preservation was concerned.

Despite this, lots of people died, including Bryce's mother. He called me the day she passed away, in tears. I felt so sorry for him. If I could have, I would have gone to him, but the lockdown was strict. Lots of people lost their jobs, and lots of companies that the guys had shorted went under. Lots more they'd piled into made record profits. Paolo said on one call that the Boss had doubled his fortune since February.

Bragg, I have to give him credit, handled it all well. He embraced the advice of the CDC, launched the vaccination initiative, promised to have it ready by September, no fail, and that reassured everyone. He was fast becoming a national hero even to the people who didn't vote for him and his ratings were going through the atmosphere and out into space. All our other world leaders were also faring well.

The Boss had summoned Dr Z to come to New York for a briefing. Bryce flew down to pick her up and the Boss and I met them at the airport in the limo. The Boss said drive and Max headed out of town. Soon we were on a winding country road heading east.

'Where are we going, if I may ask?' Dr Z said, wiggling down into her dress. She'd worn one of her power suits, a tight-fitting knee-length dress with a matching hussar jacket, but it kept riding up on her and she kept having to yank it down at the hem.

'I thought we'd take a little drive, get some air,' said the Boss.

I'd booked a meeting room at the Sheraton downtown. We were already well into the Catskills.

'So, tell me about progress,' said the Boss.

Dr Z told him. 'We've just done a second release, to accelerate things.'

The Boss nodded. 'Good. And the vaccine?'

'Ready. Three billion doses stockpiled. Effectiveness over ninety percent.'

'Excellent.' He scrolled his phone a moment. 'And what about subsequent mutations?'

She raised an eyebrow. 'Our team is geared up for whatever may come next by way of variants.'

'Good,' said the Boss. 'Turn here, Max.'

Max nodded once and turned onto a gravel road leading away into the forest. No one spoke. After a while we crossed a small one-lane bridge and came to a place where the road narrowed.

'Just pull over here, Max,' said the Boss. 'There is a nice walk here by the river.'

The car rolled to a stop. Max got out and opened the doors for the Boss and then for Dr Z and me. The air was cool and smelled of pine needles, the forest dark and thick around us.

Dr Z stood there on the gravel, tottering on her four-inch heels that made her taller than the Boss.

'Come on,' said the Boss, starting off into the woods. I took off my heels, but Dr Z insisted on keeping hers on. We followed him along a narrow winding trail. The dirt was cool under my feet and it reminded me of being a little girl and our summer place near the lake. Once in a while we had to stop and wait for Dr Z, who by now was looking distinctly dishevelled and more than a bit pissed off as she struggled over the rough ground. This was typical of the Boss, make people uncomfortable by putting them in situations way outside of what they were prepared for.

After a while we came to a small clearing in the woods with a lovely view of the river.

'I love this spot,' said the Boss. 'So peaceful. Sometimes I come here when I need to think.'

Dr Z and I stood looking at the river.

'So overall, Amie, I would say it has been a job well done.'

Dr Z smiled, obviously relieved. 'Why thank—'

She never got to say the last word of that sentence. Instead, she slumped to the ground with the front of her face missing. The Boss looked at me, just a glance, the gun still smoking in his hand. Before I could say a word, Max appeared with a plastic body bag and a shovel. I stood watching, unable to speak or move. Within a few minutes Dr Z's body and the layer of soil around where she fell had been zipped into the bag and thrown over Max's broad shoulder like a sack of ... what? Bones? Unwanted flesh? Shit? Take your pick. Her body was never found.

Lioness

Every day now I watch the sea, waiting for the winds to change, the seas to calm. If we can reach Cape Town before the end of December, we can catch the northeast trades from the Cape to the Gulf of Guinea and Takoradi, where my father was born and raised and where, according to Mum, many of his family still lived when they lost contact with them over thirty years ago. Only 2,590 nautical miles, according to *Ocean Passages*. Only.

I would have left a long time ago, if it was up to me. The longer we stay here, the more Julie and Leo become settled. I was going to write 'indoctrinated', but maybe that's too harsh. I can't deny that they are flourishing. Leo is growing big and strong, seemingly day by day, already talking to me about when he can join me and the other men 'outside', as everyone here calls it. Not that women and girls aren't allowed outside. They run the place, they can go where they like, but the philosophy makes the separation of roles quite clear. Women rule, men protect. Women are protected, men are ruled. Outside is dangerous and wild. Inside is safe and civilised.

And the longer we stay, the more I can feel Julie and I drifting apart. Despite having it out a few weeks ago, Julie shows no signs of wanting to change things or leave. She has been elected a member of the council, and now spends as much time hearing petitions and passing judgement on disputes and infractions as she does on doctoring. At home, she insists that I follow the rules to the letter. She still spends several evenings a week at the First Governess's place, getting home late, slipping into bed warm and willing. We haven't talked about Amsterdam since that day after I got back from the patrol, and since he was wounded I haven't seen him on patrol. I know that they are still seeing each other, if only within the rules of this society. But I have taken her at her word that she loves me and no one else. Her ardour with me is unabated, has grown even as this other distance between us somehow widens.

Part of me, a big part – the sane, thinking part – is happy for her, glad to see her growing in confidence and capability as a doctor, as a leader, as a woman. And there's a dark, tortured thrill I get, thinking of her enjoying herself, being pleasured, as she calls it. But another part of me – the insane, primal part – burns. Rage, jealousy, self-reproach, all boil up inside me, and sometimes at night when I know she is at First Governess's I want to walk over there fully clothed and smash the place up and grab her by the hand and walk her out of there. But then I see her smile, or she kisses me that way she does, or I hear her laugh at something Leo has said, and it all subsides, back to that dark, animal place.

When the time comes, will she agree to leave? Becky is out there somewhere, and there are questions we must answer. She knows this.

Outside, I work hard, farming and fishing, cutting and hauling wood. I've done a couple more patrols, both uneventful. Zana is all healed up and still leads our team, has learned to use his third digit as his trigger finger. The other day he told me that one of the other teams had ambushed and killed two scouts not far from the Village of the Dead. Used Claymore mines to shred them. Village of Peace. Inside, maybe.

◉

As the days pass, the southwesterlies intensify rather than abate, blowing gale force from the pole and across the forties. *Providence* handles the weather well, out there lonely and waiting on her anchor, pitching in the waves that bend around the point as if straining against her bonds, as anxious as I am to leave. Over the last week I've found time to scrape the hull clean, check the sails and lines and rigging, and grease the rudder mechanism. I time my visits to *Providence* to coincide with Sparkplug's transmissions, sit there in the cabin with our little receiver, shaking my head as I listen to her voice, wondering at the cruelty and selfishness in men's souls. I wonder where she might be and how she has managed to survive this long, with all she has seen, and it is as if our stories are slowly intertwining, like climbers on a vine. Everything is ready to go, and it is time. All I need to do is convince Julie.

One night she gets home late. She gives me a quick kiss on the lips, and in the candlelight I can see that her face is flushed. 'I'm exhausted,' she says. 'I'm going to bed.'

'I was hoping we could talk.'

She brushes her hair back and arches her back like a lioness. 'Can't it wait, Kwe? It's been a long day.'

'Not really, no.' I can tell from the smell of her that she's been with Amsterdam.

She straightens and stands looking at me. 'I am going to have a shower. You can speak to me after.' And then she turns and walks into our room, leaving me alone.

It has become increasingly like that, our relationship, as she takes her role as governess and head of household increasingly seriously. She dictates and I obey. Until now, I've treated it as she has asked me to, as an experiment, something to be open-minded about. She said it would bring us closer together, and we agreed to give it time, to try to make it work. But now I can see that this way of living is driving us apart, and it is getting harder for me to hold back the darkness that lurks inside me. I sit on the balcony and look out across the bay, listen to the wind in the treetops and the sound of falling water from our bedroom.

After a while she calls my name, and I blow out the candles and walk across the stone floor to our room. When I enter, she is sitting in her chair swaddled in a blue robe, her hair pulled back tight, purring. Her skin shines in the lamplight and her lips are dark and moist. She has placed a cushion on the floor in front of her chair as she has done before and I know what it means.

'Come and speak to me, husband,' she says, her voice catching. As she says it, she lets her robe slip down so that one shoulder glows pale in the lamplight.

I take a breath. 'Do we really have to do it this way, Julie?'

Her eyes flash momentarily. 'You said you wanted to talk to me. You know the rules.'

'Her rules, Julie. Not mine.'

'Please, Kwe. We agreed. Our rules.'

I kneel on the cushion facing her, my hands behind my back.

Julie smiles that smile of hers that she knows has always enchanted me and looks me up and down, lingering on my obvious enlargement. 'You like the rules well enough, from what I can see.'

'Julie, please. This is serious.'

Her smile softens and I know she is listening. 'It's time to go,' I say.

She is quiet and doesn't respond for a long time, and when she does her voice is very faint, almost a whisper. 'I want to stay.'

'You know that this isn't real, don't you? All of this. It's a big game of make-believe.'

I can see her catching her breath, calming herself.

'You're wrong, Kwe. Who's to say that this isn't as real as any other way of living? In many ways it's more sane, more real, as you call it, than any of the disastrous experiments at living we've read about, or seen for that matter.'

'She's brainwashing you.'

She leans forward in her chair. 'Do you really think I'm that weak, Kweku? That easily manipulated? You must, or you wouldn't have said such a thing.'

'Look at us, Julie. Is this really us? Is this really you? I don't think it is.' I stand, walk to the window. 'No, Julie. The winds are going to turn soon. And when they do, we're leaving. We agreed before we left, we were going to find what's left of my family in Africa, and we were going to try to find Becky and the people who killed Mum and Lewis and Mandy. And that's what we're going to do. That's why we're out here.'

All the blood has drained from Julie's face, and she jerks her robe up over her shoulder and pulls it close across her chest. 'Don't walk away from me while we're talking. And don't tell me what to do.'

I stay over by the window. 'If we don't make Cape Town before January, the winds for the run to West Africa might not be favourable again for another year.'

'Fine. We'll stay another year and we can discuss it again next December.'

'I'm not staying another year, Julie. Becky can't wait that long.'

She sits resolute. 'Come back here if you want to talk to me. Otherwise, I'm going to bed.'

I take a few deep breaths, and then comply.

'Oh, Kwe, can't you see how happy we all are here? We don't even know where Becky is. She could be anywhere.'

I can see that she is crying now, big tears that well up silently and brim over onto her cheeks, each a flamed ruby. And I realise that she is frightened. I try to soften my tone. 'Please, Julie. We agreed.'

'Maybe this *is* the answer, Kwe. Did you ever think of that? Maybe this is exactly what we came out here to find.'

I raise my hands in front of my face, turn them palms in. 'I'm a murderer, Julie. That man's face is haunting me.'

'You did what you had to do.'

'It's going to get worse Julie,' I say. 'I'm worried about you and Leo, about all of us. It's dangerous here.'

'Any more dangerous than anywhere else? My God, listen to yourself, Kweku.'

'I've seen what's happening outside these walls, Julie. It's my responsibility to keep you and the kids safe. And I'm going to find my brother's daughter. We're leaving as soon as the winds change.'

'No, Kweku. That's not how things work here. It's not your decision to make.'

'Yes, it is, Julie.'

'And what if we don't want to go? What then? Are you going to pick us up and carry us away under your arms, force us away at gunpoint, just like those men did with Becky?'

'That's not fair, Julie. Don't talk garbage.'

'I'm serious,' she says. 'Can't you hear yourself? This is exactly the reason we need this society, so that brute strength and force are no longer—'

I cut her off before she can finish, a cardinal sin. 'I don't want one of her sermons right now, Julie.'

'How dare you,' she hisses, the tears gone now, her eyes narrowed, unblinking. 'I thought you understood. You promised me that you would give this a try.'

'I have, Julie. Open your eyes.'

She stands, turns towards the bed. 'I'm going to bed. You can sleep out there.'

Next morning at breakfast, sitting together at the table, she asks Leo if he wants to leave, take another long journey on the boat. I expect tears and remonstrations, but all I get is a curt no.

That day we do a patrol to the west. Amsterdam is back with us, his arm healed now. He acknowledges me with a nod, but otherwise we avoid each other. Zana leads us up into the mountains, four hours straight uphill to a lookout point that dominates the next valley, the mountains ridging out deep blue for as far as we can see with no sign of human habitation. We stay for two hours, see nothing, and come back down.

When I get home, Julie kisses me. She apologises for losing her temper with me the night before, says that we'll find a way to work it out. I know she loves me, worries whenever I am on patrol. She says that tomorrow we have a special audience with First Governess. I ask what she wants to speak to us about, but Julie says she doesn't know, and I don't press her. It is day four for me, mid-cycle for her, and that night her passion is unbridled.

September 2026

After Dr Z's second, posthumous, virus release, propagation was much faster. Like everyone else I watched in horror as the reports came in from around the world. And though my shame grew with each news broadcast, I now knew, clearly and unequivocally, the price of any defiance. Dr Z had been one of the team, had abandoned her medical ethics as easily as one would let go of a slightly embarrassing and not-very-good-looking boyfriend. Her only sin had been that she knew too much, and would be highly credible on a witness stand. Maybe that was all that was keeping me alive now – I was just some ditzy secretary with big boobs who spent a lot of her time sucking the Boss's cock, and his associates' cocks for that matter. I realised that it was more important now than ever for me just to shut up and play dumb and keep sucking. But I would keep writing my journal, just paper and pen, one copy only, absolutely no digital trail. I would photocopy no documents, forward no files. This handwritten account would have to be good enough. Whenever the time might come, people were just going to have to trust me, cum-drinking airhead that I was.

The vaccine was deployed later that month to much fanfare, instant world-wide relief, and much Braggian self-congratulation. Death rates plummeted within weeks, and the Boss and the new CEO of his eponymous pharma company became instant uber-celebrities. Their faces were everywhere, along with Bragg's and the other world leaders who had pulled off this miracle of modern medicine.

I was there backstage when the Boss was interviewed on one of the major networks, live. The hostess was masked up and the Boss sat in an appropriately distanced armchair in his dubious skeleton-face mask, waiting for the cue to start.

The director gave them a signal and they removed their masks, oriented themselves towards the live camera and put on their smiles.

'I'm here with Derek Argent,' the woman began, her hair a rigid, concreted missile silo about her face. 'He is the majority shareholder and chairman of Argent Pharmaceuticals, part of the global consortium that cracked the viral code and raced life-saving vaccines to the world in record time.' She turned to face the Boss. 'Welcome.'

The Boss smiled that killer smile of his, made sure the camera got a good look at his eyes. 'Thanks, Gwen. I just want to say to everyone watching here today that it wasn't easy. We put a lot into it, went for broke really. I'm glad it worked out.'

'Well, the effect certainly has been amazing. We can only thank you.'

The Boss was loving this puffery. 'You're welcome, everyone. We're saving millions of lives, literally. And I am pleased to announce today that we will be providing the vaccine, and the curative products we've developed, to developing nations at no cost.'

The set erupted in spontaneous applause, cameramen and mic-boom girls and producers and gofers all clapping away. I could read their lips as they turned to each other: wow, so generous, what a guy, what a great thing to do.

'I'd like to thank all the world leaders, especially President Bragg and the president of the Russian Federation for their support. Without their resources and belief, we could never have pulled this off. We are lucky to have them as leaders at this critical point in history.'

On the way back from the studio the Boss wanted me to go down on him and I made sure it was the experience of his life.

Patricia

The next evening, we are shown to a small walled garden shaded with grape vines. Julie is seated on a wickerwork stool. I stand by her side, facing a large, high-backed chair set a step above the rest of the garden on a cut-stone platform. I am still reeling from the realisation that Sparkplug's boss was Derek Argent, the man who was responsible for my father's death. I have yet to share this with Julie.

After what may be half an hour but feels longer, First Governess emerges from the house and sits in the chair. She smiles and nods to Julie, who beams in return. Then she turns her gaze on me, head to foot and back up to my eyes. 'Your wife has told me you are writing a history.'

'Yes. Trying.'

She nods. 'This is very important. We can only shape the future by understanding what came before, and why. I would like to tell you the story of my country, and how we came to be here, as we are.'

Julie reaches for my hand, squeezes it. A gesture of reassurance, or perhaps encouragement. She hands me my journal and a pencil, then looks up and says: 'Thank you, Patricia. Please tell us.'

First Governess gathers her robes about her and begins. I write it as she goes.

'The early part of the century in my country was a time of optimism. Population growth was slowing as women were educated and empowered. We'd slowed deforestation and created new protected zones for our native species. My father was a successful businessman, and he established one of the first solar-energy companies in the country. By the time I entered the university, I knew I wanted to be part of it.'

First Governess leans forward in her chair and fixes her gaze on me. 'And then everything started to change.' Her eyes are dark, pulsing with a strange intensity. 'The more progress we made, the more viciously the people who represented the old ways fought. I came to see that the progress we thought we had achieved was nothing more than illusion.'

She waits for me to catch up. 'And then the pandemic came and my mother was killed by the virus. Not long after, our government was overthrown by a despot called Antimando and his cabal of reactionaries. The new regime quickly took control with support from the army, and set about reshaping public opinion. It was a very simple message, based on fear and greed. Anyone who protested was taken away. Many simply disappeared. School curricula were changed. Old mines were recommissioned, new ones opened in national parks. Forests that had been protected were logged. Fossil fuels were mined and burned like never before.'

'The Repudiation,' I say. 'My father wrote about it.'

'Yes,' says First Governess. 'I have heard it called that. Of course, it was before either of you were born. It feels like a long time ago now.' She pauses, looked at the backs of her hands. 'And then my father and sister were killed in a car bomb and I was alone.'

She closes her eyes and sits for a time as if in quiet meditation. We wait. When she opens her eyes again there are tears wicking her eyelashes. She blinks a few times and continues. 'Forgive me,' she says. 'That was when I met Zana. He'd been wounded fighting the insurgents. In hospital, he came to reject everything the government stood for. He quit the army. We fell in love. Together, we started developing our philosophy of a new way to live. We had both observed, even back when society seemed to be making some progress, the final victory of the masculine over the feminine. We watched appalled as women were made to aspire to the masculine virtues, were incentivised and subtly pressured to be more like men, to be hyper-aggressive, to play combat-imitating sport, to embrace conflict and conquest in the male way and to reject the primal female instincts of caring and cooperation and nurturing. Subtly, women had unwittingly given up their essential power for a feeble and ultimately pitiful imitation of the power of men. Society, and the world, thus became unbalanced, ungoverned, the masculine running riot, the feminine lost. We determined that we would chart a new direction, re-establish balance in the world, the balance between human and nature, between woman and man. Others joined us, bound by a new vision for the future.'

She stops, gathers breath. I can see she is giving us time to consider the depth of what she has set out to do. There is something familiar about her story that I can't place.

'Zana and I were married. He took my name as a symbol of the new order we were trying to establish. We had a baby together. A little girl. But then the disasters struck. We'd heard about the fires and floods and heatwaves in other countries, but we never thought it could happen here. We lost our child in the first killing heatwave and watched as millions died. It went on and on, year after year. I cannot describe to you how horrible it was. Did your parents speak to you of this?'

Julie glances at me. 'My parents both died when I was young,' she says. 'It was at about the same time.'

First Governess nods. 'I am sorry,' she says before continuing. 'Antimando was eventually assassinated by a rival gang and our once-beautiful island home, what was left of it, descended into anarchy.'

Julie sits forward on her stool. 'Thank you, First Governess. From both of us. It is part of the reason we came here, my husband and I, to learn the truth of what happened then, and why.'

First Governess folds her hands in her lap, glances at me and then addresses Julie again. 'Before you go, there is one more thing I have to say to you both. You have made a valuable contribution to our society. We are grateful for all you have brought. Your son, too. It is a very important time for us. There are many challenges, and we have big plans. Our society is the hope for humanity's future. I know your husband wishes to leave, he has made that very plain.' She shoots me a sidelong glance before continuing. 'I will make this clear,' she says, fixing her gaze on Julie, holding it. 'We need you here. Both of you. And so, I have decided that it is time for you to have another baby. You are young and strong, and we must grow our society.'

Her words hang there as we process them. I put down my journal. Perhaps I haven't heard right. 'You've decided what?'

First Governess repeats her words. Julie sits beside me, silent. I try to catch her eye, but she is looking straight ahead, at the woman on the dais.

'Julie and I have already talked about this,' I say barely controlling my anger, 'before we left Australia. We agreed that we're not having any more children until we get home. Tell her, Julie.'

First Governess smiles, raises her hand. 'Please, Kweku. Our genetic diversity is important. I have selected a second husband for her. He will father her next child.'

I stand, speechless, not believing what I've heard, my knees collapsing beneath me, waiting for Julie to come to my rescue, set this insane woman straight. But there she sits, silent and unmoved, as if none of this is a surprise to her. And then I realise. It isn't.

October 2026

Later that month, Bryce flew me and the Boss and Paolo to meet with Leopold. For five days before we left, he and the Boss had been talking over the secure line. Leopold had sounded angry and erratic, going on about his wife getting sick and the lack of vaccine supply for his people. He demanded that the Boss come and see him in person, and would not be dissuaded. To me, sitting there and listening, it sounded like the guy was on drugs. Or maybe it was me. The Boss and I had been going through a lot of coke lately. It helped a lot.

Finally, though, the Boss gave in and agreed to go. It was then that I realised just how powerful Leopold had become within the consortium. Either that, or there was something he had that the Boss needed badly enough to swallow the planet of his ego and traipse halfway around the globe. Just like I had to swallow him on the flight out there, twice.

We landed in Antananarivo and were picked up by a convoy of armoured trucks and driven north. The countryside was beautiful, but had that run-down, overexploited look I'd seen before in other parts of Africa. After two hours we reached Leopold's palace. Yes, another palace, this one even larger and if possible, more luxurious than the one in the Seychelles. The scale of this guy's wealth was beyond anything I could ever have imagined, even on drugs.

Led by Leopold's chief aide, a man with a strangely high-pitched voice, pockmarked face and in-turned feet, we were ushered through gate after gate, penetrating further and further into the palace, through layers of hierarchy. It was almost as if the closer we got to the inner sanctum, the further back in time we went. We walked long corridors draped with fine tapestries, the floor under our feet paved with handmade silk rugs. Uniformed guards stood at each door, dressed as Ottoman janissaries, armed with curved daggers. Here was the Sublime Porte remade, complete with what Leopold's aide pointed out as a harem, which contained over one hundred of the most beautiful women in the world. Even the Boss was impressed.

Finally, we came to a huge open-air space with what looked like a king-sized bed set up on a sort of throne in the centre. There were posts at each corner of the bed and a silk canopy above it so that it looked like a little house with the curtains tied open. Leopold was sitting up on the bed with two young and modestly attired women by his side. All three were dressed in black. We approached and the aide invited us to sit, indicating the large cushions strewn on the floor around the throne.

Paolo and I sat. The Boss remained standing.

'These are my daughters,' Leopold said, looking fondly at each of the young women seated beside him. 'Beatrice and Patricia.'

The Boss glanced at the young women. 'We're here,' he said. 'It better be for a damn good reason, Leopold.'

Leopold shrugged, not a sultan at that moment, just a tired old man. 'Thank you for coming,' he said, his voice very quiet, thinner than before. He clapped his hands and four of the men dressed as janissaries came into the room carrying a wooden board the size of a door. Atop was a body draped in plain black silk. The men placed the board carefully on a pair of trestles beside the throne and stood to attention on each side of it.

'My wife,' Leopold said. 'She died four days ago of the virus.'

The Boss frowned. 'You brought me all this way for that? Looks to me like you got plenty more wives where she came from.'

Leopold frowned. 'She had been vaccinated, twice, along with my entire family and staff. With your vaccine.'

The Boss glanced in the direction of the body. 'I told you all, ninety-five-plus percent effective. I didn't say a hundred percent.'

'I don't care about the ninety-five, I care about this one.'

The Boss shook his head, did that thing he does when he's had enough. 'Tough shit, Leopold. We all ran the same risks. Move on.'

'I intend to,' said Leopold, regaining some attitude. 'I have a proposition I would like to discuss with you, in private. The risks will be greater than your ninety-five percent, but the rewards will be infinitely higher, and much longer term. This is nothing.' He waved towards the janissaries, and they picked up the board and carried it away. 'Leave us now, girls,' he said.

His two daughters descended from the throne. As they did the younger and prettier of the two met my gaze, and for a moment we were looking right at each other. And you know, I saw fury in those eyes. Not sadness or bereavement, but boiling anger. It surprised me. And then she looked away, and she and her sister followed the janissaries from the room.

'I'm listening,' said the Boss.

'I said in private.'

'Whatever you have to say, you can say in front of my people.' Another power play. If the other guy wanted it one way, the Boss wanted it the other. It was the principle that mattered, he liked to say.

It only took five minutes for Leopold to spell it out. He wanted the Boss's support. Together, they could sway the rest of the consortium. There were still details to be worked out, and he needed Trig and his team to do it, but he would be ready to put forward the motion formally at their planned January meeting.

The Boss stood there a moment considering what he'd heard. Me, I was becoming numb to it by then. You build one pyramid to last a million years, and then you've got to build a bigger one that will last two. Except in this case, it wasn't about building. 'I'll let you know,' the Boss said.

We stayed a couple of days at the palace. The Boss and Paolo each selected a couple of companions to keep them company, and I stayed in my room and watched Netflix. Bryce flew us home the next day in the Gulfstream. I'd never been to Madagascar before.

Lotus Eaters

I storm out of the meeting, march through the darkness back to our house. I wait for Julie to follow, but after an hour I realise that she isn't coming. We are among the Lotus Eaters, blinded by a flawed vision of utopia. Is Julie really so spellbound by this woman that she will agree to such a thing? Before leaving the so-called audience, I made it very clear what I thought about these plans for Julie, and told them both that we were leaving as soon as the winds changed. I determine then that whatever it takes, I am going to get her and the kids away from this nightmare. I can now see this place for what it is: a prison, run by a tyrant.

That night I row out to *Providence*, tune into Sparkplug's regular transmission, about Leopold losing his wife, about his two daughters, one named Patricia. After, I try to sleep, but tumble in a restless undertow, unable to escape the horror unfolding in her story and in my life.

By morning, Julie is still not home. Fema and I get Leo ready for school, and then I go outside and report to Sabre, who sends me with two other men to cut wood. At midday, Sabre comes to check on us, sits on a rock and watches as we haul the logs back to the village, AK47 across his knees. If they really want to keep us here, they can just scuttle *Providence*, or pull up her anchor and let her float away. The weather still hasn't broken, but it doesn't matter anymore. Anywhere is better than here. I am going to have to be smart, think this through.

When I get home, it is already dark. Julie is back, conciliatory. She tells me she spent the rest of the night talking with First Governess, and had got her to agree to back away from her plans. I don't have to worry, she says.

'We're leaving,' I reply.

Julie smiles but her eyes are cold.

'I won't have a baby with another man, but I'm not leaving. And neither is Leo. You can't force us.'

'You tell that crazy woman that we're leaving, Julie. Two days. Get ready. I'm not discussing it with you. I'm telling you.'

She stands there looking at me as if I have just committed mass murder. When she speaks, her voice is very even and controlled. 'I would never have believed that you could say something like that to me. Never. It's everything that's wrong with the world. Your mother would be appalled.' And then she turns and walks out.

🌑

The next morning, Julie still hasn't returned. In our five years of marriage, this is the first time we've ever really been at odds over anything serious, and it is boring a hole through me. We are at an impasse. She's fallen so far under First Governess's spell that she can't see what is happening to us, how she is being manipulated. And I am sure she is thinking the same about me, that I refuse to acknowledge the obvious benefits of further integrating into this community. Doubt is pulling me apart. Why not stay another year? She asked me to try, give this place a chance, and I promised her I would. I trust her, and have since the first time I met her. In all our time together, she's never misled or lied to me. She has tried repeatedly to reassure me about Amsterdam, has convinced First Governess to back away from her plans. Maybe if I just let it go everything will be fine. I don't want to push her into an ultimatum. If it comes down to it, I know that I will stay rather than leave without her, even with Becky out there. The winds haven't turned yet. I decide to give her time.

I report to Sabre for the day's work. He tells me that my team has been assigned a long-range patrol, leaving immediately. Julie will be informed. We draw our weapons, ammunition, food, and water, and head east and then north along the usual route. Zana and Amsterdam are subdued, Bird the opposite, talking incessantly about his new wife, one of the older women. He is husband number two, but it doesn't seem to dim his enthusiasm any. First Governess has made sure that there are significantly more men here than women, plenty of protection and labour.

We reach Blown-Bridge River without incident. All seems quiet. That night we camp upstream of the bridge. We eat, set the watch rotation, settle down to sleep, no indication that anything is wrong.

Next morning, Zana says we are going to go down into the village. We check our gear and ready our weapons. Zana sends Bird ahead. We watch as he picks his way down the ridge, disappears behind a clutch of boulders and then re-emerges further down the hill.

Then Zana turns to me. 'Put your rifle on the ground, Kwek.'

'What?'

Zana nudges the muzzle of his rifle up slightly so that it is pointing at the ground between us. His eyes are set hard. 'You heard me. Right there.'

Amsterdam is standing off to one side, pretending not to hear.

'What's going on?' I say.

'Just do it.' His muzzle moves up another notch.

I lay my rifle on the ground, all that this means coming at me in a rush.

'Now that pistol of yours.'

I do as he says.

'Amsterdam,' says Zana.

Amsterdam sidles over and picks up my weapons.

'Let's go,' says Zana. 'Follow Bird.'

We pick our way down the ridge, me in front, Zana and Amsterdam behind, until we come to a small clearing.

'Stop,' Zana says.

I turn to face him.

He throws an army shovel on the ground in front of me. 'Dig.'

His meaning is clear but I can't bring myself to believe it. 'Is this what I think it is?'

'Just do it.'

'No,' I say, standing my ground.

'Dig,' says Zana, raising his rifle so it is aimed at my chest.

'So, this is your peace?'

Zana's eyes are set hard. 'You died during a skirmish with a patrol from one of the gangs. The First Governess has decided.'

I try to spit at them but nothing comes. 'You and your philosophy. And I suppose you get to father Julie's child now, do you, Amsterdam? I should have left you to bleed out back there.'

Amsterdam shakes his head. 'Not me, Kwek. Some older guy, one of the originals. His reward for loyalty. I'm sorry.'

These men, my comrades in arms, beholden to a higher power. And I realise at that moment that I don't feel fear, or hate, or betrayal, but simply a profound sense of regret that I will never see my wife and son again.

'Dig,' says Zana.

'I am not going to dig my own grave. You can shoot me where I stand.'

'Have it your way.' Zana chambers a round.

'Before you do it, tell me Zana, what is your married name?'

He looks at me as if surprised that this is my final request. 'Leopold,' he says.

And suddenly the sky is very blue, bluer than I have ever seen it before. Of course. It all makes sense. It all fits together. A sea breeze whispers across my face, caresses my hair. I can feel all of it, the living, breathing world and the deep promise therein and everything that is to come. Zana sets his stance, raises his rifle. I can see him tightening his third finger on the trigger. It is over.

And then Amsterdam steps forward and puts his hand on Zana's shoulder, leans in and whispers something in his ear. I watch Zana's expression change, as if a sudden realisation has come over him. Slowly, the muzzle of his AK lowers.

Zana nods. 'It could work,' he says. 'Until...'

'Blame me,' says Amsterdam. 'I don't give a damn.'

Zana thinks this over, wavers, unsure.

'It's not right,' says Amsterdam. 'You said so yourself. Kwek's done nothing wrong. And his family...'

'No. We must be resolute.'

Zana starts to raise his rifle again, stares down its length at me. 'Stay, Kwek. Promise to stay and we can turn around now and all will be forgotten.'

'I can't do that, Zana. I won't live like this. I won't have my wife bred like some cow. You say you wanted freedom to live the way you choose. That's all I am asking for. Let me go.'

'First Governess...'

'Is a fucking hypocrite. I know what she did, what you did. I know, Zana.'

Zana looks stunned. He hesitates, the rifle wavering in his hands.

And then Amsterdam raises his own rifle, swings it towards the river and fires off two quick rounds. The sound echoes away across the valley. 'There. It's done. Come on, Zana. We'll go get Bird, go home. Stay here tonight, Kwek, and meet me in three days' time out by the point where the freighter is anchored. There's a cave in the rocks there. And keep out of sight.'

Zana shrugs.

'Sorry, Kwek,' Amsterdam mumbles before turning away and disappearing into the forest.

I sit under the trees, alone in the fading light, the events of the last few days spinning like a cyclone in my head. Can I trust them to maintain the lie, at least until I can get Julie and Leo out of there? And now that they're aware that I know their secret, will they betray me again, show up in three days at the cave and shoot me there? And what will Julie think when they tell her I've been killed by scouts, which they surely will? What will she do? And Leo. Imagining my own death, and the reaction of others to it, is not something I have ever done before. A pointless exercise I soon abandon as sleep takes me.

March 2027

By now the pandemic was pretty much over, in the sense that deaths had tailed off. New variants appeared on a regular basis, but did far less damage overall. Boss Pharma kept pumping out new vaccines to keep pace, and the profits were eyewatering. The new CEO was well paid and compliant, blissfully unaware of why his company was doing so well. He thought it was because of his new leadership culture programme.

To be honest, when I'd first heard their plans for the pandemic at that meeting in the Seychelles, I'd imagined much worse. Shit, how could I even think that. Thirty million people died. The drugs were frying my brain, I knew, but at that stage they were the only thing keeping me sane. I know that sounds insane. Maybe it was. Hatred was too tame a word for how I felt about myself. I'd thought about ending it, but to be frank, I was far too scared to even try, and I was having way too much fun. Not this stuff at work, but away from that. Life was great, sort of. I was making more money than I'd ever imagined. I had a great new car and a bigger place. Somehow, I even had time for a couple of boyfriends, regular hookups would be a better term for them, nice guys who wanted to treat me well when what I thought I really needed was a good thrashing. I was so fucked up.

And then towards the end of the month we flew down to Grenada. Valliant was setting up a new place there with the profits from the pandemic, at the recommendation of Trig apparently. Leopold was going to unveil his big idea, and the Boss had been canvassing for it in the background for the last few months. Valliant was already on board and had offered to host.

I didn't want to go. I knew what was coming. It was all too much. The morning that we were supposed to leave I called the Boss and told him I was too sick to travel. It was the truth. I was so hungover and strung out I could barely move, let alone pack for a trip. Looking in the mirror that morning I scared the shit out of myself. Literally. I spent the next half-hour in the toilet purging myself. I was twenty-three and I felt like a fifty-three-year-old, or what I imagined a fifty-three-year-old menopausal woman must feel like. I was so fucked up and so thin from the drugs and starving myself that my periods were becoming erratic and sometimes didn't come at all.

But the Boss wouldn't have it. No one knew how to blow him like I could. He even said it on the phone. 'You're getting on that plane. No one can blow me like you can.' My minutes weren't bad either, and after all we'd done together, he trusted me, called me his good-luck chick. Twenty minutes later Max the driver was at my apartment helping me dress and pack. He made me a protein shake in the blender and handed me some ibuprofen and a couple of Valium and some other stuff that he said would help, and basically carried me to the car. By the time we pulled up at the airstrip, Bryce had the engines going and Max helped me up the stairs and into my seat and did up my seatbelt. Five minutes after take-off I stumbled to the toilet and puked my guts out.

I'll never forget that meeting. Valliant's new place in Grenada was still taking shape, half built. Not what we were used to. Trig started off with an update on the same stuff he had been telling us since 2024. There was only so much of that you could hear before you just went numb to it. Drugs helped. But then it was Leopold's turn. I was told to take minutes, so I was able to record it verbatim.

'Gentlemen,' he began. 'The time has come for us to decide, once and for all, the future of the planet and the human race. We are now at a unique point in history, and the opportunity that presents itself will likely never come again.'

He looked around the room, rolled his shoulders. He had everyone's attention. 'The pandemic and the response to the crisis have been a huge success. Not only do we here now control the majority of the wealth on the planet, we also control, directly or indirectly, all of the most powerful governments in the world, and a huge part of its media. The governments we control have used their popularity and the fear generated by the pandemic to pass sweeping new laws that have limited the ability of the public to protest, appeal, and otherwise stand in the way of our activities. For the moment, those that have always resisted us – even while they have been largely unaware of our existence as a collective – so call it instead those who have resisted our policies, have been neutralised. Well done, everyone.'

Maddisson glowed as if he had assumed that this was praise largely directed at him. Li sat implacable as usual. Yu Wan was grinning like a viper, his tongue darting red and thin between his teeth. The Boss knew what was coming and had that smug look on his face that everyone hated. The rest of them looked like a bunch of old men waiting for the stripper to pop out of the cake.

And she did. In the form of a plan to move the world decisively, once and for all, towards a purely anthropocentric state of being, where resources were to be exploited for the wealth of humanity. Prosperity would be the watchword, income generation, security, whipped cream dripping from her big fat tits and her wide, oh so fecund hips. The environmental movement would be outlawed and discredited utterly. Huge incentives would be put in place to accelerate development. They would ride the wave of gold for as long as they could before the system tanked, which they now knew it would.

Leopold asked Trig to come up again. A map of the world was projected on the screen. Overlaid on the map were coloured pixels. Red for bad, and blue for good.

'We have modelled the best places that will remain on Earth as the temperature rises,' said Trig. He ran through the slides for two degrees, already reached, then three, then four. Most of the globe started going deep red. A few places stayed white, some remained blue. He kept going. Five degrees, then six. Small pinpoints of blue in the central Pacific, the southern Caribbean and Central America, southern Africa, the southern tip of Madagascar, big parts of Chile, New Zealand, and the south coast of Australia, including Tasmania. The Northern Hemisphere was pretty much as red as my favourite lipstick.

'Here they are. The refuges. Places where conditions will be largely favourable for growing food, harvesting resources, and life in general.'

He sat and Leopold continued. 'Buy up these places. Move out whoever currently lives there. Get ready.'

The Repudiation had commenced.

Athena

Sometime later I wake in the dark, covered in sweat, that vision come to me again. Mum and me and the little copper-skinned girl, splashing in the pale blue of the lagoon. New details emerge, the little girl's dark eyes and teak-coloured ringlets, the red welted stripes across my mother's back. And that flight along a dark street, my mother's voice a tense whisper, big gates looming up before us in the darkness.

And then another, more powerful goddess, born fully grown and suited in the finest armour, aegis shield in hand, adorned with the image of Medusa. A protectress in times of peril. Goddess of wisdom and warfare and the feminine arts. Goddess of justice. But we are long past the time of gods, or God even. Replaced with what? Knowledge. Science. Logic? How well that experiment has worked for us.

Sparkplug's voice echoes in my head. It does not seem possible. The manufactured pandemic, the plans for a huge sanctuary in Madagascar where Leopold and his progeny could live out their lives. How much of Patricia Leopold's autobiography was true? A rebel acting against her father's wishes, or a cynical opportunist who saw the chance to create her own version of her father's vision, with herself at the top?

Three days to wait, the bitter acid of worry eating away every sane part of me. Mistress of disguise, transform me as you did Odysseus. That I might walk into the village as Zana himself and reclaim what is mine. Lift the veil of confusion from my beloved's eyes, that she might see the truth.

Goddess, guide me.

●

The weather has finally turned. Over the last two days the winds have calmed and then slowly, surely, veered. When I reach the point two days later *Providence* is still there at anchor. I half expected her to be gone. It doesn't take me long to find the cave. Its entrance is sheltered by low green scrub and a screen of boulders. There is a fire pit near the edge of the overhang and a small supply of dry wood. A few overturned crates and other salvage from the freighter make it passably comfortable.

I look across the bay towards the village. Julie and the kids are up there somewhere – thinking what? Will Amsterdam show tomorrow as promised? And if he does, what news will he bring? I read Homer, plan, pace the confines of the cave. At times the urge to swim out to *Providence*, pull out my AK and storm in there and carry them away is almost too much to bear.

Night comes, another tortured one, then grey, worried dawn.

I scan the freighter with my binoculars. Superficially, she looks in bad shape, but there are telltale signs of careful maintenance recently performed that I haven't noticed before. Smudges of grease in hoist bushings. Anchor rode unfouled and clean. Traces of soot at the edges of the stack. Amsterdam lied that first day when I met him. This vessel is operational, ready to go at a moment's notice.

The sun rises, also, makes slow transit across a clear-blue sky, that same sky I saw for the first time with Zana's rifle pointed at my chest, a different colour somehow, a different intensity. I break out the last of my rations, sip at the water left in my bottle.

The sound of rustling vegetation sends me spinning around. I freeze.

'Kwek, you there?'

I peer out of the cave.

It is Amsterdam. He is alone. 'Settled in nicely, I see.'

'Right.'

'You look like hell.'

'Are they here?'

'Hold up, Kwek. We're not there yet.'

'Julie?'

'Not good. When First Governess told her you'd been killed, she went berserk.'

'And now? Will she leave?'

'Yes. She's ready. Hasn't told your kid yet. You can talk to her about it. I don't have long. Sabre is watching me.'

'When?'

'Tonight. Just after sunset. I'll get them out. Bring them here. You need to get your dinghy, bring it over. Be ready. I've already loaded *Providence* with as much fresh food as she'll carry.'

'And Zana?'

'Don't worry about him.'

'What will happen when First Governess realises they're gone?'

'That's my problem.'

'You lied to me about the freighter.'

Amsterdam paws at the ground with one foot. 'She's very shrewd, our leader. You don't think she'd just wait here with no exit plan, do you? It's our lifeboat. The whole community. We can up and go and find somewhere else if we have to.'

'That's good. I'm glad.'

'Sure,' says Amsterdam with a flick of his upper lip.

'You look surprised,' I say.

'Well, after everything. I'm sorry about what happened back there, Kwek. Really.'

I've been through it so many times in my head, it doesn't matter anymore. 'The world needs more places like this. Just not for us. Not right now. Just get rid of the death penalty. Other than that, good.'

Amsterdam flicks me a quick smile. 'Come with me. Something we have to do.'

I follow him out of the cave and down to the water. We swim over to the freighter. A rope ladder hangs down the port side and we climb up to the deck in the bright sunshine. Amsterdam leads me to the bridge and then to the radio room. He sits at the console, flicks a switch and the radio lights up.

'Someone wants to talk to you.'

I stand open-mouthed as he dials in 4.75 megahertz. The line hisses a while, warbles. Amsterdam speaks into the microphone. We wait. And then that voice comes, so familiar now, like an old friend.

'*The Forcing*, from Australia?'

'Yes. Here. Good to hear your voice, Sparkplug.'

'You've gone quiet. I was worried.'

'We were attacked. Our transmitter was destroyed.'

A gap, the band hissing.

'I know what you are looking for.'

I look at Amsterdam. He shrugs. 'I've been listening to her for months,' he says. 'Told her awhile back about your niece.'

'Go to Grenada, in the Caribbean, if you can,' says Sparkplug. 'There is an Alpha Omega slave market there for children. It's your best bet. Find Elvira.'

'Elvira who?'

'That's all I can give you. Time to move again. Good luck, Australia.'

'Wait, what is *alpha omega*?'

But there is no answer. She is gone.

We swim back to the cave and Amsterdam turns to leave. 'Tonight,' he says. And then he is gone and I am alone.

The minutes and hours drag by, seconds of angle, the sun moving slowly towards the horizon. The dinghy is tied up nearby and ready to go. The western sky blushes in latent anger, that overhead darkening. The first stars appear, the world in its ceaseless spinning, night coming. Anytime now.

An hour passes, another. I think about Becky, finally a glimmer of hope, a trail that might lead us to her. I think of Mum, and Papa's son, Lachie Ashworth. He would want to read his father's story. If I can get him a copy of the manuscript maybe he can fill in some of the blanks for me. If he can't then no one can. Maybe he could even help me get it published.

Midnight comes and lapses into history. I stand at the mouth of the cave, looking out along the arc of the bay. But there is nothing. Just the splash of the spiked moon across the dark water, the village walls a faint swath of silver moonlight above the clifftop, the dark mountains rising jagged in the distance. Everything, the whole world, but nothing. Something has happened. They aren't coming.

'Kwek.' A whisper in the half-darkness. I must have fallen asleep.

'Kwek.' Again.

I jump to my feet, suddenly alert, run to the front of the cave. The first grey light is showing through the trees. Up on the clifftop where the village is, a faint orange glow of fire reflects from the trees, smoke rising thick into the air. And there they are. Amsterdam, swollen lip, blood dribbling from his nose and a long gash across his right arm, clutching his rifle. Julie, hair in tangles, tears in her eyes, Leo sleepy-eyed, staring up at me. Fema is there too, bags slung across her shoulders.

I pull Julie into my arms.

'You have to go,' Amsterdam says. 'Now. They're coming.'

I start towards the dinghy, help Julie and Leo in. Then Fema. They are silent, compliant.

I shake Amsterdam's hand. 'Thank you.'

He hands me my pistol, the one he'd picked up from the ground back at the bridge. 'Don't thank me,' he says. 'I did it for her. Now go.'

I breathe out. 'What will you do?'

'Haven't thought that far. I don't care. Just go.'

I wade into the dark water, get into the dinghy, grab the oars. Amsterdam stands on the rocks, watching us go.

We reach *Providence*, get everyone aboard. Fema takes Leo below. I raise the anchor, set the jib, get some boat speed up and throw in a jibe, head towards the gap in the reef. When I look back, Amsterdam is still standing where we left him. Julie stands with one arm wrapped around the mizzen mast, staring back in Amsterdam's direction. In the light from the fire in the village, now burning bright, the flames high, we see a group of men emerge from the trees beneath the village cliffs and start running towards the cave. Amsterdam waves. Julie waves back. He is still waving when we round the point and set sail for the Cape.

Mortals

Cape Town

Twenty-three days after leaving the village, we sight the Cape of Good Hope.

I don't know what happened here, besides the obvious. What led to this, who decided to do this thing and why, will surely be pondered over by historians in some happier future. Me, I have no narrative account, no testimony of witness, no first-hand reports. I have no time for detailed exploration, for scholarship. No books about this exist that I can read, or likely ever will. And yet what happened here requires some mark of passing, some acknowledgement of those who were ended by it.

It is a beautiful place, despite everything. That cloud-draped tabletop visible from sixty nautical miles, growing as we get closer, steepening, catching the light as the sun turns low on the horizon. Julie stands next to me in the cockpit, takes my hand. The Cape of Good Hope, the strange resonance of that name, the joy I feel at her touch, all that is unspoken in that simple gesture.

It is the stillness we notice first. The silence. The lack of birdsong, the absence of cavorting gulls, of the high sweep of broad-spanned albatross. A sense that we are alone here, completely alone.

Nothing remains of the city. It is as if it has been razed from the surface of the Earth, scoured of buildings, the flanks of the hills wiped clean. Dozens of ships of all sizes lie scuttled across the great harbour, bows thrust skyward. Not a fire, a concussion. The push of a finger on a button.

As we come closer, details emerge. The strange orderliness of what remains, concrete walls and pillars and entire buildings flattened out, smeared across the land in pebble beach imbrication. The way the vessels pattern the hills like driftwood thrown up on a beach, the giant vitrified mirror of its epicentre glowing in the late-afternoon sun.

I heard Mum and Papa talk about nuclear weapons. Papa even taught Lewis and me the principles of atomic fission and fusion. The sheer stupidity of it wells up inside my chest as if to drown me. It seems beyond possibility that this, spread out before us in all its dazzling, ordered desolation, was a *decision*. Presumably a rational, well-considered deliberation, perhaps by a committee, advised by experts, with consequences weighed, results predicted, reactions anticipated. The result of a similar decision made elsewhere? A retaliation or a warning? Who knows. Men behaving as gods.

August 2027

That summer was the worst yet. The temperature hadn't dropped below ninety-nine (that's thirty-seven Celsius for the rest of the world) for five weeks, even at night. During the day it was killer, literally. In New York alone thousands died from heat stroke and dehydration. Not a good time to be old, infirm, or very young. People flocked to shopping malls and train stations, anywhere that had AC, and rich people ran theirs constantly so that there were rolling brown-outs across the whole northeast.

The Boss and the wife had escaped to the ranch in Wyoming, which was a lot cooler due to the altitude, but the rest of us office staff had to keep the organisational wheels turning at headquarters. And that was what was so amazing about it all. We all showed up each morning, hot and irritable, yes, but we showed up anyway and did our jobs. We answered phones, made transactions and compiled reports, grateful for the office AC, breaking for iced coffees and Slurpees every once in a while, and then going back to it until it was time to go home. And so did everyone else. The restaurants and bars were full after work, the trains and buses crowded as usual. It was as if people didn't know what was happening, didn't know that they were all fucked. As if they didn't know that the decisions had already been made. And here they all were – here we all were – pretending that everything could just go on as it always had, sleepwalking towards the edge of the cliff.

Despite Maddisson and Yu Wan's best efforts over the last few years, it was still pretty easy to get a picture of what was going on. I mean, what was *really* going on. Most of what Trig had been briefing us about was available with a short Google search. Sure, the first answers that would come up now were the bogus narratives that our flunky 'scientists' – my fingers again – were putting out there, but scroll a little further down and it was all there. Hannah Arendt, my favourite philosopher, was right. Power is communication, not coercion, and can only be exercised by people acting in concert. In an age when we were all taught to be individuals and to value individuality above all else, we'd lost the ability or desire to act collectively. And the guys had basically set it up so that we were all eating an exclusive, self-imposed, low-carb diet of lies. Their lies. And now it was too late.

Matriarchy

The ghost of Cape Town is a thousand nautical miles behind us, but here still aboard somehow, lurking in the troubled faces of my wife and son, the disbelief I feel within myself. It's one thing to read about something like that, another to see the aftermath.

Whatever is waiting for us in West Africa, that is where we are going. The home of my ancestors, the family I have never known, if any remain. Mum met some of them, a long time ago, all that were left. Two brothers, both older: Abeiku, who died in the war shortly after, and Tano. And a sister, Xoese, the youngest. And after, if we are able, we will cross the Atlantic, sail to Grenada, and try to find Becky.

The cold waters of the Benguela current well up beneath us, carrying us along. And everywhere, there is life. Fur seals frolic in the water around us. We see little African penguins twisting and flashing beneath us, black-and-white darts scooping up fish. Dolphins, too, are regular companions, riding our bow wave, delighting Leo, who sits at the bow as I once did long ago on this same boat, talking to these intelligent, graceful creatures.

And yet, despite this abundance, we have seen no fishing trawlers, none of the massive factory freezer ships Papa told us about. We are alone. I keep thinking about what First Governess said: ninety percent of the human population of her island gone in the last forty years. Papa's book mentions several cities extinguished in this same abrupt, irrevocable way, but not Cape Town. How many more cities have met this fate? Can it really be that the rest of Africa has been similarly depopulated – the world too? Those bones stacked by the roadside in haunting, ordered pattern, the ditch cobbled with skulls.

Later, we pass through a gyre of garbage, plastic floating around us for as far as we can see, a heartbreaking array of containers, dismembered plastic chairs, disintegrating bags flapping just below the surface like giant medusa in strange suspension, countless moulded shapes of unknown purpose and origin, a universe of extruded single-use disposability. We watch it go by in numb awe, hour after hour. So much of it, this waste somehow testament to the millions who it had outlasted, a metaphor perhaps, of that other time.

Julie sits in the cockpit with me, the African coast dark to starboard, the South Atlantic slipping away beneath us, cold and quiet. I know she is trying to make sense of everything that has happened. So am I. Madagascar seems so long ago now, almost as if it never happened, so strange it all was. And yet, the echoes of that time surround us every day. Leo's afternoon drawings regularly feature the village, its small canals and gardens, the flowers, pictures of women in long, flowing robes, men armed and walking through the jungle. First Governess's insistence that each meal should begin with a statement of thanks is being maintained on board *Providence*, as are other customs.

Julie laces her hand in mine. 'He was an orphan, you know. Like me.'

'Amsterdam.'

'Yes. He ran away from the orphanage at fourteen and joined one of the few merchant ships still running, as a cabin boy. He was only eighteen when First Governess bought the ship. He signed on. They loaded gold bullion in Lisbon, paid their way through the Suez Canal, picked up weapons and extra fuel in Aden, and sailed for Madagascar. He chose that life.'

It is dark now. Starlight glows in her eyes.

'You love him,' I say.

'Yes.' There is no hesitation in her voice, no equivocation. Just yes.

I say nothing, listen to the hiss of the water over *Providence's* hull.

She squeezes my hand. 'But I never stopped loving you.'

'I know.'

'That's what I've learned, Kwe. We can love more than one person. Our capacity for love is huge. Infinite. All we have to do is open ourselves to it. And that's what's going to save us, Kwe. All of us. Becky too.'

'Our capacity for hate isn't far behind. Just look around you. She was going to have me killed.'

Tears well up in her eyes, splinter Rigel's ancient light.

'When he told me, I didn't believe it.'

'I never thanked him,' I say. 'If it wasn't for him, I'd be dead. He saved my life, in more ways than one.'

We sit for a long time, staring out at the stars hurling themselves against the dark waves for as far as we can see, the warm breeze streaming her hair about her face, the tears shining on her cheeks.

'What happened that night, Julie?'

She takes a long, deep breath. 'Ever since you told me about that patrol, I had known it might happen, that it was a possibility. I learned to live with it. But when they told me you'd been killed, it was as if I'd died too. I wanted to die. I thought of drowning myself. Rowing to *Providence* and shackling the spare anchor to my leg and jumping over the side. But then I thought of Leo, and I knew I couldn't. I had to be there for him. He was going to need me more than ever.'

Tears flow from her eyes, drip to her chest. She sniffs and tries to wipe them away. 'A day passed, and then another. I cried until it hurt, until there was nothing left. And then on that third night, very late, Amsterdam came to see me. He told me what had happened by the river, all of it, that you were alive and were waiting for us. I didn't believe him. It seemed crazy that First Governess would order such a thing done. I knew that you'd been angry, that you'd threatened to leave, but I always thought we would work it out, all of us, find some compromise.'

It has been so long since she's opened up to me like this that I let her talk.

'And when he told me that First Governess had selected someone else as my second husband, I knew he was telling the truth. I always thought it would be him, when the time came. Part of me thought we would stay there forever, Kwe. Really. That we would all be so happy. I'm sorry, but I did. It seemed so, so ... I don't know ... perfect.'

She hides her face in her hands. Sobs come in deep waves now, overpowering her. 'That she would do such a thing ... the thought of you lying out there with a bullet inside you...' She convulses again, overwhelmed.

It is a long time before she can continue.

'He told me to be ready the next day, at sunset. He would come for us at dusk and lead us to you. Part of me didn't believe him, but if there was even a chance you were still alive, I had to take it. That afternoon, we were all ready. I told Leo we were going for a short trip, but decided to trust Fema. I told her that it was her choice, that she could stay or go. She didn't hesitate for a moment.

'We waited. Dusk came and went, and Amsterdam didn't come. Leo was getting sleepy. I was pacing the house like a madwoman, trying to decide what to do. It got late. Leo couldn't stay awake any longer so I put him to bed, fully clothed, ready if Amsterdam should come. And then well after midnight, there was a knock at the door. My heart jumped. I ran to the door, flung it open. But it wasn't him. Two women from the council stood in the darkness, disapproval creasing their faces. They told me to come with them. Fema stayed with Leo.

'First Governess was in her chair on the dais, Zana standing next to her. She had a gun in her hand, your gun, the pistol Papa gave you when he died. First Governess told me that she knew all about what had happened, that Amsterdam was going to come for me tonight. But it wasn't what I thought, she said. He wasn't taking me to you, he was going to take me for himself. Angry at not being made my second husband, he had decided to leave in *Providence*, abandoning the village and all it stood for. But his plans had been uncovered in time, and he'd fled into the forest. You were dead, just as I had been told, killed by raiders from the north. Your gun was here as proof.'

She pauses, as if just bringing back the memory is pushing her to the edge of some cliff.

'It was all too much to take in,' she says, her voice breaking. 'Like a dream you can't wake from. I think I must have been in shock. First you were dead, and then you weren't, and now you were dead again. I didn't know what to believe. I trusted them both. I knew Amsterdam was in love with me. And I loved him. And yet, I knew he was furious about First Governess's decision. And the thought of your execution, it was as unthinkable as when I'd first heard it. I sat there, paralysed, defeated.'

A new wave of anguish shudders through her and she doubles over, hands covering her face. I put my hand on her shoulder, feel the sobs racking her body. She takes my hand, composes herself.

'And then Amsterdam burst in, covered in blood, armed, carrying a torch. He pointed his rifle at First Governess, told her to drop your gun and kick it over to him. He grabbed my hand, and before I could say a word, he pulled me out into the street. We ran back to the house, got Leo and Fema. As we passed the main workshop, he threw the torch onto the roof. Flames burst from the thatch, and within seconds the courtyard was choked in orange smoke. He screamed, "Fire!" In the confusion we slipped out of the main gate and ran all the way to where you were hiding. Until the moment I saw you there in the cave, I was convinced you were dead.'

She sits up and pushes herself into me, threads her arms around my neck, pulls me close. 'I wonder what happened to him, Kwe.'

'I don't know, Julie.'

'They've killed him, haven't they?'

'We'll never know.'

'It was my fault. I should never have—'

'Don't, Julie. You can't think like that. By then he knew about Patricia Leopold, about the sanctuary, the mass murder. He was listening to the same transmissions I was. He made his own decisions.'

She buries her face in my chest, sobs. 'How naive I've been, Kwe. How stupid. Will you ever forgive me?'

I hold her for a long time. 'There is nothing to forgive,' I say.

We are all flawed, doing the best we can in a world gone crazy.

September 2027

The heatwave was still going on when the Boss summoned me and some of the team to Wyoming. Bryce came to pick us up in the Gulfstream. As usual, he came back into the cabin after take-off to welcome the passengers. The last time we'd spoken was just after the wife's warning. I'd called him on his mobile and relayed our conversation. We'd agreed to break it off once and for all, and since then we'd kept to it. That day in the cabin he seemed different, distracted, not his usual engaging, confident pilot self. I tried to catch his eye but he studiously avoided me.

Paolo and I and a couple of the others did lines in the back, and I was glad of the distraction. It was nice to take a flight and actually sit in a chair, rather than spending a big part of it on my knees. By the time we arrived at the ranch – it had its own airstrip – it was night and I was pretty much out of it. Paolo helped me to the limo and they dropped us each at our own private cabin in the woods. I loved these places, had stayed in them before. There were twelve in total, scattered around the ranch, each with its own pool and sauna and huge stone fireplace. They sat empty most of the year. I dumped my bag in the entrance and the butler came and carried it to my room, where the maid would be waiting to put my clothes away and iron whatever needed to be ironed. Then he came back down and fixed me a G&T and took my order for dinner, and I sat on the deck looking out across the dark mountains and let the cool alpine air flow over me. It was times like these that working for the Boss was worth all the hassle, all the worry, all the *knowledge*.

That night I lay in bed and thought about Bryce, in a cabin just like this one maybe a mile away through the woods. I thought maybe he'd come to me, walk over here, throw a stone at my window and I'd rush down the stairs and out into the cool night air and we'd walk hand in hand down to the lake. But he didn't come.

The next morning, we were all at the main ranch house for buffet breakfast and an early meeting. I sat next to Paolo, who'd piled his plate with pancakes and bacon and scrambled eggs. I was trying to watch my weight, which had ballooned a bit recently, and sat there staring at a plate that was mostly white porcelain, adorned with a couple of strawberries and a slice of melon. Not fair.

The Boss stood at the head of the table. A man I'd never seen before stood at his side, dressed in a dark suit and tie. 'This is Murray Nailor. Retired General Nailor, US Army, my new chief of security. He is here to brief us all on an emerging issue.'

The Boss sat and the retired general stood and looked at us. The Boss hadn't mentioned anything to me about a new chief of security. He didn't look like a general. He was short, overweight and balding. He looked more like an accountant to me. Sorry, Paolo.

'Yesterday in Madagascar, Auguste Leopold, the country's leading businessman, was assassinated near his home. His eldest daughter was with him at the time and she was also killed.' The general paused for effect. If he was after sympathy, he didn't get any. Thank God, was all I could think.

'And today, the Direct Green Action Brigades – they call themselves De-GRAB – claimed responsibility. This is a terrorist organisation that we have been tracking for a while now. They are led by a group of radical deep-green and Marxist intellectuals dedicated to stopping economic progress, and according to their own propaganda, "ridding the world of the deathly scourge of runaway neoliberal capitalism and the governments who support it".' He changed intonation to make the inverted commas, made it sound as if a five-year-old was speaking.

'That's us,' said the Boss. As if we didn't know.

'This represents a new and material threat to our organisation and what we are trying to achieve,' said the retired general. 'De-GRAB has grown quickly around the world, and has recruited a lot of very dangerous ex-special-forces types and other disgruntled extremists. They have warned that more assassinations and attacks on assets are to come. Leopold's security was top notch. As good as ours. But these people are fanatics. The man who detonated the bomb that killed Leopold was sitting inside the car with him. It was the driver.'

The retired general paused for effect. He didn't need to. We were all listening. 'And so, from here on in, we are going to up our game. Over the coming few weeks, you will all be issued with detailed instructions and will be provided with enhanced security training. We are going to put an impregnable wall around the Boss and all his operations.'

We all breathed in.

'All employment contracts will be torn up and new ones issued tomorrow. The new terms will include mandatory annual lie-detector tests, restrictions on membership of certain organisations, new requirements for disclosure of personal financial dealings, and pre-screening of all personal relationships.'

The room was silent. One of the secretaries, Marcie, dropped a knife on the floor. I could see Bryce sitting at the far end of the table looking as if he'd just swallowed a handful of gravel.

Then the retired general reached into his suit jacket and pulled out a pistol. 'Who knows how to use one of these?'

Paolo choked on his eggs. A few people put up their hands, the Boss, Bryce.

'Over the next few days, we are going to teach you how. The best defence is a good offence.'

That was the line Bragg used when he'd introduced the new Federal gun laws a couple of months earlier, not long after Congress and the Senate repealed the twenty-second amendment and he announced he would run for a third term. The new gun law required all teachers, public officials, and federal employees to carry firearms and wear body armour. 'Make America Safe Again' was the campaign slogan. The gun lobby was delighted. Civil-rights groups, as far as they still existed, not so much.

We stayed at the ranch for four more days, learning how to shoot a gun and signing our new agreements. Everyone signed. I couldn't hit a thing. And Bryce never came to see me.

Takoradi

We reach Takoradi on the coast of West Africa on January 3rd, 2067. After a night of pounding rain, which more than fills our tanks, morning breaks with sun streaming across the harbour from between frothing pillars of white cumulus. We can hear the rumbling of thunder in the distance, reverberating across the dark country. I check the anchor and scan the harbour. A few canoes pulled up among the fingered roots of remnant mangroves, or tied to the submerged trunks of long-drowned trees. Half a dozen people squatting on overturned crates tending what look like fishing nets on a newly deposited beach of alluvium near the mouth of a muddy creek. Mud-brick houses scattered ramshackle around the bowl of the bay, the occasional slow flap of laundry drying in the sun, threads of smoke drifting aimlessly skyward.

We lock up *Providence*, check our gear, load everyone into the dinghy and start rowing for shore. If the people on the beach are aware of our presence, they show no sign until we pull up not far from where they sit. They turn our way and stare. I wave to them but get no response. We all get out and start walking towards them. There are five men, older. As we approach, they regard us through narrowed bloodshot eyes.

'*Agoo*,' I say. Hello in Twi, one of the few words of my father's language that Mum taught me.

The men glance at me, but fix on Julie and Leo.

'We speak English,' one of them says. As he speaks the flesh around his mouth flaps open in strange delay and I can see that a gap has been cut from his upper lip to his nose, and from his lower lip to his chin, revealing the broken stumps of black teeth, as if he's been abandoned mid-procedure during some botched surgery.

'We are looking for someone,' I say. 'A relative. My father is from here, from Takoradi.'

This gets their interest. The man with the carved mouth stands. 'What's your name?' he flaps.

'Abachwa. My father's name was Kwesi Abachwa, he left here during the war.'

The man turns to his companions. They exchange a few desultory words. 'No one here called that anymore. Not since the war.'

'He had a brother,' I say. 'Tano. Tano Abachwa.'

The man shakes his head. One of the other men seated at the back says: 'Tano. I remember him. Died in the war. He had a sister, I think.'

'Yes,' says another. 'Xoese was her name.'

The incisions in the man's face part like curtains on a stage as a hideous four-pointed smile forms beneath his eyes. He lisps something to his colleagues in Twi. They smile too. 'Yes, I remember her,' he says.

'Is she still here?'

'Don't know,' says the other man. 'Maybe. Lots aren't.'

'Up there,' the first man says, as if struck by a sudden moment of clarity. He points up the hill. 'Main square. Ask for Kofi. He's chief here. He might know about your aunty.'

'Please, is there anywhere we can get fresh food?' says Julie.

The men are very serious now, looking at Julie and Leo, frowns creasing their dark, leathered faces. They seem confused, disoriented.

'We can trade,' she says.

They continue to stare at her, at Leo, mouths open, eyes drifting in darkly recessed sockets.

'Please,' she says.

'There is food up there also,' says one of the others. 'At the market.'

Steam rises from the puddled street and the rusted sheet-metal roofs. The few people we see on the road stare but keep their distance. Some stop mid-stride to gaze at us with that same confused look. By the time we reach the square and look back across the town and down to the muddy bay, we are all drenched in sweat.

It is there that we see the first armoured vehicles, rusted-out hulks scattered across the town, lying with unspooled tracks by the roadside, turretless and holed like the carapaces of huge, long-dead sea turtles. A large building dominates the square, its façade pock-marked with peeling concrete and studded with exposed rebar. I ask an old woman sitting under a palm-frond shelter if she knows where we can find the chief. She looks at me through purposeless eyes and points to the main building, where a queue has formed. It stretches from inside the main doors and down a corridor. All the people are old. Many are afflicted with weeping, flesh-coloured lesions around the neck and arms and feet, seething pink eruptions that ooze pus. They stare openly at Julie and Leo, as if confronted with something beyond their comprehension. Sweat films their faces and runs across their ravaged necks and arms. The humidity is stifling, and inside the crowded corridor there is no air. The smell is unbearable. We shuffle along with everyone else, past doorless offices littered with broken furniture and the empty maws of toppled filing cabinets.

'Mum,' says Leo, tugging on Julie's sleeve. 'Where are all the children?'

'In school, I should think, baby.'

'I'm hot, Mum,' says Leo. He looks pale and his skin is moist. He slumps to the floor at Julie's feet.

Julie picks him up. 'I'm taking Leo outside,' she says, alarm in her voice. 'I'm going to find some shade, and give him something to drink. Poor darling, he's exhausted. You wait in the queue. I'll ask Fema to go and look for food.'

'Hopefully it won't be too long,' I say, feeling Leo's forehead. 'He's burning up.'

Julie frowns. 'See you soon.'

The queue creeps along. Finally, after almost an hour's wait, I am ushered into a corner office. The chief is a very large man, with a wispy grey beard and thick forearms. Unlike the people we saw on the street and in the corridor outside, he seems in good health. He sits considering my question, running thick fingers through the fine hairs that sprout from his chin.

'Yes,' he says. 'Xoese Boateng. Second wife of Nkrumah Boateng. She is here.'

'Please, where can I find her?'

The chief taps his desk with a thick forefinger. 'This is very valuable information, is it not, Kweku Abachwa? Locating lost relatives.'

'It is. And I thank you for it.'

He leans back in his chair. 'Some exchange is customary in such circumstances.'

'Of course.' I place a small coin on his desk.

'What is this?'

'One-eighth of an ounce of pure Canadian gold.'

The chief reaches for the coin, hefts it in his palm. 'She lives on the outskirts, about a kilometre from here. Past the market, near the top of the small hill shaped like a woman's breast.' He points back across his shoulder. 'That way.'

Outside, the streets steam. Thunderclouds are massing inland, towering into the sky, dark and heavy. The smell of rain fills the air. I look around for Julie and Leo but can't see them anywhere. I walk to a big mango tree at the edge of the square, thinking they might be sitting in the shade on the far side, but they aren't there. The streets are quiet. An older couple loiters out of the sun under an open stairwell. A woman crosses the square, one hand plucking the side of her dress to lift the hem from the mud, the other balancing a large jug on the top of her head. I sprint to the far side of the square, scan the road that leads down to the harbour. I shout Julie's name. A few people look at me, most do not.

If she decided to go back to the boat, she would have come and told me, or sent Fema to tell me. Maybe they're at the market, bartering for food, and let the time get away. I decide to wait back at the building. Whatever they are doing they will come back here eventually. That is our protocol, always has been. Go back to the last place we were together. She has gold, and I made her take the gun in her bag. She will be okay.

The rain comes, a torrent, churning the streets red, guttering from the roof. I sit on the front step of the administration building, watch people running for cover, the hand of my watch turning slowly on its dial. The rain ends as quickly as it started, leaving the square a half-flooded morass. Darkness is only a couple of hours away. Maybe Julie decided to take Leo back to the boat, where he could sleep. But then why didn't she come and tell me? The threads of argument and counter-argument twist in my mind until only a knot is left, unable to be prised open. I decide to wait until just before dark, follow our protocol, and if she isn't back by then, head back to *Providence*.

Minutes creep by like long, empty days. Every appearance on the square makes my heart jump against my ribs. Only about forty minutes to sunset now. I stand. Someone is running across the square towards me. A woman, alone.

I run out to meet her.

It is Fema. She is soaked, breathless. 'Kweku,' she gasps. 'It's Julie and Leo.' She bursts into tears.

I grab her shoulders. 'Settle down, Fema. What happened? Tell me.'

She takes a few deep breaths, wipes the back of her hand across her eyes. 'We were in the market, buying oranges. Three men came and picked them up and carried them away. I followed them for as long as I could. Down to the harbour. The last I saw the men had taken them into a big stone building down by the water. They're still there, I think. I came back as soon as I could.'

April 2028

When he called me that Sunday morning and asked me to meet him, I was so wrecked that I fell back into a stupor the second he hung up. When I finally woke up again two hours later all that remained was a vague recollection of Bryce's voice urging me to see him, but I couldn't remember where or when. I fumbled with my phone, furious with the thing, and popped a couple of Sinequan, which calmed me down. Then I told my bed-mate for the night to pick up his clothes, which were scattered all over my bedroom floor, and fuck off.

I wasn't a nice person anymore. I had been, once, I thought. But by now, in my own mind anyway, I had become less a person than a receptacle. A place where others could dump their shit. Bad food, drugs, meds, insecurities, secrets, cum. And it was poisoning me. All those things I used to dream about when I was young, before I met the Boss, had somehow faded away to mere outlines, like an old photograph where all the colour has gone to blue and all the faces have blurred away almost to nothing.

I sat on the edge of the bed and tried to tap out a message to Bryce, but my fingers felt like fat sausages, and about as nimble. We were using Signal now. Supposedly it was end-to-end encrypted, although I doubted it was secure. Nothing was anymore from what I'd heard our retired general saying. We both knew it was a risk, but we did it anyway. We had a code, of sorts, based on references to things and places we'd experienced together or joked about, and emojis of course, just not the ones you'd expect. Sex was 'tennis', from a YouTube video we'd both watched. Work was 'down under', from the song we both liked. You get it.

Where and when? I managed to code. *Would love to see you.*

I staggered to the bathroom, put myself under the shower, stood there catatonic, the water streaming over my body. My phone buzzed on the countertop. I reached for a towel, wiped my face, looked at the screen. *I'll call,* was all it said.

I dressed, drank one of my breakfast shakes, swallowed a couple of

OxyContin, sat on the balcony of my apartment and stared at my phone, willing him to call. He didn't. I messaged him again. *Call. Now.* By now I was even more of a wreck than I'd been when he called me that morning. I was looking in my purse for my Valium when my phone rang.

'Hi.' His voice. That voice. I realised that I didn't care anymore. I really just didn't give a fuck. I loved this guy and I didn't care what the Boss and his stupid rules said I could and couldn't do.

'Hi,' I croaked. 'Sorry, I was a bit spaced out when you called me before. I'm not feeling that good.' I've always been good at under-statement.

'Sorry to hear that. How's your aim?'

He knew that I'd just recently completed my pistol refresher. 'Good. At twenty-five metres I got exactly zero bullets on the target.'

'Not bad.'

'I'm quite proud, actually. No one else managed it.'

I could hear him laughing.

Seriously, I *was* proud. The whole gun thing was ridiculous. I left mine at home locked in the bathroom drawer.

'I need to see you,' he said. 'It's important.'

'What about new clause sixteen? Can't we just talk now?'

'I need to *see* you. In person.'

I was bursting inside. 'Where and when?'

He told me.

Three hours later we were on Bryce's little sailboat in Sandy Hook Bay. He had the sails up and the water was flat and blue, and little white cartoon clouds floated above us in an otherwise clear sky. We sat in the cockpit, Bryce at the tiller, me next to him but not touching. It was cool, and I snuggled into my Argent Industries fleece shell. The shore was far away now, just a long line between the sky and the water.

'Are you still keeping your diary?' he said. Until then, we'd only talked about boat stuff: hold on to that, turn this, careful there. It was not what I expected.

'How do you know about my diary?'

'I know, that's all.'

I shook my head. 'That's not fair.'

'Don't worry,' he said. 'If I haven't said anything all this time, I'm not about to now.' He reached an arm out and put it around my shoulder. I moved into him.

'Only occasionally now. Once every few months. I've been too busy.'

'You need to keep going,' he said. 'It's important.'

I looked up at him, into his eyes. 'Why?'

'You know damn well why. Because of what's happening.'

'It's just for me. I'm not sharing it with anyone.'

He leaned away from me. His look was deadly serious now. 'One day, you are going to have to.' And then he kissed me.

I kissed him back. It went on for a long time, longer than that first time in the cockpit. Fat hummingbird girl, who I'd thought had gone extinct, was back. And then he did something with the sails and the rudder and the boat kind of just stopped and sat there calm on the water and he took me below and still kissing me he slipped off my clothes and nothing was ever the same again.

Xoese

We run down the hill, narrow-eyed through the rain, lightning close and deafening overhead. The building hulks dark against the water, two storeys with an upper railed balcony and a walled courtyard on the landward side. The upper windows are shuttered, and the front gate is closed.

Fema points. 'They took them in there.'

'Wait here,' I say. 'I'll be back here in fifteen minutes. If they leave, follow them. Come back here when you can. I'll be waiting.'

I run through the rivered town to where I left the dinghy, rain stinging my eyes, and then row as fast and smoothly as I can towards *Providence*, scenes of murderous nightmare crowding in on me. I've killed before. The stain is there, indelible. And now I know, I will again.

As I approach *Providence* a thunderbolt launches oblique across the rain-pelted harbour, lighting up the undersides of the lowest clouds. A fortress with white ramparts set at the far point of the bay appears and then is gone. And in that brief illumination, I see two dark shapes clambering aboard *Providence*.

I shout out against the storm, a warning. And then the sound of two splashes, the men diving into the water, swimming away, lost in the darkness. A moment later I grab *Providence's* railing and jump aboard. In the darkness I fumble with the lock, but get it open, slide back the main hatch and jump below. Every second matters now. I find the windup torch, light up the cabin, find the key to the gun locker, open it and unwrap Papa's AK47 from its grease cloth. I grab two full magazines, seat one, sling the rifle over my shoulder and clamber back into the cockpit. My heart is beating so hard, for a second I think it might burst.

I jump into the dinghy and row back to shore. Seconds tick away, whole lifetimes, the future rushing towards me with each breath, each stroke of the oars. By the time I reach the shore the rain has relented. A half-moon shines through a gap in the clouds, lights their vapoured edges. The building is there, a light showing in the upstairs window, a beacon. I've just tied up the dinghy when a dark form emerges from the clutch of trees in front of me.

'Kweku Abachwa?' A woman's voice.

I swing the AK around.

'Kweku, is that you?' The same voice, heavily accented. Not Fema.

'Who are you?'

'I am Xoese. You father's sister.'

I let the rifle swing muzzle-down on its sling. 'Xoese?'

The woman steps forward. In the moonlight I can see that she is very dark-skinned, almost as broad-shouldered as me.

'I knew it was you,' she says. 'As soon as I heard.' She takes my hand. 'How much you look like him.'

'Please,' I say. 'My wife and son are in there. They've been taken.'

'Yes, I know. That's why I'm come.' She glances at my rifle. 'You won't need that. Please, Kweku. Trust in me. Leave it here.'

'If you don't mind, I'm keeping it.'

She shrugs, and still holding me by the hand leads me through the trees to where Fema is waiting. We cross the road, walk up to the front gate, and Xoese knocks on the front door. 'I know this man,' she says as we wait. 'The one who took your wife and son. Please, do not worry.'

It's like asking a fish not to swim. My heart is racing. I chamber a round. Just then the door swings open and a middle-aged man, my height and build, stands looking out at us. I level the rifle at his chest. His takes a step back, eyes widening.

Xoese says something in Twi and the man backs away slowly, eyeing my rifle. We cross the courtyard and Xoese leads us through a door and up a flight of stairs. I flick the selector to auto, check the safety. When the time comes, I won't hesitate. Whether this woman really is my aunt or not makes not a shred of difference.

Xoese leads us through another door into a large room. Two lamps burn in their glass sleeves. A large man in traditional dress sits on a divan near the centre of the room, attended by two middle-aged women. And there, facing the man, seated on plush cushions, my pistol in her lap, is Julie. Leo is sitting next to her. She has a cup in her hand, as does the man. She looks up at me. They are having tea.

Leo jumps up and runs to me and wraps himself around my leg. I run my hand through his curls. The skin of his face is hot to the touch.

The man eyes my weapon, frowns.

Julie smiles. 'Oh, there you are, husband,' she says, as composed as I've ever seen her. 'This is Mister Kojo. We met at the market.'

Kojo inclines his head, smiles a gap-toothed smile.

'They told us you would come,' Julie continues. 'Apparently, this gentleman wishes to purchase us. Me and Leo. I have tried to tell him that we are not for sale.'

'Kojo,' says Xoese.

'Xoese. How is your husband?'

'I'm not here to talk about that. This is Kweku, the son of my brother.'

The man runs his hand along his jaw. His hands are huge, each of the fingers and the thumb enringed in gold. 'And he is the husband?'

'He is.'

'My wife is correct,' I say, slipping my hand around the AK's pistol grip. 'They are not for sale.'

'I can offer you a very good price. Gold, beasts, land. Whatever you wish.'

'Not for sale, Kojo.' Xoese steps forward and crouches in front of Leo.

The big man's face creases. He looks away.

'Please,' says Xoese, looking at me. 'He is not a bad man, just a desperate one.'

'This is over,' I say.

Polite misunderstanding or not, I am getting them out of there. I hoist Leo into my arms, take Julie's hand, and start for the door. No one tries to stop us.

We spend the rest of that night and all of the following day in a large compound that Xoese shares with her husband and his two other wives on the inland slope of the hill shaped like a woman's breast. I tell Xoese that I should go back to the boat to check on things, that I am worried about people trying to break in, but she waves this away.

'Everyone knows now that you are Xoese's nephew,' she says. 'One of our own. No one will touch your boat. Quite the contrary, they will watch it for you. Keep it safe.'

The rain continues, broken by short bursts of sunshine. Thunder rumbles across the green and gullied country. We sit under a pergola outside Xoese's quarters and watch the clouds flash and boil on the horizon, listen to the rain drip from the thatch ends and patter onto the dirt. The impacts leave small holes in the hard-swept iron-oxide clay that traces the boundaries of her domain. She lives alone, like the other wives, but receives many guests and visitors. She is well known and her advice is highly sought.

'I remember the last time I saw your father,' says Xoese, pouring tea. 'He just married to your mother, and they come home to see any of us who were left before going to America. He was very frail-looking, weak from wounds, them scars still big and raw across his body. So big, they were, your mother's work, she the one who'd removed all that hateful metal from his body. Your mother was very beautiful, when I seen her, but broken. You could tell it in her eyes. All dull and faraway lookin' except when my brother around. As if in savin' him she'd broken herself.'

She smooths her skirt, adjusts her headdress. Then she picks up Leo and sits him on her lap. He squirms but she holds him tight.

'Even so,' she continues, 'I could see they were in love. Everyone could. The way they could not go more than a few moments without looking one at the other, without touching in some way, holding hands, standing pushed up against the other, hands and eyes and feet and legs, anything, just so they was touchin'. People would laugh about it, tease 'em, but they didn't care. Just their way with each other. And with the war, seein' that, well it made you feel like maybe there was hope.'

Xoese pauses, strokes Leo's hair. 'And now, seein' you here, this beautiful boy so like Kwesi when he was just small, we growin' up together, well it brings me to thinkin' that maybe there is.'

Xoese takes Julie's hand in hers, runs her old woman's fingers lengthwise along the bluish veins that show through the pale skin of Julie's wrist. 'And you so like her, so fair, like milk.'

'Did you ever have children of your own, Xoese?'

'No babies born here or anywhere to anyone since the war.'

'None?'

'None alive or whole or livin' long enough to be named.'

I lean forward. 'Was it Kejabil? My mother said something about a camp at Kejabil, near here, where something terrible happened.'

Xoese shakes her head. 'No, no. That was later.'

'Do you know what happened there, Xoese?'

'It was somethin' people were chosin'. For the virus. The pandemic was going again. So they all trudged out there and lined up. I didn't go. But my friend Effia did.'

'Is she still...' I stumble, aware of my indiscretion. 'Sorry, Aunty. Is she still alive?'

'Yes, I think so.'

'Can we talk to her?'

'I haven't spoken to her for a long time. Long time.'

We sit in silence, watch the rain pelting the hard clay, running rivulets across the compound.

Julie is caressing my aunty's wrists with her thumbs, back and forth to the rhythm of the rain on the roof. 'No children, Xoese? Really?'

'This is why Kojo wanted you. He saw you in the market with the little one. Like everyone, he wants sons and daughters. He wants a future. The men here still believe that it's the women's bodies not workin' proper. But it's both just the same. You wouldn't do him no good. No babies coming from him.'

Julie presses the old woman's hands in her own, palm to palm. 'What happened, Xoese?'

'It was the war. Fighting right here, fierce fighting. I remember the streets filled with dead soldiers. And then the Americans pushed the others out, and engineers and doctors came surveyin' and plantin' and such. A company came and gave out free medicine for the worm. Everyone took it. I took it. I still have some.'

Xoese sets Leo on the ground and then stands and goes inside, leaving us under the pergola. We look into each other's eyes but say nothing. What was there to say?

After a while Julie says: 'Write it, Kwe. Write it all.'

Xoese returns and puts a small glass vial in Julie's hand. 'This, in a needle in your arm.' She points to her shoulder. 'Here. Just one.'

Julie turns the vial in her fingers and passes it to me. 'Look at the label.'

'Jesus in Heaven,' I say.

Argent Pharmaceuticals, it reads. Derek Argent's company. The man in Papa's manuscript, the one who saved my mother's life, Sparkplug's boss.

'And after, no more babies,' Xoese says. 'Just miscarriages and still births. They said it was the water and the bombs, but I know it was those jabs.' She hides her face in her hands.

'Did my mother and father know about this?'

'I don't know. Maybe. They were leavin' and it was just startin'. And then someone bombed Lagos, I don't even know who. The land and water everywhere got poisoned with radiation. And no more children, for anyone. Ever again. Stronger than any *juju*. After us, no one.'

Xoese kisses Julie's hands. 'Except you.'

January 2029

Not surprisingly, Bragg won a third term as president of the United States. When all the numbers were in, he'd won a crushing majority of the Electoral College and the popular vote. There were a few cries about tampering, the usual accusations that Russian actors had worked to swing public opinion, but in the end everyone just accepted it as the inevitability that it had always been.

Shortly after the election the Boss called me into his office and told me that he was flying to Grenada to meet Vaillant. It wasn't in the diary.

'Last-minute decision,' the Boss said.

'Do you need me, Boss?' I said.

'Not this time,' he said.

Ever since Leopold's murder, the Boss had become increasingly paranoid about De-GRAB, and our retired general had pushed security precautions into orbit. Being unpredictable was one of them. I never quite got my head around making us all carry guns, particularly when we then had to hand them over whenever we were about to go in and see the Boss. Still, I know about as much about security as I do about drywalling. Some guy comes and you pay him for it and he does it for you. After my last pistol refresher, I asked to be given dispensation not to carry, and to everyone's relief it was granted. I handed back my gun and ammunition and I was very happy.

Two hours later I got a call from the Boss. He was downstairs in the limo and had changed his mind. I was going. I grabbed my purse and headed for the elevators. The two identical armoured limos were there waiting, engines running. One of the doors opened and I jumped in. These things were designed to survive a nuclear blast – literally. A small one anyway.

The new driver, who looked so much like Max everyone thought we'd gone out and hired his twin, was at the wheel. The Boss was in the car that real Max was driving, and body double Boss was here with me. That meant that body double me, who looked a lot like me I had to admit, but not as good-looking obviously, and a little shorter for that matter, and maybe one cup size smaller – just saying – was with the Boss. It was all very disorienting for everyone, and more than a little creepy. Fifty minutes later we were at the airport, and you guessed it, two new Gulfstream G900 jets were waiting on the tarmac for us. They didn't get Bryce right, thank God, that would have been too much.

Our retired general was there to see us off, and he personally supervised the individual body searches of everyone except the Boss before we boarded. After we were in our seats the two jets taxied side by side. I could see fake me sitting in the window, looking out at real me. Then we slowed down and tucked in behind them and we turned onto the runway and Bryce and the other pilot started accelerating, and soon we were blasting down the runway in formation, just like I'd seen the military pilots do at airshows, and I was so glad that it was Bryce up there flying us. We climbed up into the sky side by side. Fake me looked out of her window and waved at me and I could see she was smiling and just as I went to wave back, she disappeared.

We lurched away from the fireball so hard that even strapped into my seatbelt my head whipped to one side and hit the window. The engines screamed as Bryce put the plane into a near-vertical climb. Bottles and papers and food flew through the cabin, front to back, ricocheting off seats and windows and crashing into the rear galley. The new stewardess, Chloe was her name, was pinned against the rear bulkhead. I could hear her screaming over the engines as Bryce powered us into the upper atmosphere. Paolo had caught something in the head and a gash had opened up on his brow like a big red rose. I looked over at the Boss and he looked at me. We were both pinned back in our seats and the G-force was pulling our faces into strange simian grins. And then, straining his facial muscles against the force of our two screaming Rolls-Royce turbines, he smiled at me. And then I realised, he was enjoying this.

Ten minutes later we levelled out and we were cruising higher above the Earth than I had ever been, and I swear we were right at the edge of the atmosphere and the sky above us was very dark, almost like night, and you could see the planet curving away below us like some distant dream. It was scary and exhilarating at the same time. When Bryce came back to check on us, he looked as calm as he always did.

He helped Chloe up and sat her down and checked her for injuries but she seemed okay, and then he bandaged Paolo's head.

He came over and asked if I was okay.

'Fine,' I said. 'Just a little shaken up.' It wouldn't hit me until later.

The Boss was apoplectic. 'What the fuck just happened?' he shouted, those neck veins of his doing a war dance.

'Not sure, Boss,' said Bryce, his voice even and composed. 'I didn't see anything external. We were wingtip to wingtip. It wasn't a missile. My guess it was internal.'

The Boss raked his hand through his hair. 'Jesus Christ Almighty. Everyone was checked.'

'Could have been planted before we showed up. Maybe one of the maintenance crew.'

'Get Nailor on the radio. Now.'

'Will do, Boss. Where to now?'

The Boss narrowed his eyes and shook his head, his are-you-fucking-kidding-me look. 'We were going to Grenada, last time I checked.'

Bryce nodded and headed back to the cockpit.

The meeting with Valliant went ahead as planned. We drove from the airport to Valliant's mansion above St George's harbour. Unlike the last time we were here, it was almost finished. It was not nearly as grand as Leopold's palace in Madagascar – I couldn't imagine anything ever being more OTT than that was – but still amazing. They talked as we walked around the grounds. I didn't catch everything they said, but I did hear them talking about De-GRAB and the near miss we'd just had. That G900 the Boss lost was worth a small fortune.

And then Valliant came to the point. 'I hear you are setting up a sanctuary in Belize.'

The Boss nodded. 'And another in New Zealand. South Island.'

'Good choice. And what, may I ask, are you going to do about the locals?'

'I've bought up the land, and well, basically, we're evicting them.'

'Not so easy on an island,' said Valliant, looking about. 'At least not on one this size. I need something easy and, let's say, humane.'

'Not my problem,' said the Boss.

'Of course. But I would like to make it your opportunity.'

Then they moved out of earshot and I didn't hear any more about it. We left two days later and flew back to New York and the hurricane of press wanting to know about the plane getting blown up. The attempted assassination of Derek Argent was blamed on green terrorists, and within the hour De-GRAB had obliged and claimed responsibility. President Bragg directed the full resources of the US military against the terrorists, and promised to root them out, wherever they might be hiding.

Kejabil

We walk up the track in the rain. The mud is heavy and red and sticks to our shoes. Julie shelters herself under Xoese's patched and incomplete umbrella. I carry Leo on my shoulders, my poncho over his head so it covers us both. Xoese trudges ahead of us, holding a piece of laminated cardboard over her head, the rain sluicing from its edges. Beside her, an old woman trudges barefoot through the mud. The hem of her dress is heavy with thick, liquid laterite. She is holding a black umbrella above her head and a stout walking cane in the other, which she stabs into the mud with each second step, probing for the hard ground beneath.

Since leaving Xoese's compound we've seen few people and no cars or vehicles. After a while the rain relents and steam rises from the ponded red depressions and hangs in the air heavy about us, and then the rain comes again and we keep going, deeper into the scrubland. We reach a large clearing about the size of a flattened city block. A rusty chain-link fence wanders lazily around the perimeter. We approach what might once have been a front entranceway, a few toppled signs, the foundations of a guardhouse, the fibreglass sandbags spilt and photodegraded.

The old woman stops, stares past the fence into the compound. All I can see inside is grass, a few scrub trees. 'Here,' she says. 'This is the place.' Her eyes are cloudy, cataracts floating there in murky suspension. 'Most of us came that day, those from Kejabil who had received the paper. We were told to come for injections that would protect us from the virus. We didn't know then the effect the first jab, the one we'd had against the worm, was having.' She points back along the road. 'We waited here. I was near the end of the queue. We waited a long time. The line moved very slowly. As people were let inside, they were led to tents where doctors and nurses took their names and prepared them. We watched through the fence. After each person was given the shot, they were led outside and told to lie down on the grass. It was a dry day, cool. Nurses came by with drinks, checking people's blood pressure and examining them. It all looked very normal. There were lots of children, back then. No babies, though.'

She stops, looks about a moment. Xoese takes her arm, whispers something to her in Twi.

'Yes,' the old woman says. 'And then they were full and they closed the gates. There were about ten of us left outside. We walked home. Later, when no one came home, someone said there had been an accident. I waited a day, and then walked back out here, but by the time I arrived the place was empty, all the tents gone, track marks like the ones tanks and bulldozers leave crisscrossing the whole compound and only the fence still up, with signs saying *Danger Do Not Enter*.'

She points to a faded metal placard hanging from one corner of the gate, the skull and crossbones symbol still visible. 'Later someone came and said that the people had been moved to another part of the country as part of a relocation programme, because of the war. No one ever heard from any of them ever again.'

'Mum must have arrived here before the bulldozers were sent in,' I say.

No one speaks. We trudge back to Xoese's place. Thankfully, the rain stays away.

July 2029

By then it was becoming pretty clear to everyone, despite the government's calls for calm, that North America, Europe and Russia were experiencing a massive crop failure. It hadn't rained properly anywhere in the Northern Hemisphere since February, already depleted aquifers were being pumped to the limit and dry riverbeds sucked of mud, but it wasn't enough. Not nearly. Not to worry, though, said Bragg and other world leaders, the world had stockpiled enough grain to keep everyone fed for three months.

Of course, what they didn't say was that could just as easily mean six months for half of the people, or even two years for every tenth person, with some scrimping. Simple math. We were okay, though. By we, I mean all of us who worked for the Boss, his inner circle. We had stockpiles for twenty years. Yes, twenty. Everything. Laid up in special warehouses on his properties and now in the two new sanctuaries that were being built.

But even then, the cities hummed along as normal, and you couldn't even tell that anything had changed or that things were starting to go badly wrong. People just kept sleepwalking along, certain that the government and the big all-knowing 'they' would sort it all out and everyone would be okay. Netflix kept pumping out great series, and you could still order pizzas and go to a drive-thru and get your burger and fries. A little more expensive, sure, but still. A Big Whack is a Big Whack.

By then I was not only doing my old job as the Boss's executive assistant – don't laugh – I was also working directly with the Boss's newly appointed chief of staff, a guy called Singh, a tall, good-looking Sikh from the Punjab who'd emigrated to America in the early twenties after getting his MBA from Columbia. He was sharp, polite, and I liked him. It was me, him and the Boss that day when we met with Bragg and his team in the Oval Office.

'This is bad,' said Bragg, pacing around the office, his tie flapping around his haunches. He'd put on a lot of weight since I'd last seen him, and his face had that puffy look that bodybuilders get when they are doing too many steroids. He looked way older than eighty-three. 'People are getting worried. We need more food.'

'The Southern Hemisphere continues to fare well,' said Lewison, Bragg's security adviser. 'They say that harvests throughout Africa will be at or near record levels.'

'So we can buy it from them. Make a deal.' Bragg looked around the room. 'I'm great at making deals. Get their president on the phone.'

'There are several, Mister President,' said Nancy Mitchell, secretary of state.

'I know that, Nancy, for Christ's sake. Get 'em all on the phone.'

'We've tried,' said Mitchell. 'The Russians, the Chinese, the Europeans are all trying to buy from them. Prices are going through the roof.'

'Well, how much can they sell us?'

'About a month's worth.'

'That's it?' Bragg looked as if he was being told he couldn't have a fourth term.

All his advisers nodded.

Bragg turned to the Boss. 'Can you help?'

The Boss jutted his chin towards Singh.

Singh nodded. 'Over the last six months, we've quadrupled production from all of our synthetic food operations. We can double that again by the end of the year. If we have the contracts in place.'

'Great,' said Bragg. 'Great. Done.'

'That's not nearly enough, Mister President,' said Lewison.

The Boss leant forward so he was sitting on the edge of the couch. 'I've been thinking about this,' he said. 'Seems to me, it's pretty simple. They have food, you need it.'

'That's the situation.'

'So go and take it from them.'

And that was pretty much it. The start of the war. No one called it the Third World War or anything, it wasn't like that at all. It just sort of happened, unfolded slowly over years, and after a while no one could remember who had started it or why or even in some cases who was on which side, or even if there really were sides in the conventional sense. It was all kind of medieval in that way. Big boys jostling for position in ill-fitting armour with swords way too big for their brains.

Grandmother

According to Xoese the barrenness has afflicted every part of Africa, or as much as she has received news of. The population is in freefall. No one from outside dares venture here, lest they too fall victim to the sickness that killed the future in the slowest, most sorrowful way imaginable. And what the infertility sickness didn't accomplish, the weather has. Tribes to the north, beyond the forests, succumbed to a drought that lasted longer than most who were left can remember – thirty years some said. And here, in the greatest of climatic ironies, they perished from flooding, regularly receiving as much rain in a day as they once did in a year.

'You must leave,' says Xoese. 'There is nothing for you here except disease and death and the end of things.'

I don't argue. I have done my best to keep my promise to Mum. And now we have to keep our promise to Becky. I am now absolutely certain that she is out there, somewhere. In such a world, a beautiful child like her surely is the greatest treasure.

Over the next few days Xoese helps us get all the fresh food we need. I offer her gold, which she refuses. Julie sketches a portrait of Leo for her instead. She kisses the paper and puts it on a little table next to her bed. Then we say goodbye.

That last time we see her, there on the flooded shore of that silt-laden harbour, the sky strangely blue, she kisses and hugs Leo and gives him two small dolls fashioned in coloured cloth. One has a white face and arms, two brown beads for eyes and yellow cloth hair, and carries a small water gourd on its head. The other wields a wooden spear, the black sacking of its face adorned with two little white eyes and a red-stitched mouth.

'These are your father's mother and father,' she says. 'Your grandparents. You can talk to them, and they will hear you.'

Xoese holds Julie for a long time, stroking her hair as if it is a rare and precious treasure. Then she takes my hands and looks deep into my eyes. 'It is as if I am looking at my own brother,' she says to me.

'Please, Aunty, come with us.'

She shakes her head. We asked her before, but she has remained adamant. 'This is your journey, not mine.'

I nod, kiss her cheek.

'Good boy,' she says, tears streaming across her cheeks. Then she leans forward so her lips are touching my ear. Her whisper is so faint I can barely make out the words. 'Nothing could be worth this,' she says. 'Nothing. Hear me, Kweku, Born on Wednesday. The price was too great. Nothing can weigh against this payment. Ever. I beg you, my nephew, the only part of my blood to go into the future, learn from this, and teach the children.' Then she collapses in my arms.

As we row to *Providence* under a clear sky, I realise that I left the main hatch open the night Kojo invited Julie and Leo for tea – that's what we are calling it now, at Xoese's insistence. I haven't been back to the boat since. Despite Xoese's assurances, visions of a ransacked cabin careen before me, books strewn, tools and charts and supplies gone. Julie sees it too, but doesn't say a word. We tie up and climb aboard, fearing the worst. The cabin is ankle deep in water, but otherwise nothing has been touched.

We transfer the food from the dinghy to the cockpit and set about drying out the boat. Everything is soaked, cushions and bedding saturated, books swollen and bursting their bindings. It takes us the rest of the day to strip everything out and air it up on deck. Bedsheets flung over the boom, clothes pinned along every lifeline, foredeck covered in lifejackets and books and kitchen implements, the tropic sun and a fair breeze slowly drying everything out. Julie mops the cabin out, bucket after bucket, saying the old girl needed a good clean anyway. Leo helps, too – he is feeling much better – shuttling wet items up and dried ones back down, Julie and Fema itemising and re-stowing everything.

By late afternoon we've made good progress. I am refolding the dried charts in the cockpit when I hear Julie shout out. A moment later she appears in the gangway, looking up at me. Her face is smeared with grease, her hair escaping in wisps from under her cap. That big smile of hers, the one I've always loved.

She holds up a blue hard-bound book. 'Look what I found.' She hands it up to me.

I open the book to the first page. I peel the page away slowly, supporting the paper with my palm. There, in that familiar up-and-down scrawl, the ink faded and run out to a pale-sunset indigo, the words: *Log of* Providence, *2040.* The year I was born.

Julie holds up a thick plastic container smeared in algae. 'I found it in this, in the forward bilge. Jammed up under one of the spars. There are three more just like it.'

Providence's missing logs.

We set sail that evening, bound for Grenada.

August 2029

It had been four months now since the plane with my double on it was blown out of the sky in front of my eyes. I was still having nightmares about it, and my doctor had prescribed Xanax, but it wasn't helping much. Work was crazy busy, with so much going on. We'd just taken order of a new specially modified G900 to replace the one we'd lost, and we'd hired new body doubles who knew nothing about what had happened to their predecessors, so the Boss was back to flying as much as he ever had.

And then one day the Boss called me to his office. I put on fresh lipstick, plumped my hair, prepared myself for another session. Since the explosion the Boss had taken that shine to me again, and I was again spending a lot of time … well, you know. But when I got to his office, Paolo was there with him.

'Close the door,' he said. 'Take a seat.'

I sat next to Paolo. I could see the Boss eyeing up my dress, checking to see if I was wearing the half-cup bra he liked me to wear. He smiled. I was.

'I have a special assignment for the two of you,' he said, Boss in Boss mode. He pulled a thick file from a drawer and dropped it on his desk. 'As you know I asked Nailor to conduct a full investigation into the plane bombing. This is it.'

He paused. We waited.

'Basically, it tells us shit. Could have been anything, according to him. No leads. No suspects. He's cleared everyone internal. All he's concluded for sure is that those assholes De-GRAB, or whatever they call themselves, are to blame.' He pushed the dossier towards us. 'No shit, I told him. They claimed responsibility, numb-nuts. He just sat there looking stupid. Which I am seriously beginning to believe he is. I fucking know they're to blame, but how did they get to me? At this point, I don't trust the bastard. He may even have been behind it.'

Paolo whistled through his teeth.

'Fucking right,' said the Boss. 'So, the only people I can trust are the ones who were on that plane with me that day, the ones who were that fucking close to having their asses torched. That means you two, plus Chloe, Stephenson, and his new co-pilot, what's his name.'

'Green,' I said.

The Boss nodded. 'I didn't even decide to fly down to Grenada that day until a few hours before. Valiant was such a pain in the ass on the phone. Seriously, you'd think that guy had nothing better to do than pester me about his shitty little island.'

We sat there and blinked.

'And here's the thing: after we got to the airport, I told the pilots to switch planes. Last minute, literally.' He let us hang again. 'It was an inside job,' he said. 'Had to be.'

I swallowed, realising just how close I had come to oblivion.

'So here is what you are going to do,' said the Boss. 'You two are going to read this piece of crap, and then you are very carefully going to find out who our mole is. Between you, you have the two special skills that are perfect for this job. I've always said that in any investigation, there are only two things you have to follow: the money and the sex. Start now.'

Paolo and I left the Boss's office and walked down the corridor to the coffee place and asked the barista to make us each a double cappuccino.

Paolo looked at me and I looked at him.

'Detective,' I said, raising my cup.

We clinked. 'Detective.'

Jumelle

After a good start, we drift for days, the sought current missing, diverted to some other depth or latitude, the world's ocean circulations altered through the shifting of haloclines, the melting of planetary volumes of ice.

Africa lies behind us now like a bad dream that you wake from and realise it was real. We are working our way south as best we can, the Guinea Current pushing us ever eastward towards the place once called Lagos, now a flattened atomic desert.

Evening comes. Leo is in his bunk reading. Fema is below, repairing a tear in the storm jib. Dark thunderheads crowd the horizon. *Providence* is trimmed up and ploughing through a muddy chop. She's a good boat, steady and dependable. Her full keel and heavy iron ballast keep her true and solid even in heavy seas.

Julie joins me in the cockpit, touches my hand. 'Husband,' she says. She sits next to me, our sides touching. 'Do you think it was intentional?'

We haven't talked about Africa since we left.

'The more of Sparkplug's story I hear, the more I think it must have been.' I can feel the anger eating away at something important within me – patience perhaps, or tolerance. 'One person might know. Lachie Ashworth.'

Julie squeezes my hand. 'Maybe he can help us.'

'Maybe.'

'It's a long way to go to find out.'

'Becky first.'

'Becky first.'

Julie reaches into her pocket and produces a small glass vial. The Argent Pharmaceuticals Guinea worm inoculation Xoese showed us, viced longways between her thumb and forefinger. 'And if what they say is true, and America is starting to rebuild, then maybe he can help us find out what's in this. It may not help anyone now, but at least the world can know the truth.'

The next afternoon I glass a ship on the horizon, some sort of freighter, big enough, with a huge kite flying ahead of it and far above, pulling it along, headed south. Where she is from and what she might be carrying I do not know.

The days pass and we make good progress across this vast Atlantic. Distance and time spool out fore and aft to every visible horizon. A hundred and ten nautical miles yesterday. A hundred and forty the day before that, utterly alone.

Evenings, *Providence* squared away for night running, Julie and I sit in the cockpit and she reads to me aloud from the missing logs. I stand at the wheel, the breeze on my face, and think about Papa sitting in this same boat, snatching moments between star sights and watches, writing these words that Julie now speaks.

Some entries are short, limited to position and weather only. Others are longer, detailing events of the day and sometimes more – reflections on the journey, his fears and hopes for the future.

Julie reads:

February 2nd, 2040. With each passing day Francoise grows bigger. It is harder now for her to move around the ship, to help with the sails. She is well into her third trimester, she says. Sometimes I catch her sitting below, cradling her belly, whispering to herself or perhaps to the child she carries. She has been through so much. We all have. How we are going to cope with what is to come, I don't know.

Each night we trace their journey of a quarter-of-a-century ago from Belize, east through the Caribbean and along the northeast coast of South America, in strange parallel to our own track, which will, with luck, take us in the opposite direction through some of the same waters.

And then one night we are sitting in the cockpit, and Julie comes to a place in the log where the ink has run badly and she is struggling to decipher the entry. The sails are nicely trimmed up, and we have been able to start tracking north again, back across the Equator as the trades veer south and we approach the coast of Brazil, all of the future before us in those darkening waters. She moves to the next entry, starts reading. And then she stops, reads on in silence. I watch her come to the end of the page, turn to the next, and keep reading. After a while she flips the page back and re-reads the entry again, still in silence.

She closes the log book on her lap and looks up at me. 'You're not going to believe this,' she says after a time.

'What?'

'When your mother gave birth to you, Papa acted as midwife.'

'I've heard that story.'

'She directed him. There were complications.'

'That one too. A difficult birth.'

'Yes, but did she ever tell you why?'

'Not especially. I never asked.'

'It's because there were two of you, Kwe.'

I hadn't heard right. 'What did you say?'

'You had a twin, Kwe. A sister.'

A cold shiver runs through me, all the things my mother never told me, her strange reticence, the defensiveness that grew over the years as my questions probed more deeply into the past now there in cold evidence. And the dreams. A sister.

'They named her Akua: Born on Wednesday.'

Prisoners

Paramaribo

Finally, a day of fair weather. I have slept only in snatches of a few minutes at a time, the storms of the past weeks so violent that I had to remain at the wheel almost continuously, Julie shuttling me up coffee and soup, Fema and Leo confined below. Waves bigger than I had ever seen buried us more than once, huge mountains of grey water that crashed over *Providence's* deck so that I was standing up to my thighs as the cockpit drained. But below, all remained secure and reasonably dry, and more than once I found myself giving thanks to fortune or physics or the goddesses or just luck for this vessel that Papa found all that time ago.

We continue on towards the Windward Islands and Grenada. Pierre Valliant's Grenada? The site of an international market in child slaves, as Sparkplug said? We must be prepared for whatever awaits us.

I have a twin sister. To have lived this long only to have learned this now is almost beyond reckoning. Each day that passes, my anger towards Papa's son grows, this man who sentenced my father to death and my mother to a life of hardship. He even sent his own parents away, his own mother to her death. And his attempt, later, to right his wrongs by helping his parents escape I have come to see as an act of pure selfishness. I realise I need more than answers.

The inundated lowlands of northern Brazil slip away to port, towns erased, coastlines redrawn. Beyond, mountains loom, dark and wreathed in cloud, and we can see the distant flash of storms, but no sound comes. We have charts for this coast, but so much has been altered they often bear little resemblance to what we find.

Later, we sight smoke on the horizon and then a few tall buildings wavering in the distance like a mirage. Paramaribo, according to the chart, a meandering river meeting the ocean, an embayment and perhaps a port. Exhausted from the storms, low on supplies and longing to stand on dry ground, we jibe and make for the coast.

What remains of the city lies prostrate and wreathed in grey-blue smoke that drifts among the buildings and the low, burnt hills beyond.

We slow, reduce sail, and approach the river mouth, the deep blue of the ocean gone, the water beneath us laden with brown mica that shimmers in the sun. Charred branches float by, and all manner of plastic. As the wind shifts the smell of the city engulfs us, a rank miasma of sulphur and methane. There are no other vessels we can see, and the city and the country about is bare of plants or shrubs or trees, save the charcoaled trunks of long-dead palms and kapok. We continue upriver towards the city and we can make out the now-familiar signs of retreat and abandonment, and the hurried attempts to rebuild further inland.

As we move upriver, figures emerge from the maws of darkened ruins and begin limping down to the seafront, phantoms in the smoke. We come to a place where the river doglegs and narrows so we turn back and anchor off what remains of the city. By then a group of perhaps twenty people has congregated on the shore opposite.

We drop anchor and I set to go ashore.

Julie raises the binoculars to her eyes, scans the city. 'The crowd's growing,' she says. 'They all look...' she hesitates '...sick. Diseased.'

I pocket a few small gold coins, slide the handgun into my waistband and untie the dinghy. A low moan rises across the water.

Julie is beside me now, medical kit in hand. 'I'm coming with you. Those people need help.'

Julie gives instructions to Fema while I bring the dinghy alongside, then we climb in and set out. I row with my back to the shore, Julie in the stern facing me. Another collective groan rises across the water as if from parched, wasted lungs, the stench growing more unbearable as we near the shore. I watch Julie's expression change.

'My God, Kwe,' she says, choking on the words, pulling a cloth from her bag and holding it to her nose.

I turn the dinghy side on to shore. We are no more than a few metres from the water's edge now. There must be a hundred of them, crowding towards us, mouths agape, their blackened rags hanging from jutting clavicles and the sharp runes of hips and pelvic bones. They reach out to us with fingers splayed, frail like kindling wood, their eyes crazed, imploring us from within deep, bony sockets.

'We need to go back and get food,' says Julie.

Suddenly the mass surges towards us. A few of the creatures stagger into the water and start wading towards us, rags and wasted skin and flailing bones.

'Stay back,' I shout, pulling on the oars.

One of the men reaches for the dinghy's gunwale, grabs hold. I swing the oar and hit him in the head and he falls back into the shallow water, a shock of red blood welling up from his skull. Then the others descend on him, clawing and tearing.

Julie gasps. 'Do something, Kwe,' she shouts. 'They're ... My God.'

By the time we get back to *Providence* the body is gone and all that remains is a red cloud in the muddy river water and the mass of people snarling blood-faced in the sun.

Sept 2029

After three weeks of rain that didn't stop, the new levees they'd built around the city broke. This coming after a summer that had dried everything out, turned the forests inland into smoking deserts and left thousands dead from heat stroke in New York alone. But it wasn't the rain that did it. It was Greenland. I heard Trig telling the Boss over Zoom that a huge part of the Greenland ice sheet had broken away and was sliding into the ocean. Billions of tons of ice that were on land would now be floating in the seas. His best guess was that over the next month, sea levels would go up by about a foot and a half. It didn't sound like much, but on the last day of September my ground-floor apartment flooded.

I did my best to save as much of my stuff as I could, and a couple of girlfriends who'd had the good sense to buy higher up came to help me, but I still lost a lot. My favourite couch. The armoire that my aunty gave me after her husband died in the pandemic. Some great clothes and shoes. A bunch of books I really liked, blown up to twice their normal size, turned to mush.

I rented a storage unit and Bryce came with his pickup – one of the team helping another – and we moved it all across town and wedged into this dark little space that looked way too small but in the end we got it all in. When we'd finished it was late, dark, and Bryce took my hand and pulled me close and kissed me for a long time. We'd been getting careless these last few weeks, taking more boat trips together, even screwing in his truck one time somewhere out by the highway.

The Boss offered me a room in the penthouse and so I moved in. It was only temporary, I told him, and told myself.

I kept working. More meetings with Bragg's team, a couple of flights to Grenada. And of course, there was the investigation. Paolo and I thought we were making progress, but so far, we hadn't been able to find anything on our retired general, the Boss's chief suspect.

Every night I sat in the penthouse living room watching the Maddisson news. The war in Africa wasn't going well, and Bragg was having trouble aligning the narrative with what we were seeing on our screens. He'd sent in the marines first, then the army, under the guise of a peace and stabilisation mission – one of Maddisson's ideas – but nothing had gone as planned. The Russians and the Chinese had also sent forces, and soon the land grab was on, everyone trying to secure these fertile, crop-growing areas as quickly as they could. Some African countries had cut cooperation deals with one or more of the big powers, but others fought back hard against the incursions. With their outdated weapons they were blasted to pieces. NGOs like Médecins Sans Frontières sent teams, living up to their name, going anywhere they were needed regardless of who happened to be in charge, and tried to treat the hundreds of thousands of military and civilian casualties that piled up on those oh so fertile territories. I gave them a five-hundred-dollar donation.

And then one day a US army regiment operating in Ghana, near the Nigerian border, was attacked by a Chinese mechanised division, and hell broke all its chains. Or whatever chains were still left holding it in place by then. Casualties on both sides were horrific. Bragg called it blatant aggression, but claimed victory, and put his nuclear forces on alert. For a few days there we were all holding our breath, but in the end the Chinese backed away.

At least the food was coming and the stores were again reasonably stocked, so everyone could go back to pretending that things were normal, if you could call this slow creep towards the abyss normal. People sat on the train scrolling their phones, piled out at one stop, piled on at another. Women bought new shoes and handbags. The high-end clothes stores were packed. Taxi drivers yelled at bike couriers. It was almost as if the sleepwalk had become a collective exercise in waking denial.

Trust

As the winds abate, I trim *Providence* for a five-knot reach, tell Julie to hold her on a steady northwest course, and then I sleep. It is not the deep, drugged sleep of exhaustion, but a tortured journey of nightmare and half-conscious horror that leaves me parched and bruised.

When I finally wake two days later, the island of Grenada looms before us. Green mountains rise up from a pale-blue sea, puffy white cumulus ribbon out across a clear sky. We steer for St George's harbour, round the point late that morning, Leo at the rail with Fema, Julie at the helm. The water of the harbour is clean and clear, and we can see straight to the bottom. The land rises up around us in a close semi-circle of steep green hills and vined cliffsides. Small, white-painted houses perch on the hillside overlooking the outer harbour, and above, a huge palace, shimmering in the sun, its balconies cascading masses of pink and red flowers. I stand at the rail, shattered. That two such places can exist simultaneously within a few days' journey of each other is beyond my comprehension.

As we slow and ready the anchor, a high-pitched whine cuts the breeze. We look up in the direction of the sound. At first, I think it must be some sort of insect, an outsized dragonfly perhaps, hovering high above the masthead. But as it comes closer, I can see its four radial arms and the whirring propeller set in each, and beneath, a dark and swivelling eye.

'It's a drone,' says Fema. 'It's watching us.'

We look up at the strange creature hanging over us. Leo waves. After a while it moves away. We load the dinghy, lock up the boat and row to town. Whoever runs this place, they know we are here.

His name is Enrico. He is there waiting for us as I row the dinghy up to the dock. He is tall, good-looking, with long, dark, wavy hair and a quick smile. He crouches and holds the dinghy steady as I tie up. Then he reaches a hand and helps Julie onto the concrete dock, and does the same for Fema and Leo.

'You are with *Providence*, yes?' he says.

Julie throws me a warning glance: be careful. 'Yes,' I say.

'We are expecting you.'

I take a step back, put myself between him and Julie and Leo.

'Please, very safe here,' he says, seeing me eye the people milling around the dock and the adjoining wharves and buildings. 'No worries here. You are with Enrico now.'

'We are looking for someone,' I say.

'Yes, I know. You are looking for my mother, Elvira. Is this not so?'

Julie sets her eyes in a hard stare. 'That is so.'

'I will take you. Come.'

'We saw a drone before,' says Julie. 'It stopped over our boat.'

Enrico frowns. 'From the other side. They are always watching, but there is nothing to worry about.'

'The other side?' I say.

'The other side of the island. Come,' says Enrico. 'We can talk about this later.' He leads us along a narrow lane to a busy market three streets back from the harbourfront. Stalls piled high with fresh vegetables and fruits, people jostling around the tables, reaching out fistfuls of paper notes and retrieving clutches of bananas and string bags of oranges and big yellow papayas, slabs of meat hanging hooked and dried and ribbed, so much of everything.

Julie stops before a stall piled with ripe mangoes, picks one up and holds it to her nose. She closes her eyes. 'I haven't had one of these in such a long time.'

Enrico shakes his head from side to side. 'Come with me. Not far now.'

He leads us further into the depths of the market. By now our mouths are wet with anticipation, our stomachs hollow with want. Enrico stops in front of a large stall set in the open front of a three-storey cinderblock building. The front tables here are heaped with produce, too. He leads us between a gap in the tables and into the cool of an open-fronted shop. Shelves of goods run in parallel ranks towards the back. A fan turns slowly overhead, and deeper within, an electric light glows from an open doorway. A woman sits on a wood-framed chair set just inside the shopfront.

'This is Elvira, my mother.'

The woman nods, looking at us each in turn, and then smiles at Leo. She looks to be the age of my own mother, perhaps younger. Her dark hair is wisped with grey and pulled back tight behind her ears, accentuating sharp cheekbones and a square jaw. Her skin is dark and set about the eyes with creases that tighten when she smiles, which she does every time she looks at Leo.

'Welcome,' she says in Latin-accented English. 'We get few visitors. Sit.'

Enrico brings chairs and places them in a semi-circle before his mother. We sit down.

'Tell us what you need.'

'We are looking for a little girl. My brother's daughter. She is four years old now. About the same age as my son here.'

Enrico says something to his mother in Spanish much too rapid for my ear.

'We can find most things,' says Elvira.

'We have been told that there is a … a slave market here, for children,' says Julie.

Elvira closes her eyes. 'That is correct.'

It is then that I see it. By the look on Julie's face, she's seen it too. A small mark on the inside of the woman's wrist. A tattoo perhaps, or a brand. The symbols we saw painted on the bridge window aboard *Ocean Transporter* all those months ago in the middle of the Indian Ocean. $\alpha\Omega$. The symbols on the playing cards I still carry with me.

I say nothing, indicate with my eyes that Julie should do the same. We are on dangerous ground. Have we been sold into a trap? We are going to have to be smart, and very careful.

The old woman reaches for Julie's hand as she gazes at Leo. 'And what is your name, little boy?'

Leo introduces himself in that formal way he loves. The woman reaches behind her and hands Leo a ripe orange. Before Julie can take it away, he tears into it greedily and the woman smiles, seeing it. When he is done, his chin dripping juice and his fingers sticky, she wets a cloth and dabs his face and washes his hands with practised efficiency.

I stand and pull Leo towards me, take a step back towards the entrance, check the alley both ways. The handgun is there at the small of my back, with a full magazine in the handle. The woman sits back in her chair and folds her hands in her lap.

'Please,' she says, 'there is nothing to fear. If your niece is here, we will help you find her.'

I reach into my pocket, set a one-ounce Krugerrand on the counter, one of those Papa had taken from Argent's Belize hideaway before I was born.

She picks it up, turns it over in her fingers. 'It has been a long time since I've seen one of these.' She hands it back to me. 'That will not be necessary.'

'We are leaving now,' I say, hoisting Leo to my hip.

'At least take some fresh fruit, some vegetables,' she says.

Julie nods and Enrico puts some mangoes and bananas and fresh peas in a bag and leads us back to the dinghy. As he promised, the dinghy is where and as we left it. We clamber in. Enrico hands me down the bag and I set to the oars.

'I will be here tomorrow, if you need me,' he says as we pull away.

Back aboard *Providence* we square away for sea. Night is coming. These have been the only few hours we've had on land in months, but I am spooked.

'Did you see the sign?' said Fema.

I nod.

'It was on everyone,' says Julie.

I shake my head. I didn't think to look.

'Enrico had it. Every person I saw in the market. Right wrist.'

'Are you sure?'

'Put it this way: I didn't see anyone who didn't have it.'

October 2029

I'll never forget the day when he said it. We'd known each other for over five years by then, and we'd danced around the subject through the occasional dalliance and long periods of enforced separation. Clause sixteen notwithstanding, we'd been seeing quite a lot of each other recently. And it was going well. I really liked him, and I knew he liked me. It felt easy being together, and the more we talked about what we liked and didn't like and the things we dared to hope we might do in the future – the future! – the more we both realised that we had become more than just friends and fuck-buddies.

The wife hadn't said a word to me since her warning shot a couple of years back, and Bryce said that everyone's attention was now so focused on keeping the Boss safe from De-GRAB's threats, that our relationship was the last thing they were going to be monitoring. I hoped he was right, but part of me cared less and less every day.

So that day when the Boss told me to fly to North Carolina to meet with the CEO of Boss Pharma, hand him some documents in person, make sure he read them, and get him to sign, I hoped Bryce would be the one to fly me. I arrived at the airport with hummingbird wingtips fluttering away in my tummy, and when I saw Bryce walking down the G900 stairs I nearly passed out. I thanked Max and tried to walk as slowly as I could across the tarmac. Bryce took my bag and stowed it aft and I took my seat and soon we were whispering our way to Raleigh. Those G900s were so quiet inside you barely knew there were engines attached. Unless you were in a power climb after a bomb attack, that is.

As usual, Bryce came back after we'd levelled off, left Green up there at the controls. It was just us in the aft cabin. Both the stewardesses had covid. He led me to the aft suite, opened the door and walked me in. Then he closed the door and locked it and without saying a word took me in his arms. We kissed and he manoeuvred me to the bed and I lay back and he lay beside me and kissed me and moved his hand down and pushed my dress up and slowly moved my legs apart and ran his hands up my thighs and when he found my lust pearl I sighed and arched into him and not long after I came.

After, I went to go down on him but he stopped me and lay there on his back with his head in the crook of his arm.

'What's wrong?' I said.

'Nothing. I just want to talk.'

I snuggled into him. 'So, talk.'

'How is the investigation coming along?'

'That.'

'I was wondering if you and Paolo had made any headway.'

'It's not Nailor. We've been able to determine that for sure.'

'The Boss will be pissed.'

'Only if we don't find the real culprit.'

'Any leads?'

'We've pretty much narrowed it down to one of two people.'

Bryce sat up. 'Really? Who?'

'It was either the other pilot, the one who died that day, or you.' There, I'd said it. It had been weighing on me for weeks now.

Bryce stiffened next to me. 'Me?'

'No one else could have had enough time to put anything in place once the Boss decided to fly, and no one else knew about the Boss's last-minute switch – only the two of you. You said yourself there was no missile, so it could only have been a device onboard. Nailor supervised the searches of all the passengers and luggage himself, so no one could have brought a bomb on board, even strapped to themselves.'

'Makes sense,' he said.

'So the bomb must have been pre-planted, waiting for the next flight. All of the ground staff checked out clean.' I was getting into it now, talking like a detective in one of the cop books I loved. 'Only the two pilots had the opportunity, the access, the knowledge, and the means to do it. The only thing I am trying to work out is motive.'

'I never trusted that guy,' said Bryce.

I turned to face him, gazed deep into those beautiful eyes of his. 'You can drop it now,' I said. 'I know it was you.'

He lay there beside me for a long time, not moving, his arm still around me.

'You weren't supposed to be on the flight,' he said finally. 'When I saw you get out of the car, I switched, just like the Boss said. I was supposed to fly fake Boss and the doubles. I told the other pilot I would fly real Boss. So I just directed the passengers to the other plane. I'm senior pilot, so he went along with it. The doubles all piled into the rigged plane and off we went. The detonator was set for a thousand feet.'

'And what if I hadn't showed up?'

'Either way, I would have made sure the Boss got on the rigged plane.'

'Even if you had to fly it.'

Bryce lay there next to me and I could feel his heart beating against my chest.

'You're with De-GRAB aren't you?' I said.

'No. They claimed responsibility, but it wasn't them.'

'Then who, Bryce?'

'It's better that you don't know.'

We landed an hour later and I went to my meeting with the CEO of Boss Pharma, and he read the documents and sat there staring past me for a while and then finally he signed. On the way back, Bryce greeted me as usual as if nothing had happened, and we didn't say a word to each other the whole way home.

Elvira

We stay on *Providence* that night. Julie and I lie out in the cockpit under the stars, the lights of the town dancing across the water. This place has electricity and running water. Food is plentiful, and the people we saw seemed healthy and happy. Was this the sanctuary Valliant had set up all those years ago, or some evolution of it?

We talk until late, trying to decide if we should leave or stay. There is no moon and the tide is slack, a perfect time to weigh anchor and slip away in the darkness. But Becky could be out there, just over that darkened ridge, maybe up in the palace on the hill. We agree that Enrico and Elvira seem trustworthy. If they wanted to do us any harm, they'd had plenty of opportunity. If the population was somehow aligned in some dark confederacy, they could easily have overpowered us. Julie remains suspicious, says I am too trusting, but as I remind her, I am not alone.

By the time we agree, a sickle moon is rising over the island. We will go back to town first thing in the morning, push them to help us find Becky. We will take gold, pay whatever it takes. Leo will come with us, and we'll leave Fema to look after the boat. And we will be careful.

When we arrive back at the dock next morning, Enrico is waiting for us. The market is even busier than it was the day before. Enrico leads us through the throng, holding Leo by the hand, talking to him. Soon we are at the store.

Elvira greets us, smiles at Leo. 'We have made enquiries,' she says. 'We can help you.'

'Good,' I say.

'My daughter has come from the other side today. We will discuss it with her. She is upstairs. Come.'

We follow Elvira and Enrico up concrete stairs to a large room on the first floor. Big doors open onto a balcony overlooking a treed garden. The smells of orange blossom and freshly baked bread swirl through the house. A carved crucifix is set on one white-painted wall, Jesus with hands and feet staked, head to one side, eyes heavenward in supplication, the thorns of his crown drawing blood. A big dining table has been set with fresh linen and plates and glasses and steel cutlery and a big glass jug of orange juice.

Elvira sits at the head of the table, a young woman on her right. 'This is my daughter, Isabella.'

Her daughter nods but does not smile. There is a dark circle under one of her eyes and her lower lip is cut down the middle and swollen. Her eyes are dark and she is very beautiful, like her mother, despite the damage.

We say our names, each in turn.

'Now, please, sit. Join us for breakfast.'

I am impatient to get going but with a glance Julie beckons me sit. Elvira and Isabella go to the kitchen and reappear shortly after with bowls of fruit salad, thick slices of toasted bread smothered in butter, fried chicken's eggs, and big bowls of strong coffee with milk. We eat without speaking, with eyes closed, the three of us lost, conquered.

After we have finished and Isabella has refilled our mugs, we sit looking outside at the parrots fluttering in the trees.

Elvira dabs the corner of her mouth with a napkin. 'Did the drone return?'

'No,' I say.

'That is good.'

'Thank you for this wonderful meal,' says Julie. 'It's been a long time since we've enjoyed anything quite so good.'

Elvira smiles, inclines her head.

'We have questions,' I say.

'As do we.'

'Where is the slave market?'

Elvira glances at her daughter. 'It is on the other side.'

'Is there a way to find out if my brother's daughter has been through it?'

'Yes,' says Isabella.

Julie glances at me again. 'Are you all from here?' she says. 'From Grenada.'

'No one is from here,' says Elvira.

'And the marks on your wrists?' says Julie.

Elvira runs the index finger of her left hand along her wrist and looks at her daughter. 'I come from Cuba. I was just married when they came, looking for people to work for them. The testing was very rigorous, and they took only a few, the most attractive and intelligent. My husband and I were selected.' She hangs her head. 'You must understand, things in Cuba were very bad by then. Very bad. We were starving. It was a way out. And that was when they gave us these,' she says, rubbing her wrist. 'We were put on a ship and a few days later we arrived here. We were assigned this house. My husband and I worked in the farms. Others were taken to the other side. We made a life for ourselves, started this shop. Enrico and Isabella were born. And then my husband was killed in an accident on the other side.' She looks at the backs of her hands. 'A long time ago now.'

'What about the people who lived here before?' says Julie.

'It was empty when we arrived.'

Julie and I look at each other. 'What, all of it?' she says.

'We were among the first. The whole of the town, all of this side, was empty. They said it was the pandemic. Of the other side, I do not know. I have never been.'

'The other side was empty also,' says Enrico.

'You do not know this,' his mother says. 'You were not here.'

'I know people who were here and worked on the other side in the early days.'

'Which people? I know everyone who was here at the beginning.'

'The old man.'

'A drunk and a liar.'

'Oh, Mother,' says Isabella, pushing her chair back. 'Do we have to go through this again?' She faces Leo. 'Would you like to see my pet parrot?'

Leo nods vigorously. 'Can I, Mum?'

Julie smiles. 'Be good.'

After they leave the room Elvira says: 'She is a good girl, but I worry about her, working on the other side.'

'What does she do there?' says Julie.

'She works as a housemaid for the officer who is in charge of the guards. We call him the Colonel.'

'What is on the other side?'

'Them.'

We wait for her to continue.

'Eminence and his family, and the people that protect and serve him,' says Enrico. 'We live here in the town and the fields around, but the airport and the southern part of the town and all of the rest of the island is for them. We farm and provide them food, and they send us electricity from their power station and water from their treatment plant. No one can cross to the other side without permission.'

'Your sister has permission.'

He glances at the floor. 'Yes. She is chipped. Only those who are chipped may enter.'

Elvira makes the sign of the cross. 'Now I have told you about my family,' she says. 'Please, tell us of the outside world.'

Julie tells her some of what we have seen over these last months, provides a stark account of Becky's disappearance. Elvira and her son listen in silence.

'This is why we need to find her,' I say. 'As soon as possible.'

Elvira contemplates this a moment, then starts clearing the table. Julie and I go downstairs with Enrico to the garden. Leo is feeding a red-and-green parrot that is perched on Isabella's hand.

Enrico stands beside me. 'I can take you to someone who can tell you more. A person who was here at the beginning, even before my mother. He is a doctor. He is able to … to communicate.'

'Yes. Let's go. Now would be good.'

He glances up towards the kitchen window and then pushes up his right sleeve and taps the mark on his wrist. 'You asked about this.'

'What does it mean, Enrico?'

He frowns and pushes his sleeve back down again. 'It means we are slaves. Or dead.'

May 2030

Even then, despite all that was happening, all the turmoil, the war, the now-incessant rolling natural disasters as we were all told to call them, people still found ways to resist. People like Dahlberg, still out there campaigning for a different way of living, still leading protests, despite the warning shot we'd given her, and the other ones since. People like Electra deVilliers, a politician from South Africa who was trying to rekindle the idea of a global tax on carbon and environmental destruction more broadly. Industry was waging a balls-out campaign against her, and the guys had put out a 'destroy' order on her, but so far, she hadn't been silenced, and actually seemed to be gaining support. Still, what news could you trust, with Yu Wan and Maddisson on the job?

One thing I did know, completely and without doubt: Bryce's revelation had changed everything for me. I'd realised that day flying back from Raleigh that not only did I admire him, I loved him. I wanted to be with him. I wanted a future for us. And I wanted kids.

And so that day when we flew to a little island in the middle of the Pacific called Bora Bora for a meeting of the consortium, I realised what I had to do.

Yu Wan called the meeting to order. Most of the guys were there. It was a chance to have a look at Yu Wan's new sanctuary. He'd just started working on it, had recently concluded a deal with the government to purchase most of the national park, which included the high volcanic peak and a couple of beaches, as his private estate. Trig's team had identified this area in particular as one which would experience long-term upwelling of deeper, cooler water, which would keep it relatively healthy, even as many of the other Pacific islands suffered and disappeared under water.

'The subject for today is the continuing resistance from those who advocate for taxes on free enterprise, action to curb greenhouse gas emissions, and new legislation to protect the natural world. In short, colleagues, socialism.'

General agreement around the table.

'The war in Africa has actually been more successful than we thought it would be. And with the demand for steel, energy, and minerals of all kinds going through the roof, profits are up. And with everyone fighting everyone else, no one is focusing on us. Except deVilliers and Dahlberg. I don't know about you, gentlemen, but I have run out of patience.'

'They've been warned,' said Li.

'Several times,' said Maddisson.

'I move for immediate termination,' said the Boss.

There was a show of hands.

We pissed around in Bora Bora for a few more days, mostly so the guys could party and congratulate themselves and compare toys, and then we flew home. Both targets were dead within the week. Dahlberg had a seizure at home and died on the way to hospital. DeVilliers' helicopter crashed as she toured a national park in Botswana that was being gazetted for mining.

I was a twenty-six-year-old woman in love, and I'd had enough. I couldn't do much, but I had my diary, and I knew how things worked. That was the day, after half a decade of denial and self-interested rationalisation, that I joined the ranks of the people who gave a fuck.

Grenada

Enrico leads us through the town, past tall, bleached buildings that glow in the morning sun, through long, cool streets where every kind of tree and flower and foodplant grows from the places where the concrete has been ripped up. We come to a small bridge that spans a deep-sided ravine of black porphyry, cross over and keep walking along a footpath between plots of vegetables and orchards. Enrico stops and points to the hillside where a twined fence line runs away inland for as far as we can see. Cameras like the one we saw under the drone swivel on tall towers set at regular intervals along the fence.

'The other side,' he says.

Against my judgement, Julie convinced me that it would be better to leave Leo with Elvira and Isabella, and the two women seemed delighted to spend some time with him. I am already beginning to regret it. I console myself with the thought that I have my gun, and I have her son.

We keep going. Eventually we come to a small cluster of houses set among gardens and fruit trees. Enrico knocks on the door of the first house and a moment later an old man answers. He steps back without a word and leads us through the darkened building and out the back door to a stone-tiled veranda that overlooks the harbour. Crates and empty bottles lay strewn across the stone, and a big black cat with yellow eyes sits on a disused brickwork oven, its tail flicking back and forth as its fur rustles in the breeze. We sit on wood-plank benches and the man pours us each a drink from a dark bottle, the twin symbols there on his wrist, his hand unsteady.

'Beer,' he says, voice like gravel. 'Make it myself.'

We drink. The beer is bitter but cuts our thirst.

'Enrico tells me y'all are looking for someone.' The man's accent is like Papa's: North American, stronger.

'A four-year-old girl. Becky Ashworth. Taken from Australia almost a year ago.' I point to his wrist. 'The people who took her left calling cards with that symbol on them.'

The man closes his eyes. He has a long grey beard and his hair is roughly shorn, as if someone has taken a set of shears to his skull. 'One thing I can tell y'all, they keep damn good records. If she's been through here, you'll know.'

'How can we access the records?'

'You have to go inside.' The old man takes a long drink of his beer.

'Where inside?' says Enrico. 'We need precise details.'

'Those I can give you,' says the old man. 'But y'all need to know that what happened here, it done happened in many places, I reckon. This here is not the only guilty place, not by a long throw.'

'Belize?' I say.

'So some say. Not that far from here.'

'Africa?'

'Now that's another story.'

The man pours more beer into our glasses. 'What I can tell y'all is that this island is not as it used to be. I know this because I was one of them that had a part in it.'

He rubs the top of his head as if to scrub off some ancient affliction and drinks down what remains of his beer. 'Truth told I really don't give a God damn what they do to me anymore. Done lived my life, as good and mostly bad as it were. Stuck here on this fucked-up island in the middle of this fucked-up world.'

'Enrico told us you were a doctor,' says Julie.

'Combat medic. Eight years in the marine corps. Two tours in Africa. Fuckin' nightmare, all I'll say about that. By the time I got out I was so fucked up couldn't rightly tell you who I even was. Not who I'd planned to be, that's for damn sure.'

Julie sets Xoese's vial on the table. 'Have you ever seen anything like this?'

The man regards the vial askance for a while but does not pick it up. 'Done seen many. Not the same by way of label, mind, but similar.'

'Where?'

The man drinks down the contents of his glass and refills it, holding the bottle on the vertical to harvest the last few drops. Most fall to the table. 'Here. It was here. I reckon there were damn near one hundred and fifty thousand people here when we arrived. They picked the place

special, like they did them other places, to outlast the climate changin'
an' all ... Kid, go get me that bottle of whisky sitting on the table inside
the door. Never believed any of it about them greenhouse gases heating
the place up. No one in the military did. We believed what we was told
to believe. And then my hometown of Abilene done burned up one
summer and then my pappy's farm dried up all together, and all those
round and by likewise, and then he died rather than live on with
everything he worked for his whole life gone.'

Enrico returns and hands him the whisky bottle. He gestures to my
glass but I shake my head, no, cover it with my hand. He gets the same
reaction from Julie. He pours himself a glass and drinks it down.

'By then, like I said, I was too fucked up for any clear thinkin' or
much else besides. They were promisin' work and money, and some
others ex-corps I knew joined 'em, so I did too. Word was they'd come
here and just bought the whole place, paid the government some
insane amount. When you got that much, who cares, right? Them
government types all shipped out with wives and kids and such, and
that was it, so I was told. And then they sent us. A few of us medics
and a bunch of engineers and other surly and fucked-up types, likewise
ex-military, who'd done their tour in Africa. Over about two weeks I
reckon we travelled the island top to bottom inoculating everyone
against the pandemic – y'all is too young to remember it. Then a
month later we drove all throughout the self-same places, burying all
the bodies. So, by the time the first workers started showin' up there
was no one here but us who'd done that evil work. No trace of all them
graves well buried and us with nowhere to go. All them others I done
it with are long dead, but here I am somehow still rememberin' and
not dying, despite my best attempts, on account of me not being as
successful as them others. Like them Carib Indians who lived here
before in sixteen hundred and some such throwin' themselves every
last man woman and child from that cliff in Sauters, leaving the whole
place similar as now to the French or whoever it was, don't really
matter anymore.'

The old man hangs his head and pushes his face into his hands.

'Please,' says Enrico. 'The records.'

Without looking up, the man says into his hands, 'Blue Quarter.

Section five. Administration of Human Assets. Ask for Karpok. He likes gold.'

And that was it. Julie and I stare at each other. She takes the vial from the table and replaces it in her pocket. The old man is still like that when we leave.

November 2030

With the war going badly in Africa, at least as far as the US government was concerned, the Boss was asked to meet with the head of the army and some of his advisers. We flew to DC and drove out to the Pentagon. It was my first time there, and all I remember now is long corridors and lots of elevators. As far as meeting rooms went, the one we used that day was definitely way below par.

The Boss wanted me there because he'd insisted on having his own minutes taken, and by now he didn't trust anyone else. A bunch of officers in uniform were there waiting for us around the table, women and men, and there were a couple of other guys in suits who sat in the back of the room looking ominous and didn't introduce themselves when everyone else did.

The general in charge came the point. 'We have a problem, Mister Argent, that we need your help on.' The general looked to his left at the officer who had introduced herself as Colonel Sperling.

'Given your firm's exemplary service to the government during the pandemic, we are willing to directly contract you to develop a new product to assist with our campaign in Africa. The work would of course be highly classified.' She opened a folder and handed us each a document, me, the Boss, and the CEO of Boss Pharma. 'What you have before you is a standard non-disclosure agreement of the kind you have signed before, specific to this project.'

The Boss nodded and signed and we signed, too. I was already in so deep, what did one more NDA matter, right?

With that out of the way, the briefing began. Another colonel gave us a PowerPoint presentation on the demographics in Africa. Populations by country, age distributions, birth rates, overlaid with food export requirements to maintain North American demand, local consumption, and Trig-like projections of the effects of ongoing and future changes in rainfall, temperature and evapotranspiration. 'In short,' he said, 'we need to control the population growth rate across the whole continent.'

'Have you tried educating the women?' I said.

The room went silent. The Boss scowled at me. The rest of them just stared at me as if I was wearing my panties as a face mask.

'It is not simply a matter of control,' said the general, eyeing me. 'We need a permanent reduction in fertility.'

Everyone knew what he was saying, but no one said it.

'We need delivery by mid-2031 at the latest, and there will be bonuses for early successful deployment. We can offer unrestricted human-trial opportunities. Can you do it, Mister Argent?'

The Boss leaned over and whispered in our CEO's ear. Our CEO nodded enthusiastically. 'We can do it,' said the Boss. 'But it's gonna cost you.'

'Name it,' said the general, looking relieved.

The Boss took out his Cartier pen, a gift from the Malaysian industry minister, just four years ago now, celebrating the opening of Argent Energy's newest power station in KL. At the time, it was the biggest coal-fired plant in the country, over two gigawatts. It turned a massive profit in its first year of operation, and he sold it the year after for almost twice what he had put into it. The Boss scrawled a number on a piece of paper and pushed it across the table to the general. It was a big number.

The general glanced down at the paper. 'You have a deal. Start work immediately.'

There were big bonuses at Boss Pharma that Christmas.

Nemesis

We return the way we came, silent and brooding on all the old man has told us. Though the sun is still high and the sky blue, the hills take on an ominous aspect, as if a dark cloud shrouds the island. The Goddess Nemesis at work here, her vengeful fury palpable. If you believe in such things.

'We must hurry,' says Enrico as we reach the lane. 'We need to catch my sister before she goes back to the other side. She is the one who can get the information you need.'

'And if she finds Becky, then what?' I say.

'That will be more difficult,' he says. 'But there are possibilities.'

I take a deep breath, keep walking. When we reach Elvira's store we find it closed up. Enrico reaches a key from behind a notch in one of the cinderblocks, unlocks the steel door, swings it open, and calls to his mother and sister. Inside, it is dark. He flicks a switch and a light comes on. We follow him upstairs to the main room, but it is empty. Julie calls Leo's name, running to the balcony, leaning over the railing and peering down into the garden.

'Perhaps they are sleeping,' says Enrico.

Enrico climbs the stairs to the second floor, where the bedrooms are. Julie races down to the garden. I check the kitchen, but it is empty. By the time I return to the main room Julie is standing with Enrico. Her face is flushed and she is breathing hard.

'They're not here,' she says.

Dread wells up inside me. I should never have agreed to let Leo stay. I stop myself saying anything about being too trusting. 'Where can they be?'

Enrico frowns. 'Mother would normally leave a note if she was going out unexpectedly. Maybe they took your boy to the playground. There is a small one just near here.' His tone is so earnest, his distress so genuine, I decide to believe him.

'Show us.'

Julie is halfway down the stairs before the two of us can follow. We run down the lane, almost deserted now, and come to a small park with some big trees and a children's playground set behind a screen of shrubs in the shade at the far corner. We can hear the excited shrieks of children, the laughter of adults. Julie sprints across the grass towards the playground. Enrico and I follow. When we catch up to her, she is staring at the children with her head in her hands. None of them is Leo. She turns to me, tears welling up in her eyes.

'Don't worry,' I say, not convincing myself, every dread demon running in my head. 'We'll find them.' And then to Enrico: 'Where else could they have gone?'

'The library, maybe. Follow me.' We set off again at a run. We check the library, the store that sells sweets. We check the little beach near the point where people who live on this side like to swim. We run through the streets calling his name. By the time night falls we are exhausted and frightened. Julie is beside herself, wringing her hands one over the other again and again, her breathing so fast I worry she will hyperventilate and pass out.

We track our way back to the house. The light Enrico switched on earlier is still burning in the shop. The house is as we left it.

'What about the hospital?' says Julie. 'We haven't checked the hospital. Is there one?'

'Yes,' says Enrico. 'On the point.'

It takes us a quarter of an hour to reach it, running through the darkened streets, the hopeful glow of lamplight behind half-shuttered windows, tree limbs throwing dark shadows across the houses and the road. The hospital is set on the north point of the harbour, a large colonial building with wide verandas. We burst through the main doors and approach a uniformed attendant who is sitting behind a desk.

'Elvira and Isabella Ramez,' says Enrico. 'Are they here?' – all in Spanish.

The attendant runs his finger down a handwritten list. '*Con un niño*,' I hear him say.

Enrico nods. '*Si.*'

The man says something in rapid-fire Spanish.

Julie grabs my arm. 'What did he say?'

Enrico frowns. 'They were taken to emergency surgery two hours ago.'

Julie stands a moment, her lower lip trembling, the blood draining from her face.

'Come,' says Enrico.

I take Julie's arm and we follow him down the corridor, the attendant shouting after us.

We find them in a room at the far end of the hospital. A bare bulb glows from a fixture in the whitewashed ceiling. A wheeled cot sits empty along one wall, the sheets rumpled and displaced. Elvira sits in a chair at the side of the bed nearest the window. She looks up as we enter. Her face is set hard and we can see she has been crying.

'I'm so sorry,' she says in English. 'I should have left a note but there was no time.'

Julie pushes past me. 'Is he alright?'

Elvira raises her index finger to her lips and pushes back her chair and glances down. There on the floor beside her, curled up on a blanket, his little chest rising and falling, Leo. Julie runs to him, bundles him in her arms. He is fine, just a little sleepy.

Sometimes, you need to trust.

❦

While we were meeting with the old Marine, Isabella suffered her third miscarriage in five years. The doctors said she might never be able to have children again.

Enrico paces the room, fists clenched by his sides, shaking his head back and forth. 'This is what she does over there, Mother. You have never wanted to believe it. It's not some secret lover she has, as she has told you. She is the Colonel's concubine. That is how she gets the information.'

'Shut your mouth,' said Elvira.

'I know what goes on there, Mother.'

'How can you know? You know nothing. Be quiet. Do you want people to hear?'

'She told me herself.'

Elvira closes her eyes and shakes her head and then crosses herself.

'No. I don't believe it.'

'The Colonel gives her to his friends, to the men who work with him. Even to the Eminence. She fucks for a living, Mother.'

Elvira stands, rage pouring from her eyes. 'How dare you?' she hisses. 'You will not use language like that in my presence. It's not true. Not my Isabella. Never.'

'It's not her fault. She has no choice. This is what she must do.'

Elvira puts her hands over her ears. 'I won't hear it. Get out. Get out. How dare you, with your sister like this, unable to speak for herself. Get out.'

Enrico shakes his head and stands limp.

'Get out,' she screams.

February 2031

I had delayed it for as long as possible. But now the Boss was insisting. It had been over a year and a half since he'd asked us to investigate the plane bombing, and I'd run out of excuses. Paolo had pretty well let me run the thing, and I'd conducted a massive interview campaign, redoing a lot of what our retired general had done himself, ostensibly to check for evidence that he had misrepresented testimony. He hadn't.

Bryce and I hadn't spoken about it since that time in the rear cabin of the Gulfstream. But over the past few months De-GRAB had repeated its public warning to the Boss: change your ways, stop destroying the planet in the name of profit, or next time, that will be you.

So, there we were, in the Boss's office, Paolo and me.

'So, who did it?' said the Boss, chewing on an unlit cigar. This was a new thing he had started doing recently. No one knew why.

I looked at Paolo and he looked at me.

'Well?'

'It wasn't Nailor,' I said.

The Boss stood, paced around the office. 'Are you sure? I could have sworn the bastard was in on it.'

'Pretty sure,' said Paolo. 'He did everything he was supposed to. There is nothing that points to him.'

'So who the fuck was it?'

'The pilot who died in the explosion. His name was Richternse.'

'Fuck, I knew it,' said the Boss. 'You fucking can't trust anyone. Was he Be-CRAP?' That's what he called them now.

'We think so,' Paolo said. I'd managed to force enough evidence in this direction to convince him.

'It was your idea to switch planes at the last minute that saved us,' I said. Stroke. Always a good tactic with Boss.

'Damn right.'

'Thanks, Boss,' said Paolo.

The Boss bit the end off his cigar, spat it across the room. 'Call Stephenson,' he said. 'Get the jet ready. We're flying to Belize.'

'The new sanctuary?' said Paolo.

'Shangri-La, I'm going to call it. When it's finished that is.'

'When, Boss?' I said.

'Now.'

Four hours later we were wheels up and speeding south. The other G900 with new fake Boss on board turned back once we reached Florida. The Boss briefed us on the way down. This was a special meeting of the group, the last that would be held face to face for some time.

'And I want minutes,' said the Boss. 'This is going to be historic. It needs to be recorded.'

The airstrip still hadn't been paved, and the road through the jungle to the main complex was rough and potholed. We bounced around in the armoured Land Cruiser for an hour before we reached the main gates. Still, the countryside was stunning, mountains and thick forest. The others wouldn't be arriving for another day, and we had a lot of work to do to get things ready.

The place was huge. I'd seen plans, but there is nothing like seeing the actual thing. Construction crews were everywhere, and most of the buildings were still in various stages of completion. The main house with its big veranda would be the site of the meeting, and the guests would each have their own bungalow in the forest, with everyone's support staff staying together in the personnel accommodation building, which wasn't quite finished yet, but would work. Not Leopold levels of luxury, but comfortable enough.

I worked through the night to make sure everything was prepared. Menus were agreed, wines and spirits readied according to each of the guests' tastes – always particular and expensive – and the full agenda for the two days finalised with Singh and the other chiefs of staff and their advance parties. The night before the big shots arrived, the staff had a big bash at the personnel building that went late into the night. Bryce and I stole away from the party within twenty minutes of each other and met as agreed around the back of the building, where it was dark. We climbed over a construction barrier and found an empty room in one of the unfinished wings. Bryce laid his jacket on the floor and then he kissed me and lowered me down very gently and made love to me there in the dark among the stacked lumber and the exposed wiring and the stars shining bright though the empty windows.

Next afternoon, Yu Wan called the group to attention. 'Gentlemen, the time has come,' he began. 'Over the past decade, we have quite literally changed the world. Now, it is time to finish the job.' He inclined his head towards his assistant, a very young woman – girl? she looked barely pubescent – who walked around the room distributing a dossier to each principal. She was dressed like a high-school cheerleader in a tiny, pleated skirt and a halter top, and she was very beautiful, and when she leaned over to put the paper in front of the Boss, I noticed that she wasn't wearing anything under her skirt.

'This is a draft manifesto, for your consideration, which I have worked up with a number of you. It sets out the key principles for the formation of an organisation that solidifies and goes beyond our current informal partnership.'

There was silence in the room as everyone read the document.

Yu Wan signalled to his bare-assed hairless cheerleader-assistant who disappeared into the adjoining room and returned with my least-favourite scientist, Dr Trig. Correction, my least favourite scientists were the ones that we paid to spout garbage to the ignorant and wilfully lazy populace. Trig at least was telling us the truth. Not that I had the ethics market cornered, by any stretch. But at least now, I had a plan, a partner, and a reason to care about the future. I was three months pregnant.

Trig's presentation, delivered without slides, was stark and straight-forward. In the last five years, greenhouse gas emissions had grown by more than a third, and the rate of warming had jumped significantly. Positive feedback loops in the system were now well established and could not be reversed. We were now on track to hit three degrees Celsius of increase over pre-industrial levels by 2040, and nothing anyone could do was going to change that. The sanctuaries his team had previously identified had been confirmed.

Trig straightened, adjusted his tie. 'My work for you is over,' he said, with a slight catch in his voice. 'There is nothing more that I can tell you. I had hoped that armed with this information, you might have altered your views, used your power to change direction. But now, for better or worse – and believe me, there is no upside to this – the die is cast.' And then he turned and walked away.

The guys sat a moment in silence, looking at each other, blinking. And then the Boss started laughing, that big booming laugh of his, and soon everyone was laughing and it went on and on. I remember feeling sorry for Trig. It was a brave gesture, but he wasn't going to get far, and I was sure that wherever he was he could hear the laughter coming from the veranda.

After the mirth had died down, Yu Wan stood. 'Gentlemen, as our renegade doctor has explained, there is now no way to stop catastrophic climate change in our lifetimes. As people come to this realisation – and they will, despite our efforts – they will seek to destroy our businesses, our position, and our wealth. In short, they will seek to destroy us to save themselves. But they cannot be saved. On that basis, there is only one course of action open to us.'

The Boss stood. His turn now. 'We push as hard as we can for as long as we can. We short everything, and push the system to failure. At the right time, we retreat to our sanctuaries and let it all collapse around us. When the dust clears in a couple of decades or so, we, and our descendants, emerge as the new rulers of a cleansed and empty world.'

Even for these guys, the vision was breathtaking. You had to admit. They all took a breath. And then Maddisson started clapping and soon everyone was clapping and even we stupid low-level accomplices in the back seats were clapping and hoping that we and our descendants might also be invited into these arks.

The Alpha-Omega was born.

Isabella

Enrico's sister was noticed very young. Her mother did her best to hide it, but soon it was impossible to conceal what was obvious: Isabella was becoming a remarkably attractive woman. Her intelligence, too, was exceptional, and Elvira did as much as she could, teaching the young woman from her own knowledge, borrowing books from friends for her to read, and purchasing an old upright piano the girl could play on. She practised for hours, rapidly eclipsing the abilities of the few teachers available to her, filling the neighbourhood with the strains of Ravel and Beethoven and her favourite, Schubert's *Impromptu* Number 3 in G-flat major.

And then one day a notice was delivered. Isabella had been selected to work on the other side. She was instructed to report at the main crossing point in two days for an interview. She was sixteen.

Her mother went with her as far as the crossing, kissed her and watched her walk through the opening in the outer fence, the gate swinging closed behind her. Though her mother was crying, Isabella remained composed and stood patiently while the cameras verified her identity. Then the inner gate tracked open, and she looked back at her mother and waved and walked across to the other side, where a black vehicle was waiting. A guard opened the door for her, and she got in and the vehicle sped away.

Isabella didn't tell her mother what happened that day, but she was never the same again. She worked five days on the other side, and returned on the sixth morning to spend two days with her mother before going back again. She would not be drawn into any discussion of what she did there. Her time at home was spent in the garden with her pet birds or sitting in her room with a book open on her lap, gazing out of the window. Sometimes she would play the piano, the music pouring out in a fury her mother and brother had never heard before.

'That is when I decided,' Isabella tells us. 'I was going to do something to fight back. I started by collecting small pieces of information – the dates of shipments of cargo, the names of key people in Eminence's team, like this.'

'And we communicated them to the world,' says Enrico. 'There are people who want to know these things. It was my sister who learned about the market for children. And it is I who transmitted this information, with the help of my friend.'

It has been three days now since Isabella's miscarriage and already she looks much better. 'I know you are anxious to find your niece,' she says, offering her parrot a small piece of fruit, which it nibbles happily. 'Tomorrow I will go back and speak with Mister Karpok. I have met him before. He is ugly and venal.'

'We have gold,' I say.

'Good,' she says. 'Bring it tonight. I will leave early.'

I row out to *Providence* just after sunset. Fema is there waiting and in good spirits. All is calm. I unload the supplies that Enrico packed for me, fresh fruit and vegetables, flour, tinned goods, and Fema helps me stow everything. I check the anchor and then go below and open the strong box where I keep the AK and ammunition. I pull out one complete belt of gold Sovereigns, twenty in all, a fifth of our reserve, and strap it around my waist. Then I grab the log books, the ones Julie and I have been working our way through, and drop them in my bag. I tell Fema to make ready to leave in a hurry – I will be back to check on her tomorrow.

I am about to row back to shore when I hear the drone. I watch it through the binoculars as it jerks in a 360-degree arc around us, at one point descending low and just abeam the cockpit. The camera eye swivels towards me, and for a moment it hovers there just out of reach, staring at me like some cycloptic insect. After a time, it loses interest and flies off.

That night we sleep at Elvira's house. It is our first night on land in sixty-two days, and I dream that I am still aboard *Providence* and that we have beached on a shoal of dead coral winnowed into a broad arc in a clear sea, and when I step out onto the shoal to push the boat free I can see that the sand is made not of coral but of smashed femurs and caged ribs and the stacked vertebrae and holed skulls of people long dead, their bones washed to sea from the high plateaux of their killing in great rivers of sediment that spill into widespan deltas, their remnants smashed into rubble against ancient rocks, tumbling and disaggregating ball from socket and tooth from jaw, shoaling up over the days and years of our history to rest now, here, beneath my feet. And in all my dreaming I am not alone, but shadowed by a parallel presence, a person unknown but known, and when I wake, I know that the person in the dream is my twin.

By then, Isabella is gone, back over to the other side, and we wait. I work on my book, write all of this. I realise what day it is and row back out to *Providence* and listen to Sparkplug's transmission – the decision to sterilise an entire race, the world's slow sleepwalk towards ruin guided by Argent and Yu Wan and Valliant and Li. And we, now, live the result. And we wait.

We sit in the garden and while Leo plays with Isabella's parrot, Julie and I keep reading through the logs. The year 2041 arrives and the two babies – me and my twin sister Akua – are growing strong and healthy. Progress down the coast is slow, often against prevailing winds and currents, the continent a smoky, burnt-out, depopulated presence to starboard. They have documents taken from Derek Argent's refuge that indicate parts of the Southern Hemisphere may remain habitable. Just what we've heard in Sparkplug's transmissions. They – we – are on our way to The Hope. There are glimpses of the growing bond between Papa and Mum, of the joy he takes in these children. The year 2042 comes and Mum is pregnant again. They spend time in a small community on the south coast of Argentina, meet some kind and generous people. Lewis is born there. Months pass. They become part of the community. Mum starts doctoring again. Papa helps build a school for the children of the community, starts to teach them science in his rapidly improving Spanish.

We come to the log for 2043. Akua and I are almost three years old, and by all accounts thriving. Lewis has just had his first birthday. The entries are steady and predictable as *Providence* crosses the Pacific. They stop at Easter Island, find it deserted, and make their way towards Polynesia, following the trade winds. *Providence* makes landfall at Bora Bora on March 16th, 2043. Papa describes it as a mountain thrust from the sea, with dark volcanic cliffs and thick vegetation and a fringing coral reef that has somehow managed to survive the warming oceans. They go ashore. They are greeted by the inhabitants, who seem friendly. They buy food and water. Akua and I swim in the lagoon with Mum while Papa watches Lewis. They spend a quiet night on the boat, safely anchored, and then decide to stay a few days longer, enjoying the peaceful beauty of the place.

Julie turns the pages, stares at the next entry for a moment, flicks the page back, and then forward again, leafing quickly through the next several pages.

'What is it?'

'Something happened.'

'What, Julie? Tell me.'

'The next entry isn't until September of 2044,' she says. 'Between, there's nothing.' She looks up at me. 'Eighteen months. Nothing.'

She hands me the log book. She's right. Once the logs restart in 2044, there is not a single mention of my sister. Not anywhere. It is as if she vanished, not only from the boat, but from their memories. And when we arrived at The Hope almost a year later, she was gone, never to be spoken of again.

❂

That night we are sitting in Elvira's living room reading under electric light when Enrico walks in. He is out of breath and sweating heavily.

'Quickly,' he says. 'Gather your things.'

I stand. 'What's happened?'

He looks into my eyes. 'You must leave now. I have heard things.'

'What things?'

'They are becoming agitated. You have stayed too long. They know you went with me to speak with the old doctor.'

I put my hand on his shoulder. 'I hope we have not put you in danger.'

'I will explain on the way. There is no more time.'

Julie has already packed away our few things into our bag and has Leo in her arms. We kiss Elvira goodbye and she cries, and we follow Enrico down the stairs. We hurry through the darkened streets.

'One day I'm going to leave this place too,' he says.

'Where will you go?'

'Anywhere but here.'

'Come with us,' says Julie. 'There is room.'

He shakes his head. 'Thank you but no. It would be too dangerous for you. Many of my friends have tried. None have been successful. Some are brought back, most are not. They own us. My mother does not want to admit this.' He wipes the tears from his eyes. 'I cannot leave them, not now. But one day, I will find a way for us to go together.'

Enrico leads us down to the quayside. The town is quiet. A few lights flicker through the swaying vegetation. We find the dinghy and I pass Leo down to Julie.

I shake Enrico's hand and thank him. 'I am very sorry,' I say. 'About everything.'

He shakes his head. 'No, please. There is nothing you can do.' He is still holding my hand. 'Before you go.'

'What is it, Enrico?'

'I heard from my sister,' he says. 'Your niece was sold in the market here three months ago to a man called Yu Wan. One of the Eminences.'

My heart jumps into my throat and stays there, hammering away.

'According to the records, she was taken to an island in the Pacific, Yu Wan's sanctuary. I am not sure the name of it. I am sorry.'

'Bora Bora.'

'Pardon?'

'That's where she is. Bora Bora, in the Pacific.'

'How do you know this?'

'A friend of mine told me, over the radio.'

Enrico narrows his eyes.

'It doesn't matter. How can we ever thank you?'

'By telling the world what is happening.' He flashes the hint of a smile. 'Julie told me about your book.'

'I will try.'

'And one more thing. Our friend the old marine also has a message for you. He says go to Panama. Someone from the USA government will meet you there, at the canal. I told him about your step-brother.'

I get into the dinghy, and lock the oars. So much to say but no way to say it and no time. Enrico pushes us off and stands and waves, but it is very dark and I don't know if he sees me wave back.

Orphans

Hecate

A door has closed behind us and we are approaching a crossroads, boundaries manifest in these liminal spaces. A thousand miles west the canal beckons, and a transit to the Pacific, and Becky? Dare we hope? Enrico was clear. She was taken to the Pacific, to Yu Wan's sanctuary. According to Sparkplug, that means Bora Bora. Could it be that Akua and Becky are in the same place?

Suddenly, the place of my sister's erasure crowds in on me, the images of that brief, joined childhood clearer now, the memories released and bubbling to the surface. My sister lying next to me, the shadow of my mother's face above us, a candle in her hand, its glow diffusing through white, diaphanous netting. Standing in a kitchen, a pale-green sky showing through an open window, Akua beside me holding my hand.

I read somewhere about history being the chronicle of the victors. If that is true then perhaps this story that I am writing is not history but a testament to those who have paid that price Xoese spoke of, the one that no possible outcome can ever justify. For surely, we are not the victors, if indeed there are any. I wonder, do those on Grenada's so-called 'other side' consider themselves among the victorious? Perhaps, but if so, what have they won but the right to build a prison and put themselves inside it?

☽

They knew we were coming.

We sail into the broad, muddy expanse of Limón Bay in Panama with the sun rising behind us and anchor in the lee of the Cristobal breakwater, a modest swell surging between the abandoned buildings and winnowed spires of Colón.

Not long after, a military launch is planing out from Cristobal harbour to meet us. Leo sits in his usual spot at the bow and watches the vessel approach, white spume flying in its wake. Its hull and super-structure are painted dull wartime grey, and we can see the colourful pennants flying from its tower, and as it veers to come alongside, the American flag fluttering at the stern. The deck gun is unmanned and secured. An officer in crisp fatigues is standing on the flying bridge. The vessel slows, settles into the water and eases up to within hailing distance.

'*Providence* from Australia, bound for the Pacific?' the officer calls down to us.

I wave. 'That's us.'

'Mister Abachwa?'

'That's me.'

'Welcome to Panama, sir. Captain Matthew Hargreaves, United States marine corps. Permission to come aboard?'

He turns and says something to the helmsman, who starts to manoeuvre the launch towards *Providence*, and then a moment later he steps from the launch onto our deck. He turns to Leo at the bow and gives him a quick salute, which Leo returns with a grin. Then he walks to the cockpit, takes off his cap and inclines his head to Julie. 'Ma'am.'

He is our age, maybe younger, cleanshaven and brushcut, with piercing eyes the colour of storm clouds. We shake hands. I invite him to sit, which he does.

'Sir, ma'am, I have been assigned to see you safely through the canal.'

'Julie and Kweku, please,' I say.

He glances towards the bow. 'He reminds me of my little ones back home. How old is he?'

'Three and a half,' says Julie.

'Mine are four and eighteen months. Haven't seen them for almost a year.'

'It must be very hard on your wife,' says Julie.

He seems to drift away for a moment and then catches himself. He pulls a sheaf of papers from his pocket. 'Here are your transit papers. I know you don't have an engine, so we'll tow you across the lake and whenever otherwise necessary.'

'Thank you,' I say.

Just then the sound of thunder rolls across the sound. Captain Hargreaves looks back towards the hills and frowns. 'I must warn you that we only retook the canal zone six months ago. Insurgents are still active along the whole length of the zone, particularly on the Pacific side. We will do everything we can to protect you, but you must know that there are dangers.'

Julie glances at me and puts her hand on mine. 'We understand, Captain,' she says. 'We thank you for your protection.'

Hargreaves inclines his head. 'We'll tow you to Gatŭn, raft up and transit the first lock. There are three chambers, which will step us up to the lake. And then across the lake and three more chambers down to the other side. If everything goes smoothly, we should have you through to the Pacific and on your way by the day after tomorrow. Better if the boy stays in the cockpit from here on.'

He stands, straightens his uniform jacket. 'But before we set off, there are some people in San Cris that want to talk to you, Mister Abachwa. It shouldn't take long. We'll tow you in.'

January 2032

My daughter Ruby was born during the killing heatwave of July 2031. They said over a hundred million people died all over the world. If you were old or very young or poor your chances of dying were ten times higher, the experts said. Strange how Trig – relatively young still, he was only fifty-one – bucked the odds. They found him alone in his apartment, in bed, a copy of Yuval's banned book open face down on his chest. We were okay, though. The power to the private hospital I delivered in never faltered. It was one of the Boss's businesses.

The official story was that I had decided to have a baby with one of my casual boyfriends, but wanted to raise it on my own. I moved into a seventh-floor apartment close to where Bryce lived, hired a full-time nanny and was back at work, on the Boss's insistence, by September. We decided that the best place to hide was in plain sight. Bryce would meet me and Ruby every Saturday afternoon in the park and we'd walk around together in our masks on account of the smoke from the fires burning in Canada and the rolling outbreaks of the virus, and Bryce would hold her awhile and we'd talk, and you know, I was so happy. Despite all the shit, all the disasters, the death, the war, I was happy just to be with the man I loved and my beautiful, perfect little baby girl.

Winter came and with it a bit of a respite from the heat and the smoke. Russia finally declared victory in Ukraine after securing eighty percent of the country, but only after three million people had been swallowed up and shit into shallow graves from Bakhmut to Lvov. And then in January Bragg did what everyone had predicted he would do. He suspended the 2032 election.

I'll never forget the day he came on TV and addressed the nation. Even with all the makeup, his octogenarian skin sagged and wobbled as he spoke. I watched his mouth moving and I heard the words but they seemed to go right through me, like some kind of weird aural x-ray. The world was now a very dangerous place, he told us. The war in Africa was entering a new and dangerous phase. The global order was crumbling. Natural disasters were threatening the viability of American society. What the country needed now was unity and focus, not the divisiveness of a presidential campaign, which he would win anyway. He knew Africa better than anyone, knew how to deal with the weather better than anyone. In her time of peril, America needed strong leadership. Leadership that only he could provide. Such a gentleman, a knight in shining body armour.

I never thought I'd see it, not here in America. A president for life. The only question was, whose life?

Panama

Captain Hargreaves tows us in and we tie up along a newly poured concrete dock in the centre of the otherwise inundated city. After we are safely alongside, Hargreaves' launch turns and powers away, back towards the Gulf.

Two men in dark fatigues are waiting for us on the dock. They are big men, tall and powerfully built. One of them flashes a badge. I don't have time to read it.

'We're here to speak to Mr Abachwa,' one of them says.

'You're speaking to him.'

'Please can you ask your crew to disembark.'

I don't like his tone. 'On whose authority?'

'Please, sir,' says the other man. 'This does not have to be a problem. It's up to you.'

'It's alright,' says Julie, calling for Fema and Leo. Soon we are all standing on the dock.

One of the men boards the vessel and goes below. We can see him moving through the cabin, opening lockers, rifling through shelves, sweeping with some sort of device. I see him reach down and put something into the bag he is carrying.

'What are you doing?' I say, angry now.

'Security,' says the man on the dock. 'Just routine.'

'What are you looking for?' says Julie.

This time the man does not answer. A few minutes later his colleague reappears and jumps to the dock. He is holding my pistol. He drops the magazine and thrusts it and the gun into his pocket without saying a word.

'What's wrong, Mummy?' says Leo.

'Nothing, sweetie,' she says, holding him close, kissing him on the top of the head.

The man who has my gun says: 'Can you come with us, please, Mr Abachwa?'

'Where are we going?'

'Not we. Just you. Your family can stay.'

I stand my ground. 'Tell me where you are taking me.'

'I'm not asking,' he says.

The other man pulls a pair of handcuffs from his jacket. 'Don't have to use these things. Your choice.'

'What is this about?' says Julie, her voice flaring. 'He hasn't done anything wrong. Captain Hargreaves said this would only take a short time.'

'It will,' says the other man. 'If you cooperate.'

I breathe, assess. I don't want to inflame the situation any further, not with Leo and Julie here. 'It's okay, Julie,' I say. 'I'm sure it's just a mistake. At least tell me where we're going.'

The first man juts his chin toward me and his colleague steps towards me opening the cuffs.

Ten minutes later I am being led blindfolded and handcuffed down what from the echo of our steps on the floor I assume is a long corridor. Then the blindfold comes off and I am in a small room with bare walls, two chairs and a table. One of the chairs is bolted to the concrete floor, and I am pushed into it and my handcuffs attached to the chair behind my back. The guards leave and I am alone. I wait. Sometime later the door opens, and the two men who took me from the boat step inside and position themselves on either side of the door, facing me. They stand expressionless.

The man who follows them in a few moments later is tall and thin, and has grey hair and dark eyes the colour of the eastern sky just after the sun has set. His face is cleanshaven and the skin is deeply lined around the eyes and mouth. He is dressed in a plain-blue suit with a blue tie and carries a brown leather briefcase. He sits in the chair opposite and looks at me from across the table.

'Kwesi Abachwa,' he says after a time.

'Yes.'

He reaches into the briefcase, withdraws a red folder, places it on the table and opens it. He taps the stack of papers with two fingers. It is Papa's manuscript. The top page has *THE FORCING* written on it in Mum's hand. 'Where did you get this?' he says.

'It's mine.'

'Who gave it to you?'

'The man who wrote it.'

'David Ashworth.'

'Yes.'

'Also known as Teacher.'

'Yes.'

The man claws a long-fingered hand through his hair, front to back, and closes the file. 'Are there any other copies?'

'No,' I lie. The other is buried ten thousand miles away, underneath my house.

'Is he still alive?'

'No.'

'Did you see him die?'

'I was with him, yes.'

'And his wife – your mother?'

'She's dead. Bandits came and killed her. My brother too. They took his daughter. Her name is Rebecca. Rebecca Ashworth.'

The man purses his lips. There is a strange curve to his mouth, as if frozen in contemplation of something not to be fathomed in this lifetime. 'Who is they?'

'Alpha Omega,' I say. 'They left a calling card.'

The curve of the man's mouth does not change, but he tilts his head slightly to the left and exhales.

Anger jets inside me. 'What is this about?'

'Routine, as these gentlemen told you. All you have to do is cooperate.'

'I am cooperating.'

'Well then.'

I fill my lungs and hold it awhile, blow the air out.

The man produces the glass vial that Xoese gave Julie and sets it endwise on the table between us. 'Where did you get this?'

'In Africa.'

'Who gave it to you?'

'Someone I know there.'

The man closes his eyes a while, then reopens them. 'And what is your business with the United States government?'

I shake my head. 'What?'

'We were told you had urgent business.'

'If you read that manuscript, you will know that my mother was married to President Ashworth's father. My brother was the president's half-brother. And the little girl I am trying to find is his niece.' I jut my chin at the file. 'It's all in there.'

'And so?'

'I have a message for him.'

'You can tell me.'

'And you are?'

The man glances at his watch. 'You're running out of time.'

I squirm in my chair. The cuffs bite into my wrists. 'I have questions for him,' I say. 'I was hoping for some answers.'

The man sits gazing at me, eyes narrowed.

'Why did he send his own parents to a concentration camp?'

The man's face is as expressionless as the two men standing behind him. 'It was a government decision made in a time of crisis. The original policy of the LeJeune government was designed to be humane and fair, and guaranteed those displaced similar accommodation and work.'

'But it didn't turn out that way, did it?'

'There was a power struggle within the cabinet. It was a government of youth, very inexperienced. LeJeune was an idealist. His original vision was fair and humane. But radicals took control.'

'The president's own mother died in that camp. Many more besides.'

'It was not supposed to be like that.' The man rakes his claw through his hair again, glances at his watch.

'My own father died there too.'

'My condolences.'

'You tell the president for me that his policy was wrong.'

The man sits impassive. Then he reaches into his briefcase and puts a book on the table and pushes it toward me. 'Yuval,' he says. 'Read it.'

I ignore the book. 'Tell me about Alpha Omega.'

The man contemplates this for a long time. 'We are aware of them.'

'What can you tell me about them?'

'They have territories scattered all over the globe, in the remote tropics and the Southern Hemisphere mostly. They are expanding, acquiring weapons and territory.'

'Places like Grenada.'

'Yes.'

'And Bora Bora?'

'Not that I know.'

'And Derek Argent, he was one of them?'

'He was.'

I glance at the vial. 'And Argent Pharmaceuticals supplied inoculants to the US government for use in Africa, is that right?'

'Yes, during the war. The LeJeune government discontinued that programme after it took power.'

'But the war went on.'

'For two more years, yes.'

'And what would happen to me if I inoculated myself with that stuff right now?'

'That's classified.'

'Was it for depopulation, sterilisation?'

He turned the vial over in his hand but did not answer.

'And what happened in Kejabil? Was that Argent also?'

The man locks my gaze and stares deep into my eyes. Then he stands, places the vial and the manuscript into his briefcase. 'These men will take you back to your family. Leave, now. Go home.'

'Are you keeping those?' I say, as he reaches the door.

'Have a good life, Mister Abachwa,' he says, then turns, thrusts the briefcase under his arm and walks out. 'I hope you find your niece.'

December 2032

That Christmas I told the Boss I was taking some time off, and Bryce and I went to his father's cabin up in Ontario on a lake in Muskoka. There was lots of snow on the ground and that area hadn't burned since 2025 so there were trees and deer in the woods, and it was even cold enough to skate on a little rink one of the neighbours made on the lake, and at night we'd sit outside by the fire, snug in our winter coats and blankets with the big fat flakes falling over us like confetti, Ruby there between us with the firelight shining in her big eyes, and it was perfect, just perfect.

It reminded me of an exchange between the Boss and Trig way back in the early twenties. The Boss had challenged the scientist with the observation that if the planet was warming why were we getting so much snow? The Boss always loved gotchas like that. Then Trig had very carefully explained, like a teacher to a not-so-bright pupil, that it only needed to get to zero Celsius for it to snow. And warmer air held more moisture. So, if winter temperatures were on average now minus one instead of minus ten – a lot warmer – you'd get a lot more snow. The Boss was furious, but he knew Trig was right. I think that was when he started to believe it, all the climate-change stuff.

Still, being up there everything seemed so far away, all of the shit with the Boss, the fighting and the anger and the fear, and we were so in love that I wanted every single day to stretch out forever, every moment. I wanted time to stop, right there, forever. But of course, it didn't, it just kept going, and no matter how hard I tried the world kept intruding.

And then one evening after we'd put Ruby to sleep, we were sitting by the fire in the main room, the snow falling outside, and Bryce finally told me what I knew he'd been holding back from me all this time.

'You asked me that day on the way to Raleigh who I was working with,' he said. 'I haven't told you all this time, because I wanted to protect you. But now…' he glanced to our room where Ruby was asleep in her cot. He took my hands in his. '…You need to know.'

I hadn't pushed him because I knew that he would tell me when he was ready.

'Everything's going to shit,' he said. 'Fast. So fast it may not be retrievable, no matter what we do. And now, with Bragg suspending the election, even our right to protest is being taken away. We have to change things, and we have to do it soon, or Ruby will have no chance of a decent life.'

I had been providing Bryce with transcripts of all the Boss's meetings for over a year now. None of this was new. 'So, what do we do?'

'We need to overthrow the government, take back power, not just here in America, but everywhere.' This wasn't pilot Bryce anymore, and this wasn't his usual even, unflappable, pilot's voice. Passion and anger boiled in every word. 'And who has the power? The same people who have the money, that sit on all the boards and own the companies and run the countries. Old fuckers, that's who. They've gotten obscenely wealthy and have lived like emperors for decades by knowingly trashing the place, sucking every last drop of juice from the future. Everyone over fifty-five is guilty of a collective crime against humanity greater than any other ever perpetrated.'

I could feel my heart beating faster. Finally, the real talk.

'And so, we are going to take them down,' he said. 'And then we are going to make them pay. Every last one of them. Starting with Argent.'

Over the next hour he told me all about his long affiliation with the new 'government of youth' movement, how he'd been recruited to provide information from inside Argent's operation, track the movements of other members of his circle of associates. At first, he'd thought me naive and indulgent, a bit of a skank. But all that had changed.

'And now we have to do it together,' he said. 'For Ruby.'

I kissed him. My heart was bursting. It was as if my whole life had changed. And it had. Finally, I had a purpose that mattered. Mother, wife, and saviour. We were going to save the world.

'For Ruby,' I said. 'And all the other children.'

Marlin

They return me to the dock. I jump aboard *Providence*. The three of us stand there in the cockpit for a long time just holding on to each other.

Not long after, Captain Hargreaves returns in his launch and tows us out into the bay, towards the first lock. We wait as a US navy patrol vessel transiting in the other direction clears the canal, and then, rafted up to Hargreaves' launch, we enter the first chamber, looking up as if from the bottom of a huge concrete coffin. The gates close and the chamber starts to flood, lifting us skyward. Then again, and another time after that, carried up by this marvel of human ingenuity twenty-five metres to Gatŭn Lake. That we could conceive and build marvels such as this and yet not have had the foresight, the courage, to avert disaster when the time came is an incongruity impossible for me to process, let alone understand, despite Sparkplug's transmissions, her unfolding story of the descent. Some things cannot be explained with facts alone.

❂

Two days later, we emerge into the broad sweep of Panama Bay, the Pacific Ocean stretching out before us. Hargreaves tows us to the protected lee of the three-mile-long newly raised breakwater that curls from the river mouth to the edge of the city. Then he wishes us luck and we watch as his launch turns back towards the canal. We drop anchor in the bay off Panama City and set about preparing for the crossing.

The next afternoon, I am sitting in the bosun's chair near the top of the mainmast, checking the anchor block and the triatic stay. Below me, *Providence* rocks gently on a hint of Pacific swell that refracts around the point and into the harbour. That morning, Julie and Fema rowed into the city to buy supplies, and I can see the place where I lost sight of them going in, and beyond the raised seawall and white office buildings and apartment complexes of the city. Below me on the foredeck, Leo sits dangling a line from the fishing rod I gave him for his birthday. The water here is very blue and though I measured out seven fathoms of chain and the same of rope, the colour of it is that of the deep ocean.

Just then there is a shout from the deck. I look down. Leo is standing at the bow, the rod in his hands bending deep towards the water so that its tip is nearly at the surface. Droplets of water spring from the line as he fights to keep hold. I can see the place where the line cuts through the surface as the fish pulls in wide circles, and the tangent of the line splicing down through the blue prismed water.

'Daddy,' he shouts, 'what do I do?'

Whatever it is, it's big, and it's going to pull him in. 'Give him line,' I shout, releasing the bosun's chair and starting to rappel down the mainmast.

Leo glances back at me. His dark eyes flash, then he whips his head around, dark curls lashing the breeze. He braces his feet against the deck rail and leans back and pulls on the rod so I can see the veins and tendons in his little neck bulging taut as the tip of the rod rises slowly from the surface. And then, just when I think the rod will snap, he lets the tip fall back until it is just under the shimmering surface and then he quickly pulls the rod up again, grabbing the reel in his little hand and turning the handle, regaining a metre or so of line. The fish hits again, and for a moment I think it will pull him right over, but he steadies and lets the fish take line, the reel spinning away, his hand guiding the tension until the line bounces and goes slack, and he starts reeling in again.

By then I am at his side, ready to cut the line or take the rod from his hands. He looks up at me, turning the handle, reeling in line. That same look, very old – from another time. 'He's mine,' he says.

I stand next to him and watch him fight the fish. After half an hour, both fish and boy are tiring. Spasms shake his body and tremors run the length of his little arms, but the circles the fish is making are tightening, and its runs have become shorter and slower, and I can see in the way the rod bends and from the tension on the line that it is slowly coming to surface.

When the fish jumps, he comes out of the water just off the starboard bow. He is so close we can see his big black eye and the long curve of his big, blue dorsal fin and the shine of the sun across the blue curve of his back and the leader deep in his mouth and the long spike of his bill pointed skyward.

Leo stands with the rod in his hands, eyes wide, staring at the beautiful fish seemingly suspended there above the water. And when he hits the surface, the boy lets out a cry so that I flinch and move towards him, thinking that he has been hurt, but he steps away from me and dips the rod to the water and reels hard. Blood is dripping from the base of the reel and I can see the places on his hands where the skin has rubbed free and the glistening flesh beneath.

I reach for the rod. 'Son,' I say.

Leo jerks the rod away from me. His face is dripping with sweat and his mouth is set in a hard line. His gaze meets mine and for that instant it is as if we are looking into each other's souls, and I know then that he knows. That nothing we have seen these past months has escaped him and that he understands it all.

And then the fish is alongside, huge and ancient, looking up at us through the blue, clear water, that eye black and strangely impassive, his flank turned to us very blue and ridged and silver-bellied, and the big sickle tail tremoring and the spear of the bill piercing the surface. I reach down with the gaff and coil my forearms to drive the hook deep into the side of the fish, but just as I do he shakes his great head and flashes his tail and dives again so that we can see him below us, dark and huge and magnificent. Three times Leo brings the fish alongside and three times it dives away, just beyond our reach.

By now the boy is exhausted. I know it is over. 'Do you want him?' I ask.

The boy looks up at me as if from a very far place.

'We can cut him loose if you want. Let him live.'

Leo closes his eyes, the rod shaking in his ruined hands, the fish there just below us, hulking and blue against the darker blue of the water. And then he looks at me and nods, just a single drop of the chin.

I pull out my knife, grab the line as close to the water as I can, place the blade against the line, and cut the fish free. It hovers there a moment, unaware, and then with one flick of its tail it is gone.

Leo collapses to the deck, his little legs folding up beneath him. He sits staring at his hands and out at the ocean and back at his hands and at the rod there on the cockpit floor. I think he will cry, but no tears come, and he is very quiet all the time I am bandaging his hands and he never says a word again about the fish.

☙

Julie and Fema return from the city as dusk is colouring the horizon. By then, Leo is asleep below. We load the supplies, and Fema sets to preserving as much of the fresh fruit and vegetables as possible. I tell Julie about Leo's marlin, and she listens in silence when I tell her about his hands.

We are sitting together in the cockpit when we see a launch round the breakwater and start speeding towards us. Its masthead light blinks over the darkening water and the red and green navigation lights shine against the coastline. We sit and watch it approach on a steady course. Soon we can make out the superstructure and the pennants flying, and the deck gun and a solitary figure standing on the flying bridge. It is Hargreaves' launch, the one that brought us through the canal.

Soon the launch is alongside and Hargreaves steps aboard carrying a big duffel bag slung over each shoulder. We go below and he puts the bags on the saloon table.

'I have a message for you,' Hargreaves says. 'It came in today on the classified wire.' He opens the satchel slung crosswise over his right shoulder and produces a single sheet of paper.

He reads: '"Status, Bora Bora: do not approach. Extreme danger to navigation and life. Island believed controlled in entirety by Alpha Omega. High probability Yu Wan Junior present. If approach imperative, seek contact Freyja on west coast of the island of Taha'a, Sandrine boatbuilders, Ruutia harbour. Recognition code prompt: last stem of the Norse rose. Response: a lost fable five times never told."'

He looks across the table at us. 'Got it?'

I nod.

'Are you sure?' He folds the paper. 'I cannot leave this with you.'

Julie and I repeat the message back.

Hargreaves replaces the paper in his satchel. 'And there is this.' He places a red waterproof bag on the table, opens it and takes out a dossier, which he places on the table. There is a crest on the front with the words Central Intelligence Agency inscribed in the outer circumference. 'You sure must have friends in high places.'

We both shrug.

'Anyway, it's none of my business. But please be careful, whatever it is you have to do. I brought a few things to help you on your way.'

He reaches into the first duffel bag and withdraws two cardboard boxes and puts them on the table. 'MREs,' he says. 'Meals, ready to eat. These ones are my favourite. M&Ms with peanuts, for the boy. It's candy.'

'Leo will be so happy,' says Julie. 'Thank you, Captain.'

From the second bag he produces a large military backpack. 'It's a complete medical trauma kit,' he says. 'Oh, yeah, and I nearly forgot.' He sets a magazine on the table. It is a copy of *Time*, dated two and a half years ago, dog-eared and greasy. The faded front cover features a photograph of a tired-looking man with the caption: "Can President Ashworth lead us out of this?"

I stare at the cover a long time. It is the man from the interrogation room in San Cris. We sit in the cockpit and watch the launch move away and disappear behind the breakwater.

We set sail for Bora Bora next morning. That evening, after Leo is in bed, we set the self-steering gear and go through the contents of the CIA dossier. The first document is marked *CLASSIFIED*. It is heavily redacted, dated from the early years of the African War. The title page is emblazoned with the words *Operation Tirade*. We read in silence, side by side. The chief contractor, Argent Pharmaceuticals, is tasked with the development and deployment of a new drug whose stated purpose is to cause reproductive sterilisation of the patient, male or female. Two hundred million doses were delivered in the first phase and subsequently administered to the entire population of Ghana, Ivory Coast, Nigeria, Togo and Benin, regardless of age or current fertility. The document states that the purpose of Operation Tirade is to prevent further suffering through alleviation of resource scarcity in selected territories, and to secure agricultural production potential for export.

Julie stares at me across the table, horror in her eyes. 'Xoese,' is all she manages to say.

The second file, also classified, is very short, just two redacted pages. It refers to a trial conducted by Argent Pharmaceuticals in a small village in Ghana called Kejabil. The date of the trial has been redacted. A new drug was being tested, the purpose of which is not mentioned. One thousand, three hundred and fifty-two people of all ages and both sexes were inoculated and observed over a period of twelve hours. The trial was classified as a failure. All of the subjects perished within three hours of being inoculated.

We stare at the paper, overwhelmed.

The last file contains a copy of a recent cabinet briefing entitled *Global Situation Report*. Julie and I read in silence. The CIA estimates the current global population as eight hundred million, less than one fifteenth of the Repudiation peak. Of these, less than a hundred million are likely to be fertile females. Functioning, democratic or semi-democratic governments remain in a few countries. The United States itself, severely weakened by the protracted civil war, remains one of the dominant global powers. Fractured totalitarian regimes make up most of the other semi-functioning states. The majority of the world's population now lives in small, isolated communities with a variety of local governing systems. No functioning Earth-orbiting satellites are believed to exist.

After the first page we both just stop reading. Julie folds the papers in half and puts them back into the bag. 'Thank you, Mister President,' she says. 'But we don't need this. We are living it.'

'He took Papa's manuscript,' I say. 'And your vial.'

'Probably because they were too damaging to him personally, and to the prestige of the United States,' Julie says. 'Imagine if it got out.'

We sit a moment, side by side, and then I go on deck to check the self-steering gear.

May 2033

That spring, more than eleven years after launching his special military operation in Ukraine, the Russian Federation's president-for-life died of cancer in hospital in Lausanne, Switzerland. All that wealth, of course, in the end, couldn't stop the inevitable. The day he died, his successor launched a new offensive to capture the last strip of independent Ukraine that remained along the border with Slovakia. It seems we have war in our DNA.

By then a new pandemic, this time not launched by Boss Pharma, but caused by a natural mutation of the initial Operation Red virus, was burning across the world like an out-of-control wildfire. There were a lot of those burning, too. Australia had just suffered its worst summer fire season in history, with over half of the country burned to ash and thousands of people dead. According to the UN, a mere rump by then, global population had peaked and was now dropping. That was also the month that Canada voted in a Bragg-inspired referendum to join the USA. They were small, scared and wanted Big Brother's protection. It was almost Orwellian. Bryce was right. It was all going to shit.

I was sitting in my office when I got a coded text from Bryce. I waited ten minutes, grabbed my purse and left the building and walked to the coffee place where we would pretend to bump into one another, hiding in plain sight. We feigned delight and sat down with our lattes. The place was packed with sleepwalkers. We grabbed a table outside, where it was nice and noisy.

He put his foot next to mine, applied some pressure. 'Tell me about Kejabil.'

I'd read the documents that I had delivered to the CEO of Boss Pharma that day, of course, and later heard the Boss talking on the phone about a test gone wrong. 'From what I can tell, it was an accident. Pharma was testing a new inoculant. It didn't work right.'

'What do you mean?'

'It wasn't supposed to work that fast.'

Bryce leaned forward, lowered his voice. 'That fast?'

'Yeah. They all died within a few hours. It was supposed to take a few weeks and look like botulism, you know, the plague.' Shame burned through me like a runaway infection, and I could feel the tears building behind my eyes, a dam ready to burst.

'My God,' said Bryce. 'Fucking animals.'

The dam burst. Bryce handed me a napkin, let me work through it.

'I've heard that the group is going to be meeting soon,' Bryce said after a while. 'Sometime in the next few months. The Pacific, I'm told.'

'I haven't heard anything about it,' I said, blowing my nose.

'You will.'

'What do you want me to do?'

'As soon as you hear anything, let me know.'

I smiled, pretended to chit chat. You never know who's snooping. 'Sure.'

'It's getting close. We need a big story, one we can share with the world. One that will knock them all out of their stupor.'

'Bigger than Kejabil?'

'Way bigger. You need to keep notes, but you also need to get a voice record of it. All of it.'

I blanched. 'The Boss never allows it. Never has.'

'Well, you're going to have to find a way. We need this. I'm counting on you. We all are.'

'Jesus, Bryce. I don't know if I can. Can't someone else do it?' I was feeling distinctly wobbly.

He grabbed my hand. Anyone could have seen us. 'There is no one else. Don't you understand? It's taken us years to get inside the Boss's organisation, and no one else has been able to penetrate to your level of access in any of the other organisations. You've told me yourself. You are Alpha Omega's de-facto secretary.'

I could feel the blood draining from my head. Everything was going dark around the edges. 'I don't feel well,' I said, putting my head in my hands.

'Keep it together, bae. We need you.'

I was high-key not happy.

'Don't worry,' Bryce said. 'You're going to slay this.'

I let it pass through me, opened my eyes. I squeezed his hand and then pulled mine away, regained some composure. 'Okay, I'll think about it. About how to do it, I mean. And I'll let you know as soon as I hear anything.'

The fightback was about to begin. And I was going to be on point.

Wife

I stand at the wheel and watch the slow progress of the clouds across the water and the changing colour of the thrown shadows and the way the rain cells shift and disappear and then appear again from the base of the clouds and how the sunlight refracts across the overwhelming, bursting, emptiness of it.

The Pacific lives with us, and we with her, the incongruity of our existence manifest in each cloud-strewn dawn, each night's quantum shattering of stars. Night comes like a law of physics, and it is as if blinds are being drawn and suddenly we can see forever, all the way back to the beginning of time, and it is almost too much to bear so far is it from any real human understanding. And each night I stand at the wheel, piloting our small vessel through this impossibility, and I think that it is like being dead and living forever.

I read Yuval's *Years of Warning*, the book Lachie Ashworth gave me that day in Panama. It covers the crucial years from 2020 to 2025 and was published just before the start of the Repudiation. In it, he talks of the increasing instability of the global economic system, how national debt in the major countries continued to balloon, with real wealth increasingly concentrated in the hands of a very small and increasingly powerful group of people scattered around the globe. The average person in the developed world worked harder for less, with more of their effort going towards financing the debt owed to that same group of mega-rich individuals. He writes of the rising impact of climate change and what he describes as the completely inadequate, conscience-assuaging efforts to combat it, a series of empty national pledges and a concerted effort to unload the cost of mitigation and adaptation onto those least able to pay and least able to object – the young, the poor, and future generations. Yuval reserves special disdain for corporate boards, whose efforts to appear to be acting for good while actively lobbying against meaningful change he describes as shameful and duplicitous. Despite decades of so-called action to reduce emissions, through the 2020s global greenhouse-gas emissions actually rise. The plight of the poorer nations receives special attention, two chapters detailing the hopelessly inadequate pledges of aid, largely never delivered, and the subsequent rise of radical autocracies in those countries, supported by the big northern dictatorships such as Russia, China, and North Korea. The war in Ukraine dragged on, consuming more lives and more of the democracies' precious resources, contributing to growing worldwide food shortages and diverting effort and money that could have been spent fighting climate change. The last chapter warns of a global rise in fascism, and the perils of not acting decisively to reduce global greenhouse-gas emissions. The final sentence of Yuval's book is: 'But there is still time, if we work together, to avert the worst of these consequences, and create a world in which we can all live decent lives.'

I put the book down and look up into the cockpit. Julie is there at the wheel. Her hair blows in the breeze. White clouds pearl the horizon behind her, and the sun shines on the brown skin of her face and shoulders and bare arms, her long legs supple and responsive to the surging rhythm of the ocean beneath her.

She glances down into the cabin, perhaps sensing I am looking at her, smiles at me a moment, and then looks away to the horizon. I sit watching her guide *Providence* over the running current that foams and pulses beneath us. She is wearing a pair of loose khaki shorts slung low on her hips and a white T-shirt which she has tied up tight under her breasts so that the topography and colour of her shows through the thin cotton.

I join her in the cockpit.

After a while she says: 'Do you ever wonder what happened to them?'

'Who?'

'Everyone at the *Village de la Paix*.'

'Sometimes.'

'I was happy there. Really happy.' She looks at me for a moment and then back to the horizon. 'At first, I was ashamed of feeling that way. But not anymore. Especially after listening to those radio transmissions. I hope it survives.'

'Me too.'

'And you know something else?' she says. 'You and Leo would have been happy there too. I know you would have.'

'Maybe, Julie. Maybe. But we have a job to do.'

'I know, and I'm with you, Kwe. I always have been. We'll find Becky. I believe that. And after, we have to find a way to live, just like Papa said.'

'We can go home.'

'Home. I don't even know what that is anymore.'

That afternoon I am dozing in our cabin, the sea air flowing over me soft and cool, Julie at the wheel and Fema forward with Leo watching for flying fish, when a change of course wakes me. I can hear Leo and Fema talking excitedly and Julie answering back from the cockpit. And then the feeling through the boat as Julie spills power from the main and *Providence* suddenly slows. I jump up and clamber into the cockpit.

'What's wrong?'

Julie points. There, about four or five miles off the port bow, a ship of some sort.

'Leo spotted it about an hour ago, and we've been getting closer to it ever since. It doesn't look like it's moving.'

Julie hands me the binoculars and I glass the horizon, focusing in. It is a cargo ship, large, with a superstructure and stack and open foredeck. A Panamax, similar in configuration to *Ocean Transporter*. No markings or flags that I can see, and no wake.

'Looks like she's adrift.'

Julie and I look at each other, both thinking the same thing, or versions of it.

'They may need help,' I say. 'Stay this course.'

She frowns, bites her lower lip.

Half an hour later and we can see a thin ribbon of smoke drifting from what looks like a hole in the ship's bow, just above the waterline. The forward cargo holds are all open.

'What's that sound?' says Julie.

I turn my ear but all I can hear is the sound of the hull moving through the water and the wind in the sails.

'There it is again,' she says. 'It sounds like...' She hesitates. 'Like guns.'

I raise the binoculars again, scan the ship again. 'Fall off,' I say.

Julie turns the wheel and eases the main, and *Providence* picks up speed. Slowly the far side of the ship's hull comes into view.

'There are two ships,' I say. 'A smaller one is tied up alongside.'

'Maybe they're providing assistance.'

Then I hear it, the distinct staccato sound of gun fire – automatic weapons. 'Not assistance. They've been boarded.'

Julie gasps. 'What should we do?'

'Fema,' I shout.

She turns and looks back at me.

'Get Leo below.'

She starts to unclip Leo's lifejacket from the lifeline.

'Hold this course, Julie. We'll pass astern and keep going. This is our fastest point of sail. Hopefully they won't bother with us.'

She frowns, holds the wheel steady, trims up the jib and mizzen. *Providence* is flying now, and as we close astern we can see the neck and gaping jaws of a bucket crane biting into the hold of the stricken ship and then pivoting back to discharge the contents into the second ship. We are about a mile and a half away now and can see figures moving about on the deck of the stricken ship. The crane swings back to the smaller ship and folds itself down onto the deck. A thick cloud of black smoke belches from the smaller ship's stack, and the figures start moving back to the smaller ship. And then the two vessels part.

We are closer now, cutting across the larger vessel's stern quarter. Suddenly there is a loud hiss and then a flash near the larger ship's bow followed by an air-splitting detonation. Black smoke pours from the stricken ship. Then the smaller vessel turns away and gathers speed and soon it is only a smudge on the horizon.

January 2034

I hated leaving Ruby. Going to work every day was bad enough, but these longer trips were just hard AF. Kleo, my nanny, was great, though. She was only nineteen but super responsible and switched on. She'd lost both her parents to the first pandemic and her older brother was in the army, fighting in Africa. Every night she watched the news and cried, even though they'd stopped showing anything much about the war a long time ago. She loved Ruby, and I could tell the way she looked after her that she wanted a baby of her own one day, but we never talked about it, and I never saw boys coming around.

Over the last few months we hadn't travelled so much. The Boss had stayed close to home, and other than a quick trip to the ranch in Wyoming back in September, I'd stayed in New York. Truth, Boss was worried. Yu Wan had narrowly escaped being turned to mush when the armoured limo he was travelling in was clipped by a Javelin. The car in front, which was carrying two of his very young wives, took the missile full on, but the force of the blast flipped his car over and he broke his collarbone and messed up his face. He'd set up the wives' car as a decoy. It was the only thing that saved him. De-GRAB claimed responsibility, but again they claimed responsibility for everything these days whether they'd done it or not.

And the faster the economy roared, and the warmer it got, the more money we made. But by now everyone could see it. The planet was dying in front of our eyes, and we were dying with it. After a while the news stopped reporting it and people stopped talking about it – at least in public. But in darkened rooms, in basements and back alleys, everyone knew. We were fucked. But the problem was, no one knew how to change it, and after almost a decade of being told that we couldn't change it, our imaginations just didn't work properly anymore. And we were scared. I mean, *terrified*. And so most of us did what normal people do when faced with a terrifying situation they think they can't change. We ignored it. Got on with life. Partied. Fucked. Watched lifetimes of TV. Did drugs and drank ourselves blind. Anything but stare it right in the eyes.

Not me. Not anymore. I'd dumped most of the pills I had been taking down the toilet. Got clean. Started running again. In one fit of rage I threw most of my shoes and clothes over the balcony into the alley. They were all gone by morning. Over that previous six months I'd experimented with all kinds of ways to secretly record the meeting that Bryce had said was coming. Getting a reasonable, decipherable recording wasn't a problem. Smart phone was the best way – all kinds of apps for that. Just turn it on, stuff it in your purse, or down your underwear. But Nailor was scanning everything these days. There was no chance of getting a phone in, unless I was part of the advance party, like I'd been at the meeting in Wyoming, now that would have been easy. A thousand places to hide a device beforehand, Bluetooth it active before going in. I mean, I wasn't a spy. I didn't have access to the technology those guys had. At one point I started thinking about excusing myself and standing outside the room and putting a cup on the wall. Even an internal device was risky. What if the Boss decided to explore me under the table like he did sometimes? What's this, bae, some bougie new vibrator?

The meeting was called, like Bryce said it would be. Wherever he was getting his information, it was good. We left for Bora Bora two days later. After the missile attack Yu Wan had pretty much locked himself inside his Pacific Island fortress. I'd settled on a very small dictation machine that I'd bought on line. It was about the size of a AAA battery, and could fit inside one of my old MAC lipstick holders. A bit of pissing around and I got it so I could switch the recorder on from the bottom and still use the lipstick. I even made sure it had my favourite shade in there. I tested it a couple of times there on my kitchen table, speaking normally, and it worked fine.

We arrived a day early so the Boss could relax and prepare. That evening I walked down to the lagoon with Bryce and Green and Singh. The breeze from the ocean was gentle and I watched it playing with Bryce's cowlick as he waded in the shallow, clear water with his trousers rolled up to knees. We could hear the waves crashing against the reef and the first stars came out and it was very beautiful. The lipstick was in my purse – it had made it past Nailor – but suddenly all the shit seemed very far away, like a bad dream. Surely things couldn't be as bad as we believed. They sky was still blue. The air was clean and fresh.

The stars shone brilliant in the night sky as they always had. All you had to do was look around. Look. This one little pixel.

The day of the meeting I put on my tightest, sexiest dress, the one the Boss loves to see me in, and my candy-apple-red stilettos to match my lipstick, and I marched to the meeting room and up to the security guys and put my purse and heels on a tray and walked through the CT scanner. The Boss was there with me and after I was through the scanner, he came up to me and grabbed my ass.

'Like it,' he said, referring to my lack of underwear. 'The sparkplugs, too.' That's what he called them.

My purse came through and one of the security guys, a huge man with burly shoulders and a savage, bearded face, rummaged through it and pulled out my lipstick. 'What's this?' he grunted.

'Lipstick.'

He fumbled with the top, took it off, sniffed at the little red tumour.

'Matches my shoes,' I said.

'It's got something inside,' he said, staring at the screen next to him.

'It's a little heating device,' I said. 'To keep the lipstick at just the right temperature.' I flashed him the sluttiest look I could find. 'Hot.' I glanced at the Boss. He was liking me again these days. A lot. Called me his MILF-plus.

The security guy grunted, replaced the top. 'I don't know,' he said.

Just then the Boss leaned in. 'Let her have her lipstick, or you'll be wearing it.'

It was a big meeting. Everyone was there. Some of the guys had brought their sons, the heirs to their empires. Yu Wan's son, Yu Wan Junior was there. He looked about fifteen, smooth-skinned and smaller than his father, but with those same unsettling eyes and Dad's arrogant swag. Maddisson's son was there too, tall, good-looking, with a burgeoning Monaco playboy persona that he was already starting to flaunt in the tabloids. I sat next to the Boss, Paolo to his right, and put my pad and pencil on the table in front of me, ready to take minutes. I reached into my purse and put my lipstick next to my pencil.

Yu Wan called us to order, and after the usual preliminaries, got to it. It was time. I picked up my lipstick, pushed the bottom to start the recording, pulled off the cap, and applied myself a nice kiss of my favourite shade. This is a particularly feminine act, and quite sensual, I know, and more than a few guys watched me do it.

'Gentlemen,' Yu Wan said, and I wrote, 'matters are unfolding more quickly than we anticipated. The late Doctor Trig's predictions were, while geographically accurate, as you can see, too conservative. Global temperatures continue to rise and the Earth system, as he liked to call it, is reacting much more strongly and quickly than he said it would. We need to advance our plans, all of us.'

Valliant raised his hand and was recognised. 'Some of us have not been able to make the progress on our sanctuaries that you have.'

'Then I suggest you accelerate your efforts.'

The Boss scrawled a note on a bit of paper and told me to walk it over to Valliant. I did. It said: *I can help. Have something that will solve your problem. Good price. Contact me after.*

'How much time do we have?' said Li.

'Five years, maybe ten at most. Some of the tipping points the unfortunate Doctor Trig told us about have already been reached.'

Maddisson was recognised. 'We may not have that long. This new youth movement is gathering steam. Nothing we do is slowing it down. People are angry.'

'Anger without power is a weeping woman,' said Yu Wan's son.

'They are getting stronger,' said Maddisson. 'I don't know how long we can hold them back.'

Until then the Boss hadn't said much. Now he stood, and without waiting for Yu Wan to give him the floor he said: 'Stop fucking whining about it, Maddisson, and do your job. As for the rest of you, keep pushing everything as hard as it will go. We made the decision and here we are. This is the future.' He pointed out of the window. 'So get the fuck ready.' He sat back down.

Li started clapping, and then Yu Wan, and soon everyone was applauding, even Maddisson.

Three days later we were back home. I went back to my apartment, removed the recording device from the lipstick container and plugged it into my laptop and downloaded the file. I took a breath and hit play. There was a loud bang and then a parrot screech and then a long hiss that continued for an hour and a half. I sat there and cried for about as long.

Orion Star

It is Julie who insists.

We approach the ship from astern. She is taking on water and starting to list. We come alongside where one of the ship's lifeboats floats, all its lines still attached, dangling from the davits. An aborted escape attempt? We lower sail, lie rolling in the swell next to the huge ship, the smoke from the bow darkening the sky above us. I swim over with a line, pull *Providence* in and tie her alongside the lifeboat. Then I shimmy up the rope to the deck with my pistol in my belt and an empty duffel bag over my shoulder.

The deck is quiet, just the open cargo-hold doors and the smoke rising into the blue sky. The acrid smell of burning rubber and scorched steel fills my nostrils. It doesn't take me long to find one of the escape ladders. I make it fast to the deck rail and let it unroll over the side. Julie follows me up, Hargreaves' new trauma kit on her back.

We climb to the bridge. Grey-bellied clouds float above the horizon, undersides sheeting curtains of rain. On the bridge I grab a few charts and put them in my bag, half expecting to find some marking or sign, as on *Ocean Transporter*, but there is nothing. We move down through the decks. The first crewman we find is on E deck, an officer by the uniform, dead, shot through the chest. We find two more on D deck. We make our way down to C deck, the ship groaning around us as water floods her lower levels, this the new law of the sea. History folding back on itself. We reach the crew lounge, find toppled chairs and four bodies in a slick of blood, piled behind an upended table sieved with bullet holes. Empty cartridge cases litter the floor. I double over and retch.

We keep going, scanning the darkened insides of the dying ship with the beam of our torch. Fire extinguishers in their cradles. Crew notices on walls. A child's painting taped to a cabin door. We find more bodies, twelve crew in all and four mercenaries, armed guards. All dead.

We make our way to the galley. I fill the duffel bags with canned and packaged goods. 'We'll come back and get more,' I say.

Julie nods in the darkness. I feel it more than see it. We are about to start back up to the main deck when we are stopped dead by a human voice.

'Whoever you are, don't move.'

We freeze.

'Put down the gun. Slow. Keep your hands where I can see them, both of you.' A man's voice, wheezing, laboured. An American accent.

I put the pistol on the deck.

'The torch too, shining forward. Now turn around.'

We turn in the direction of the voice. The man is sitting on the floor, propped up against a bulkhead, holding a handgun. 'Kick the gun over here,' he says. 'And now the torch.'

As the dying beam swings towards him, we can see that he is holding a bloodied compress to his neck. Another is strapped around his bare torso, and there is a tourniquet around his right leg, just above the knee. He nudges the torch around so the beam is directed at us, but the light is almost gone.

'You have to wind it,' I say.

He lets go of the compress on his neck and wedges the torch between his knees and cranks the handle. The light brightens.

'Who are you?' he says.

'We're here to help,' says Julie. 'I'm a doctor.'

The man coughs, a deep rattle in his chest. Blood foams at his mouth.

'Your lung has collapsed,' says Julie.

'No shit.'

'Let me help you, please.'

She starts to shrug the medical kit off her back.

'Stop,' he says. 'Answer my question.'

I tell him our names and the name of our vessel, and its dimensions and means of propulsion and our destination. We wait as the light begins to dim again.

'Okay,' he says, motioning with the pistol. 'Doctor Julie, you come here. You, Husband Kweku, stay over there by the wall.'

Julie lays the trauma kit on the floor and crouches next to the man. 'Please,' she says, 'let my husband have the torch so he can give me light.'

He nods, and she takes the torch from him and walks it back to where I am standing and gives it to me. As she does, she whispers: 'Don't worry, it's fine.'

I crank the torch and play the light over them. The deck around the man is slick with blood and littered with torn-open medical packaging and spent cartridge brass. His assault rifle is propped against the bulkhead next to him and his chest rig lies shucked nearby like an unwanted carapace.

Julie crouches next to him and scans his body. 'You are going to have to put down that gun and trust me.' Her voice is very calm and authoritative, and I think of how much she has changed over the last few months.

I can see the man's eyes starting to close. He sets his gun on the floor. 'Go ahead, Doc. I'm in your hands.'

Julie works quickly, cutting away his clothes and searching every part of his body for wounds. He doesn't resist, just lies there and lets her work. He is a big man, broad-shouldered and heavily muscled, young still, maybe a little older than me. His skin is much darker than mine, more like Xoese's, African.

He is in bad shape. One round has sliced through his neck, narrowly missing the carotid artery. Another has blown a hole in the back of his calf. A third passed through the lower part of his right lung and out through his back, missing the spine by about two inches. There are smaller lacerations all over both his arms and he has lost a lot of blood.

Julie packs and bandages the leg wound, irrigates the furrow in his neck and applies some temporary sutures and a clean compress, and sets chest seals on the wounds in his torso. When she is done, she looks at me and says: 'We have to get him back to the boat.' Her face is streaked with blood. 'If we leave him here, he'll die, one way or another.'

Together, one under each shoulder, we lift him to his feet. He is groggy from loss of blood and drags along between us, swinging the damaged leg from the hip, barely conscious. By the time we get him up to the main deck the ship is listing badly to port and the sky is blown apart by stars. I've never seen so many. Strange what you notice.

I rig a harness and strap him in. Julie climbs down to the boat. When she is ready, I lower the man down, belaying the line around a stanchion, bracing the rope against my back. I follow with the duffel bags and together we get him to *Providence*, where we lay him on the cockpit bench and put a blanket over him. We are both exhausted.

'I'm going back for more food,' I say.

I grab an empty duffel bag and am about to jump over to the lifeboat when Julie takes my arm.

'There's a nick in the artery in the leg,' she says. 'I am going to have to operate, soon. That tourniquet has already been on too long. Be quick.'

🌑

By the time I return from *Orion Star*, Julie has cleared the saloon table and laid out what she needs for the operation. Both oil lamps are burning, and the kettle is boiling on the stove. I dump the duffel bags and the man's rifle and chest rig in the cockpit, untie *Providence* and let her drift away from the drowning ship. She is very low in the water now, listing almost thirty degrees, great hollow groans echoing through her hull.

I raise the sails and set course west, for Bora Bora. Soon we are foaming along under a blanket of stars, a small speck of light on the ocean, lost in the vast reflected mirror of the heavens.

Julie comes on deck, scrubbed and ready. 'We have to do it now.'

I set the self-steering gear and help the wounded man down the gangway. He groans in pain as we lay him naked on the table.

Julie takes position near the man's head, bends over him and says: 'I am going to operate on your leg. If I don't, you'll die.'

He inclines his head and closes his eyes.

Julie gives him a dose of morphine and soon he is out, breathing steadily. We turn him on his side so Julie can access the back of his calf. You can see where the tourniquet has cinched in against the muscle and the change in colour where the circulation was stopped. With Fema and I moving the lights and assisting as directed, Julie works. She finds the cut artery and clamps it and then removes the tourniquet. Blood begins to ooze from the wound. She repacks the hole around the clamp and then tears open a package and withdraws a small synthetic patch no bigger than her small fingernail with a pair of tweezers. She reaches into the wound and positions the patch, and with her other hand applies a smaller clamp and then another to hold everything in place.

She looks up at me. Sweat beads her forehead and runs across her cheeks and neck. I reach for a cloth and wipe her face.

'Time two minutes for me, Kwe.'

I start my stopwatch.

'New technology,' she says. 'Developed during the African wars. An adaptable biological adhesive that quickly mimics the cellular structure of the tissue it's applied to and bonds with it. Amazing, really.'

She sees the amazement on my face, points to the packaging. 'I'm a fast reader.'

On two minutes she checks the graft and then releases the tourniquet. Blood oozes from the wound, but the graft holds. She applies three internal dissolvable sutures and then closes and sews up the exit wound, then the smaller entry wound, and then bandages it all with care.

The lung is more difficult, and takes much longer. She inserts a chest drain to bleed off the air in the chest cavity and then goes in under the lowermost rib and, using the same patching compound, seals the puncture in the lung and then reinflates it with her own breath.

When it's over and the man is resting in the forward port berth, Julie and I sit in the cockpit with mugs of hot tea. Dawn is only an hour away and light tinges the eastern sky.

'Will he survive?' I ask.

Julie sips her drink. 'Definitely. He's strong.' She kisses me on the forehead. 'It feels good,' she says. 'And now, I'm going to sleep.'

April 2035

Bryce and I were in the park with Ruby enjoying a clear, warm day when we heard the news. A city ratchet came by scrolling on his phone, head bowed, glancing up now and again to avoid colliding with other equally device-absorbed pedestrians. As he passed us, he suddenly stopped and stood there staring at his screen.

After a while he looked over at us and said: 'Hey, did you hear? Bragg just died. Deadass.' Then he walked away, thumb flicking across his screen.

We sat there a while, Ruby in her stroller not realising that history was unfolding around her.

'You know what this means,' said Bryce.

'Elections back on.'

'Roger that.'

'Ending the wars.' That's what we called them, now, just 'the wars'. As more countries piled in, each with their own grievances, their own strategic objectives, the conflict became more and more confusing. A giant fucked-up melee, the Boss called it.

'Maybe,' said Bryce.

I remembered the day the Boss said those words to Bragg in the Oval Office: 'so go and take it from them.' Well, he did. And look where we ended up. Who says words don't matter?

Bryce turned to me. 'It's time, bae,' he said. 'Finally. After all these years. I just hope it's not too late.'

'Sorry I didn't get that recording,' I said for the hundredth time.

'It doesn't matter. We have your journal. That will have to do.'

We sat there on that bench, holding hands, not caring who saw us or what they might say or who they might report us to. It was as if the whole world had changed.

A couple of weeks later I met Anton LeJeune and Lachie Ashworth for the first time in a basement club in Manhattan. Bryce and I were there together, and he introduced me to them. They were both very young, early twenties, handsome and full of fire. They were the brains behind the youth movement that had slowly and carefully been building political power across the country over the last few years, holding secret meetings, staying one step ahead of Bragg's police, rallying young people with a simple message.

The place was packed with all sorts of people, young, all races, men, women, even grey-hairs. Now Bragg was dead, it was as if the lid had come off. They didn't even try to keep it secret.

LeJeune stood on a chair, Ashworth there beside him, and the room went quiet. 'Thanks for coming, everyone,' he began. His voice resonated through the room. 'Our message is simple. The future, our future, is being destroyed by a powerful group of supremely wealthy people – old people. People like Bragg.'

A loud cheer went up. LeJeune raised his hand and the room went quiet.

'And they are doing it with the mute acquiescence of an entire generation, those old enough to have done something about it. The future of the planet and the human race depends on us taking back control and changing course, peacefully if possible, violently if necessary, and doing it quickly.'

More cheers, cries of 'burn the fuckers'.

LeJeune continued. 'We have proof that Bragg and his cronies were in secret collaboration with a group of uber-rich businessmen and foreign leaders who conspired to enrich themselves at the expense of the planet and its people. Together, they are responsible for starting the wars in Africa, dismantling all of the legislation built up over decades to protect our environment, the destabilisation of our climate and the systematic elimination of anyone who stood in their way.'

The room erupted. Bryce squeezed my hand. I knew he was proud of me.

'But none of that matters,' said LeJeune, his voice rising above the din, calming it, quietening it. 'What matters is now. We call for the immediate re-establishment of free elections, not only here but around the world. And, if the people support us, we intend to set up a new government of youth that will govern as if the future matters, as if we need to keep the planet healthy if we want a future on it. I urge you all to get out there and tell the world what you want.'

'We want the future back,' someone shouted from the audience.

'Make the fuckers pay,' came another voice. Soon the room exploded with cries until a thousand voices were chanting in unison. And what they were chanting would have made the Boss shiver.

Beloved

As the days pass, the stranger grows stronger, watched over by Julie and Fema. *Providence's* daily rhythm re-established, we move across the ever-changing ocean, progress measured in the subtle shifting of the stars. The memories come to me, sometimes as dreams and other times not, the copper-skinned girl with the big dark eyes, and our mother as a young woman, always in sunshine, watching over us.

Six days after leaving the big cargo ship to her fate, the stranger takes his first limping walk about the cabin. Two days later he is able to sit with us at the saloon table for dinner. He is very quiet and eats ravenously, occasionally glancing at Fema, who glances back, her face reddening.

He says his name is Treyvon and that he is from Philadelphia in the US of A.

'What happened back there, Treyvon?' says Julie.

'I reckon you saw.'

'We did.'

'They came from nowhere,' he says, eyes on his plate. 'Crippled the ship with rockets.'

'Who was it?' I ask.

He shakes his head, chews his food. 'Didn't ask 'em.'

Julie glances at me, tilts her head.

He refills his glass and drinks the water down in one go. 'You get my gear?'

'No,' I say. 'We got you.'

'Thanks, man,' he says, pushing himself to his feet. 'Can I ask, where are you headed?'

'French Polynesia. If the winds hold, we'll be there in a few days. We can leave you there if you like.'

'That would suit me fine,' he says before limping off to his cabin.

Over the next few days we make rapid progress, passing sunken atolls curved and pale as sky against the darker blue of the abyss. Treyvon and Fema are spending more and more time together, sitting next to each other on the foredeck with Leo for hours at a time as *Providence* cuts through the sparkling sea. We can hear their voices and occasionally a ring of laughter from Fema. Treyvon does endless pull-ups in the pulpit and once his leg can handle it, push-ups on the forward deck. He eats copiously and seems to be gaining muscle before our eyes. I find his presence increasingly unsettling.

Fema tells Julie that Treyvon fought with the US army during the later stages of the civil war in the late forties and was discharged after being wounded. All of his family are gone, and he joined a shipping company as a security guard. She likes him and he likes her. Over the days, they have come to know each other well enough to see that they have a future together. He has asked her to come with him, and she is thinking about it. She wanted Julie to know.

'I told her to follow her heart,' Julie tells me. 'Life is short.'

Five days later we make landfall on Taha'a island. Bora Bora is only a few miles away. We navigate a passage through the outer reef and anchor in Ruutia harbour. Forested mountains rise from the sea around us. The only signs of habitation are a few small docks and a couple of ramshackle houses visible through the trees.

Julie and I and Leo row to shore, leaving Fema and Treyvon on board. We tie up at the dock. After so long at sea we stagger like drunks, laughing as we sway and totter. At the end of the dock is a dirt road that runs parallel to the shore, and beyond, a house with a broad tin roof and some grass in front. The place looks deserted.

We come to a place where the bay narrows and the road splits off into a boat ramp and, adjacent, a wood-plank dock with a few wooden dories floating nearby. Landward, a windowless weatherboard building hulk in the sun. There are no signs or markings on the building.

'Sandrine Boat Builders,' says Julie. 'That's what Captain Hargreaves said. Do you think this could be it?'

'I'm going to find out.'

Julie takes Leo back to the dock, and I walk up the white coral drive towards the main building. The drive is lined with red flowering hibiscus. Twin doors large enough for a vehicle to pass lie ajar. The smells of wood oil and fresh-cut timber flow through the gap, and the air inside is cool. I can hear the trade winds rattling the roof iron. I push the door open enough to pass through, step inside and call out, my eyes adjusting to the dark. The ribbed skeleton of a timber-frame boat sits up on trestles, the far wall hung with hand tools above a long workbench with vices and a hand lathe and several drill presses. I walk towards the back of the building and call out again.

'I'm looking for Freyja. My name is Kweku Abachwa.' I wait but there is only the sound of the surf breaking on the reef and the breeze in the palms.

I check the other buildings, peer through a window into a small office, the desk strewn with papers and ledgers, another building that looks like a storehouse, the gravel pathways between set with empty olive-oil tins sprouting flowers and clay pots and basins overflowing with tomato plants and bright-red chillies. I return the way I've come and walk back to the dock where Julie and Leo are sitting with their legs dangling over the side.

I sit next to Julie. 'Couldn't find anyone,' I say.

Leo points. 'Look at all the fish, Daddy. Tomorrow I am going to bring my rod.'

When we get back to *Providence*, we find Fema and Treyvan asleep together in Fema's bunk. The door to her cabin is open and they obviously haven't heard us climb aboard. Treyvan grins, broad-toothed, and Fema reddens as she pulls the sheet to her chin and reaches for the door and closes it quietly.

Later that afternoon they go ashore, and by nightfall they still aren't back.

We put Leo to bed and Julie makes tea, and we sit in the cockpit together and watch the stars rise over the island and the reef.

'I'm happy for her,' says Julie.

'It's been good having her around.'

'Yes, it has. But now we're going to have to cope on our own, just as we did before.'

I am about to answer when a voice skips over the water. '*Providence*?'

We turn in the direction of the voice. A wooden rowboat floats a few metres off our stern quarter. In the starlight we can make out one person only aboard.

'This is she,' I call back.

'You came by our place. Are you looking for someone?' A woman's voice, or a boy's.

'Yes, I did. We are looking for Freyja.'

The sound of the surf on the reef, and then after a moment: 'Do you have something for me?'

I give the recognition code. The voice replies: 'A lost fable five times never told.'

Freyja stands about five feet tall and can't weigh more than forty-five kilos. In the darkness, her eyes seem very large and there are deep hollows in her cheeks that catch the shadow so that in the starlight she takes on the aspect of a yet-living inmate of some hunger camp.

Julie pours her a mug of tea and she sits with us in the cockpit.

'We need to go to Bora Bora,' I say.

She frowns. 'Now that is a very dangerous place. Why, may I ask, would you want to go to that God-forsaken hell hole?'

I tell her the story, all of it. 'If Becky is there, I want to get her out. We are not leaving here without her.'

Freyja sips her tea, considers this. 'And your sister? Twenty-eight years is a long time.'

'So is twelve months.'

She tilts her head to one side. 'So it is. A lifetime.'

'Can you help us?'

'I can get you there, but we can't stay long, a few hours at most. The longer we stay the higher our chance of detection.' She thinks about this for a time. 'There might be a way. How important is it to you?'

I open my hands. 'What can I say? I've told you the story. I suppose it's of no significance whatsoever to the world, but it's everything to me. To us.'

Freyja smiles. It is just her eyes that do it, but it changes her countenance wholly. 'That's good enough for me,' she says.

'We can pay.'

Freyja lifts her hand. 'This is a no-pay service,' she says. 'Let me do some checking. We'll go tomorrow night, if I can arrange it. One of you only.'

December 2036

With Bragg gone, the election went ahead. LeJeune won the biggest majority in living memory, and his youth party took commanding positions in the House and the Senate. The way was open for rapid reform, and LeJeune took it. Within weeks of being sworn in, on a sunny, smoky day in August, new legislation taxing carbon and diverting the proceeds into renewable energy projects was in place. Huge areas were set aside for natural regeneration, and national parks – which under previous administrations had been eaten away piecemeal for mining and oil exploration and new highways and tourist developments – were slowly reconstituted. Huge new climate-adaptation projects were started, including building seawalls, re-establishing coastal wetlands, and re-greening cities to keep them cool. Everything that had needed to be done back in the beginning of the century for prevention was now being implemented as cure. And what they were finding is that it was way, way more expensive, and way harder to fix something after it broke than to prevent it from breaking in the first place. Sorry, but duh. Facepalm.

In the end, LeJeune and Ashworth and their advisers decided not to release any of my diary publicly. They were using the information I was providing to position against Alpha Omega, and they didn't want to blow my cover. Not yet. Once they did, I knew that I would be marked. And the mark would be termination. I also knew that the Boss's network was still dangerously active. In many ways, they were more powerful than ever, with these inexperienced youth governments struggling to keep civilisation from flying apart, still coming to terms with the scale of the problems they had inherited. Be careful what you ask for, you might just end up getting all of it dumped on you at once.

I was kneeling in the Boss's office when they burst in. The sound of the door being smashed open was so loud I bumped my head on the top of the desk. I could see at least a dozen booted feet moving towards us, the Boss yelling while he tried to hike up his pants. Me, I just curled up and stayed there under the desk, hoping no one would notice me, the bimbo airhead personal assistant cocksucker. So much for over-throwing the patriarchy, right?

Anyway, they did find me, and with knowing smiles flashed between them, the cops led me and the Boss down to the street and into the back of a truck, and a few minutes later we were in separate adjoining cells in a lockup somewhere in Newark.

The Boss was standing within touching distance of the cell bars, but seemed to be resisting the temptation of reaching out and grabbing a bar in each fist. He wasn't going to give the bastards the satisfaction that the gesture would surely relay, nor was he willing to acknowledge the barrier that was holding him there. That's the way he was.

After a while, a middle-aged man in a dark suit and tie arrived and stood outside the Boss's cell. A uniformed agent was beside him. 'I'm Special Agent Tresscott,' he said.

'About goddam time,' the Boss said. 'I've been promised a call and I want it now.'

'Open them up,' Tresscott said to the uniform.

'Did your checking?' said the Boss.

'Follow me.'

The Boss winked at me and I followed him, and he followed Tresscott, down a corridor into a cramped office. Tresscott sat behind his desk and we sat in two chairs facing him.

The Boss rocked back in his chair. In the harsh fluorescent light, he looked older than he did back at the office, his eyes not quite so piercing, his brow gullied in a way I hadn't really noticed before.

Tresscott slammed an old push-button phone down on his desk. 'One call, Mister Argent.'

The Boss reached for the receiver, but as he did Tresscott grabbed his wrist and tightened down. I could see the Boss struggling, but the guy was strong.

'I don't know how you've done it, Mister Argent,' he said. 'Contacts in high places, obviously. But I can tell you this, I'm not going to make this easy for you. The charges may have been dropped, but you're not going to get away with it. I'm going to make damn sure of that.'

The Boss relaxed his arm and leaned in towards Tresscott so that he was staring right into the other man's eyes. That's what he did. He let him see what was inside. And no shit, it was enough to break most men. 'You don't look that much younger than my wife, Tresscott,' he said, steady. 'Mid-forties?'

'Young enough that I couldn't vote when you bastards should all have known better.' Tresscott released his grip and they separated like two fighters at the bell. 'Old enough to know a criminal when I see one.'

The Boss picked up the handset. 'The depth of your hypocrisy cannot be measured, Agent Tresscott. Think because you have a badge that it changes a thing? You're just a cog, a very small and compliant part of a machine that I run. I am going to make sure you never work again.'

Tresscott closed his eyes, ran his hand across the stubble on his jaw. All the energy seemed to have drained out of him. 'Just make your call.'

The Boss punched in a number, ran his gaze over the newspaper that lay half folded on Tresscott's desk. I could hear the landline click, ring, then connect.

'Yeah, Boss?' came the voice. Paolo.

'It's me.' Lagos destroyed.

'Code in.'

'Fuck you.' Millions perish.

Silence for a moment, and then: 'What's up, Boss?'

Tresscott was standing within earshot, watching him. The Boss covered his mouth, lowered his voice. 'I'm in custody. Some place in Newark.'

'I heard.'

'Fix it.' Calls for immediate ceasefire. 'Then have Max come and get me.'

'We got the charges dropped, but this…' I could hear from his voice that Paolo was deeply stressed. He always got that way when the Boss asked him to do things he figured the legal team should be handling.

'But what?'

'Well, it seems it's local. You'll have to try to deal with it there.'

'Fuck.'

Dead space on the line, and then Paolo saying: 'Boss, there's something you need to know. Singh is dead. Shot through the head outside his house this morning.'

'Get Samantha to cover.' Leaders call for calm.

'You got it, Boss. Don't worry.'

'Good. One more thing.'

'Listening, Boss.'

'Whatever happens, the plan continues. No deviations. Keep going for as long as you can. I'll get back to the office as soon as I deal with these pecker heads.'

'Understood.'

The Boss put down the phone, leaned back in his chair, stared at the man across the desk. 'You married, Agent Tresscott? Got kids?'

Agent Tresscott pulled out a cigarette, lit it, and blew a stream of smoke ceilingward. 'None of your business what I've got. Get up.'

The Boss stayed where he was, signalled me to do the same. 'You're an intelligent man, Tresscott. I can see that. You know what's happening here.' He glanced at the newspaper. 'You *understand*.'

Tresscott planted both fists on the desk and leaned toward us. 'Why, Argent? That's what I'd like to know. It was so clear what was happening, even back then. So why persist? You could have changed direction, found a way to do some good.'

The Boss stared back. 'I can't change the past. I did what I did. The question is, what do we do now? Or more specifically, what do *you* do now?'

Tresscott took a long draw on his cigarette, narrowed his eyes.

'It's going to get very difficult, very soon, Special Agent Tresscott. I can help you and your family get through it.'

Tresscott examined the burning end of his cigarette a moment. 'What exactly do you think is going on here, Mister Argent?'

'Enlightenment, Agent Tresscott. That's what I *know* is going on here.'

'I haven't heard that word in quite a while.'

'No.'

'So, enlighten me.'

'You don't need me for that, Tresscott. You already know. The question you have to ask yourself is, what are you going to do about it?'

Tresscott took another drag on his smoke. 'You're right, Mister Argent. I do know. I've known for a long time. That's why I'm still here, sitting with you now. It's the reason I haven't taken you out back and put a bullet through your head.'

The Boss smiled that fuck-you smile of his. 'But you know that's what's coming, don't you? Exactly that, on a grand scale.'

'Perhaps. I hope not.'

'Look around you.'

Tresscott frowned. 'I've been a cop for twenty years, Mister Argent.'

'So, you know. It isn't abstract.'

'No.'

'But you've never seen anything like what's coming.'

Tresscott glanced at the newspaper, shook his head. 'None of us have.'

'The offer stands, Special Agent Tresscott. Now's your chance. What are you going to do?'

Tresscott broke eye contact, turned his head away, stood looking towards the west-facing windows and the darkened streets beyond. He remained like that for a long time, the cigarette between his right index finger and thumb slowly burning down, fighting that never-ending battle, waged in darkness, the one that you can never fully share. The one that tells you, finally and forever, who you really are.

Finally, Tresscott broke free of his trance, turned and faced us. 'Here's what I am going to do, Mister Argent. I'm going to keep doing my job. Despite everything that's happening, I'm going to do my duty.' He pinched the filter of his smoke and flared away the last of the tobacco, then stubbed out the butt in an ashtray. 'I'm going to let the two of you go. I can't hold you. Not legally. And then I'm going to spend whatever time I have left making sure people like you get what they deserve.'

Max picked us up twenty minutes later and we were back at the penthouse drinking champagne in time to see the sunset.

Akua

Freyja sits at the tiller, her face obscured in star shadow as the little boat slips quietly through the gap in the reef. Crates of coconuts and bananas piled to the gunwales barely leave room for the two of us. In the darkness I can just make out *Providence* snug in the little bay, and below us the pale, living rock of the coral. Clear of the reef, Freyja sets course northwest, the first spray hitting my face as she increases speed, the electric motor humming beneath us. Fifteen miles away, Bora Bora's volcanic spire hulks above the star-strewn ocean.

I rub the place on my forearm where a few hours before, Freyja implanted a microchip. Bora Bora is under heavy and almost continuous surveillance, she explained. Drones patrol regularly and a network of sensor arrays and cameras covers most of the island. Everyone who lives there or visits has to be chipped. She does a regular run selling fresh produce and hand-crafted boat parts to the community. When I ask about the chip, all she says is that it belonged to someone who doesn't need it anymore.

'I made some enquiries yesterday,' Freyja shouts over the wind and spray. 'A friend has a contact who may know something about your sister. If she agrees to help, she will meet us tonight.' She pauses. 'And here's the really good news. Your niece is definitely on the island. We are going to try to get her out. It's all set. But you must understand that we will all be taking a big risk, especially your niece.' She shows me a small device that looks like a mobile phone. 'When the time comes, you are going to have to make the call. We are only going to get one shot at this.'

By now I am shaking with adrenaline. 'I understand.'

'Breathe,' she says.

I do. 'What about that,' I ask, pointing at the cargo.

'The fruit is in case we are spotted. At least we'll have a story. But the idea is to get in undetected. There are blank spots in the sensor coverage, and the drones have regular routes. I've done it before. We meet my contact about your sister, and then we make the call about Becky. If we are able to get them out of the palace, and we decide to go, then all hell will break loose. So be ready. Don't freak on me. Stay cool.'

All I can do is nod and hope that I will stay calm when the time comes. 'And if we find them, can we get them out?'

'We'll cut out their chips and leave the way we came in.' Freyja shrugs. 'That's the plan, anyway.'

Two hours later we can see the phosphorescent arc of the surf on the outer reef and the island rising buttressed and fortress-like within. A new moon is rising in the east, its pale light scattering shards across the dark ocean and the flanks of the mountaintop. A few faint lights flicker halfway up the spire, along the rim of a long cliff.

'That's where the palace is,' Freyja says, slowing the boat. 'Where the Eminence and his harem live.'

'Jesus.'

'Most of the senior advisers and functionaries also have their own, smaller harems. This island is eighty percent female. And lots of kids. They're busy breeding their new society. That's why they need to import food.'

'Do they tattoo everyone?'

Freyja rolls up her sleeve. 'You mean like this?' The Alpha Omega symbol, the one Elvira and her family were marked with, there on her wrist.

'You, too.'

Her mouth crimps, jagged in the shattered moonlight. 'I am one of the few that have managed to escape.'

'And you stay so close, and keep going back?'

'Let's put it this way: you're not the only one who's lost someone.'

If she wants to tell me she will. 'And what happens if we're caught?'

'Before, if they believe our story, they let us on our way.'

'And after?'

'They take us as slaves, or they kill us. Me, they'll probably kill. Not sexy enough. You, a slave probably. Work you to death.'

'Nice.' All of this I try to lock away so one day I can write it.

Freyja points to a place where the reef joins a narrow spit. The tide is almost high and the surf over this part of the reef is much reduced.

'Piti Aau,' she says. 'We'll cross the reef there. There's a little hook where we can hide the boat. Then we swim to the main island.' She looks up at me. 'I hope you can swim.'

Soon we are across the reef and around the end of the spit. Freyja beaches the boat and we jump into the water and pull the boat up the sand, covering it with palm fronds. Freyja peels off her jacket, revealing a top that hugs her wiry contours. 'Okay, now we swim. Follow me and stay close. Stay quiet. There are sharks, but they won't bother us.' And with that she is into the water and powering ahead in an elegant, almost-silent crawl.

I grew up in the water, swam as soon as I could walk, before actually. But this woman is a fish. Buoyant and with a small surface area, she slides through the water without effort, her feet flicking like a tail. I follow as best I can, tracking her wake, pushing up a bow wave that makes me feel like a barge in comparison. I am making far too much noise.

By the time we reach the main island, I am breathing hard. We slide out of the water and walk up the sand into a grove of palms. The moon is higher now and sends long shadows spearing across the sand. Water drips from my body and the salt stings my eyes and the places where the lagoon coral has nicked my skin. My heart is pumping at twice its normal rate and the noise of it fills my ears.

'Follow me,' whispers Freyja, setting off into the trees.

I follow her to a place where the palms end and there is a rocky outcrop and dense jungle foliage spilling over. It is very dark, and the way underfoot is littered with thorns and sharp rocks and fallen fronds that bite into my bare soles. She climbs up through a channel in the rock to a ledge where we can see back out over the lagoon, bright now in the risen moon with the white of the surf on the reef crest and the dark water of the Pacific beyond.

'We wait here,' she says, looking at the hands of her watch. 'If she's not here by two, we start back.'

Towards one-fifteen we hear the whine of a drone and crouch in the undergrowth as the thing flies past, its little red operating lights flashing in the darkness. By one-thirty Freyja is getting restless, checking her watch every few minutes, and I am starting to worry. Another quarter of an hour creeps by.

'Come on,' I hear her mutter under her breath.

I think of Becky, ripped from her mother's arms, brought halfway around the world. I can't even imagine the terror she must have felt. I think of Akua, of all the years that separate us, of the bifurcation in our lives that happened here. I think of this woman putting her own life at risk so that I can be here, on this island where Papa stopped recording his log entries so long ago, not to begin again until a year and a half later. Enough time for a little girl to disappear, for her life to change irrevocably and for her to forget, as I had, all of her short existence before.

There is a rustling of vegetation next to us.

'Freyja,' calls a voice in the hushed, strangled tones of fear. 'Is that you?'

'Camille.'

A woman emerges from the foliage. She is petite, with long dark hair. 'Sorry I'm late,' she says. The two women hug.

'We don't have long,' says Freyja. 'This is Kweku, the one I told you about.'

The woman called Camille inclines her head. I can see in the moonlight that she is very pretty, with an oval face of striking symmetry. 'How old are you?' she says.

I tell her.

She looks me over, runs her hand through my hair. 'There was a girl called Akua who came to the island many years ago. She was three years old.'

'Yes,' I say, the words catching in my throat. 'That would be right. Is she still here?'

'She is.'

It feels as if my chest will explode. 'Can I—' I begin, too loud.

'Quiet!' Camille cuts me short.

'Can you take me to her?'

'Yes, but you won't like it.'

I shake my head. 'What do you mean?'

'She is buried not far from here. She died two years ago.' Camille hands me a small metal tube with a cap on one end. 'As much as we can tell you about her. One of her friends wrote it for me.'

I pocket the tube, still in shock. 'What about Rebecca?'

Camille looks at Freyja. 'She's ready. But we are going to need a diversion to get her out.'

Frejya reaches into her shorts and pulls out the device I'd seen her with before. 'Your decision,' she says, her thumb hovering over a red button. 'No way back once we start this, you understand? Your niece is here, she is safe and healthy. They keep them that way, for obvious reasons. Once we do this, there are no guarantees. She will be in danger.'

I look Freyja in the eyes, take a deep breath. I know exactly what Lewis would have wanted. 'Do it.'

Freya pushes the button. A moment later a series of bright flashes lights up the horizon. Four burning stars streak up into the sky trailing comet tails, red against the night sky. We watch them arc up and then start a gentle downward curve. They are coming straight for us.

'Come on,' says Freyja, moving away into the bush. We follow her until she comes to a dirt track. She stops, looks both ways, and then starts away down the path at a sprint. Camille and I race after her in the moonlight. Moments later the jungle lights up in a blinding flash that sends crazed phosphorous shadows hurtling over us, and then another and again in quick succession and then the shock wave thunder of the detonations that stun our ears and leave us gasping for breath.

'That's it,' says Frejya, 'just up ahead. The rendezvous point.'

We run on through the stunned aftermath, the wail of sirens now reaching out over the island, the glow of fires starting to gather momentum up on the mountainside. We continue on through the fire-stained jungle until we reach a small hut where the path splits.

'Wait here,' says Camille. 'If they've made it out, they'll be here soon.'

In the fires' glow I can see Freyja checking her watch. 'If they're not here in twenty minutes, we have to leave. The tide is starting to ebb.'

After all this time, after so many miles, to have it come down to just this. I check my watch, scan the path. Ten minutes creep by. The fires have intensified and from up the hill we can hear the roar of the flames and the shouts of those trying to control it. Drones zip above us like angry insects. Surely if they are fitted with infrared detectors, they will have spotted us. How we are going to get back to the boat and across the reef I have no idea.

Another five minutes go by.

'I'm going to see what's happened,' says Camille. She kisses Freyja and runs off down the path.

Time ticks down. Three minutes left. Two. Jesus, she's not coming.

Freyja puts her hand on my shoulder. 'I'm sorry,' she says. 'We have to leave.'

'Five more minutes,' I say. 'Please.'

'We aren't going to be able to get the boat over the reef. We'll be stranded here. You don't want that, believe me.'

'What about Becky?'

'We're just going to have to hope that the diversion has created enough confusion up there that the people who are helping us can protect her, and themselves. Come on.' Freyja starts back down the way we came.

I take a last look back down the path and shake my head. None of it seems real. Then I turn and follow Freyja, stumbling along, half blind, dumb, mute, every emotion I've ever felt heaving there inside me, over-whelming me.

We reach the beach and Freyja looks across the lagoon to where we've hidden the boat. She wades into the water. 'Let's go.'

I follow her. We are waist deep and about to launch ourselves in when a voice reaches out to us from the trees. We turn. Camille is there. There is a bright cut across her forehead. She is holding a small bundle in her arms. She staggers to the water's edge, and thrusts the bundle at Freyja. 'Go,' she says. 'They are coming.'

Freyja looks at the bundle, passes it carefully to me. From within a dark blanket, two eyes peer out at me, big like the eyes of an owlet waiting for her mother's return. It's Becky, my darling little Rebecca, trembling in fear.

'It's me, Becky,' I say to her. 'Uncle Kweku. I'm here to take you home. Do you understand?'

She gazes up at me and I can see that she doesn't understand, and there is only fear in those huge, innocent eyes. It's going to take time, and time is the one thing we don't have.

Camille hugs Freyja and runs off into the jungle. Freyja takes the device and looks at me and presses the red button. Two more flashes light up the horizon. 'Let's go,' she says. 'She's going to have to swim.'

And then she is in and powering across the lagoon. I unwrap Becky and put her on my back and fold her arms around my neck. 'Hold tight, Becky. You're going to have to hold on as tight as you can and not let go.'

I can feel her arms cinch up around my neck.

'Good girl.' I wade into the water and push off. 'Here we go. Keep your head up, sweetheart. Breathe.' I can feel the warmth of her there on my back, her little arms like a vice around me, the tremors flickering through her body. Two huge explosions erupt on the hill and the sound crashes over us like a wave. It is as if the volcano has awakened. Flame and smoke pour into the night sky. Screams fill the air. The water of the lagoon shimmers red in the flamelight.

I swim as fast as I can, breast stroke so that I can keep Becky's head out of the water. Freyja is well ahead and reaches the shore and darts behind the headland.

'Almost there, Becky,' I say, breathing hard.

As I swim I can feel her head moving slowly, up and down, a little nod against the back of my neck.

September 2037

All through '36 and the first months of '37, the pressure on the Boss and his businesses was unrelenting. Paolo was going crazy trying to manage all the new taxes the LeJeune government was hitting us with, taxes on carbon, as promised, but on every other kind of environmental and social harm caused by our activities, too. The Boss fought back everywhere he could, and the wife was busier than ever, filing a new law suit against the government almost every day so that the courts were so clogged up she said that it would take a hundred years for all the cases to be heard.

With the new tax on luxury jets and aviation fuel, Bryce was flying less than ever and the Boss even decided to sell one of the G900s. He was supremely salty when Paolo told him how much he'd got for it. We all just sat there and let him rage.

Not long after that Bryce took Ruby and me out on the boat. It was a weekend and the weather was fine, just like autumn used to be. By then it was pretty well known in the organisation that we were a couple, and we had given up hiding it. We weren't overt about it at work, but Bryce had moved in with me and we pretty much spent every weekend together. The Boss had cooled on me again by then, thankfully, and I promised myself and Bryce that I wouldn't go back to being his whore. No matter how important the information I was proving was, I'd had enough.

After hearing about Lagos, the first city to be destroyed by a nuclear weapon since Nagasaki, and then Marseilles shortly after, we'd decided that we weren't going to wait any longer to start our real life together. They could do to us what they wanted. We'd both saved up enough so that we could get by, and Bryce had his dad's place up in Ontario if we needed to hunker down and go survivalist. By then Bryce was convinced that it was coming to that, and had set about preparing. He was going to make sure, he told me one night, that whatever happened, the three of us would be able to survive. Live out whatever was coming. And you know, I believed him.

We'd had a nice picnic on the boat. Ruby was growing fast and she loved being out on the water, and loved to swim. It was everything we could do to keep her from throwing herself into the water whenever she could. We were all sitting in the cockpit, tootling away on a nice easy reach, when Ruby pointed to the eastern sky.

'What's that, Mommy?' she said.

We both looked to where she was pointing. It was just after noon, but the eastern horizon was blushing a strange shade of yellow-green. We sat there watching. The colouring was faint at first, and as we watched it slowly intensified and spread towards us. Soon half the sky was the colour of puke.

'Holy shit,' said Bryce. 'Is that what I think it is?'

'It's getting bigger, Daddy,' said Ruby. And it was.

Bryce hardened up the sails and we headed back to shore as quickly as we could. By the time we reached land the sky was green for as far as we could see and we didn't know it at the time but it would stay that way for the next ten years.

When we got back to the car, we heard on the radio that the Chinese had unilaterally decided to implement global, large-scale atmospheric seeding with sulphur-dioxide, in a last-ditch attempt to cool the planet. Genius.

Rebecca

Becky clings to my back as if she will never let go. We pull the boat down to the water and Freyja starts the engine and we get in and soon we are around the hook and across the reef and speeding our way back to Taha'a. Behind us, the island that bears my sister's grave burns, and above us the stars shine bright through the smoke.

Neither of us speaks as the island sinks into the horizon behind us and another rises up before us. We look back, but there is no sign of pursuit.

'They will not risk coming after us now,' Freyja says.

I hold Becky close. 'We are very grateful to you,' I say.

'Thank the US navy. That was them out there tonight.'

I breathe silent thanks to Becky's uncle.

'I'm sorry about your sister,' Freyja says. 'That place is a graveyard. So many good people buried there.' And then a long silence, just the sound of the boat moving through the water. 'What will you do now?'

'Go home. Try to find a way to live. Raise our kids. Try to tell these stories so people know what happened, so they can learn, and hopefully we can find a way to make this all work.'

'That's a good plan,' she says. 'I like it.'

'What about you?'

'I'll keep doing what I do.'

'For her, that person you talked about?'

'I didn't say her.'

I ask her about her home and how she has come to be here and to be doing what she does, but she just waves this away and won't be drawn in.

It is dawn by the time we pass through the gap in the reef. *Providence* is there at anchor as we left her. Freyja pulls alongside and I jump aboard, Becky in my arms. I tread lightly so I won't wake those sleeping below deck. I stand in the cockpit and wave as Freyja motors up the little harbour and past the submerged rocks of the point and pulls in at her dock.

It is then that I notice that *Providence's* dinghy isn't tied up in its usual spot astern. Nor is it stowed atop the cabin. I scan the shore and spot it pulled up on a notch of sand halfway to Freyja's dock. Someone has gone ashore.

I am holding Becky in my arms, and Akua's story in my head. I want to share it all first with Julie, and then maybe later, when it is not so raw and unforgivingly immediate, I will try to write it. I carry Becky below and sit her on the settee and pour her some water and watch her drink it down. Morning light shines through the portholes, yellow and clean, lights up her little face. The ship breathes easy on her rode. I open the door to our berth and look inside. Rumpled bedding, pillows folded up against the bulkhead, books lining the shelf, this place so familiar. But no Julie. She must have gone ashore for supplies.

I walk forward and open Leo's cabin. It is empty also. I call out for Fema, but she doesn't answer. I knock on Treyvon's cabin door but it swings open to reveal another empty bunk. They are all together. Good. Or maybe Fema and Treyvon have already gone their own way. I check the strong box where I put Treyvon's AK and sidearm and chest rig, and find it secure. I will leave a note and swim to shore with Becky and try to find them.

I ruler a strip of paper from the back of the log book and start to write a note for Julie in case she returns when I am out looking for her. I am halfway through when a loud thump echoes through the ship. The dinghy bumping *Providence's* hull. They're back. I jump up and stick my head out of the gangway, but there is no dinghy. I am still there looking around the harbour when I hear it again, two thuds in quick succession. It's coming from below, forward. I jump down and go to Fema's cabin and throw open the door. There she is, lying on her side, trussed and gagged. Her eyes scream out at me as she works her jaws around the gag, moaning in frustration. Julie.

I grab my knife and cut away the gag. She splutters and chokes as I pull it from her mouth.

'Leo,' she croaks. 'He's taken Leo.'

The words hit me as if fired from a gun. 'What?' I stammer. 'Who did?'

'Treyvon, that monster.'

'When?'

'Last night. Not long after you left. He and Fema. He has your gun.'

I start cutting Julie free, guilt running riot. Her wrists and ankles have been tied together, her legs folded back behind her so her hands are almost touching her feet. The rope work is comprehensive and expert, and it takes me a long time to cut it away, the knife shaking in my hands as the reality of what she's told me punches through me, an overdose of adrenaline. After a while I have to stop and steady myself or risk cutting her.

When I finally sever the bond between her ankles and wrists she groans in pain as she unfolds and lies panting and covered in sweat as if in the throes of childbirth. 'We've got to find them, Kwe,' she breathes through the spasms.

I cut away the rope around her wrists, revealing red skin chafed through and bleeding from her struggle.

'He's Alpha Omega, Kwe. He told me so himself. He wasn't there protecting that ship, he was part of the boarding party. He said he was going to kill me but decided not to because I'd saved his life.' She gasps as I cut away the rope around her ankles.

I help her up and she hisses with the pain.

'Where did they go? Do you know?'

She shakes her head. 'No idea.'

I walk to the strong box and unlock it and pull out my AK47, slam in a magazine and take Treyvon's sidearm and his chest rig and put it all in a dry bag along with two lifejackets, then roll the bag closed with plenty of air. 'We have to swim,' I say.

It's then that Julie sees Becky. She staggers back, mouth wide.

'Say hi to your niece,' I say.

Julie bursts into tears and scoops Becky up in her arms and showers her with kisses. Becky looks mildly irritated.

'She has to come with us,' I say. 'More swimming, Becky, like last time, okay?'

She tilts her chin slowly down and then back up.

Julie lets go of Becky and gets her medical kit and her hat and water and some food and puts it all into another dry bag. When we get to shore, I pull out the rifle, snap a round into the chamber and thrust the pistol into my belt. Then I lower the chest rig over Julie's head and close the clasps at her side. She winces as I tighten the ballistic plate down hard across her breasts.

'Come on,' I say. 'I know someone who can help.'

March 2038

In February the Marshank-Watson Bill was finally passed. It was LeJeune's big policy initiative, and as a result, the Intergenerational Equity Commission was formed, and a new era of social justice began. That was the plan anyway.

The Boss's wife, Samantha Tyler-Argent, had led the Supreme Court challenge against the bill, but she'd failed at the last hurdle. Despite years of stacking the court with elderly conservatives, so many had died during the last few years that a whole new demographic was in place by the time it came to a vote.

If the Boss thought it was bad before, he was about to learn just how the rest of the world felt, what was left of it. The cost of responding to endless disasters, cope with rising sea levels and chronic food shortages was bleeding the Treasury dry. The gold standard had been re-introduced and every marginal deposit in the country was being mined as fast as they could blast the tunnels and leach the piles. But it wasn't enough, not even close.

'Fucking payback,' the Boss shouted at New York's skyline. 'That's what this is. A fucking reparations programme, just like 1919. That didn't turn out so good, did it?'

One by one we watched as his major assets were confiscated or closed down, the power stations, the oilfields. We employed an army of accountants and lawyers, directed mostly now by the wife, trying to stay as many moves ahead of the government as possible, moving funds, launching counter-suits, opening and closing shell companies, diverting accounts, nesting trusts within holding companies, making maximum use of the offshore banking system in friendly countries, places that blamed the USA for most of what was happening and for its blatantly colonialist response to the unfolding crisis, hiding in the complexity of a splintering global economic system. The wife, Sam, had managed to save a large portion of the value of the Boss's conglomerate, much of it now converted to gold, held in half a dozen countries, much of it in his new sanctuaries. But he'd lost a lot.

'And now this fucking relocation programme they've just announced,' he shouted. 'Can you fucking believe it?' He was laughing now, pitching hysterically between rage and mirth. 'They've even picked a date, a "cut-off date" they call it. If you were born before 1988, you're out.' He looked around at us, wild-eyed. 'That's right. You're out, Paolo. You too, Sam. They're going to confiscate all your assets and move you to so-called equivalent accommodation further south, where you can live out your life as a fucking pauper.' He looked right at me, held my gaze hard. 'Actually, I pity whoever has to stay behind in this fucking madhouse. It's time to go. Get the Gulfstream ready.'

That night Bryce and I agreed. Finally, after all these years of hiding and scraping and doing what we were told, it was time.

Freyja

She sits in the little office and crosses her hands in her lap. Tell me.

'He said he was going to sell the children.' Julie sounds as if she is being strangled. 'He laughed about it. I screamed at him, and he hit me so hard I fell down. He made me show him where we kept our gold. Kwe's gun was in there too. All that time Fema was sitting there with her arms around Leo, talking to him. Leo went after him when he hit me, but Fema grabbed him and pulled him to her.'

'Do you think she's in league with him?'

'I would never have believed that she could do anything to harm Leo.' Julie touches the bandage on her wrist. 'Maybe he's controlling her. Maybe she thinks she's in love. I don't know.'

'There's not much that happens on this island that we don't know about,' Freyja says, reaching into a drawer and withdrawing a small device, a phone of some sort, like the one I saw her use on Bora Bora. She touches a button and brings the device to life. 'This may take a while.'

We sit and listen as Freyja connects. We can hear the person's voice on the other end. The conversation is short, obviously coded, largely conducted in French. She shakes her head and starts again. Two more times she calls off and shakes her head. And then on the next, she stops and her eyes widen and she nods, listening to whoever is on the other end.

She turns off the phone and replaces it in the desk. 'They've been sighted in Ha'amene. It's not far from here. A black man and an Asian woman with a white boy. Hard to miss. He's been trying to arrange transport off the island.'

I stand. 'Let's go.'

'Hold on,' says Frejya. 'Last sighted he's with a man called Devereux. He owns a place up the hill from Ha'amene. He's Alpha Omega, and very dangerous. We are going to have to be smart about this.'

'We?'

'You don't think I'm going to let you do this alone, do you?'

'Please,' says Julie. 'We wouldn't want to—'

'On this there will be no discussion,' says Freyja before Julie can finish. 'Devereux is an unprincipled coward. It sounds like they both are. We'll use that against them.'

Freyja leads us to a shed where a number of bicycles are stored. There is even one with a child seat. I don't ask. We mount up, Becky with me, and set off along the dirt track towards Ha'amene. We cover the two and a half kilometres across the island in a few minutes and pass through the settlement and start up a steep hill. Near the top Freyja dismounts and pushes her bicycle into the forest at the side of the road. We follow her.

'From here, on foot.'

We follow a narrow trail, single file, up through screens of climbing, broad-leafed vines and huge trees that flare into a thick canopy high above. After a while we come to a clearing with a large, steel-roofed house at the far end.

'That's it,' says Freyja. 'We'll skirt the edge of the clearing from here. Stay out of sight, for now.'

Julie takes Becky's hand. I unsling my AK.

Freyja glances at my rifle. 'Do you know how to use that?'

'I do.'

'Good,' she says, pulling a square-barrelled black pistol from the pocket of her vest.

Soon we are close. We crouch in the underbrush, the house less than fifty metres away. Its broad veranda sweeps around three sides with a view across the island and out to the lagoon.

Freyja stands. 'Okay. Here we go. Follow me.'

We follow her out of the cover of the forest and across the open grass towards the house, Freyja walking as if she is on an afternoon stroll, unhurried and steady. When she reaches the veranda, she climbs the steps and walks in the front door. We follow her up and in.

'Monsieur Devereux,' she calls in a singsong voice, 'it's Beatrice.'

Noise from deeper in the house, and then footsteps approaching. A man in his sixties stands in a doorway. He is overweight with burst-blood-vessel skin and greying hair swept in wisps across a sunburnt pate. He looks at Freyja, at us, at the gun in Freyja's hand.

'Beatrice, always a pleasure.' He smiles unconvincingly, showing a row of uneven, yellowing teeth. 'But we are not until Wednesday, no?'

Freyja squirms, points her pistol at his chest. 'This is not a business call. I believe you have guests.'

The man seems unimpressed. 'As a matter of fact, yes. How is this of interest to you?'

'These are the parents of the boy. Bring him to us and we leave, no questions asked, and our meeting of Wednesday will procced as planned.'

A frown forms on his face, slowly as the calculus of the situation unfolds in his mind. I can see him thinking it through, his eyes darting towards Julie, to me and my AK, and then back to Freyja and her pistol.

'And if I were to agree, what would be to my advantage?' he says.

'Well, two things.' Freyja shifts her weight from one foot to the other. 'First, you get to maintain your happy relationship with me, and second, you get to retain the use of your balls.' She lowers her gun so it is pointed at his crotch.

He takes a step back, all that cool suddenly gone. 'I don't know the gentleman, I assure you. He came to me.'

'You share an affiliation.'

'A non-binding one, as you know.'

'I'm not sure your employer shares that view.'

'I was about to send them away.'

'I am sure you were.'

By now my patience has run out. My boy is in that house somewhere and these two are carrying on like a pair of old enemies met on a neutral street. I step forward, raise the AK. 'I want to see my son now or your balls won't be all you're missing.'

Devereux stumbles back. 'In there,' he stammers, pointing towards the back of the house. 'The kitchen.'

I push past Freyja, march down the corridor and kick the door open.

Leo is sitting at the table spooning something into his mouth, Fema beside him. Treyvan is leaning on the kitchen counter next to them with a beer in one hand and my handgun in the other. Empty beer bottles are scattered across the counter. Milk drips from the corner of Leo's mouth. Beyond, windows and a kitchen door leading outside.

I level the AK at Treyvon's chest. 'Put down the gun and move away from them.'

If he's surprised, he shows no sign. He stands, takes a swig of beer and places the bottle on the counter. 'Well, I reckon with your boy right behind me there's no way you're gonna shoot.'

Just then Julie appears in the doorway behind me, strapped into the vest, sweating, bandaged, holding Becky by the hand. 'Leo,' she cries.

'Mum,' Leo shouts.

'Stay right there, Doc,' says Treyvan, raising the pistol. 'Or I'll do what I should've done first go. Fema, you keep the boy right where he is so no one gets hurt accidental.'

Fema puts her arms around Leo and pulls him close. Leo's bowl spills and falls to the floor with a clatter. Becky starts crying.

'Just give me the boy and you can go on your way,' I say. 'I don't care what you do after.'

'Please,' cries Julie. 'Let him go. We'll give you whatever you want.'

Treyvon smiles and steps slowly back so that he is now standing next to Fema. 'I reckon I already got all you got to give.'

'There's more,' says Julie. 'I only showed you where we keep our ready-for-use. There's a lot more.'

Treyvon's eyes widen for a moment, a flicker, and then narrow again and then, so quickly we barely register the movement, he scoops up Leo in his free arm and presses the gun's muzzle against his temple. 'I don't believe you, Doc. Anyway, this here can bring more than I need.' He caresses my son's head with the gun's muzzle. 'So healthy and pretty.'

Julie is shaking now, every sinew in her body taut and shivering.

'Now we're just going to back out of here,' Treyvon continues. 'If you all try to follow, I promise you it won't turn out good. We'll find your boy a good home and you can be happy knowing he's alive. Come on, Fema.'

Fema stands next to him and they start stepping back towards the outside door, the muzzle of Treyvon's pistol still pushed into the side of Leo's head. Becky is screaming now, and Julie is trying to calm her, rocking her back and forth.

'Daddy,' says Leo, tears welling up in his big dark eyes.

Just then there is a flash of movement outside, and I see Freyja dart to the doorway. As she does, Treyvan wheels and crouches and fires. The kitchen window shatters and Becky lets out a high-pitched scream. In that moment I see Fema grab Treyvon's pistol so that her body is between Leo and the gun. They struggle a moment entwined and Leo is flung free. I charge, hitting Treyvon with a full body tackle, carrying Fema back with us. As the table collapses under us, the gun goes off and Treyvon wheezes as I land full weight on his chest, the AK between us. As we grapple I try to find his gun arm, but he is strong and experienced and I am tangled in my own weapon. He spins out from under me, reaches across Fema's motionless body. His gun must have been knocked free as we struggled. It is there on the floor, close. He lurches over Fema, stretching out his hand, reaching for the gun, a fingertip away. Just then Julie stamps her foot down hard on the gun and sweeps it away. Then she picks it up, and very calmly, as a surgeon might, she shoots Treyvon three times in the chest.

We find Freyja outside the kitchen, lying in the grass holding her side, blood pulsing up between her fingers, barely conscious. We carry her to the kitchen and lay her on the countertop, and Julie gives her morphine and cuts away her clothing and finds the place where the bullet entered and the exit wound, larger, just below her ribcage. Blood wells up and seeps from the holes. It seems impossible that so much blood can be brought forth from someone so small.

Leo and Becky huddle together in the corner, staring wide-eyed at the bodies of Treyvon and Fema leaking blood onto the tile, and I am thinking that I should move them to a place where they do not have to witness this carnage, but Julie shouts for me to boil water and look for towels and other means to staunch the flow of blood from Freyja's spasming body, so I leave them.

By the time Julie has debrided and disinfected the wound, cauterised the torn vessels and sutured the holes, the sun is low in the sky. Julie takes one of the bags of plasma from the kit Hargreaves gave her and sets up a drip. 'She's stable,' Julie says. 'But she can't stay here.'

I find Devereux in the front room. He is sitting in one of the armchairs with a cold drink, staring out of the window. There is a deep cut on his forehead, and when he sees me and the gun in my hand and the rifle slung over my shoulder and the blood covering my clothing he cries out and spills some of his drink.

'I had nothing to do with this,' he stammers, his voice trembling. 'It is not my affair. I have never seen these people before in my life.'

'It's okay,' I say. 'I know.'

His eyes widen and he reaches for the gash on his head, wincing as his fingers trace the damage. 'She hit me.'

'Do you have a car?'

'What? Yes. Behind the house.'

'I need it. Freyja's been wounded.'

'Who?'

'Beatrice.'

'That bitch. I should have killed her myself.'

'Where are the keys?'

He points to a table just inside the front door and continues sipping his drink.

I open the drawer. Inside there are some papers and an old watch and a small pair of binoculars and a handgun. 'No keys,' I say.

'Underneath.'

I reach under the table and grab the fob hanging from a hook.

'Be careful with it,' he says. 'It's the only one on the island.'

We carry Freyja to the car and lay her in the back. Julie sits next to her patient and the kids in the front with me. I'd driven a car only once before, in Albany when I was nineteen, and this one looked totally different, inside and out. I push what appears to be the start button and the instrument panel blinks to life. I move a lever set in the centre console to D, which I assume is drive, push the pedal and we are rolling.

It only takes a few minutes to reach Freyja's house. When we arrive, an older man is there to meet us. He touches Freyja's head and shows us to a ground-floor room where we lay Freyja on a bed.

I drive back, bury Treyvon and Fema in a small clearing behind Devereux's house. Devereux helps me. Then we sluice the blood from his kitchen floor. It takes us a long time and we work in silence. By the time we are done it is dark and a waxing moon has risen. We stand looking across the dark lagoon to the sea beyond.

'How is she?'

'She's lost a lot of blood, but my wife says she'll live.'

He takes a breath and lets it escape between pursed lips. 'Good.' He sees my reaction and says: 'We have an understanding. There are not many of us here, and we must all get along, whatever our apparent allegiances.'

I leave him there on the veranda and ride back to Ruutia.

Witnesses

The Hope

We arrive back at The Hope on September 13th, 2067, after a journey of 470 days that has taken us right around this troubled planet.

We tie *Providence* to her mooring, row to our little shingle beach, and climb the hill to Mum and Papa's house, the first one we built on that lonely shore, two years after we abandoned Akua in the Pacific. It is midday and the sun shines on the bay and parrots swoop and screech in the trees, and the sound of it and the blue water stretching across to The Hope are as they have always been.

Mother's vegetable garden lies untended, vines withered and brown, the faces of dead sunflowers pushed into dry, once-loved ground. I climb the wood-plank steps to the veranda where Papa liked to sit in the afternoons and look across the sound. Inside, the house is dark and still, and there are signs of mice and the leavings of lizards and other small creatures. I go back out to the veranda and wave to Julie. She is standing outside our house with the granite pillars behind and the ruins of our radio hut further up and beyond, the ridge where Papa and Mum and Lewis lie buried and further along the place where the bones of Mum's baby lie, shallow and bleached and re-buried.

Julie waves back and I watch the kids run down the hill towards Lewis and Mandy's home, built at the same time as ours, after the four of us returned from Albany newly married, each son to an orphan girl. I walk up the path towards our house, where Julie is waiting.

We hang on for a time, trying to re-establish our former lives. I work on this history, this complement to Papa's story, harvest the fruit that is ready, clear leaves and dead insects from the collection basin where our spring continues to bubble, clear and cool, as it has since the day we arrived, and fish the sound for dhufish and emperor. Julie clears the vegetable plots of stalk and resuscitates the plants that can be saved, seeds the ground anew. We take turns with the kids' lessons, walk evenings up to Chicken-Head Rock and look out across the sound to the far hills where Uncle Liberty's mob have their summer camp. Occasionally we see a thread of far-off smoke or catch a whiff of burning jarrah, or at night a faint glint of firelight.

'We should go,' Julie says one evening.

'We should.'

'Well then, let's do it. We can start tomorrow.'

I stand there looking across the water at the place I know the camp is.

'What's wrong, Kwe?'

I tell her it's nothing.

'It's your mum, isn't it?'

And though I deny it, I know she's right. We travelled so far to end up back here. We found Akua and we rescued Becky. And now we have our whole lives to live. But still, questions remain.

A week later I hide the guns and the gold in the safe store under our house, lock up *Providence*, and the four of us start the long walk to Uncle Liberty's summer camp. We set out early, before sunrise, when the air is still cool, and walk until lunchtime. Then we sleep under the shade of some windblown sheoak and continue on in the afternoon. Leo walks, uncomplaining. I carry little Becky on my shoulders most of the way, which I can tell she loves.

By dusk we are approaching the outskirts of the camp. We've just passed through a copse of ancient jarrah set in a protected valley behind the dunes, when we hear a familiar voice.

'Been a while, Born on Wednesday.'

Uncle Liberty's son steps out from behind the wind-shorn trunk of a greying tuart. He is naked except for a pair of faded shorts, in the manner of his father, and a big smile shines on his face.

'Born on Sunday,' I say. 'Sure has.'

We shake hands and he kisses Julie on the cheek, ruffles the kids' hair. 'You got her back. Good on you, Kwe. Always knew you would. Ripper.' He eyes the backpacks Julie and I are carrying. 'Planning on staying a while?'

'If you'll have us.'

'We'll make do.'

'We've missed you,' says Julie.

'Gone a long time,' he says. 'A lot's happened.'

'How is Uncle Liberty?'

'Sorry business. He asked for you. Always loved you. I shouldn't say it.'

I don't realise then just how hard it will hit me later.

That night I sit by the fire with Kwesi, watching our wives talking in the kitchen with the other women. I tell him about Akua, about some of what we learned. A while later Aunty Jennifer sits next to me. She's aged since I last saw her, and her hands seem very small and frail in mine.

'I'm sorry about—' I begin.

She pushes a bony finger to my lips. 'Hush,' she says. 'Don't say it.'

'I had a twin sister,' I say, pulling a rolled-up paper from the small metal cylinder Camille gave me that night on Bora Bora. 'I want you to read it,' I say.

Jenny unrolls the papers and reads. I know each word by heart, read it in my head with her. Akua was adopted by one of the original wives who was unable to bear her own children. Her childhood was a happy one and soon the memory of her previous life dimmed and then was lost altogether. She made friends, learned to read and write, and do work such as sewing and cooking, and she played games in the cool of the afternoons and swam in the warm water of the lagoon and ran along the beaches. Akua kept a pet tortoise and loved to look at the birds and the fish. She had a beguiling voice and would sing to the animals in songs of her own composition. By the time she reached puberty she had already been earmarked for childbearing. Akua was very beautiful with clear copper-coloured skin and big dark eyes. She was assigned to one of the senior administrators on the island. He was much older than her, but he treated her well and beat her only occasionally, and even then not harshly. She had her first child at sixteen, a little boy who died of fever before his first birthday. She had a baby girl three years later, who was named Calliope, and a boy two years after that, called Benjamin, both of whom were still living on the island. After her third child, another girl, Akua's relationship with her master began to deteriorate. As with so many of the deaths on the island, little was known of the circumstances around hers. She was buried in the servants' graveyard on the northern side of the island.

When she is finished reading, Jenny hands me back the scroll. There are tears in her eyes.

'Did Mum ever tell you about her, about what happened?'

'Your mother was the best friend I ever had, Kwe. Every time I needed her, she'd make the trek out here and stay as long as she had to. She was an amazing woman. What she went through.'

'How much did she tell you?'

'Everything.'

A cold shiver runs across the backs of my arms and through into my wrists and fingers. 'All of it?'

'Yes, Kweku. All of it.'

I sit a moment watching the flames burning up the hardwood. 'Why didn't you tell me before, when I asked you?'

'She made me promise a long time ago never to tell anyone what happened. And then with Becky being taken and you deciding to go after her, I thought it was the last thing you needed, all of that terrible past dredged up. It seemed better just to let it lie.'

I stare into the fire. 'You thought I wouldn't come back.'

'No, Kwe. No.' She was crying. 'But now your mum's gone and my husband too. You deserve to know.'

February 2039

'What's taking so long, God damn it?' The Boss paced the linoleum floor of the waiting room. Outside, on the apron, Bryce was getting the G900 ready to leave. I watched him walking through the drifting snow, collar up, checking the plane's undercarriage and wings and engines. When he was done, he crossed the apron and opened the door. A cold gust filled the room.

'Weather's turned bad, Boss,' he said. 'But we're fuelling up now. We should be airborne in forty-five minutes.'

'Did you switch out the transponder?'

'Yes, sir.'

'And the registration?'

Bryce pointed out of the window. 'Did it yesterday.'

'And the cargo?'

'Already loaded.'

The Boss grunted, looked at his watch. 'The bastards can have all of it. It doesn't matter now.'

'I'll file for Denver,' said Bryce. 'That won't arouse suspicion.'

'Do it. And Stephenson.'

'Yes, Boss.'

'We won't be coming back.'

'That was the deal, Boss. Understood.'

'Sure was.'

'Once we get into the mountains, we'll get low, disappear from the radar. If they're watching, it'll look like we went down. By the time they start looking, if they even bother, which I doubt they will, we'll be long gone.' Bryce threw me a look that said stay cool, zipped up his jacket and opened the door and walked out across the snow-streaked tarmac towards the plane.

The wife was bundled up in a handmade Inuit coat, holding a steaming cup of coffee between her hands. Outside, the snow was falling harder. Down in the valleys the rivers would be running wide and full. Through the flurry I saw the jet's navigation lights come on and then the landing light pulse twice. The signal.

'Let's go,' said the Boss.

Paolo and I zipped up our coats. The wife pushed up her hood.

'Are you ready for this, everyone?' the Boss said. 'A new beginning.'

'Is that what you're calling it?' said the wife.

The Boss took a step towards her and brought his face up to hers so that his chin was brushing the sable trim of her hood. 'You bet,' he said, loud enough so the rest of us could hear. 'Want to stay?'

Fear flashed in her eyes, just a pulse. 'Fuck you, Derek,' she said. 'Wouldn't miss it for anything.' She opened the door and started across the tarmac to the waiting plane.

'Damn right,' said the Boss. 'No way back now. Fucking assholes, all of them.' We weren't sure who he was talking to so we stopped and paid attention.

'All anyone ever had to do was take a look around,' he continued. 'But no. They needed to *hope*. So they believed what they were being fed, as if *belief* has ever changed a single God-damned thing.' He turned and walked out the door.

We followed him out to the waiting Gulfstream.

I was thinking: finally, after all these years. Not long now. And there was the plane, the cabin windows glowing warm in the darkening storm, Bryce up there at the controls, the engines whispering, ready to go, the airstrip empty, all the buildings shut down, the fuel and de-icing trucks gone now.

We followed the Boss up the stairs and into the cabin, brushed the snowflakes from our hair. Green, the co-pilot, was there to greet us. Paolo and the Boss and the wife took their seats, strapped in.

'Join us up front,' said Green.

I didn't look back, went into the cockpit, strapped into the jump seat, put on a pair of headphones and plugged in the jack. Bryce looked over his shoulder at me, winked.

Green strapped in and Bryce pushed the throttles forward. The engines surged and the aircraft started to roll. Outside, the snow had changed to sleet and it was coming down hard now. But inside the jet it was warm and bright. We taxied to the end of the runway, the last of the day's light slanting low through the sleet, this part of the high valley in shadow already.

Bryce slowed the jet, swung her through a 180-degree turn, lined up with the runway. The engines started to hum as he powered up, brakes on. Heavily loaded with cargo and fuel, at this altitude Bryce had told me that we would need every foot of runway.

'Ready, Boss,' Bryce said into his mic.

'Go for it,' said the Boss. 'Goodbye, losers.'

The engines screamed at full power as the jet started rolling, gaining speed, the wet tarmac flashing past. I could imagine the Boss settling back into his seat as the Gulfstream accelerated into the night, into the future, *his* future.

And then, suddenly, Bryce cut power. We were thrown forward in our seats. The jet yawed across the strip as Bryce jammed down on the brakes and hit the thrust-reversers.

The Boss's voice in my headphones: 'What the hell's going on up there?'

And then Bryce back: 'You'd better come up here, Boss.'

A moment later the cockpit door flung open and the Boss was standing there, staring past us out along the runway. Instead of the dark expanse of Montana night, the runway was crowded with red and blue flashing lights, at least three vehicles I could make out. And then, running towards us through the snow, half a dozen black-clad cops, armed.

'Shit,' muttered the Boss.

I could see the back of Bryce's neck tighten. He was smiling.

Daughters

Aunty Jennifer sits by the fire, head bowed. Kwesi is with us. Julie and I hold hands and wait. We have waited a long time, a little longer doesn't matter.

'I'll tell it to you just like she told me,' Jennifer says, head still bowed. It's as if she doesn't want to look up for fear that her best friend might appear there at the fireside, full of reproach.

'Teacher and Francoise and you three children entered the main lagoon at Bora Bora aboard *Providence* just over three years after leaving Argent's refuge in Belize. The twins were three years old and Lewis still a babe in arms. After so long at sea you were all enchanted by the island's beautiful reef and lush, green hills. It seemed a paradise. The local inhabitants, while cautious, were willing to trade, and your mum and dad stocked the boat with fresh fruits and vegetables. There were loads of fish and Teach fished the reef each day. The plan was to stay for only a few days. But after seeing so much devastation, the place was too good to leave. There was food and water and sunshine, and the chance to rest.'

Julie squeezed my hand. 'We know what that's like.'

'Soon days extended into weeks. Your mum and dad started to relax. They were happy. The kids were happy. And then one day, when Teach was spear fishing out on the reef, Francoise took the kids – you Kwe, Akua and Lewis – to the main island to swim. She was approached by a local who had food to trade. The woman led Francoise through the forest to a small house. Inside, the woman showed her shelves of preserves. They haggled for a while about the price. Francoise bought four jars and packed them into her bag, little Lewis on her hip and the twins playing outside. And then suddenly she heard you shout, Kwe, and there was a scream. She dashed to the door but by the time she got there you and your sister were gone.'

Jennifer goes quiet and leans forward, her elbows on her knees, arches her back and then stands. The orange firelight shines on her face. 'Forgive me,' she says. 'I cannot sit too long anymore. Everything starts to ache.' She shuffles stiff-legged around the fire a few times.

Kwesi leaves and reappears a few moments later with a jarrah-framed chair with a kangaroo-skin seat and places it by the fire.

'Thank you, Kwesi,' she says, settling into the chair.

'Your mum looked everywhere, calling out, running through the bush, checking all around the house. The old woman feigned ignorance but Francoise knew she'd been lured there, and she cursed herself and cursed the old woman, but she couldn't find you twins anywhere. She rowed back to *Providence* and told Teach what had happened. He got his gun and rowed back to the island. She didn't see him again for almost two years.'

I tell Jennifer of our experience on that same island, more than twenty years later. She smooths her long skirt across her lap and continues.

'Not long later, armed men came to the boat and took Francoise and Lewis. She was smart, your mum, and when she saw them coming across the lagoon, she managed to hide all the gold and the guns and ammunition, and anything else she couldn't bear to part with. At first, she assumed they were brigands, like ones they'd met before in other places, and that she would agree to pay some gold and her family would be returned. But she quickly realised that the currency here was not money or gold or goods, but souls. The way she told it to me, the people who ran the island had been observing them, and had decided that they liked what they saw. A tall, strong man, an attractive, fertile young woman with three exquisite children. Francoise was interviewed – that's the word she used when she told me about it – by the Eminence, the senior man on the island. She was stripped naked, inspected, and then when the Eminence was suitably aroused, told to pleasure him. She knew the lives of her children might depend on how well she performed, so she did what so many of us women have had to do – she pushed down her revulsion and made it the most sensual experience of this man's life.'

Jennifer stops, wipes the tears from her eyes. 'I'm sorry to have to tell you this. But this is what she told me, and you need to know the whole story.'

'Go on,' says Julie, reaching for her hand. 'Please.'

'She was taken into the Eminence's harem and allowed to keep her children with her. You and your brother and sister moved into quarters with her in the palace on the mountainside. The twins spent their days in a creche with the other children of the harem women. Francoise was very careful and adept, and managed not to fall pregnant, despite the increasing attention she attracted from the Eminence, who also began offering her to his two most senior lieutenants.

'As the months passed, she never stopped trying to find out what happened to Teacher, but none of the other women knew, or if they did, no one was telling, and none of the men she was with would tell her anything at all. And each day she would look out across the lagoon and see *Providence* there still at anchor where she'd left her, a mute reminder of her imprisonment and the hateful extortion that ensured her compliance. She feared the worst, and suffered, thinking of Lewis growing up without his father, and the twins having already lost their father and now the man who loved them as if they were his own.

'One of the men who she was now regularly required to serve was the Eminence's head of security. He was older than Francoise, and was very passionate and vigorous with her, but once his desire was sated, he was kind and accommodating. As the months went by, she realised that he was falling in love with her. She saw an opportunity, and did everything she could to promote these budding feelings in him. The other man that the Eminence allowed to use her was mean-spirited and ugly, and she started to fuel the fires of jealousy in her lover's heart, setting them against each other.

'As the head of security's love for her blossomed, and his resentment for his rival and for the Eminence grew, she started to introduce the idea of escaping the island together, so they could live only for each other. By then, the Eminence seemed to have become aware that something was changing in her demeanour, and started to restrict the head of security's access to her. Most nights now, Eminence would call for her himself, sending her back to her quarters in the early light of dawn.'

I sit staring into the fire. It is hard to hear. I think of poor Isabelle, tied to the same fate, still living it.

'What about Papa?' says Julie.

'He had become a labourer. All that time he had been working in the gardens and orchards and unloading the barges that sometimes came with supplies. He was also put to work building the huge electric fence that would eventually seal off the main part of the island from the small coastal area where the workers lived. By then he knew that Francoise was in the palace. Each day he went and worked on the fence and each day it closed around his family. He knew that if he was going to get them out, he would have to do it before the fence was completed.'

Jennifer pauses and stretches again, then stands and does another circuit of the fire. One of her daughters brings us mugs of steaming tea. Jennifer sips and gazes into the fire, and I can see her face in the flamelight and the sorrow in the creasing of her eyelids and the way the words catch in her throat.

'They were both working to the same purpose,' Jennifer says, 'without knowledge of the other. Teacher knew that his rifles were still aboard *Providence*. He'd heard that the men hadn't found anything of interest on board when they'd searched. And *Providence* was still there in the lagoon, where he'd anchored her all those months ago, perhaps waiting to be sold or used by one of the rulers. He had identified that there was only one fast patrol boat in the harbour. All he needed was to find out where Francoise and the kids were and how to reach them. He'd shoot his way out if he had to.

'By now, Francoise had realised that she was pregnant, and she was sure the baby was the Eminence's. But she told the head of security that the child inside her was his, that they needed to leave together. He agreed, and they started to make plans. They would leave aboard *Providence*, with the children. They picked the night of the next new moon, three weeks away. Francoise knew that she had to take this chance, even if it meant leaving Teacher behind. She knew that's what he would want. She started to prepare.

'Then one afternoon, two weeks before the planned escape, while she was dozing in her quarters, Lewis asleep in his cot beside her, you and your sister at the creche, there was a knock at the door. Francoise opened it. One of the servant women, plain-looking and haggard, stood in the hall.

'"Please, Mistress Francoise, I must speak with you," she said.

'Francoise opened the door and the woman stepped inside. "I have a message for you," she said. "From a man called Teacher."

'Francoise gasped. She felt as if she was going to collapse, but steadied herself. "He's alive?"

'"Yes. He is working on the fence. Soon it will be complete. He says to be ready to leave in two days' time, just before midnight. He is going to come and take you and the children. You must find a way to meet him at the lower west gate. He says it is your only chance, so you must be ready." And then the woman was gone, scurrying down the hallway.

'That night, the head of security came to her and she pleaded with him. They had to leave in two days' time, she said. Eminence had called for her to attend to him at a special party on the day after. They both knew what the words 'special party' meant – one of the Eminence's increasingly frequent and often sadistic bouts of orgiastic debauchery that left guests in a state of shock for weeks. Francoise was lying, of course, but he agreed.

'Everything was ready. The day came, and that afternoon Francoise went to collect the twins at the creche. You ran to her, Kweku, and jumped into her arms. "Where's your sister?" your mum asked, scanning the room.'

Suddenly, I am back there. The memories, repressed for decades, leap out at me from the flames. 'And I told her that Akua had been taken away with some of the other girls,' I say.

'Oh my God,' says Julie.

I swallow hard.

Jennifer continues.

'Your mum spoke to the woman who ran the creche and she said that the girls, four of them, had been taken to the Eminence's quarters and would not be returned until Friday. Beside herself, your mum returned to her room and tried to get word to the head of security via one of the palace cleaning women. She wasn't going to leave without Akua. She had to get her back. She racked her brains. Had Eminence heard something, caught some whiff of her impending betrayal, and taken Akua to ensure her compliance? By eight o'clock she still hadn't heard back from the head of security. By then, Teacher had slipped from the workers' quarters, swum out to *Providence* and had started to make the boat ready to sail. He got his rifle and his knife and some gold, and swam back and made his way to the place where the patrol boat was kept. He slit the guard's throat and disabled the motor, then started towards the lower west gate.'

I exhale long. Part of me doesn't quite believe what I am hearing, but the memories are coming fast now.

'At eleven o'clock the head of security finally came to Francoise's room. By then she was a wreck, pacing back and forth, you two sitting there on the bed, staring at her as if she'd gone mad. He told her that he'd tried to have Akua released but the Eminence would not hear of it. She was a beautiful child and he wanted her for a tableau he had planned. "Then we are not leaving," she said. He pleaded with her. They had no choice. He'd paid the bribes, everything was ready. If they didn't go then, Eminence would find out and would have them all killed.'

By now the fire has almost burned down. Jennifer pauses and looks at us both from across the glowing pile of coals. She takes a deep breath, holds it a long time and then exhales slowly.

'This is why your mother could never tell you. She had to make an impossible decision that night, one no mother should ever have to make. She decided to sacrifice her daughter to save you and your brother.'

February 2039 – final entry

Bryce rolled the Gulfstream to a stop.

The Boss gazed through the cockpit window down the runway at the fast-approaching vehicles, three in all, two police cruisers and something that looked like a Humvee, National Guard maybe.

'Someone has tipped them off.' The Boss turned and called to the wife. 'Sam, you better get up here. We're going to need your skills here pretty shortly, baby.'

By now the vehicles had surrounded the plane. The Boss told Bryce to shut down the engines, keep the APU going for the onboard systems. Bryce did it, unbuckled his shoulder straps and eased himself out of his seat. 'Fucking de-icing guy,' he said. 'I knew we couldn't trust him.'

'How do you know it was him?' said the Boss.

'Just a feeling. He kept asking all kinds of questions. Where you headed? Whose plane? That kind of stuff.'

The Boss grunted. Of course, it could have been anyone.

'What now, Boss?' Bryce said.

'Let them sit,' said the Boss, fury starting to boil and jump in those neck veins of his. 'And be ready to move when I give the word.'

The wife stuck her head into the cockpit. 'Seems someone doesn't want us to leave without saying goodbye.'

'So, let's say goodbye,' said the Boss. 'Bring me my case.'

Samantha stepped back out of the cockpit.

Outside, the snow had started again, thick white sheets that almost obscured the vehicles sitting just a few metres away on the concrete.

'We can't wait too long, Boss,' said Bryce, 'unless you want to get that de-icing unit back here. Ice builds up on our wings, we'll never get off the ground.'

'Always got to do everything my God-dammed self,' grunted the Boss. 'Well then get him on the radio and get him back here. Offer him whatever he wants. If it was him, we can make it worth his while. This may take some time.'

'We'll try,' said Bryce. 'I don't think he'll want to come back.'

'I'll scrape the ice off the fucking wings myself if I have to.' The Boss turned and disappeared into the aft compartment, returning a moment later with a big, nickel-plated handgun. The wife was waiting at the front door. She handed the Boss his case. He grabbed it and put the gun inside his jacket.

'Let's go,' the Boss said. Bryce lowered the stairs and a cold gust of wind blew over us. Flakes spun into the cabin. Two men were standing on the runway a few metres away, looking up at the aircraft. One was uniformed and had on a big, fur-hooded parka and mittens. The other was dressed in a dark suit and tie with a long dark overcoat.

'You come with us,' the Boss said to me as he stepped down to the runway. I shrugged and followed.

'Gentlemen,' the Boss opened. 'You're blocking my runway.'

'Not your runway,' said the main in the suit, stamping his feet and blowing into his bare hands. 'The property of the good state of Montana.'

I recognised him immediately, that voice, those eyes. It was Tresscott.

The Boss recognised him too. 'Fuck me,' he said. 'Look who crawled out of the shit pile.'

'And who are you?' said the wife, stepping forward and throwing off her hood.

Tresscott produced a battered wallet, flicked it open. 'Special Agent Tresscott, double S double T. And this is Sergeant Watson.' The man in the parka inclined his head, blew steam from under his hood.

'What's your first name, Agent Tresscott?' asked the wife.

'It's Tom, ma'am.'

'Well then, Agent Tom, can I ask what it is that you want?'

'Well ma'am, what we want is you.'

'And what exactly do you want us for, Agent Tom?'

'You are under arrest for attempting to leave the country illegally.'

'Do you have a warrant for this?'

The sergeant in the parka fumbled with his mittens, pulled one off, dropped it to the snow, recovered it, fished a piece of paper from a zipped outside pocket, passed it to Tresscott.

The wife inspected it a moment, handed it back. 'I am afraid this does not apply to us,' she said, reaching into her pocket and extracting two passports. 'If you check your records, Tom, you will find that as of five weeks ago, we both ceased to be citizens of the United States. Our citizenships were officially and legally revoked. Check with District Court in Washington, D.C., and the Embassy of Belize if you like. As you can see, we are citizens of Belize. Your warrant has no legal validity. We are foreign nationals returning to our own country. I am assuming, of course, that the rule of law still holds sway?'

Tresscott stood blinking in the blue and red flashing lights, snow accumulating on his hair. He shuffled his feet, looked over at the sergeant.

Sam reached out her hand. 'Our passports, please?'

Tresscott handed back the dark-blue booklets.

Sam continued. 'We understand that the relocation programme is primarily about property.' She handed Tresscott a thick document. 'This deed officially relinquishes title of our properties in Montana and Colorado, and all of their contents, to the government. This, I believe, is what you are after.'

Tresscott scanned the document, flipped through the pages.

'You can even have the fucking helicopter,' said Argent.

Sam shot him a bolt. 'So, if you would please move your vehicles, Tom, we will be on our way.'

Tresscott considered her, silent, the documents hanging in his hand. The Boss turned and started back to the plane. I followed.

'Mister Argent,' said Tresscott. 'I wouldn't be getting too comfortable, if I were you. I am going to have to check this out.'

The Boss kept walking without looking back, raised a finger, and bounded up the stairs into the cabin. 'Pog,' I heard him say, and then as soon as he was inside: 'Any luck on the de-icing, Stephenson?'

'Can't raise him,' said Bryce. 'I'm not surprised.'

'Well then get out there, you and Green, and start doing it by hand. Sam'll have these cunts sorted out pretty quick.'

Bryce hesitated, just for a moment, and I saw the Boss tilt his head to one side, his eyes glittering. And that was when I realised that he knew. Right there, just that moment of hesitation, that millisecond of disappointment on Bryce's face, was enough. And I knew Bryce knew, too.

'Well?' said the Boss.

'Just going now, Boss. Come on, Rob.' Bryce and Green threw on their jackets and went outside.

Samantha was still outside talking to Tresscott. Twenty minutes passed and they were still at it. At least they'd turned off the strobe lights. The Boss was pacing the cabin, back and forth.

'Come with me,' he said to me, opening the door.

'Me?' I said. I'd blurted it out. He'd caught me off guard. I wanted to stay here, with the plane, with Bryce. That was the plan. But now the Boss was giving me that look. And I realised, shit, he knew.

He patted his jacket, the bulge where the gun was. 'Get your ass out there.'

I zipped up my jacket and flipped up my hood. What else could I do? I followed him across the snow-swept runway to where Tresscott and the wife were standing.

'What the hell is going on?' said the Boss.

'Calm down, Argent,' said Tresscott. 'We've just checked with head-quarters, and, notwithstanding your citizenship, we've been told to bring you in.'

'This is not legal, Tom, and you know it,' said Sam.

The Boss reached into his jacket. The sergeant shook his head, put his hand on his sidearm.

'Don't worry,' said the Boss.

'Nice and slow.'

The Boss pulled out a coin and tossed it to Tresscott. It tumbled through the air, catching the light. 'Krugerrand,' he said. 'One ounce of pure gold. The only currency that's going to be worth anything pretty soon. That one coin there is worth seventy-thousand dollars. There's twenty of 'em here in my jacket. Just take it, son, with my blessing, and let's both be on our way to a better future.'

Tresscott turned the coin in his fingers a while, then closed his fist around it.

'You're smart,' said the Boss. 'Take it. Look after yourself. No one else will.'

I looked back towards the plane. Bryce and his co-pilot were scraping ice from the wings.

Tresscott put the coin in his pocket and stood a bit taller. 'Derek

Argent, Samantha Argent,' he said, his voice steady. 'You are under arrest. The officers will read you your rights.' And then he looked at me. 'You too, miss.'

I sat in the back of the police cruiser between the Boss and the wife and watched Bryce board the jet and pull the door closed. The G900 powered up and started taxiing back to the far end of the runway. Soon the Gulfstream with the love of my life at the controls was at the end of the runway. It swung around and started its take-off run. It really was a beautiful aircraft. It made me sad to see it accelerating down the runway, sad that our plan hadn't worked out the way we'd thought it would. Still, I knew that Bryce wouldn't leave without me. He'd get me out of jail, or wherever they were taking us. After all, it was me that had tipped off the authorities that the Boss was planning to bolt. I'd provided the evidence that would convict him and many others of dozens of crimes. And when he did, we'd get Ruby and go up to Ontario like we'd planned, and live our lives.

I watched the Gulfstream leave the runway and claw its way into the air, full fuel, full cargo, three fewer passengers. And then the Boss reached for his belt buckle and flipped it open and pressed down with his thumb.

Half a second later the Gulfstream disappeared in an orange fireball that streaked like a meteor into the dark forest a mile beyond the end of the runway.

Earth

I sit in silence, staring into the coals, the meaning of Jennifer's words coursing through every part of me. For I was there, witness to these events. There in that room as those words were spoken and our mother thought through the horrible alternatives and came to a decision. I think of the tiny skeleton she buried that night up on the ridge a few months later, its father, how it came to be born. In that moment I understand what she did and why she chose to keep it from us all those years. Whether it was remorse or guilt or sadness, or a profound sense of shame that led her to bury all of this doesn't matter now. She made her decisions and she lived with them.

The head of security led Mum, me and Lewis to the gate in the darkness as Papa was reaching it from the other side. I can remember it now, walking along that darkened alleyway. When we emerged and Papa confronted him, there was a silent struggle and when it was over the other man lay mortally wounded. I can remember, now, the sight of the two of them, giants, wrestling silently in the starlight. After, Papa led Mum weeping to *Providence* and together we slipped through the reef and set sail west without being pursued, leaving Akua to her fate as we had come to know it.

Aunty Jenny kisses each of us, her lips lingering on the skin of our foreheads as if we are infants, and then disappears without another word, leaving Julie and I staring into the dying fire.

We live with Jennifer and her mob now, all of us together, working for harmony and balance in our lives. We watch as each year the birds and the animals and the whales return in greater numbers, and rejoice in this healing of nature. Once in a while we take *Providence* out and sail the sound, and sometimes we go further up the coast to Albany, but we always come back.

Julie is busy with her doctoring and has become one of the leaders of our community. Leo has become quite a fisherman under Kwesi's tutelage. He still has the rag dolls that Xoese gave him, and he still talks to his grandparents sometimes. Becky seems to have overcome her ordeal, though I know better than most the echoes that she will always carry. She says she wants to write books like her uncle, which makes me very proud. And though we can no longer transmit, my plan is to one day find a place that will publish and print copies of both *The Forcing*, and my book, which I am calling *The Descent*.

We still listen to the short-wave radio and hear news of the world outside, of the slow progress and the setbacks as what remains of humanity struggles to shape a future. Although we have not heard any more transmissions from Sparkplug, I still think about her and wonder where she is and if, one day, she will continue her broadcasts. I will always be grateful to her for sharing her story, so strangely entwined with my own. Alpha Omega are still out there somewhere, and I still have those playing cards as reminders of the danger that we all still face.

By any reckoning, our descent was swift. And while predicted by some, it seems to have been wholly unexpected by most. We are witnesses now to the aftermath, as others were to the fall, and all we have seen and the stories we have heard form part of this acknowledgement. And while this collective act of murderous folly may have been directed by a small group of immensely wealthy and inordinately powerful men, they only succeeded through the acquiescence of the compliant majority. People like my mother and Uncle Liberty and Papa and Patricia and Sparkplug fought against it, each in their own way, but they were far too few, and unarmed in every way that mattered. Perhaps in that sense, this course of history *was* inevitable. But it matters not. History, like time, unfolds at its own discretion, deaf to the petitions of men and blind to the tears of women.

Sometimes Julie and I walk back to The Hope and we stop at the graves along the ridge. Along the way we talk about everything that has happened and try to make some sense of it. We remember the people we've met and loved, and hope that they are well and happy, and we mourn those the world has lost. We reflect on the ways in which they have changed us and the ways in which we will honour them through the conduct of our own lives. And in all of this we have determined that the world remains a very beautiful place, and that despite our failings and hauntings, there is an infinite capacity for love in each of us, and so there must also be hope for us all, here on this immense, vanishingly small, fragile, and oh so precious Earth.

Acknowledgements

his book came together quickly once we decided it needed to be written. As usual, anything like this depends on many people. The writer toils away by the grace of those wonderful souls who edit, publish, support, mentor, feed, love, and inspire him. To all of them, my deepest gratitude. And through this process, I have come to realise that the only thing that matters in the world is love, and anything that increases the amount of love in the world, and decreases the totality of suffering, is to be treasured.